"This big-hearted story about small-town Maine captivated me from the first page. Filled with humor and poetry and complicated characters who love foolishly and too much, *The From-Aways* is about putting down roots and gazing up at the stars in a place where the rhythms of life are as constant and yet unpredictable as the surf on the shore."

—Christina Baker Kline, *New York Times* bestselling author of *Orphan Train*

"In *The From-Aways,* CJ Hauser introduces us to Menamon, Maine, a town of wisecracking fishermen, activist waitresses, and secret fathers, with such deftness we immediately know and care for it like locals. At its heart, *The From-Aways* is the story of a hesitant friendship between Quinn, a Bernstein looking for her Woodward, and Leah, a newcomer to Menamon and her marriage to one of its prodigal sons. These compelling, unlikely women rub the sorry states of their lives together to ignite a breathless chain of events that whips clean through to an explosive conclusion that resonated with me for days. I loved spending time in Menamon, and was sorry when I had to go."

—Marie-Helene Bertino, author of *Safe as Houses* and *2 A.M. at the Cat's Pajamas*

"*The From-Aways* is populated by twentysomethings running from and in search of family, by people passionately in pursuit of home. CJ Hauser has written a wise, lovely, luminous novel about love and work and leaving New York. It will make you want to get out your lobster pot and set forth for the coast of Maine."

—Joshua Henkin, author of *The World Without You*

"I first read CJ Hauser's work a few years ago and was immediately pulled in by the wit of her prose, her sharp dialogue, and her honesty in portraying the journey of young women trying to find their place in the world. With her enchanting debut novel, *The From-Aways*, CJ Hauser delivers on her promise of being a writer to root for, a writer to watch, a writer to read."

—Vendela Vida, author of *The Lovers* and *Let the Northern Lights Erase Your Name*

"CJ Hauser's debut novel, *The From-Aways*, is as charming, salty, and fresh as its setting in small-town Maine. Through her spunky heroines, Leah and Quinn, who have both come to Maine to find roots, Hauser tells an affecting story about lobsters, loyalty, and love."

—Elliott Holt, author of *You Are One of Them*

The From-Aways

C J HAUSER

wm

WILLIAM MORROW

An Imprint of HarperCollins*Publishers*

Designed by Diahann Sturge

Library of Congress Cataloging-in-Publication Data has been applied for.

ISBN 978-0-06-231075-0

14 15 16 17 18 OV/RRD 10 9 8 7 6 5 4 3 2

For Boo, Lemo, and Daddio—my family

I will arise and go now, for always night and day
I hear lake water lapping with low sounds by the shore;
While I stand on the roadway, or on the pavements grey,
I hear it in the deep heart's core.

W. B. YEATS

Take me down to the paradise city
where the grass is green and the girls are pretty
Oh, won't you please take me home?

GUNS N' ROSES

The From-Aways

Summer

1

Leah

I have two lobsters in my bathtub and I'm not sure I can kill them.

I'm sitting on the rim of the tub. It has curled brass feet. Everything seems alive and haunted in this house; that's my first problem.

My second problem is that I pet the lobsters. I roll up a white-buttoned sleeve and run my pinched fingers along the length of Lobster Number One's antenna. It feels sensitive and unbreakable like coiled wire. Lobster Number One knocks his crusher claw against my hand, but there's a thick pink rubber band binding it up, so I'm in no real danger. I stroke Lobster Number Two's antenna as well, so they're even.

Henry says one lobster boil won't make Maine my home, but he is wrong.

Both lobsters have dark spotted backs that remind me of Dalmatian puppies. I really should not be thinking of them as puppies.

I get a six-pack from the fridge. This is my plan: I will get blind drunk and then I will kill these lobsters. I tie my hair up in a dark knob. I use the faucet to pry the cap off my bottle. Beer geysers up and fizz plops in the water like sea foam. Henry says his mother, June, gave her lobsters beer before cooking them. She also bathed them in seawater so they'd have one last taste of home. I ask the lobsters, "Do you feel at home?"

Of course not. Some bearded yahoo caught them in a pot. Their home is long gone. As is mine, but no one snatched me up. Instead, I snatched Henry. I married him and begged for us to move to his hometown: Menamon, Maine. I broke the lease on my apartment. Quit my job at the *New York Gazette.* Donated the tangle of wires and smartphones and life-simplifying devices from my purse, because I wouldn't need them once I left New York.

People use those in Maine, you know, Henry said. *We're not going back in time. Just north.*

North!

So now I will find a way to do this, because love is boiling the lobsters your freckle-backed husband doesn't believe will grow you instant roots. My parents raised me an only child in a nineteenth-floor penthouse. No one grows roots nineteen stories deep.

I swing my legs over the side of the tub and stare at my underwater feet. My toes are painted the color the lobsters will be once I boil them. Lobster Number One and Lobster Number Two conference at the other end. I turn over my beer bottle so it glugs empty into the tub. I open another one for me.

We take turns, the lobsters and I, finishing the six-pack. I had imagined tonight so clearly. The boiled red beasts on blue plates. The melted butter in its crock. The wine bottle sweating. The sound of waves through the screen door and of Henry, laughing. A warm breeze wending through the house. I have been imagining this dinner for months. Ever since I started thinking about Maine.

The lobsters jostle around my feet. I look at the empty six-pack and know I won't be able to kill them.

I splash my feet around in the tub and devise a new plan. I'm going to name them. I get a box of salt from the kitchen and shake it over the water so it will be briny like the sea. I lie on the fuzzy bath mat and wait. It is almost six but the day is still warm. My legs stretch out past the mat and the tiles are cool.

"Leah?" Henry appears in the doorframe, searching for me. "What are you doing down there? The bathroom smells like a bar."

"Welcome to the Lobstah Bah," I tell him. Henry's face is tan and his arms are covered in small scratches. The knees of his jeans are dark-wet and dirty. He has been planting. There have been thorns. He pads over to me in sock feet. He smells sweaty and like mulch.

"Are you okay?" he says. "Why are there lobsters in the tub?"

"Meet Lavender and Leopold. They eat scurf and they have names and so we should not eat them." Still lying on the floor, I gesture toward the tub. "Don't they look at home?"

"You stubborn girl," he says. "I told you we didn't have to do this."

I sit up and Henry and I both kneel by the bath. He puts his hand on my back. Lavender and Leopold scuttle to opposite ends of the bathtub. Their carapaces are the color of dried blood and their legs are like machines and I wonder if they are married. But how would I know? I don't even know their sexes. There is no way to tell which is the boy and which is the girl unless we eat them and see who has eggs inside and who has nothing.

"There wasn't enough room in the sink," I tell Henry. "They looked crowded."

"Naturally," he says. He leans an arm on the rim of the tub and rests his chin in the crook of his elbow. He looks so much a part of this house, like another piece grown out of it. The lobsters flick their antennae around. "It's lucky you're cunning 'cause you're not much for cooking," Henry says.

"Do you want to cook them?" I say, and curl into a position like his.

"If you think I'm eating something named Leopold, you're crazy," Henry says.

I say, "Let's return them to the sea."

We remove the lobsters' rubber bands and wrap them in a beach towel. At the end of our backyard wooden steps descend to where the grass falls off into rock into sand. To our own tiny boardwalk with a dinghy tied up. To the coast.

The sun is fizzling out and I smell the musk of a small rotting carcass. The ocean stretches wide and green waves tumble in. Gulls are screaming. They have clever faces, spatter-patterned backs, mean spirits. Birds are hollow in their bones. I do not like the way they hang overhead.

I release the lobsters and Henry looks around cagily as they scuttle toward the tide line. If the neighbors see him, he will be laughed out of town. I crack up at the expression on his face.

"Oh sure, laugh," Henry says. "You're the one who's got us on this lobster mission. Guys spend half their lives buggin' and here we are dropping them back in the sea."

I count trap buoys bobbing in the deep water, each one marking a pot. It seems like a cruel trick to me. These playful hunks of foam are jail markers, guiding fishermen to the places lobsters have come to practice poor decision making. Traps my lobsters may or may not be smart enough to avoid their second time around. Lavender and Leopold march until a wave crashes and they are gone.

Henry watches the spot where his dinner disappeared. His hair and eyebrows get wild in the sea air. His face tans, so quickly, and already I can see an underglow, a darkening. This is my husband in his natural habitat, in more ways than one. Our house is Henry's childhood home. His parents passed away five and two years ago. June in an accident. Hank in a boat.

I hug on to him. "I'm sorry," I say.

"Don't be sorry," Henry says. "Jeezum, just don't buy any more, okay?"

The sun is sunk as we walk back.

THAT NIGHT, IN bed, we are quiet although neither of us is sleeping. I wriggle so Henry can feel my arm against his back, but he doesn't roll over.

I want to mention that I am good at many things. To start, I am good at writing newspaper articles, which is what I did in New York. I'm also a good cook, a fast runner, and I am excellent at loving Henry. In fact, I did such a stellar job of loving Henry that three months ago he decided to marry me despite the fact that our two ages lumped together didn't amount to half a century.

I sometimes worry what we've got ourselves into.

It was my idea to move here. Because even though I am good at many things, it wasn't until there was Henry that I enjoyed any of them. From the moment I met Henry he made everything seem realer, better. He reminded me that all the people on the streets and subways were actual people, not just a crowd to push through. He found delivery sashimi more miraculous than the moon landing. From my bed, he'd open the slatted blinds I never touched and sit cross-legged, looking out the window of my twelfth-floor apartment while totally naked. *Are you aware the neighbors can see you right now?* I'd say, pulling the covers around myself. But Henry didn't care. He'd point at the slash of cloud and blue visible between the buildings and remind me that it was incredible, us floating twelve stories above the earth in a gently swaying tower.

Henry reminded me that I was a human being, on a planet, with a body. And when he put his hands on my body I felt myself returning to it. My self who too often lives only in my brain and forgets about the rest of me. Henry was always in a state of wonder about the city, my city, and he saw it in ways I never had: looking straight through the sidewalks and subway tunnels to the black earth underneath. I started seeing things Henry's way, the realer, better way, and found I wanted more of this. I thought, What could be realer or better than moving to Maine where he is from?

I knew Maine was the best place because of the stories Henry told. He lay around my apartment, hand behind his head and T-shirt riding up to expose a trail of fur, and he spun me stories. Back home, someone found a yellow diamond the size of an egg in a shark's belly. Back home, the old woman who ran the lighthouse could be seen drinking coffee with the ghost of her dead husband at night. Back home, there were moose the size of Mack trucks. Back home, everyone owned land. Back home, everyone knew each other and said hello.

I'd jump on him, clumsy because I am tall and sometimes forget what to do with my limbs. I'd pin him there and say, *It's not really like that, though, is it? Did all that really happen?*

Sure it did, bub, he'd say, and swat me on the butt. Then I'd settle into the crook of his arm and make him tell it all again. Menamon sounded magical. For months I demanded these stories over and over. Soon I could imagine Menamon so completely that I knew it was the right place to live. I practically lived there already.

Let's go there, I said.

I throw off my blanket. I can barely hear the ocean from here, but the steel bell buoys ring out a baritone song, one note for each time the waves rock the buoy. It's a deep, echoing sound I found haunting until Henry explained that the noise is meant to let ships know they're too close to shore when visibility is bad. I thought that was nice. *Dong, dong,* you're too close. *Dong, dong,* it's all right, just turn away, we're watching out.

I listen and stare at Henry's back. He is teaching me these things he already knows so that I can make a home here. I reach out and run my fingers over his back so just the finger pads are touching. Henry is still, but I trail my fingers between his shoulder blades that just barely protrude, like vestigial wings. I follow the vertebrae of his spine down to the small of his back where the bones disappear beneath the surface.

"Were you drawing a sailboat?" Henry asks.

I wasn't, but suddenly I wish I was. "A sailboat would be like this," I say, and trace a boat body shaped like lemon wedge. I add a tall mast and two triangular sails. They would be white, if they weren't invisible. I move my finger in a curved but unbroken line along his lower back.

"Those are the waves," he says. "I can feel them."

"Yes," I say. "Those are the waves."

2

Quinn

I went to find my father because my mother was the most beautiful dead woman I knew and I thought someone should tell him she was gone. If he had plans to make amends, I figured he should know it was now too damn late.

Not that I thought he had plans.

Listen, between Mom's hospital bills and my college tuition, we broke even. I got a mediocre journalism degree. She got the best care the state of Connecticut could provide and a weeping willow planted over her plot. I asked her, Couldn't we get a nice dogwood or maybe a cherry? A weeping tree seemed maudlin.

She said, *Won't you cry when I'm gone?*

I said, *Well, yeah, but could you stop being so goddamn macabre?*

She said, *I've indentured a tree to do the grieving so you won't have to.*

Okay, I said, *okay. We'll get a willow.*

Do you have any idea how hard it is to find a cemetery that will let you plant a tree over someone's grave?

I know three things about my father:

1. He used to be a folk singer.
2. He named me Quinn, after the Dylan song about the Eskimo (just what every little girl dreams: igloos, pigeons, and shitty acoustics).
3. He was born in Menamon, Maine. He moved back there to live between gigs ever since he split from my mom, right after I was born. Carter and Marta were believers in loving free and easy. No papers between them. Just me.

MY MOTHER'S OBITUARY ran in the local paper. It was the normal rigmarole about her being an art teacher and a mother and dying of cancer, but the last line was the kicker: *Marta Winters is perhaps best known as the "whiskey-eyed dame" in Carter Marks's 1960s anthem, "Leave Your Shoes Behind."*

That line was removed by the obituaries editor twice during revisions and both times Marta insisted it be put back in. I know, because I was the obituaries editor. Twenty-two-year-olds with journalism degrees often get their start in obituaries, or so I was told by the *Fairhaven Hour*. I think Marta wanted that last bit included because she hoped Carter would take notice. Like he's reading the *Hour*. Like anyone reads obituaries.

After she died, I found a note she'd left me. I braced myself. I assumed it would be a teary missive full of loving words and advice for the future. But when I tore open the envelope it wasn't even a letter. It wasn't typed or signed or dated or any of the things a deathbed mother-daughter letter should be. It was a scrap of yellow-lined paper and she'd scrawled on it, so sloppy it seemed like an afterthought: *Go see your father, please.* I put the note away in Marta's sock drawer, shoved between the balled woollies and bright hippie stripers. She'd never before suggested I do anything like this, and I felt so cheated out of a real letter, or any parting affection at all, that I came close to crumpling the paper and chalking the whole thing up to terminal delusion.

But something kept nagging at me. Yes, Marta was crazy, but hers was a crazy with reasons behind it. A month later, I was sure of it: Marta was trying to show me something. I dug the note out of her socks and I taped it to the television set so I could see it while I watched. After I sold the TV, I left it in different kitchen cabinets—next to Marta's jars of pickles, or taped to a canister of flour. Then, the house was all packed up. Sold. There were all these boxes headed for storage, and that note.

It was the *please* that got me. You've got to understand, Marta never said please. She must have spoken the word before, but when I sat there with the note in her still-unmade bed and tried to recall a single individual instance, I couldn't. So I packed one duffel bag and my father's old guitar, Marta's note slipped into the case. I decided to go find Carter—and to get a new job, at the *Menamon Star.*

THE *STAR* OFFICE is small and the staff nonexistent. A she-editor named Charley Lynch runs the place and is too young to have doomed herself with an editorial position like this. But who am I to judge with my portfolio that is, literally, DOA? I watch Charley's face for signs of approval as she looks through my folder, but what qualifies me for this job has nothing to do with my clippings. I want to say: *Listen, I've watched* All the President's Men *more than twenty times and I know everything about how this works already. I've studied Woodward. I've studied Bernstein. I'm an investigative reporter. Just watch me.* I want to say: *Those guys? The way they throw down like nothing matters? The way they fuck up left and right but always come through in the end? I am those guys. This is what qualifies me.*

"All these clips are about dead people," Charley says. She's wearing jeans so worn they're almost white and brown duck boots. Her hips are wide; they make her look battle-ready. She appraises me with a stare that leaves no barrier between her judgment and my face, and I like this. I want the respect of this woman, just to have it, like a lucky green penny in my pocket I could pull out from time to time and say, *Look, this is something I've got.*

Charley sighs. "You're hired," she says.

"What's my beat?" I ask. *No obituaries, no obituaries,* I telegraph silently.

"Beat?" Charley says. "Your beat is to find some news in this godforsaken excuse for New England idyll. And much luck to you."

I THOUGHT IT would be hard to find him but it says CARTER MARKS right on the damn mailbox. Driving from the *Star* to my new place, I'm taking a hairpin turn, braking into it and ready to zoom out with my wits about me, when I see it. I'm used to seeing his name in newspaper articles, on late-night radio shows, in used-record bins, but the mailbox is a first.

I brake. I let the car idle. The mailbox has a stuffed fox wired to the post. Its glass eyes glint at my low beams. The drive is gravel, red lollipop reflectors all bent to hell along the sides. The trees are tall and thick here and the house is surrounded by a wall of juniper bushes. Through the branches I can see that the roof dips low at its center and clots of lichen spread outward like a saddle. It looks uninhabitable.

I have an impulse to march in and do this right now, but sometimes I also feel like screaming loudly in silent movie theaters or leaping over railings at the mall. What I'm saying is that this is not a healthy impulse. Even if I got so far as knocking on his door, I wouldn't know what to do with myself. I've been working my speech over in my mind, and it's not quite done yet. Actually, it's less of a speech and more of an ode, to my mother. More of a song, really, but fuck if I'm going to sing to that man. Fuck if he'll ever hear the sound of my voice outside the tirade of life-smashing information I'm going to deliver to him like a smiting angel with a badass sword.

Maybe I won't even tell him my speech. Maybe when I do go down his creepy fox driveway, I'll go like a soldier. I'll unfold a piece of paper and eyeball it the way those sad-eyed boys do in the war movies. Carter Marks? I'll say. And when he says yes I won't even spare a glance to see if our noses are the same or if I got my green eyes from him. I'll just inform him in my most official way that Marta is dead. And that she was beautiful. And that he is a total fool for using her so cheaply. Wringing a song out of her, knocking her up, and then leaving once there was no more juice to the squeeze. That he never really loved her at all, and I want nothing to do with him.

Although I am curious about the fox. Whether or not taxidermy runs in the family is the sort of thing I'd like to know.

ROSIE AND I live above the Stationhouse Café, where she waits tables. Our apartment shakes when the local passes through, but this is nowheresville, so that's only four times daily. In the online listings, hers was the only apartment under *MENAMON (West)*. The subject read, *Area Girl of Little Means Seeks Same as Roommate.*

Rosie's room has a single bed with pink sheeting that's twisted into knots by morning because she thrashes like a demon in her sleep. She has postcards from her parents taped to the wall. Rosie grew up here but her parents moved to Florida a year back, right after she graduated from high school. She refused to go with them because she thinks Florida is where people go to die. She ticks off on her fingers: skin cancer, alligators, syphilis-carrying mosquitoes, retirement homes. "Besides," she says, "there's nothing less appealing than a man in Bermuda shorts offering you a drink made from bananas."

I think she means encephalitis-carrying mosquitoes, but I don't have the heart to correct her. Rosie is nineteen. She started working at the Stationhouse right after high school. She comes home from work smelling like coffee and the butter the café fries their eggs in. "This job is ruining my complexion," she says. Rosie says she's going to be a famous singer when she grows up, so her complexion is of paramount importance. She sings in the shower and likes to wear a shower cap because if she takes a bow at the end of a song, the drumming of water on plastic sounds like applause.

In spite of this, I hide the guitar from Rosie. The guitar was Carter's, left behind when Marta and I were left behind. The original plan was to give it back to him: *Here, the last of your shitty stuff, and I don't want it.*

But then, right before I moved, I started playing it, and now I've been practicing chords and riffs when Rosie's at work. I hide the guitar because it seems too much to explain. How bad I am. How old it is. Why I still have it at all. Because when I pick up the guitar I feel a strange sense of balance, like a missing limb has been returned to me. Because I don't know how to feel about the fact that this is obviously Carter's genetic juice, working away inside me.

THE DAYS TICK by for Rosie and me. It's seven o'clock in the morning and I'm drinking coffee with two hands, sitting cross-legged on my pullout couch. I'm mustering the strength to go to the *Star* and let Charley run me into the ground again. I've been cranking out articles for weeks but I haven't found that Woodward and Bernstein intrigue like I'd hoped to. Maybe because Charley has me covering things like the county's largest wasp's nest. My headline was COUNTY ABUZZ OVER COUNTY'S LARGEST WASP'S NEST!, which I thought was pretty great, but Charley reamed me out. Apparently you're not supposed to use the same word twice in one headline. But whatever, the intrigue will come. I'm on the beat now. Excitement is obviously right around the corner.

I drink the dregs of my coffee and get up to pour myself more.

"You?" I say to Rosie, holding up the pot. She shakes her head.

Rosie is getting ready to go to work downstairs. We have our rituals already, she and I. Weak light through the open window makes a screen shadow on the floor. Late-summer bugs rattle in the grass outside. Rosie ties her apron strings. She's the perfect waitress, she says, waiting for something better to come along.

"What do you think is going to come find you here in Menamon?" I say.

"Love," she says, looking up with a squint, like maybe she can see right through me. "People are always falling in love with waitresses."

3

Leah

There is, in Menamon, Maine, no news.

Here is what there is: One of the oldest carousels in the United States. It spins on the south side of the harbor, on a little scrap of land staked with a sign that says NEVERSINK PARK. I park the woody nearby, its hood ticking like a bomb after I cut the engine. The carousel's horses have sneering painted mouths: gums exposed and teeth too large. A brass ring, the victor's spoils, flits around the perimeter. This was one of Henry's stories: fishermen said the wooden horses came alive at night and galloped over the waves, capsizing boats and biting through mooring ropes.

A red-bearded man with dark complicated tattoos around his calves operates the carousel machinery from a folding chair in the center. He catches me staring. "You're too tall to ride," he says, and pulls a lever that makes the ghostly organ song go faster. "But give me a kiss and I might let you." It's the kind of challenge I might have accepted once, before I was married. I lock up the car and head down the boardwalk to the market.

The boardwalk runs along the shore to the docks. The beach is just a few yards of slick rock. There are a dozen piers, most for lobster boats and small fishing craft. Gulls hover; this is where the men sit and smoke and pull the guts from fish, the meat from clams, the lobsters from pots. There is a convenience store that sells ten-dollar galoshes and tiny waterproof virgins. There is a fish market that sold me Lavender and Leopold and today sells me cod. There is the hardware store where Henry loves to pilfer Red Hots from a fishbowl they keep on the counter. No one minds. The men who work the waterfront, they don't begrudge him anything. No one does. He is the prodigal son come home, saved from the city just in time. Saved from being what I am. What they call me. A From-Away.

I did that! I want to say when people smile and say they're glad he's home. I want to point a thumb at my chest and let them know Henry had no intention of coming back to Maine for another few years at least. I was the one who heard his stories about life in Menamon and knew we had to move. Of course he agreed, got excited once plans were afoot, but Henry could easily have dallied forever eating New York pizza and condescending to ladies who thought you could grow peach trees on roof decks. He was happy enough landscaping roof gardens for city matrons, until he met me. *Here is your prodigal son!* I want to say to the people of Menamon. *I have brought him home for you.*

On the drive back, the car's heat gauge rides high. I worry, because this car is Henry's baby: a wood-paneled red Buick Roadmaster with two decades of beach-pass stickers plastered on the rear windows. It belonged to Henry's father, Hank. Henry spent our first week here fluently cursing under the hood, and whatever he did worked, though we keep a tool kit in the trunk. The car is hot, but the day is hot. I can make it home.

We live south of the downtown. Beachfront, but tiny beachfront. Red-tide-twice-a-summer beachfront. Watch-out-for-the-invisible-jellyfish beachfront. Oh-those-are-just-the-sand-fleas beachfront. Closer to town, where the shore gets wide and the sand gets fine, there's a gated community called Elm Park. Those houses are all the same: Palladian windows, two-story entryways, a piano no one knows how to play in a foyer they actually call the foyer. This year the sticker pass to sit on that wide sandy beach costs eighty dollars, up from fifty. The paper said the beach-sticker hike had old-time Menamonians "in a hot-blooded fury." Who is writing this copy? I thought.

Are you *angry?* I asked Henry. He shrugged. He said, *Things change. People should get used to it.* It disappointed me that my Menamonian wasn't in a hot-blooded fury of his own.

When I get home I tell Henry the woody is running hot and that in addition to its being haunted, I think the carousel might be the secret engine of Menamon; that if something happened to the red-bearded operator, the town would grind to a halt.

"Maybe," he says, but does not sound convinced. "How hot?" I stand behind him and slip my hands into his pockets. I stick my chin on his shoulder, a tall-lady prerogative, and kiss his neck. Henry unpacks my groceries. He has white scars on the backs of his hands and arms from wrestling trees and thorny perennials. In the winter they're invisible, but with his late-summer tan they've developed like a Polaroid. Higher up, on his right arm, Henry has a tattoo. It's a circle. A single blue line, thin as the needle that inked it. I tease that he meant to get it filled in with something but couldn't handle the pain. But he says no, it was always only ever going to be a circle. Because a circle is perfect.

An artist's ideal. It's a truly boring tattoo, if you ask me, but I never thought I'd wind up married to a body with any ink at all.

I hear a car engine in the drive. "My sister's coming by," Henry says.

"What?" I say. Because she can't be. I have been excited for this moment, meeting my new sister, but in my head it happens differently. Not like this.

"She's dropping off some extra house keys," Henry says. I see what must be Charley's Jeep. It has stalactites of red mud hanging from its undercarriage and a bumper sticker that says SAVE THE LOONS!

I say, "You know I hate unexpected guests."

Henry palms my neck and rubs his thumb beneath my ear. He once trained as an EMT and sometimes I think he is secretly taking my pulse when he does this, seeing how worked up I actually am.

"Family don't count as guests," Henry says, and as he does, Charley comes around back, through the kitchen door, with a box of beers.

She and Henry smile at each other with their mouths closed, then hug each other. Charley claps Henry on the back. The older sister.

"Charley, this is Leah," Henry says.

"Hi," I say. "Let me help you with that box." Charley checks out my arms like she doesn't trust me not to drop it. She has an expressive forehead and the thick blond hair of a well-cared-for horse. I've been told she and Henry resemble their mother.

"Hi," she says, and hands over the box. Seadog Ale. "Welcome home," she says to Henry, and hands him two sets of keys.

"Stay for a beer?" says Henry.

"Just one," Charley says.

Charley and I sit with beers in the yard while Henry puts

the rest in the refrigerator. The plastic chairs we found in the basement had been chewed along the legs by a long-dead dog or something more feral. The yard is encircled by tall trees and the last light comes through splotchily. I can hear the ocean. I can hear Charley's teeth clink against the glass mouth of her bottle.

Charley is a journalist too. Runs the local paper. This is the other reason I have been imagining this meeting: I want to work at the *Star*. I've got to start reporting again. If I don't find a way to write, to sweat under deadlines, to patchwork information into stories, I might go crazy.

"You grew up in this house?" I say. Charley looks at me, like she knows I'm wasting her time with questions I already know the answers to.

"Sure did," Charley says. She takes out a pack of Marlboros and lights one, staring up at the house. I regret my question. I imagine this is a sad thing for her to do, to look at this house that was her parents', and is now her little brother's. If you ask, Henry will tell you his pops was mauled by a black bear in a squabble over blueberries. He will tell you this because, if you don't already know it, the truth is none of your business. The truth is that Hank Lynch got drunk and sailed a too-small craft into a storm a few years after Henry's mother, June, died.

It seems like a good moment to ask about the newspaper.

"Charley, I'm interested in the *Star*," I say. I could swear I saw her inhale a lungful of smoke but now she is staring at me and nothing is emerging.

"What part interests you, exactly?"

"Any parts that might be hiring, actually." I had imagined we might become close in this way. Sisters, running a small paper together.

"I hired someone a few months ago," Charley says, and rakes her strawlike bangs behind her ears. "Come see me at the office."

She tips her beer backward and finishes it. "Nice to meet you, Leah," she says, and braces her palms against her knees to stand.

I HAVE TROUBLE falling asleep. Insomnia is a New Yorker's affliction.

Henry and Charley are practically their own species. They have their own grunting language and their own shared grief, parceled out generously between the two of them. They are the last Lynches of Menamon, unless you count me, which obviously no one does. I doubt I will ever truly be one of them, *family* family. It is Henry's tribe of two, and different now that he does not have Hank or June.

I loved books about orphans when I was small. Sara Crewe in *A Little Princess,* Mary Lennox in *The Secret Garden,* Pippi Longstocking with her absent pirate father, and my favorite, Harriet the Spy, with her tomato sandwiches and secrets. I pretended to be an orphan just like these girls: a sad child abandoned at a stranger's grand estate, my parents lost to a car accident or a tiger in Africa. I would mourn them at night, drifting through the hallways of the penthouse, running my hands along the sideboards, telling myself stories about what my life would be like had I not lost them.

What are you doing up? my father would say when he caught me drifting around, my hair all tangled from bed, humming little things to myself as I played out these fantasies. *Do you need something?*

Nothing, I would say. *No. I do not need anything.*

Sara, Mary, Pippi, Harriet. My orphan heroes. I now realize I didn't have any idea what I was playing at. How stupid a thing it was to wish for.

I flip my pillow. Pull the blankets higher. There is a problem with my childhood list, I realize. I think of *Harriet the Spy* along with these other orphan girl books, even though she did have parents. Because when I think of Harriet I see a girl on a busy sidewalk, big glasses, her backpack hitched high. She has her notebook in her hands because she always has her notebook in her hands. She is there to write down secrets. I see her as very much alone.

WE MOVED HERE knowing Henry would get a job at Arden Nursery. I would look for work, but with the house all paid for, his salary would be enough to float us. I drive him to pick up his new work truck. We walk along the busy rear lot where the land is writhing with green-scaled hoses that twine around the Ecuadorian yard workers' ankles like snakes. A man with a Roman nose and long black hair spilling over his shoulders comes out of a greenhouse, dragging a length of hose behind him.

"Hey, Batman, *ven conmigo*?" Henry says.

"Sure, *la casa grande*?" he asks. Batman is the yard manager at Arden. His real name is Bertilio, but because the customers have trouble saying it, the younger men have changed it to Batman, which best I understand has something to do with the way he tosses his hair over his shoulder like a cape.

"Yup," he says. *"Vámanos."* Henry speaks a little of what he calls landscaper Spanish. The men at Arden tease him for his gender confusion and accidental innuendos about hoses and cross-pollination.

"The *casa grande*?" I say.

"The house they're building out by the carousel," Henry says. "They bought two cherry trees and asked for an estimate on the back property. Forty acres of landscaping. I wanna get a look at it."

Batman whistles. "The New York people who bought the Penobscot lots," he says to me. "*That* house."

I can tell that this seems like a glamorous project to Henry. So far Arden has sent him sawing off cancerous tree arms and spraying slaughterhouse leftovers to deer-proof rose gardens. But I wonder about this job. I have been reading in the paper that people are not happy about plans for this home, larger than any other in Menamon, even the Elm Park McMansions. A home that will sit on not one but *five* recently purchased beachfront lots. They don't like how these people threw their money around to dissipate a handful of Menamon families, who, according to the local paper, "sped away from town, their trunks stuffed with out-of-state money, tails between their legs." Again, I thought, Who is writing this copy? It couldn't possibly be Charley.

"You wouldn't mind working for them?" I say. "These new people?"

"Why would I?" Henry says.

"I don't know," I say. But I am surprised. This is his town after all, the one he described to me in ways that got me dreaming about a cozy small-town kind of life. Henry in a diner on Fourteenth Street: back home a waitress would give me a talking-to for not finishing my eggs. Henry at a bar on Fifty-third: one of the fishermen got married and the bride danced on the bar in her wedding dress and a pair of boots. Henry and I at home, his feet in my face and mine in his as we lay on the couch: his parents used to spend Sundays just like this. Bow to stern, they called it. Menamon is supposed to be a place ruled by kind mothers and stoic fathers, fishermen and good folk. Henry's stories never included three-car garages or summering city people.

"Bye," Henry says, kissing me.

"Later," Batman says. Both men climb into a red F-150 that has ARDEN stenciled across the cab door and two cherry trees bungee-corded to the bed. They drive away.

NOT LONG AFTER I met Henry, we spent a day in the park. We'd stopped at a bodega and bought fruit to eat. We sat on protruding roots beneath a tree bordering Sheep Meadow, and as Henry ate his orange sections he spat the seeds into a blue paisley bandanna he'd pulled from his back pocket. I almost shook him when he did that. I almost shouted, *Don't you know you've made me love you now?* That was the moment. Those seeds in his pocket.

We thought about having a honeymoon, Henry and I. The fuss of a wedding we weren't much for, and I was afraid what sort of bridemonster my parents might make of me. I didn't want to think about tablecloths, flowers, or whose drunk uncles would fight with whose angry cousins.

A honeymoon, though, that sounded like something Henry and I would be good at. I'd been thinking of Rome. I'd seen *Roman Holiday* a dozen times and I was thinking about Henry renting a moped and buying me an ice cream cone and taking pictures on an Instamatic camera. Henry was thinking of a hot island somewhere. *With cocktails,* he said. *With class injustice,* I said. Henry groaned.

We kept talking but nothing seemed right—until we thought of Niagara Falls. We both loved the idea of shacking up in some cheap motel and writing dozens of postcards in our underwear, the pictures showing all the things we didn't do. Niagara Falls was big and dangerous and getting married was like going over it in a barrel. We bought our tickets. We thought we'd go on that boat, the *Maiden of the Mist.* We would not wear ponchos. We would stick our heads in the flume.

But then, so close to the wedding, I started thinking about the falls. Dreaming about them. I saw a picture in the brochure of a place where you could walk close to the railing at the top and peer over. I kept thinking about that picture, about the railing.

I panicked. I said, *We can't go to Niagara Falls.*

Why not? Henry said. *What are you talking about, we already booked our tickets.*

I just can't, I said.

And he was so nice to me. *Okay,* he said. *Okay. Let's just get married, huh? We don't need any honeymoon.*

Yeah, I said. *We don't.*

And Henry said, *Let's do it right now.*

Now? I said.

Sure, he said.

So we did.

I'd been crying a little, about Niagara and how I wouldn't see it after all because there was clearly something wrong with me. But I washed off my face. I wore a white dress. A sundress, eyelet cotton. Henry put on his nice jeans, and a nice shirt, and he looked so good. And that was how we did it. We already had our license, so we went to city hall and had this woman with a rubber stamp tell us that we were bound together for the rest of our lives, which was a long time considering we were both twenty-four.

And in our own bed that night we had such sex that I almost didn't care about Niagara anymore. We didn't need the falls to have a honeymoon after all.

I didn't tell Henry any more about Niagara and he never said anything. This was what good marriages were made of, I imagined. Knowing which things not to ask.

If he'd asked I would have had to say, *I am pretty sure that if we go up to Niagara I will wind up tossing myself from the falls.* When I looked at that picture in the brochure I just knew I would have gone right over the railing. I wouldn't have been sad, it wasn't that. I would have been ecstatic, so in love on that night, everything exactly the way I imagined it. But staring down at the falls, thirty-five million gallons a minute . . . who could resist a temptation like that? Imagine it, honeymoon eve, standing there almost touching the spray, ecstatic with love, who would not think: The only place to go from here is down?

4

Quinn

A fish market is a holy place. People who come from near the sea know this and my smartass people were ocean-side flotsam for certain. I grew up with my mother in Mystic, Connecticut. My grandfather was a biologist at Woods Hole. Year-round beach dwellers who weathered the winters and paid for pumps when basements got flooded.

Deep's Fish Market is in a puny building on the harbor. It's webbed over with fishing nets, skewered buoys stuck in there. A bell jangles when you open the door.

"Good day, sir!" I say to Billy, who rules the big glass shop counter. He's only seventeen and it's a marvel to see how well he plays the man. He wears a yellow slicker, necessary on rainy days but today an affectation. There's an odor of damp flannel from where Billy is sweating under the arms.

"Good day to you!" he says, smiley. A good smile, even though one of his canine teeth has fallen back and overlapped with its neighbor. Billy Deep has inky-black hair and the pale skin of the drowned. I bet his father tried to put him back the day he was born. In a fishing family, skin like that is bad luck for certain.

Billy says, "We have a special on Glidden Points. Came in this morning. D'you know what oysters do to a lady?"

Billy jokes because he knows he doesn't have a chance. It was the first time I came in with Rosie that did it. She was in the corner, quietly talking to the lobsters in the burbling tank. We were beaming at her, Billy and I, like she was the most wonderful thing we'd ever seen. Billy caught me staring, staring like *he* was staring, and just like that he understood he wasn't my type.

So now we have our rapport. This is what happens to boys once they realize they're not getting in your pants: they get fun to be around.

"Don't need any oysters, Billy."

"Well, then take some flounder and be done with it."

I watch him cut the floppy white meat into fillets. As he cuts, his gloves wrinkle. The tacky rubber cuff tugs at the dark hairs near his wrist. The slabs of fish are lined up like gems on the ice inside a case. The tuna is red and translucent as a drop of blood. The swordfish is more opaque, purplish and obscene. There's a halibut that hasn't been boned yet, its wobbly dead eye still intact. Something happens, not in the eye itself, but somewhere deeper inside, when a fish dies. You've seen it happen if you've ever watched one flop around a dock until it's dead. Some brightness or intelligence fades. I saw this happen to my mother. This very same thing.

There are plenty of examples to take from ocean beasts, if you're willing to look for them. My biologist grandfather specialized in photosynthetic plankton, which seemed infinitely less glamorous than the toothy sharks and blunt-headed belugas in the aquarium. But he showed me maps of how deep the ocean was and how only the smallest percentage of that was surface. He told me how it was the plankton grew green there and could catch the sun. This was what whales ate. Those minuscule creatures wound up in a whale's belly and made for enough nutrition to keep its lumbering heart beating.

Billy wraps the flounder in white paper and tapes the package closed. "Here you go. Hope your girl appreciates this."

Rosie always appreciates dinner. She usually says, "I used to go swimming with this?"

Rosie and I can share these small things, and I make sure to appreciate them. I turn them over in my mind real slow. I know it doesn't sound like much to go on, but I tell myself that if I lump all these small things together, they might add up to something. If I keep it up, they just might be enough to feed my big old Monstro heart.

AT HOME, I throw the fish down and say, "I'm making dinner." But Rosie says she isn't hungry. She says, "Let's go to the bar."

The Monkey's Uncle is the sort of place where people are drinking for a reason. There's no one waffling between cocktail options and definitely no chance of an anonymous encounter, which is what I thought bars were for. In the movies there's always a pretty girl with a sad face leaning against the cigarette machine, waiting for someone to save her with a scotch and soda. I've been living here for three months and I know every damn person in the Uncle right now.

Rosie normally drinks beer but she says, "I want what you're having," so I order us whiskeys with rocks. Jethro Newkirk is a couple of stools away and perks up at Rosie's voice. She has this effect on people.

"Rosie, my flower!" he says. Jethro is only fifty but takes old-man liberties: afternoon drink, self-indulgent storytelling, harmless lechery. He lays a hand on Rosie's knee. "You girls seen the new house going up?"

"It's a monster," Rosie says. "Worse than Elm Park."

That house is going up on a lot where Rosie's childhood home used to be. They tore her house down last summer, right after some out-of-staters, some *flatlanders* as Rosie says, bought her parents' lot and four more adjacent to it. Most of them beachfront, close to the shops downtown, right near the carousel. They paid a lot of money to get everyone out. If you were Rosie's parents, enough to get you to Florida twice over. Once a week Rosie takes a Polaroid of the construction site and sends it to her parents like a postcard. It usually reads something like: *Dear Traitors, I miss you. Love, Rosalind.*

"I heard it's going to have a two-story entrance and a three-car garage," I say.

"Ah-yuh," Jethro says. "I hate to see a house like that." He rubs his pink ears, flushed from booze. "But it's not getting done anytime soon. I saw the crew just sitting around this afternoon."

"Well, it's awfully hot to work that time of day, what do you want them to do?" Rosie says.

Jethro leaps off his bar stool and lifts his glass. "Burn it to the ground!" he cries. "I'd like them to burn it to the ground."

Rosie takes a sip of her whiskey and purses her lips. I can tell she doesn't like the taste. "Let it go," I say, and she dribbles it back into her cup. Beautiful girls can pull off disgusting gestures like this. And Rosie *is:* short, pale-skinned, and big-lipped with uncountable piercings along each ear. She takes another sip and stubbornly swallows.

We head for the jukebox. Rosie feeds quarters into its slot. She types in E32 and plays the same Guns N' Roses song she always plays. The one about the city that has all the pretty girls in it.

Rosie says when she's a singer she'll only sing songs like this one. I wonder if I could get good enough to play like Slash.

No way. I down the rest of my drink.

WE HEAD OUT hours later and the night smells like smoke and summer dying. We have whiskey coursing through our arms and arteries, making us strong and stupid. We walk the roads. We hear a humming. Tucked away among trees is the Menamon substation, the energy hub for most of Hancock County. We stare up at the transformers. There are metal towers with cables looping between their posts and coils of metal conducting insane amounts of wattage. The humming is incredible.

From here we can see the construction site Jethro was ranting about. Rosie points a fierce little finger at the foundation of what will certainly be a monstrously big house.

"I hate them," Rosie says.

"You don't even know them," I say.

"No one needs a house like that," Rosie says. "You should hate them too."

"Okay," I say, because with a girl like Rosie it's impossible to say no. I pick a stone up off the ground. There's nothing but a foundation to throw at and the site is too far away anyway, but I hurl the stone toward where the house will be. It flies uselessly off into the dark. "One imaginary window, smashed," I say. "Happy?"

Rosie grins and hands me another stone. I put it in my pocket. "I'll save it for real windows," I say. She squeezes my hand, my spine goes electric, and, man, am I in trouble.

"I buried a time capsule down there when I was eight," Rosie says. "In my backyard. I had every intention of digging it up and then one day there was all this cement."

"What's in there?"

She exhales irritably. Like the stuff in there isn't even the point. "Some photos. A letter I wrote to myself. A tape of me singing my favorite songs. A magic seashell."

"Magic?"

"Again, eight years old."

"Magic." I turn back to the substation.

Rosie wraps her fingers around the chain-link fence that surrounds this electric outpost. "Hmmmm," she hums, the exact same pitch as the transformer. Maybe Rosie really will become a famous singer someday. Not to be outdone, I hum an octave higher, harmonizing.

"We're going in," Rosie says, and starts to climb the fence.

"You've got a death wish," I say. "You'll be zapped."

Rosie shakes her head. "It's never the fence that's electric," she says. "It's everything inside that'll kill you." She hops it.

I follow. An obituaries writer, even a retired one of little mettle, has a duty to follow the doomed.

The ground inside rattles with gravel. Rosie lies down and stares up at the steely forest buzzing around her. I lie down too because she's fucking crazy and I might want to get close to that.

How many watts is a thousand? A million? I spread my arms wide and make a V with my legs. Then I slide them shut. I do it again, and a third time, and I might be cutting up my bare arms and thighs on the gravel but I don't care.

"Gravel angels," I tell Rosie.

"You're wicked crazy," she says, and begins to flail. "You know that?"

As we flex ourselves open and closed a cloud of dust rises around us. It hangs in the air, tiny particles. We are scuffing ourselves up in this toxic dirt. We are too close together, and as we beat our wings furiously Rosie's nails scratch my face and my fist wing catches her ribs and we're drunk and bruised and laughing.

When we're exhausted and spent we tuck our wings at our sides. There's only the sound of our alternately rasping breath and the humming. We sit up. The orange light on top of one of the transformers flicks on and light falls around us like a pumpkin, like a halo.

Rosie's bright hair catches the light and within minutes pale moths have gathered around her head. They parachute their furry bodies in arcs around her, wholly determined torpedoes. Rosie closes her eyes. A few moths settle on her head. I could stare at her like this for a long while yet. In fact, since I got here, all I want to do is stare and stare at this girl's face, and yes, I really am in trouble now. Bad trouble, I think as I watch this solar system of tiny revolving bodies orbiting Rosie's head.

[illegible]

[illegible]

[illegible]

[illegible]

Fall

5

Leah

There are dead bees on the windowsills of the *Menamon Star* office. Their legs stick up in surrender. I have been here five minutes and already I can tell, this is the kind of office where even the vermin have given up.

Charley is in a backroom office. A scrappy redhead raps on her open door to let her know I am here. Charley knows I am here. The redhead walks past me to the copier. On the breeze of her motion I smell last night's booze. She sits down at a desk that seems more appropriate for an antiques shop than an office.

"You smell like gin," I tell her.

She looks at me. Her eyes are pinkish around the rims, like a rabbit my class used to have in school. She's wearing a blue-and-white-striped button-down with the cuffs rolled up and too-big, straight-legged jeans. "What kind?" she says. Her cheekbones are high, a note of distinction in an otherwise ragamuffin exterior.

"Gordon's, maybe, but I'm only saying that based on looking at you. The smell could be Tanqueray. Could be Beefeater."

"Who are you?" she says, but then Charley emerges.

Back in her office Charley makes a big show of actually looking through my clippings. I feel nervous, which is laughable, but the real joke is that I want this small-time job as badly as I did my gig at the *Gazette,* and I'm afraid Charley won't give it to me. She lights a Marlboro, on which she takes long puffs. I can't believe her slowness. I think of all the competitive editors back in New York who would piss themselves laughing if they could see me right now. But why do we New Yorkers always think we have the best of everything? *Only in New York. Only in New York. Only in New York,* my parents told me. But one day I started wondering, Is that really true? Is all this New York hustle really that important?

The key to not blowing your life apart is not asking too many questions. But once I started, I couldn't stop—and then there was Henry. Standing there in the bar near my office downtown, the one I went to on bad days, not the celebrating pub two blocks the other way where I might see people from work. I was staring at the back of Henry's neck and waiting to order something truly potent to make the day slip away. His neck was so deeply tanned I knew he worked outside. He smelled of pine and soap, and when he turned he caught me behind him, leaning in too close. *What, do I smell or something?* he said. We sat in a vinyl booth.

Hours later, I said I hoped I wasn't keeping him from anything. He probably had somewhere else to be, I said. Everyone in New York has somewhere else to be. Henry said, *Where would I be going?* He rolled his shoulders to crack his neck and relaxed into the booth. He had tussled sandy hair, and a knobbled nose, and even though he was so young, he had white crow's-feet by his eyes from being sunburned while squinting. I could see that boring tattoo on his arm, and when he smiled he had a snaggletooth. He had *stillness,* Henry. He wasn't rushing away anywhere.

I sit with Charley now, and I see this too is a family trait. They can sit quietly, these Lynches, for what seems like an eternity.

Charley stubs out her cigarette in a coffee mug. "You're hired," she says. "Report to the redheaded felon out front."

I'm so relieved I almost laugh. It may be small, but I don't even care, I'm just so happy to be back on the beat.

6

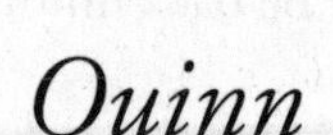

Quinn

I crane my head out our front window and catch the blue smell of wild grapes getting fat on the vines that choke the trees to death. The fall makes me so goddamn melancholy. Today is my birthday. My ex-girlfriend Sam called at midnight. She was out at some bar, *drunk but thinking of you!* I listened to her message three times.

I go downstairs and sit on the steps of the Stationhouse. Today I'm on assignment with Leah Lynch, my new partner. What a person could have done wrong in this life to wind up both related to and working for Charley Lynch I can't imagine. I thought I was hallucinating when this tall woman with a broomlike black ponytail walked into the *Star* office and sniffed the booze on me. Damn was she tall. Olivey-skinned with a wide, thin, serious mouth and eyes that showed exactly how disappointing she found the office. I listened in while Charley hired this sister-in-law, smoke drifting from her office, and I thought, Could you be the Woodward to my Bernstein? Are you the one I've been waiting for?

I operate best in units of two. Once, it was Sam and me. When Marta got sick, it became Marta and me. Imagine our family portrait: a confused and suspicious balding woman in a blue gown stares ahead as her snarling redheaded daughter crouches nearby, a protective animal. That was us. And then Marta died, leaving me alone in the frame. That wench. We were two parts of the same whole, and when she was gone I felt a lightness, a heavy weight unlashed from me. It should have been relief, not having to take care of her anymore, but instead I felt like I was floating, barely there at all.

Get me straight: I don't *need* anyone, but old habits die hard. Sometimes, when I feel too nothingy for my own good, I want to pull someone, anyone, into that empty space next to me in the family portrait. Otherwise, I'm just an old snapshot of some random girl.

Rosie is taking someone's breakfast order on the porch when she spots me sitting on the steps. Beyond the parking lot the train tracks are a rusty orange. The last of the summer weeds are busy pushing up through the gravel between the slats. How they keep from being blown to pieces when the engine goes through is a deeply fucking mysterious matter.

Rosie finishes taking the order and sits on the step above mine. She's wearing a tight white T-shirt and faded jeans. Her pouch of waitressly things is tied around her waist and makes her look marsupial. She flips through her order tickets and rips one off for me. In the section where it says *Table #* she's scribbled *Happy Birthday!* In the order section she's written, *This ticket entitles you to one highly mediocre birthday breakfast at the Menamon Stationhouse.*

"Thanks," I say.

By the time Leah gets here, I'm eating a plateful of huevos rancheros with blue birthday candles in them. Leah's ride is what my mom called a woody. It's the sort of car poor-ass surfers are always driving on cable television. Leah opens the door and scopes out the parking lot like she's trying to decide whether this is the sort of planet she wants to land on. She squints into the morning sun and jangles her car keys as she approaches.

"Nice ride," I say. "Want some eggs?" I offer a sloppy forkful of candle wax and red beans.

"I'll pass," she says, and squats on her heels so that we can talk. "It's your birthday?" I shrug and extend the red beans to her again. She waves her hand to dismiss them. "Well, happy birthday."

Over her jeans, Leah is wearing a cream-colored sweater that definitely can't go in the washing machine. More than that, I swear her black hair is in a French fucking twist. Marta used to keep her hair that way. She was one of those women who went apeshit for Audrey Hepburn, a lameness of spirit only acceptable in someone as strong as my mother.

Leah eyes my Top-Siders and green hoodie that lets her know I used to play a mean field hockey midfield. On the back it says WINTERS 19. I can tell she's questioning her sweater. She says, "I'm not quite sure how this works. I presume you know the ropes?"

"Slipknot, double cross, and superhold noose," I say. "I know them all."

Leah considers. "What percentage of the *Star*'s content would you say you write?"

"Sixty," I say. "I'm a goddamn machine."

"Sixty percent!" Leah stands up fast. She presses her fingers to her temples. Her hands are enormous. They fan out at the ends of her thin arms. "That's obscene. Why don't we divide up the work? You take this story. I'll find another one." This makes perfect sense, but what the fuck? We've barely met and already she's decided she'd rather go solo?

"Nah," I say. "You're junior editor and I'm senior editor. I need to train you."

"*Train* me?" She takes a few deep breaths. "Where does Charley fit in?"

"Charley is the Chief Amazon Lady of the Nile."

"And how long have you been with the *Star*?"

"Four months. I used to be with the *Fairhaven Hour*."

"What was your beat?"

I consider lying. I want to hang on to alpha status here, and the truth will hardly help. But I say, "Obits, you?"

"City section."

A lot more impressive than obits. I hold out hope she worked at some podunk rag. "For who?"

"The *New York Gazette*."

"Holy fuck, you wrote for the *Gazette*?" I shoot to my feet. "What are you even doing here?"

A diner shoots me a dirty look but I can't help it. The *Gazette* is real shit. I have no business giving Leah orders. I should be licking a ballpoint to facilitate her note-taking. "Does Charley know that? Can you get me a job there?"

"Charley knows," Leah says. She doesn't say whether she can get me a job. Is it that easy to tell I wouldn't be able to hang at a place like the *Gazette*?

Rosie comes out on the porch. She sticks her hand out and waits for an introduction. "Rosalind Salem," I say. "Leah Lynch."

Rosie says, "Pleasure to meet you. You want some eggs?"

"No thanks," Leah says. "Is this your place?"

"Might as well be," Rosie says. "It's my tin can coffin. Where are you headed?"

"Out to Deep's," Leah says, "though I can't imagine—"

The train signals flash and clang and the chugging of the engine approaching drowns out what she's saying.

"Eleven forty-two," Rosie calls over the racket.

Leah covers her ears and watches. Little pieces of her hair flick around her face and the sun is blazing away but she keeps her eyes open. They shudder back and forth, constantly settling on different parts of the train passing by.

7

Leah

Deep's Fish Market sits in a wide, unkempt lot of reeds. In the reeds are dead boats, moldering and full of bugs. I pull out my notebook. I always have my notebook with me. The slop and pull of the water is loud enough that Quinn raises her voice to speak to me. "The party line is disappearing marine real estate," Quinn says. "Just FYI."

FYI? "How do you know what the story is already?" I say. "How do you know the real estate is disappearing?"

Quinn points at several hand-painted signs, staked in the yard: VOTE NO ON PROP. 2! and KEEP OUR WATERS, KEEP YOUR DINNER!

"So it's an election story," I say. "Concerning the upcoming issues for the town vote."

Quinn shakes her head and pushes up her sweatshirt sleeves. "Come on, there's Billy now." She points at an anemic-looking boy with a blue knit cap pulled over his ears. He has enormous dark eyes, features too dainty for a fisherman, and a sideways smile. I present my hand for him to shake. The kid cocks his head and then smacks my hand like a high five.

"My da's in the boat," he says, already loping toward the wharf. "He's got the *Star* real clean for you. Figured she's the one you'd want."

Quinn vigorously scratches her scalp. "You have any Dramamine, Gazette?"

Down where the boats are tied up is a man Billy has no chance of equaling. Joseph Deep looks not a bit off balance as the lobster boat he stands in shifts from side to side. Fortysomething, there is a little gray in the hair that curls over his ears. He is wearing a hat like Billy's, with an embroidered logo on it that reads DEEP'S MARKET, EST. 1952. He has the brightest blue eyes and a Black Irish complexion. His jaw is set hard but there is humor in this face that might be unlocked at any second.

"Joseph. Nice to meet you," he says, and immediately grabs my hand. I watch him notice that it is approximately the size of his own. I think he's going to shake it but instead he helps me aboard, one hand on the small of my back. Squatting in the back of the boat is the boy in the cap, Billy. He is chewing something. There's an inch and a half of water sloshing around the boat bottom and my shoes soak through. The water is very cold. Billy is wearing rubber galoshes, and dozens of sunflower-seed husks are floating around his feet. He spits.

"You wanna life jacket?" he says.

"I'm an excellent swimmer," I say.

"You'll jump in and save her, though, won't you, Billy?" says Quinn. Joseph has now extended his hand to Quinn but she says, "I wasn't expecting a boat, Joe."

I look over the side of the boat and the lettering says THE ME-

NAMON STAR, next to which is an image of a compass rose. I think maybe we should use this image on the newspaper masthead. I wonder whether the paper is named for the boat. Quinn and I put on our life vests. Damp and salty, mine rides up too high on my chest. Cages are stacked in the back. Rubber bands coil in a bucket. Billy picks up a gauge from a box of metal tools and starts tweaking Quinn's waist with it. "What size we got here?" he says, and Quinn slaps him away. "Aw, Da, she's a runty one. We'll have to throw her back."

"I'll take you over with me," she says. "I swear to God I will use you as a raft."

Joseph turns the engine over and the roar eats everything up. I smell diesel and we're moving.

"How long have you been a lobsterman?" I ask.

Joseph shouts, "Since the fifties!" The engine settles. "But these days we mostly just run the shop, buy from the guys who set more traps. If we don't lose Billy overboard, we just might stay in business another generation."

"Not if they raise the rent again we won't," Billy says. "Not if those flatlanders make us move."

"Who?" I say. I look to Quinn to see if she's planning to ask some questions, but she seems bilious and distracted.

"The ladies over in the development have been complaining about the boats out front. Say we're driving down real estate prices along the rest of the waterfront," Joseph says. "But our rent has almost doubled since they changed the waterfront zoning. Cleared it for nonmarine occupancy so a developer could build those Elm Park houses on the water. And now the owners of that new house spent a fortune on a number of waterfront lots out by the carousel. Suddenly the real-estaters are thinking our shop might be more lucrative if it were owned by someone other than us." I'm writing fast to keep up with them. Joseph turns over the engine again so it roars. "This stretch of water we call the jungle," Joseph says.

"Mad lobsters out here," Billy says. The water is thick with bobbing buoys in different colors. They rise and fall with the water like a comforter on a sleeping body.

Joseph says, "There have been disputes over who has the rights to this water since the seventies."

"The lobstah wahs," Billy says in a voice like a crusty old-timer's.

Lobster wars? This is the news? I'm jotting fast to get everything down. It's not that I didn't account for this. I knew the news would be small. I just thought it would still be *news.* I try not to be too disappointed. The rent hikes, the zoning—that I could get behind. It's worth some digging. I look up from my notes. "Quinn," I say, because I want to see what she thinks of this angle. But she doesn't even hear me. She is picking at sunflower-seed shells. She is not taking notes. Is she even listening over there?

"This is one of my pots," Joseph says, and points at a floating buoy with different shades of blue in alternate stripes.

"What about that one?" I point at another buoy, tangled up and rolling around in the hull of the boat. Instead of Joseph's blues, it has green and orange stripes. A blazing happy pattern like an Easter egg.

"That's Hank's pot," Billy says.

"Henry's?" I say. I have never heard Henry called Hank before.

"Hank Senior's," he says.

I pick the buoy up and turn it over in my hands. It is spongy and smells of mildew, but not old. I knew Henry's father fished, but none of these details, these pots and lobster wars, has ever come up.

Joseph points at the floating buoy. "Why don't you get this one, Billy," he says. Billy scrambles to his feet, not so sure on them as Joseph, wobbly like a deer. He seizes the buoy and gets his back braced, ready to heave up the weight. He pulls, and when his arms give too easily, he tumbles backward. A length of rope comes onboard with nothing attached.

"Where's the lobsters, Billy?" Quinn says. Her skin is sallow and she's doing some regimented breathing. It is only now that I remember the terrible, melodramatic copy I'd spotted in the *Star* weeks ago. "Hot-blooded fury." "Tails between their legs." My stomach feels heavy.

I hiss at her, "Are you birthing a baby over there or are we writing a news story?"

She rolls her eyes. "If you don't want me to ralph on you, I'd back down."

I roll my eyes back, then realize how stupid that is. It's Quinn's fault, for getting under my skin like this and dragging me down to her level. The girl doesn't know the first thing about reporting.

"It's cut. Fucking crooks," Billy says, inspecting the rope.

"Who would have cut it?" I say. I make a big point of lifting up my pen and notebook as I anticipate his answer so Quinn can see that this is what she should be doing.

"Could have been lots of people," Joseph says.

"Quinn," I say. She's looking really green now. "We should take a picture of the cut line. Do you have the camera?"

She grimaces and pulls out a small digital camera. "Smile, Billy," she says. Billy grins and holds up the rope like a prize catch.

"I don't know that he should be smiling," I say. "I mean, it depends what angle we're taking but . . ."

Quinn snorts. "Okay, look dour, Billy."

Joseph laughs as Billy pulls a long face. "Hey, move that trap there, Leah," Quinn says. "It's ruining my shot." She points at me, then the trap. When I don't respond she points again. In New York, I used to look over my photographers' shoulders and adjust their lighting.

But clearly this is not New York. "This way?" I finally say, and drag the trap across the bottom of the boat so it splashes and soaks Quinn's pants. She wheels around, more surprised than angry. I say, "Is that the best camera the *Star* has?"

"This is a nice camera." Quinn shakes out her wet pant cuffs. "Charley got it for her birthday." She looks approvingly at the little silver machine.

When we dock, Quinn scrambles to get out of the boat. On the boardwalk, water runs off her jeans and puddles at her feet. She takes several deep breaths and seems pleased to have her legs beneath her again. I stalk back toward the shop and Quinn runs to catch up. "So," she huffs, "you take some good notes back there or what?"

I could murder her. This is the news.

In the store, we say good-bye to Joseph. Billy sits back down behind the counter. On a high shelf behind the register is a lobster mounted on a plank, standing jauntily on his legs.

"Who's that guy?" I say.

Billy looks like he's been waiting for someone to ask him this his whole life. "That would be the gentleman lobster," he says. He grins and takes the thing down from the shelf. Up close you can see the fine work of the taxidermist. The antennules are curled elegantly, framing the face, and the lobster is wearing a tiny pair of spectacles. A mustache has been appliquéd and on each of the lobster's feet is a small shoe. He is wearing spats.

I laugh, in spite of myself. I have never seen anything like it. I look to Quinn, but she doesn't seem to think it's funny. In fact, she seems enraged.

"Where would one get a taxidermied lobster like that?" Quinn asks. While I'm glad to hear her engaging in something like journalistic discourse, I can't see how we can possibly work this into our piece.

"You're in the market?" says Billy. "Carter Marks is the guy."

Quinn sets her jaw. "Let's go, Leah." She jingles her keys at me like I'm a dog and blows out the door. Billy's face falls.

"Thanks again," I say. "That thing is cool."

Billy picks it up and stares into its face. "Thanks," he says. I head out the door but peek over my shoulder as I go. I see Billy wiggle the platform back and forth. All eight lobster legs wobble, a small dance. Billy smiles.

8

Quinn

Driving Leah and me back to the *Star,* I can't help but hold the wheel like it's a neck. I might just be in the market for a gentleman lobster and it better be pretty glorious. It better be the most elegant fucking gentleman I've ever seen if that's what was keeping Carter from my mother all these years. Keeping, because I know she called him once.

When Mom was sick I spent my Sundays in the bleak-ass kitchen, paying bills and eating Cheerios. I drank coffee until my head spun because I've always been shitty at math and I didn't understand how things like taxes, hospital bills, and mortgages worked. It was on one such occasion that I spotted the scattering of calls to Menamon that Marta made right after she first got diagnosed. They were dated and numbered on the bill. Short, less than ten minutes. But there was one that lasted over an hour. I highlighted that line in yellow because it was a satisfying thing to do with evidence no one cared about.

That she would talk to him and not tell me was a maternal atrocity. I'd thought we were in things together. I thought I wasn't talking to him, seeing him, knowing him, out of some kind of solidarity with Marta. And if she was talking to him, then, well, why wasn't I? I was mad enough to spit. *Mad enough to spit* was something Marta said a lot once she got diagnosed, usually about people she imagined had slighted her: doctors, waiters, neighbors. Before she got sick, Marta was always beautiful and always angry. The way she swept around in a rage it was like the old Greek gods.

Marta had thick hair she never tied back, a deeper red than mine, and she wore long wrap skirts that orbited her as she strode. She wore sandals until the first snow and jingling silver bracelets she only took off in her pottery studio. Don't give me any of that *Ghost* shit: when Marta threw pots she straddled the wheel, her arms strong and unmoving, her tits jiggling as she pressed the pedal to spin the clay faster. She barely moved her hands; the clay just *became* what she asked of it: a vase, a bowl, a vessel.

And then, suddenly, she was tired. Tired! Tired and delusional enough to think now was a good time to call Carter. Carter who was busy with his band, and his touring, and his midlevel fame and taxidermied animals. That morning in the kitchen I hocked a ball of spit into the stainless-steel sink to see if that would make me feel better, but it didn't. Marta was asleep in the bedroom, a soporific saint for one quick minute. I checked for the evenness of her breathing before I dialed the number on the phone bill.

He didn't sound much like the recordings. All that warbling isn't the same as talking. His voice rang like a gong over the distance of the phone wires. *Hello?* He sounded suspicious. He sounded like the sort of fucker who would leave his lady and child. This, I knew even then, was a lot to read into a single hello. I also knew I had to say something to him, because he was breathing into the line. Waiting. I had a lot of options, but I panicked. All I got out was *Your refrigerator's running* before I slammed the receiver down.

And then I folded over, the breath knocked out of me, weeping like the fucking tree she wanted in Marta's doorway. What wrecked me most of all was that a person as great as her could get stuck with nobody better than *me* to look after her. What a lousy fucking deal. I stayed there for a while, listening to her breathing in and out, and paying too much attention to the minutiae of the dirty floorboards.

"WHAT ANGLE DO you think we should take?" Leah says, and I almost drive off the road. She white-knuckles the console. She says, "I was thinking we could spin it like, 'New Budget to Decide Local Lives.' Or even, 'The Disappearance of the American Fisherman.' "

I look at Leah, because this is too good. "Seriously?" I say.

"Seriously what?"

I crack a smile and relax my death grip on the steering wheel. "Charley really hates your guts," I say. My pant cuffs are still soaked where Leah splashed me and my ankles are freezing.

"What does that have to do with anything?" Her posture gets real straight, defensive. Like she knew Charley hated her but maybe thought it wasn't apparent to the rest of the world.

"What just happened," I explain, "is you got hazed. Charley sent us out there because there was no way in hell you'd find a story on the Deeps' lobster boat."

Leah looks back at her notepad, where she's been scribbling in impossibly neat handwriting. She looks sick for a minute.

"Well, I guess she was wrong," she says, and goes back to jotting. This damn woman is unshakable and I'm almost out of viable reasons to defend my senior editor status. I cut a hard left into the *Star* parking lot and Leah's pen drags across the lines. She flips the page and starts over.

THE *STAR* OFFICE is a ground-floor, two-room affair. The burgundy carpet is musty from when a pipe burst once and flooded the place. None of the furniture matches and the overall effect is more junk shop than hub-of-all-news. When Charley opens the door to her office we get the stink of the eight thousand cigarettes she smokes in there. Her face is remarkably smooth for a lady with so much rat poison in her lungs, though her long, tapered fingers are stained yellow at the tips. "Let me see if you managed to keep your thumb out of any of those photos, Winters," she says.

"I already found the best one," Leah says. I'd try to one-up her but good Christ, it's starting to look like I'm outmatched. Leah shoves the camera in front of Charley. It's the shot I took of Billy pulling a dour face next to the cut trap rope. Billy's face has come out looking serious and the angle is clear: young man can't believe after hauling and hauling he's found nothing at the end of his rope. All three of us press our heads together to look at the image on the screen.

Charley says, "Good. Now write it."

Leah sits down and spreads her notes out at a wobbly desk that might have once been a lady's makeup table. She waves me over. I shake my head and wave *her* over.

"I've got the notes," she says.

"I'm senior editor," I say.

She refuses to stand up but instead wheels her seated body over by pulling at the carpet with her heels. She rolls until she's right up in my face. She has the sort of lashes that create the illusion of an unbroken black outline around her eyes. "Okay," she says. She flips through her pad. "Why don't we lead with the budget vote?" This is a perfectly reasonable suggestion that I'm not going to take because I'm in charge.

"I think we should lead with the complaints about the dead boats in Deep's yard," I say.

"But that's minor news compared to the vote!"

In my best Barbara Walters voice I say, "I think we should lead with 'The Disappearance of the American Fisherman.'"

She gives me a deadly look.

"Who's in charge?" I say, and Leah's face crumples. It's unfair, I know, but I've been working here four months longer than her, and so I get to be Bernstein, be Dustin Hoffman. That leaves Robert Redford for Leah.

Listen, I know that in real life both of those guys went on to be successful. I know Woodward wrote books and dedicated his life to service and the news and was, after all, the one who initiated contact with Deep Throat and probably the more famous one when you really get down to it. But have you *seen* the movie? How cool Dustin Hoffman is as Bernstein? The way he flirts with ladies and shows Woodward how to edit copy? How he kicks his feet up on the desk and has a mouth no one in the newsroom can handle? Have you counted how many cups of coffee he drinks and fully appreciated the extinct sort of rogue journalist he was?

"You are in charge, Quinn." Leah puts her pen down on the desk. A white flag if ever I saw one in this office that is, in and of itself, one gigantic white flag. I look at Leah with her copious notes and straight posture. Leah with her half-decent headlines, pulled from thin air. The truth that I already know but don't want to admit is that *she* is Dustin Hoffman. She is Bernstein, who goes solo and cracks the pretty lady. Gets the interview. Runs the show. I don't stand a chance. I'll always be the guy who fumbles around and catches a few lucky breaks. Lurks in garages. I'm Woodward, goddammit. I've even got the Redford hair.

"Oh, of course we lead with the vote," I say.

Leah sits up and shouts, "Great!" I move my chair closer so I can help her. If I'm honest, I'll take this duo any way that I can get it. I'll be Woodward. Watson. Sundance. The sidekick. Anyone, just so long as my sidecar's hitched to something.

9

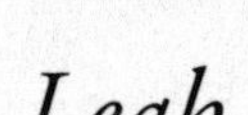

Leah

When Quinn drops me back at the Stationhouse the sun is half sunk beneath the restaurant's tarpaper roof. Henry had suggested we celebrate my first day at the family business tonight, but I know he will ask me how my day went. *It went badly. I got hazed by your gene pool. It was disappointing.*

But truthfully, even today, when I've made a fool of myself, taking notes then making sense of them on the page is good for me. I have my own ideas about what the world should be like, but when I write down actual facts in my notebook, when I smooth those facts out into a true point-A-to-point-B story, it's like a tether that keeps me from floating away. My *Gazette* editor told me this made me good at the job. I didn't just like writing the news, I *needed* it.

How was your day? Henry will ask if I go home. We never

firmly made plans. I don't want to go home and explain today, even though I should. In Maine, Henry told me, family rituals are not optional. All occasions are marked with mandatory dinners, toasts, parties. Hank used to throw a birthday party for June every year, even though she'd beg him not to. One year she wound up baking her own cake, a huge white-frosted vanilla one big enough to feed sixty guests. By two in the morning everyone had left except "the singers." The singers were two men from the docks who sat with Hank in the yard, drinking and warbling old Irish songs and Hank Williams and all the dirtiest shanties. They made June join in. At four, when the night was at its blackest, *dark as the inside of a pocket,* Henry said, she went inside, and found Henry and Charley in their pajamas, barely awake but peering out the screen window, amazed to hear their parents singing. June scooped them up and brought them to bed, where they all curled together, June still wearing her party dress. June still smelling like vanilla cake.

And yet.

"Quinn," I call. She cuts a funny profile standing on the porch. There is a sloppy elegance in the way her too-big clothes hang upon her frame. The sunset lights her hair up strawberry.

"Can I buy you birthday dinner?" I point at the Stationhouse.

She grins. Her scrawny face opens up, just like that. "Fuck no," she says. "But you can buy me a dozen drinks."

AT THE MONKEY'S Uncle there's a wooden cutout of a monkey sheepishly clutching his tail above the door. The monkey, I think, is ashamed of something he's done in this bar. Inside, the lights are low and warm. Men with muddy boots and stocking hats hold beers. Three women, all wearing cable-knit sweaters, laugh and drink from clear glasses with limes in them. Playing pool in the corner is a gang of boys with pitiful facial hair, definitely not twenty-one. They all wear shirts from the ironworks. A line of people teeter solo on bar stools.

A woman behind the bar is waiting for me to place an order by the time I make it there. Quinn says, "Buy me a Jack and ginger, Leah."

"One Jack and ginger," I say, "and do you have any drink specials?"

The bartender has silver-and-black hair pulled off her face. She says, "It's real special that we have beer *and* liquor." She is tanner than a person should be, and wirier. She wears a blue thermal with the sleeves pushed up. Her arms look winnowed down to bone and muscle alone.

I order a beer and she ducks to get it from a fridge. Quinn says to me, "Sara Riley. It's me she doesn't like, not you."

"I like you fine when you're sober," Sara says as she comes up with my beer.

Quinn wanders over to the jukebox and puts on Guns N' Roses.

When she returns to the bar a half-asleep man in a checkered shirt wakes and says to Quinn, "I knew it was you, because of the song. But you were with a different one." He points at me before laying his head back in his arms.

"Let's sit in the garden," Quinn says. "I want to smoke a cigarette." She grabs a sack of peanuts from behind the bar.

Outside there's plastic furniture in a gravel pit with a view of the parking lot and a generator shed. "I'm technically quit, an ex-smoker," Quinn says as she lights a cigarette. "So, is your husband as much of a hard-ass as Charley?" She is exhaling not only smoke but also her own breath made visible in the cold. The pink rims of her eyes are inflamed and her mouth is lively with mischief. She pulls her red hair out of the neck of her sweatshirt so it falls across her shoulder.

"I don't know what Charley is like, really," I say. "She barely talks to me."

Quinn splits a peanut in two and the nut skitters across the table. She picks bits of red skin off the table with her finger and eats it. "That's just how it goes," she says. "She rode my ass when I first started too. Sent me maple sugaring for my first assignment."

"When did she stop picking on you?" I say.

"When you showed up!" Quinn says, and laughs a rumbly cigarette laugh, coughing, letting it build and roll over.

"Maybe I should recruit another employee," I say.

"Oh yeah, just call up your friends at the *Gazette*. Tell them you've got a real great opportunity up here. Prime-time shit."

I crack a peanut and eat it. "It's like she's already made up her mind about me," I say. "Henry isn't like Charley. Henry is solid."

Quinn pinches the bridge of her nose twice, a liar's tic, and stares at me. *"Solid?"* she says, an octave too low.

"What's wrong with solid?" I say. I eat another peanut.

"Solid sounds boring." Quinn leans on her elbows. "I thought marriage was for when you found someone life re-magnetizing, or reason-for-living-producing, or good in bed."

She waits for me to respond, but I'm not sure what life re-magnetizing might mean. My old editor definitely would have struck it. She would have put a red line through Quinn's whole phrase. I grab a handful of peanuts and start lining them up on the table, rank and file. I say, "Solid is good. You'll see. Eventually you just start caring about different things in a relationship." As soon as it's out of my mouth I realize this is something my parents once told me.

"*That* is condescending as hell," Quinn says. She pulls a peanut from my line and smashes it open. "How old are you anyway?"

"Twenty-four."

"And today is my birthday, so, so am I. Are you saying I'm

going to experience revelation in my sleep? Is the archangel going to come down and give me the news that what I'm now looking for is a *solid* woman?"

"No, not like that," I say. I can't really believe we're the same age. I also wonder if I should follow up on that last bit. In spite of her total lack of journalistic skill, I find myself liking Quinn. I like the way she's testing me. So I do:

"Woman?" I say.

"Women," Quinn says. Her whiskey hovers halfway to her mouth, which is set in a challenging line.

"But never solid ones?" I say.

Quinn grins. "Never. I make a point of it."

I press my fingers to my mouth. Quinn drinks.

"I haven't been here very long," I say. "But it seems to me that Menamon is exactly the sort of place to look for unstable women."

Quinn laughs and can't keep from spitting her drink back in the cup. She wipes her mouth and smiles. "I know," she says, and shakes her head.

QUINN DROPS ME home late at night, a little worse for the wear. When we get to my house I say, "This is me."

Quinn puts a hand to her forehead and looks at the bull's-eye glass above our door. She looks at our symmetrical shrubberies. "You live here? Leah, this is a grown-up's house."

"I am very grown up," I tell her, and climb out of the car. Before I even have my keys out, Henry has opened the door. He stands in the doorway. His face is cast in darkness and the hallway light glows around his silhouette, and I think of a story he told me once:

Henry accidentally set the neighbor's barn on fire when he was twelve, a campfire experiment gone wrong. He ran home to hide before anyone found out it was him, but of course when he got there his father was already standing in the warm square of the doorway. Henry said that was the most scared he'd ever been. Hank took him back next door and made him watch the barn burn while the firemen tried to put out the blaze. Hank explained that they were too late; the barn was ruined and would need to be rebuilt. Henry rebuilt that barn all summer. Hank taught him how. It was so much work, Henry said. It was so difficult to raise a thing from the ground like that. I remember all the details Henry told me because whenever he mentions how strict his father was, I think about how he was so, so lucky.

My own parents used to catch me coming in late. I'd take my sneakers off outside the apartment, lift the doorknob as I pushed, thinking maybe I could make it past them if only I could keep walking on the balls of my feet. Mostly they caught me. My father still up and working on briefs with a red pen, sipping a tumbler of club soda for his stomach. Wearing a set of actual pajamas, light blue linen with dark blue piping. His longish black hair, gray at the temples, swept back. His papers propped on his belly like that's what he had it for. He'd look over his enormous tortoise-shell glasses and say something vaguely interested-sounding like, *Late night?* I'd kiss his forehead, hope he didn't smell the night's trespasses on me, and jaunt off to bed. In the morning it would be my mother's turn. I'd sit on a high stool at the bar in the kitchen eating too much organic cereal from a bowl that was meant for soup while my mother used the kitchen mirror to do her makeup. *Your father says you had a late night,* she'd say to herself in the mirror as she clipped on large gold-knot earrings. She had short auburn hair feathered around her face and always smelled of mature perfumes that came in frosted glass bottles. She'd pick up her matching necklace, hand it to me, and turn around. I'd do her clasp for her, and as I did it I'd say, *Yes, I did,* and that would be the end of it. I love my parents, I do, but I always felt it was as if the three of us were members of the same exclusive club that just so happened to have its headquarters in our penthouse. It was an old and dignified bond that brought us together in our blood, but like all those old clubs, we'd been at it so long we'd lost our sense of what we were there to do.

"Where the hell were you?" Henry says now, and I am delighted he is angry. That he cares I was gone. I have burned a barn and he will be strict with me! I throw my arms around him.

"You are mad!" I say. I kiss his cheek. "I was at the bar with a friend," I tell Henry. "I forgot to call. I'm sorry."

Quinn waves. "I'm the friend," she tells Henry. She rubs her hands on her jeans, as if to clean them, and sticks out her right for him to shake. "Quinn Winters. I work for your sister."

He shakes her hand. We all stand there for a minute, not sure what to do next. "Well, I'll be going, then," Quinn says. I wave awkwardly as she gets back into her car. Her tires spin out and fling bits of clamshell as she accelerates out of the driveway.

Once we are inside, Henry says, "That girl has eyes like a rabbit."

"I know," I say. "And that girl gets along with your sister."

"Listen," Henry says. "I'm not saying you can't do what you want but do you think you might call me next time you go off the grid?"

"So you can worry about me?" I say.

"So I *won't* worry about you," Henry says. "So I don't wait for you to eat and stuff. Logistics." Henry palms my head and smoothes back all the little pieces of hair from my face so he can see me.

"Yes," I tell Henry. "Of course." I should know this: When you are married you need to tell people where you are going so they don't worry, because they love you. And because of logistics.

"How was your first day?" Henry says.

"I'll tell you all about it tomorrow," I say. "Right now I am very sleepy."

Henry falls asleep easily. He is a champion sleeper. I roll around next to him for a while and then creep downstairs. Sometimes you need to stare into the refrigerator glow awhile to get ready for sleeping. But when I open the fridge I see that Henry had made enough dinner for both of us. There is a bottle in there too. Champagne, unopened. My chest constricts.

When I crawl back into bed with him he sighs but does not wake. Already this is more difficult than I'd thought it would be, being each other's family. I thought that because I loved Henry it would be easy to do the right things but sometimes I forget to be thoughtful. I forget to do what is right. Sometimes I just charge on ahead and do what it is that I want. Tonight my love cannot fix the small thing that I have ruined. I am too late. A barn burner.

I CALL MY parents.

I got a job, I say.

We're very happy for you, they say.

I'm covering all sorts of real American news, I say. Things that matter to real Americans.

Are we not real Americans? they say. The *Gazette* isn't for real Americans?

You know what I mean, I say.

How is Henry? they say.

Henry is good, I say. Fall is a busy planting season.

You missed the Hopper at MoMA, they say.

Everything here is good. Very good. So good, I say.

It's great to hear that you're doing so well, they say.

10

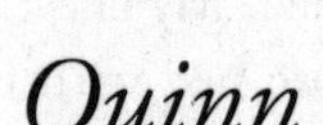

Quinn

I'm sitting on a wrought-iron bench that's radiating cold into my ass, feeling bad for myself about the fact that my mother is dead. I let myself do this about once a week. I figure, if I allot time for it, it won't come creeping up on me at other, less convenient times. This mostly works not at fucking all. I light a cigarette. They're tricky, these feelings of missing someone. They burrow like gophers, creating tunnels in the matter of your self, riddling everything with holes. I tell myself if I keep puffing I'll smoke them out eventually. I smoke and I smoke. We've just gone to print, it's not late, but the Neversink Park carousel is closed. The ancient horses are still but their eyes roll wildly, too much white exposed.

I make a pitiful face for no one. I try to conjure a tear, a slow roller, for show. When I was a kid, I used to imagine Carter could see me. Not in a crystal ball or anything, but in his mind. I reasoned that, because I had half his genetic juice, maybe he had the ability to check in. Not that he would ever do it, that he would care. But whenever I lied to my mother, or shoplifted gum, or did any of the dumb shit requisite of youth I always sort of thought Carter would know. So I acted different. I sat up straight even when no one was looking. Ever since I got to Menamon I've been doing this again. Alternately trying to look cool, like I don't give a damn, and trying to look sad, so he'll feel guilty.

I spot Billy Deep shuffling down the wharf. He has one hand in his jacket pocket and he's holding a burlap sack. His knit cap is pulled low and he keeps his head down as he walks.

"Hey," he says, and as he gets closer I see he's shifty-eyed.

"What's in the bag?" I say. The burlap wriggles.

"A cat," he says.

"The fucking proverbial cat of lore? What really?"

"It's a damn cat, Quinn, would you lower your voice?" He speaks in the hushed tone of the guilty. A mrowling from the bag confirms this.

"All right," I say, lower. I look up and down the deserted waterfront. "What are you doing with a cat?"

"Just been bagging cats is all."

"Bagging? What the fuck, Billy, why?"

"Elm Park."

I ignore the fact that Billy didn't answer my question—not my best investigative moment—and ask instead, "Billy, is that someone's pet?"

"He's got a tag says 'Ginger Boots.'"

There is almost certainly a frantic woman somewhere calling this name into the tree line, which would be hilarious if it weren't so fucking sad. "What'd you bag him for?"

"You know how much rent is at the store as of next month?" Billy says. "Four hundred dollars more than it was last month."

I don't like to see his boyish face all fevered like this. It spoils the charm. "And you know what people are paying for fish next month?"

"How much?"

"The same they're paying for it this month."

"Shit," I say. "Shit."

"Yeah," Billy says, and swooshes his black forelock under the band of his cap. "And you know why?"

"Elm Park?" I say.

"Elm Park and your new big-house neighbors."

I get what this is about. The town vote went badly this week. The school budget wasn't passed and there's been talk property taxes will be higher next year. For the issue we just closed I'd suggested GENERAL GRUMBLING IN RESPONSE TO EPIC BUDGET FAIL as a possible headline, but Leah wouldn't have it. We ran with BUDGET VOTE SHOWS NEW DEMOGRAPHIC AT PLAY IN LOCAL POLITICS.

I say, "What does the big house have to do with cats, Billy?"

He shrugs. "They get lost easy after new people move in. Just trying to let people know this is a hostile environment. Besides, there's a demand."

I knew I should have taken this kid out drinking. Boys need booze in their veins to keep them too lazy to get into trouble. Forget the YMCA.

"A demand for cats?"

"For taxidermy."

I feel nauseous. "Billy, do you sell cats to Carter Marks?" Billy scans the waterfront for eavesdroppers, like I don't write for the town paper anyway. "Billy, you can't kill that cat. You're not that kind of guy."

"I don't kill 'em. I just bag 'em."

"Give it," I say. I won't let my nonfather fuck up Billy Deep, who was an upstanding and only sometimes libidinous seafood salesman last I knew. I wrest the sack away from him and drop it.

The cat slinks out of the bag, raises its hackles, and hisses. I see rows of sharp milk teeth, the pink of its tongue. It's a calico cat covered with black and marmalade patches, including a broad one on its head like a helmet. Each foot is orange from paw up. Ginger Boots. It crouches low to the ground before darting away, a domestic bell tinkling around its neck.

"You owe me thirty bucks," Billy says.

That Carter would do something like this is sick, pathological. And the worst part of it is that lately I've been wondering about the vacancy in my family portrait. I'd started to wonder what he'd look like standing there. I'd let myself imagine showing up at his door and him crying and saying how happy he was to see me and that Crazy Marta forbade him to ever talk to me and that he didn't just use her for a shitty folk song after all and that he was so glad to have me back. But after this? Taxidermied cats? Fuck that delusion. I'm back to the original plan.

"Tell me you'll stop doing this, Billy," I say.

"Tell them to stop building that big house," he says. "Tell them not to raise my father's rent." He claps me on the back, the way an older man might. "Hell," he says. "You're a newspaper lady. Lead the call to arms."

LEAH IS SITTING at the *Star*'s computer, aggressively typing and retyping. I'm cross-legged on the desk next to her shooting pencils at the wastebasket, mostly missing. We've been arguing over this piece for half an hour and Charley's on us to finish so we can go to print and go home, but Leah and I are still at it, having too much fun fighting to compromise. The headline in question: NONMARINE OCCUPANCY ZONING LAWS CHANGING THE COAST.

"I'm so bored," I say. "You say zoning, and immediately I'm so bored I want to gouge my eyes out." I use a pencil to mime some gouging.

"You keep saying that," Leah says. "But you can't tell me what would be better. Give me one better suggestion. And don't even try bringing up—"

"Kept women!"

"No!" she says. "We've been over this. A woman supported by her husband is not necessarily a 'kept woman.' And you don't know that the Elm Park women are kept. They could be independently wealthy professionals."

"There are two papers in front of you," I say. "One says, 'Kept Women vs. the Lobstermen.' The other says, 'Boring-Ass Treatise on Zoning.'" I weigh the imaginary options in my hands. "You know I'm right," I say.

"But you're not!" Leah clonks her head down on the table, but she's laughing.

Charley appears. "Give it to me," she says. "I can't stand listening to the two of you for another second."

Leah types and clicks. "It's uploading," she says to Charley.

"You wench. You went with zoning, didn't you?" I say.

"I did," she says, standing and stretching. Pleased with herself. "Bar?"

"Sure," I say.

At the Uncle, we argue about the headline for another hour. Even though it's already gone to print. Even though Jethro covers his ears and asks us to please, please, talk about anything else.

WHEN I GET home, Rosie is sitting on the brown couch that is also my bed. She has my guitar out and is strumming an open G, over and over again. One of her breasts rests in the valley of the guitar. It never occurred to me that if I had a decent pair, they might interfere. She strums and stares at me pointedly.

"You know I love to sing and you never even told me you could play guitar?" she says.

"It's not like that," I say. "It's complicated. I don't want to talk about it." Rosie has showered recently. A warm, steamy clean hangs over the apartment like a weather system.

"Complicated how? Do you not like my singing?"

"I like your singing fine," I say, and plop on the couch next to her.

She strums again, thoughtful. "It's pretty," she says.

"A G chord is like that."

"I mean the guitar. The Dove." She runs a finger over the lacquer pick guard. It *is* a Dove, I see now.

My mother loved birds. Back in Connecticut we heard the mourning doves when we woke up, *oo-waoh,* and the barred owls dolefully hooting at night. Sometimes she'd point out an owl, sleeping in the hollow of a tree, the hole seemingly stuffed with fluff. All this was fine till she started hooting at them. She'd stand out on our wraparound deck and hoot and hoot, trying to call the owls down. I gave her a lot of shit for that. I said she was going to become the crazy bird lady of Mystic. But she kept at it. I got looks, a mix of pity and disgust, from our neighbors. From the cigar-smoking ones, the compulsive laundry-drying ones, and especially the just-clearing-sticks-from-my-yard-which-is-the-thinnest-damn-excuse-for-spying-ever ones. But fuck all of them. Did they want to take care of her?

One night, Marta slid open the glass door, her body set against the black, and said, *Pssst, Quinn, come here. Pssst, pssst.*

I went out into the dark, into the spring cold, and stood on the deck with my mother. She was barefoot and wore a white nightgown, the kind with cutouts at the bottom. The hem swirled around her ankles as she paced about the deck, calling between cupped hands *hoo, hoo, hoo hoo. It's "Who cooks for you,"* she said. *That's what it sounds like. Their calls. "Who cooks for you!"* So I sat on the deck railing, feet dangling like a child's as I smoked through half a pack of cigarettes and my mother continued hooting.

Then, dead silently, this owl the size of a football came and perched on a branch not three feet from the deck. He had drag-queen eyes that owl, rimmed in black, with a weird filmy lid that slid back and forth instead of blinking and a white mask like a Venn diagram. His head sat densely on his chest, no neck to speak of, and he did not so much cock his head as rotate it around. The strong yellow curve of his beak barely parted when he hooted, but she was right. My mother in the moonlight, her white nightgown bright in the dark, the soft bulge of her freckled arms exposed to the air, was right. This owl was asking a question.

I thought about my answer. Who cooks for you? Is that like, Who does your dirty work? Or is it more like, Who loves you? One of my mother's favorite expressions was *Can't it be both?* She resolved all manner of crises this way. I think that was the case with Who cooks for you. That it might mean both of those things.

"Play me a song," Rosie says, and slides over. She's wearing three pairs of earrings, which means today was a dark day. I know she needs more metal when she's low. A Polaroid of the big-house construction is on the kitchen table. There's a note scrawled at the bottom, a stamp in the corner. The house is growing tall, taking shape.

I found the guitar in my mother's closet when I was packing up the house. Carter's, for sure. The strings were stiff as hell. Before I left Connecticut I bought a book and a new pack. As the old strings unspooled, the whole body of the guitar seemed like it would fall apart with a groan. But the new strings bend easy now, ring clear. I've been getting better, practicing while Rosie is at work. I've even been working on a few songs of my own. Scrawling lyrics and chords in a little green notebook. I sit next to Rosie and take the guitar.

"I can't, really."

"Frankly, we're beyond me believing such crap," Rosie says. She's wearing gray sweatpants, rolled at the waist, and her hair is tied back with a red rubber band. "Sing to me." She rests her head on my shoulder, and I realize that Rosie is deeply sad these days. Outside the sun is going down an hour earlier than it used to. Rosie has weathered nineteen Menamon winters. She knows another one is coming for us now.

But damn if Marta Winters didn't ruin me for life. If loving her didn't magnetize me so I cleave to the crazy ones with sad streaks a mile wide. The birdcallers and the Polaroid senders. The late-night wanderers and radio song requesters. I reach my arm around Rosie and pull her close. I smooth her hair down. I tug on her ear. "Not the best day?" I say.

"Just the same, you know?"

And I know what that's like, because it used to be that way with Marta and me. How after she was gone, an enormous question mark floated behind my eyelids. The way it seemed impossible to wake up and do the same little necessary things all over again and how the best thing to do was not to question it. Because if you questioned it everything seemed hopeless and got you down real low.

I could tell Rosie everything I know about survival mechanisms, but what I really want to tell her is that I don't feel that way anymore. That since I came here, to town, to her house, every day I wake up clutching this private feeling of excitement like a rag in my fist. I wake up, realize where I am, and a jump start goes through my heart, like, What will she say today? Will she make me eggs? Will I buy her a drink? Will she touch my shoulder and will I think about that for days and days? Because I know that, even though half of this town is in love with Rosie, I'm the one who can love her best. The one who gets her and knows what she needs before she even needs it. The one who will cook for her. I feel a rumbling in my chest like the first pull of a lawn mower, the vacuum before the roar. Because I can't let Rosie know this. Because I don't want her to know and then feel bad that she can't give it back to me.

"All right," I say, adjusting the guitar. I play her an old tune of my father's, all the way through, without even skipping the bridge. You wouldn't believe what a new set of strings can do for an old groaning guitar. I hold the last chord down tight, letting it ring out. When I let go my fingers are string-dented.

"I like that," Rosie says. She takes my hand and squeezes each fingertip. And just like that, I sketch Rosie into my family portrait. Into the gaping hole I now know better than to save for Carter. See us there, two girls, arms looped strong together.

Rosie says, "Was that a Carter Marks song? He comes by the Stationhouse every Sunday. He's an excellent tipper."

11

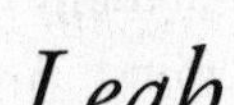

Leah

Henry sits on the sofa in our living room, which has a low ceiling supported by beams. The thick carpet is a deep green. On the windowsill is a CB radio tuned to one of the lobstermen's channels. I turn it on and hear, *She don't know I've gone buggin' and if she finds out she'll have my head*. I click the dial off.

I hear rain pelting the roof. The stone fireplace has a picture of a boat on the mantel and the room is full of armoires and sea captain's chests and things that belonged to Henry's parents. I look through them when Henry isn't home. The desk's first drawer is full of stray knobs and keys and bolts. Another had recipes in it. Plain index cards rubber-banded in a stack. The recipes were written in pencil, in what could only have been June Lynch's slanting hand. Recipes for cod bakes. Lobster rolls. Corn casserole. Blueberry slump. Whoopie pie. Strawberry rhubarb pie. There was a red splotch on the last one and I shivered when I saw it. I turned, thinking I might see June there behind me, in flour-dusted jeans with her sleeves rolled up, wanting to show me how to roll out the dough. But there was no one, and I was a little disappointed. I shut the cards in the drawer.

Most of this house spooks me most of the time, and I love it. Back in the city, when Henry and I talked about moving to Maine, we ran our mouths until it sounded like something we'd talk about forever but never actually do. His stories about Menamon grew and grew in my mind. A place with lobsters so thick in the sea you could barely go swimming, he said, tweaking me all over, a thousand lobster claws pinching. A place where lifelong grudges were held over stolen pie recipes and county fair ribbons. A place where children were tough; they raised animals for 4-H and butchered them too. They worked on boats and in fields and in shops. They learned to build things and to shoot, the value of money and how to behave at a funeral. And they were happy, these children, because no one had allergies or learning disabilities or nannies. *No one?* I said. *Surely some—*

No one, Henry said, his eyes lit up, twinkling.

He talked about his parents' house, and we dreamed about living there, but we'd have had to pay the bank a fair amount to get it, and the amount just seemed too much. So we gave up on that idea and I tried to find something on Craigslist. The people of Hancock County, it seemed, did not often use Craigslist. And then, one day, Henry showed up with a stack of photos and a ring of keys, a green ribbon tied around them. *These are for you,* he said. He was grinning, beaming, prouder than I'd ever seen him. Embarrassed too for being so proud. They were the photos of this house, his parents' house. The keys, to open its doors. *How did you—* I said, and Henry just told me he'd worked, saved, found the money to pay off the bank. He'd *made it work,* he said.

You are giving me a house? I said. *We're really going?* I have never been good at receiving gifts, they make me feel awkward and guilty and shy, and this was such an enormous gift I felt unequal to it. But whatever discomfort I felt at the hugeness of what Henry had done, the wonder of it was greater. Henry was magical. He had swum through seas of lobsters and worked since the womb and never had allergies and he had, not an apartment, but a whole house, and we were going to live in it together. We were going to have an adventure. I was holding a tinkling ring of keys in my hand.

The wonder of it has not dissipated. I still have trouble remembering that this house is mine. When I cook in June's kitchen and ask Henry if he would like salt in his eggs, I feel like I am playacting. Who is this grown-up Leah Lynch in a house with a husband cooking eggs? This woman who thanks Henry for taking out the garbage? What happened to Leah Gold, who worked all night and had an encyclopedia of delivery places in her phone?

I look at Henry now, sitting on the couch, huge papers on the coffee table, sketching the gardens of the *casa grande* into existence. He has not been shaving much and has scruff coming in all over his face. He moves his hands over the table papers to smooth them, erases something, and fills in something different. He makes a low, grumbling thinking sound like a growl, so deep you can barely hear it. But I listen for that noise. I try to catch it whenever I can.

I sit in Henry's lap and wrinkle all of his papers. He sticks his pencil behind his ear and wraps his arms around me. He slides a hand into the back of my jeans and snaps the elastic of my underwear, then picks me up from the hips and sets me on my feet. He follows me to the bedroom.

THE FIRST TIME I ever slept with Henry was in the morning. I had spent the night at his Brooklyn apartment (Brooklyn! It was a brave new borough, I'd known nothing off the island). We'd been seeing each other for two months and hadn't slept together yet. I was holding out, tormenting him, in part because I knew you never got that chance again, but also because Henry was an unknown entity: met at a bar, was from another state, lived out of borough. He had no papers.

He slept under a quilt, a yellow patchwork affair so earnestly a defense against the cold how could I not want to crawl under it? We slept in our underwear and in the morning I opened my eyes and there was Henry with his warm expanse of furred chest. Henry under this dainty quilt. I pushed up against him. From the living room came the muffled sound of grunts and whistles and penalties announced. It was winter, and his roommate seemed intent on watching every game of the football season from their living room couch.

Good morning, I said, and Henry shushed me. Snapped the elastic of my underwear. We were, for a while, like teenagers: he discreetly pressed himself against my leg while I hid my face by his ear so he could hear me breathing. I bit his earlobe and our bodies radiated the heat of a night spent under covers, and when we wriggled out of our underwear and slid together, I gasped and Henry put his palm over my mouth.

Shhh, he said again, and his face looked worried, so I bit him, and when he took his hand away I said, *Don't you shut me up.*

We moved like clock hands that circle away from each other and then meet again so it is incredible and inevitable both. His roommate shouted from outside, *Hey, what're you up to? Want to watch the game?*

Henry shouted back, *No. We're playing Scrabble.*

On the TV, a whistle was blown.

Who's winning? his roommate said.

Both of us, Henry said. And we laughed and snorted and

Henry promised he would get his roommate tickets to see a game one of these days. Would get him out of the apartment. He said, *I'll get him tickets to the damn Super Bowl if I have to.*

WE ARE STILL in bed, bow to stern, half naked and reading to each other from the newspaper, when Quinn calls.

She shouts into the receiver, "You're not going to believe this shit! Come to the office now."

12

Quinn

I'm pitching Charley the story of the Menamonian century when Leah walks in. "The Georges live in the Elm Park development. They moved in a month ago. They brought their cat with them."

"What's the cat's name?" Leah says, first thing. That wench.

"Derek Jeter," I say. "But that's not the point."

"The cat's name is Derek Jeter?" Charley says. "I hate these people already."

"They have an eight-year-old son who always wanted a dog but got a cat instead and they let him name it and so he named it Derek Jeter—Leah, if you write that down in your fucking notebook—"

She flashes me the notebook. She has, in fact, written down: *DEREK JETER = cat. Breed??*

I say, "He went missing a week ago, and this morning they found him on the front step, dead."

"Coyote?" Charley says.

"The cat was taxidermied."

"What the fuck," says Charley. "Like a belated Halloween stunt?"

"There was a note. It said 'Go home.' "

"That's sick," Leah says. "Who would do that to someone's pet?"

"We know who," I remind her. "The gentleman lobster?" The first good story since I got here, and it's about Carter. No way would Woodward give it up, so I'm not giving it up—but that means I've got to come clean.

"Carter Marks," Leah says.

"That guy?" Charley says.

I take a deep breath. "That guy," I say, "is my father."

"Then you'll have no problem getting an interview with him," Charley says. She heads into her office to fill out advertising paperwork without another word. I watch her in there, sorting through her papers, and I realize she is pretending to be busy, avoiding me. Which also means, I realize, that she knows. That Charley already fucking knew.

"Your father?" Leah says. "Is he a taxidermist?"

"Way fucking off, Leah," Charley shouts from her office. She's still not looking at me.

"Can we go get a drink?" I say. I feel nauseous.

"We'll get the story and then get a drink." Leah's face is mottled with uneven flush. "You seriously never told me that your actual, literal father lives in town?"

Leah looks pitiful and crushed, but I'm *going* to get this story. She and Charley aren't the only ones with something to contribute around here.

I leave, slamming the door behind me. I jump into my car and start the engine. Hit autolock. Leah bangs out of the office, raps on my car window. She raps again, mouthing, *I'm coming too,* but I crank the engine and leave her.

MY CAR *DING-DING-DINGS* at me, letting me know that the door is still open and that I have as yet to successfully climb out of it. Things are not going as planned. I'm not wearing the right pants and I don't have his guitar and what the hell am I going to say? In the name of the shittiest local paper in Hancock County, I charge you with one count of cat slaughter and two counts of amateur taxidermy? You never loved her and then you wrote a song telling all the world you did? I almost wish I *had* brought Leah with me. She'd know how I should handle Carter.

I stare at his slanting shack of a house. I wait until I'm angry enough. I think about my mother and Billy and those poor fucking cats. I even think about me. Then, when I've got a slow burn started, I jump out of the car, sprint to the door, and wail on the flimsy brass knocker before I can change my mind.

The man who answers the door is the man on the album jackets. I don't know why I expected otherwise. He is older, though; pretty damn old, as a matter of fact. His face is long and the slanting angles of his cheekbones are weirdly refined. They are the cheekbones of a Russian ballerina or perhaps the Penobscot ancestor he claims. His skin is loose, a little slack under the chin. His pores are so big they look like shadowy freckles across the bridge of his nose. His hair is chestnut and gray, mixed in equal parts. His nose is a bird's. It has a noble curve to it that is mysterious from the front and makes him hawkish in profile. He is tall, taller than I thought. The album covers always had him sitting, holding his guitar.

"Yes?" he says. "Can I help you?" But I don't have my shit together yet. He watches me watching him. I am greedily inventorying everything I see. He is wearing a faded denim buttondown,

Carhartt pants, and no shoes. I stare at his bare feet on the wood-planked floor. There is a largish freckle at the softly crinkled arch of his left foot. Everything else I can deal with but this one thing I cannot handle: he is not wearing shoes. It implies to me somehow that he is not ready for me. For this moment. I wouldn't want to face a moment like this without shoes.

"Can I help you?" he says again, and that's the part of him I know best, his voice, which I have been listening to for years, through various layers of record grime and dust and scratches, and now here it is, that voice, which tells me I really know nothing at all.

"Leah Lynch," I lie. "From the *Menamon Star*?" Because if I can be Leah, be competent and stubborn like she is, then I think I'll be able to say all the things I need to.

"I forgot about that," he says. "Hold up."

Forgot about what? My existence? I feel a jolt of terror as he leaves, even though he's only going deeper into this ramshackle house. When he returns, a minute later, he pulls ten bucks out of a wallet that has some beading on the front. He hands it to me.

"What is this?" I say.

"This is about my subscription, isn't it?" he says.

"No," I say. "It's about skinning cats."

His eyes widen and I feel pleased to have surprised him. "Fair enough," he says, and takes the ten dollars back. "I expect you want to be invited inside so you can harass me in my own home?"

"I'd like that," I say, making sure to convey that I'll relish it.

Just like that, I'm inside this house I've been picturing for months. For how shoddy it looks outside, it's clean and warm. The living room and kitchen share a space and there are a half-dozen copperware pots, kettles, and pans hanging tails up from a ceiling rack. There's a fire. The logs crack and resettle. There is a long wall of books, records, and CDs. There is only one chair, which makes me think about "Norwegian Wood," that Beatles song where the journeyer can't find anywhere to sit, and I wonder if this is the sort of thing Carter would be proud of if he knew I was thinking it. I scan the vinyl for *Rubber Soul,* for a sign. Next to the chair is a pile of newspapers and several inordinately large pinecones, and suddenly, inexplicably, I am enraged. I'd wanted to find him in some sad state of bachelordom. I'd wanted his life to look incomplete, like it was crying out for Marta, for me, and here instead are these fucking pinecones.

"Just 'cause I'm offering you a chair doesn't mean we're on good terms yet, all right?" Carter says, and grabs a wooden chair from the kitchen for himself. I sit in the big forest-green armchair, next to the fucking pinecones. My feet do not reach the floor.

Carter leans forward on his knees and says, "So what can I tell you?" His forearms are thick and his sleeves are rolled up and the soft hairs on his forearms all lie the same direction, like reeds underwater leaning with the tide. His hands are the eighth wonder of the world. The tendons dance up and down with his slightest movement. I can see exactly how much blood is going where and through what channel. Blue veins pop out along the backs of them. His nails are short and thick.

"You shouldn't do that to people's cats," I say feebly.

Carter pinches his stubbly chin between finger and thumb and worries the scruff there. His face is ragged, but not quite bad-looking. "They shouldn't be pushing people out of their homes and stores like that," he says. "Joseph Deep is a friend of mine, not that he has anything to do with this, don't write that down." It occurs to me that I haven't brought my steno pad with me. I can't write anything down. How will I face Leah without any notes? I really wish my feet reached the ground.

I say, "I saw him—Derek Jeter. You're not very subtle." On

crime TV they always refer to the victims by name, to humanize them.

"Are you referring to his posture or expression?" Carter says. "I think 'hackles up' conveys exactly what I wanted to say."

"I mean I don't think it's subtle to put a gentleman lobster above the shop counter at Deep's and then think you can get away with cat slaughter."

"Joseph has that still?" He chuckles. "The gentleman lobster. What a sentimental fool, keeping that around." There is something a little dreamy about his demeanor. I imagine Carter and Marta together, high out of their minds and rolling around on the orange rug beneath my chair, laughing.

"What first interested you in the slaughter and preservation of family pets?" I say, because I'm a reporter. I'm asking questions.

"The trappings of taxidermy fascinate me, if I'm honest." Carter stands and goes into the other room, and when he comes back he has a cardboard box. He hands it to me. Inside about fifty glass eyes are rattling around, staring at me from every which kind of pupil. I see the slitty eyes of an owl. The Coca-Cola brown of a deer's eye, chestnut-sized. Some regal green peas, translucent black slice in the center, make cats' eyes. The keen yellow flickering one must be for a fox.

"Special order," Carter says. "You want one?"

"Why would I?" I ask, even though I do.

"The Turks wear evil eyes. Why not one of these?"

And so it is that after my name, the second thing my father gives me is a sightless animal's eye. I slip the marble of a fake fox eye into my pocket and let my fingers linger there a moment. On the first day of first grade I accidentally called my teacher Mom and got heckled for the rest of the year. I'm terrified of making a slip like that here. The word *Dad* could just slip off my tongue. This isn't working. I resolve to try a new tack.

"Mr. Marks," I say.

"Carter," he says, which is equally weird.

"Carter," I say. "If you could be either Woodward or Bernstein, who would you be?" He looks confused. "Woodward and Bernstein as played by Robert Redford and Dustin Hoffman in the film *All the President's Men,*" I clarify.

"The Watergate guys? Either, I guess." But he's not done mulling this over yet. Unbelievably, he's taken my question seriously. This is not a man who balks. In fact, he seems to be exactly the sort of person Marta needed in her life. A man who could encompass her crazy and love her anyway. I tried to be that person for her, but I was always coming up short. Here, here is what she was missing. The third figure in the portrait to balance us out.

Carter says, "I've always thought of it as more of a Butch Cassidy versus the Sundance Kid situation. Wouldn't you know I always wanted to be Sundance? My whole life. But I'm a Cassidy through and through. Just can't shut up."

I almost tell him everything, right then. Not just because he's taking me seriously, but because he's right. I'd never really considered it before, but there are parallels. Woodward's a bit like Sundance. Stoic. And maybe an inability to blab about your feelings doesn't necessarily mean you're broken. It's too much. I've got to get us back on track.

"Why Elm Park?" I ask Carter.

"Ms. Lynch, I was born here. I've been back over twenty years, and all the good things I remember from growing up are changing. The town budget has never been voted down before, and with the recent purchase of the Penobscot lots, the majority of the town's waterfront is now controlled by out-of-staters. Are you aware that the owners of that new house control the property all the way through Neversink Park? The carousel and park have been maintained by the Sanford family for the past sixty years.

Now the Sanfords live in North Carolina. Who's going to maintain that park, Ms. Lynch? Summer people who aren't here three-quarters of the year?"

"I don't know," I say. Every time he calls me Lynch I feel a twist in my guts. He looks at me then, his head cocked, like he knows me from somewhere he can't recall. I can't stand it. I look away. There's a set of big glass doors looking out on his backyard, and through them I see a cat. A tabby with a bell, rubbing against the doorframe.

"Is that Derek Jeter?" I say.

"There are a lot cats around here," Carter says. "I put out food. They come and go."

I get up and open the door. The cat comes in and circles my ankles, purring loud. I pick it up and look at the license. *Derek Jeter.*

"Who was that on the Georges' doorstep?" I say.

Carter leans back, his shoulders relaxed. "I couldn't begin to tell you," he says. "But I give Jethro Newkirk use of my father's taxidermy studio. Perhaps you should ask him; he's the only one who's used it in years."

And sure, I'm relieved Carter hasn't done it. Relieved that it's a bait and switch and the cat is fine. But now my plan is all shot to hell. Carter starts rubbing the cat under the chin. He's too close, right next to me, and I lean in a little so our arms are touching.

Do you know what the bitch of this is? This is a man I wouldn't have wanted to hate. This is a man whose approval I desperately would have wanted to win. The irresponsible asshole who spent his days on the road while Marta went crazy back at home, the man I hate, is gone, gone, gone, and all I've got is this guy, this mild guy who, in the way of many aging men, does not quite fill out the seat of his jeans.

I take a step back. I hold the cat tight to my chest. "Well, thanks for your time, Mr. Marks. I'll just go ahead and cite you in my article. That's *M-A-R-K-S,* right?"

"You go ahead and use my name," Carter says. "Just get the quotes right. I hate to be misrepresented in print." He looks at the nothing where my notepad should be. "You think you can handle that?"

"I've got it," I say, and tap my temple.

"Real journalistic vigor," he says, and shows me out.

13

Leah

I can't believe Quinn wouldn't tell me something like this. I also can't believe she left. This was supposed to be my story too.

"Charley!" I bang into her office. "Quinn and I are supposed to be on assignment together. Where does Marks live?"

"Let her be, Leah." And Charley looks almost sad as she says it. Like for me to bother Quinn now would be an intrusion too terrible to consider. But has she read Quinn's copy lately? I like the girl but the idea of her going solo on the only interesting story to hit Menamon since I got here drives me crazy. The accusations are against her dad; there's no way she won't go easy on him. It'll be a mess. A little intruding is definitely in order.

"Always together. That's what you said," I say. I hate being kicked off a story. "Where, Charley?"

Charley leans back in her chair and says, "If you need something to do, go interview your friends in Elm Park. You can contribute quotes to the piece."

"I've never met the Georges," I say.

"I'm sure you'll hit it off, they speak Jeter," she says. Her disdain is so idle it's infuriating. This woman is my sister, and I feel cheated. I want someone to call when things are bad at work, or Henry is driving me nuts. I need a sister. Even if it's Charley.

"What would you say your problem is, Charley?" I say. "If you had to put a finger on it?"

She throws her hands up. "I don't have a problem. I just don't like it when a reporter, a damn *Gazette* reporter, who I've hired, by the way, who is on my staff, asks stupid questions. You and Henry sell Pop's boat to buy the house, you waltz around like it doesn't even matter. Fine. That's personal, I deal. But here? You work for me. You've been working with Winters for weeks now and you didn't realize she was Marks's daughter? The only semi-famous person in Menamon, she's his spitting image, and you're dumb enough to miss it? Learn your fucking beat, Leah."

The window is open and the world outside is dizzying through the screen: sea and sky chopped up into pieces. "What boat, Charley?"

I can tell she wonders if I'm screwing with her because she starts stacking papers she hasn't touched since I've worked here. Tapping the bottom out on her desk while biting her lip. "You don't know this," she decides. "Of course you don't know this. Because the two of you are *children*."

It creeps up on me. The first assignment she sent me on. The one Quinn called hazing. "The *Menamon Star,*" I say. "The lobster boat at Deep's. It was yours?"

She sighs. "How the hell did you keep a job in New York?" she says. "The *Star* was Pop's lobster boat. The paper came later.

After he died I got the paper and Henry got the boat. Family businesses. Then Henry says he's leaving. Going to New York. You know what he said? 'Just give me a few months away and I'll come back and take it over.' "

I feel seasick. I don't want to believe what she's telling me, but I can hear Henry making that vow, offering up that timetable. It's just the sort of thing he would say.

Charley smacks the table. "But he didn't, and you know why? Because he met a girl. Henry sold the *Star,* used the money to pay off the bank's share of Mom and Pop's house, and lost us our lobstering license."

I think of Henry beaming proud as he gave me that shiny ring of keys with the green ribbon. The money. He just *made it work.*

"Henry doesn't even fish!" I say. Because it's so improbable. Henry as a lobsterman. My Henry. I would have known. "He's a gardener," I say, then regret it. I wish I'd said *landscape architect.*

Charley goes back to the papers on her desk, through with me. She says, "There's a picture of the *Star* above your mantel. Unless you've been redecorating."

She sighs, pinches her crooked nose. "Just leave Winters alone on this one. That's all I was trying to say."

OUR FIREPLACE IS made of smooth rocks that Henry's grandparents picked out by hand. Riverbed rocks, schlepped back from inland, his grandparents' arms growing strong and their palms callused, Henry told me. Henry's grandfather caked them together with mortar and built this hearth. In the top right corner is a lumpy stone that Henry says his grandmother made his granddad dive for. The family legend is that she claimed it was shaped like a heart, asked for it to make her husband show he loved her. He dove for it and now love is cemented in with stones. History.

Everything that has happened to this town, everything that has happened to Henry's family, the local celebrities and their obvious estranged children . . . this unknown history comes between me and everyone I am trying to reach.

Like Charley said, resting on the mantel is an architectural drawing of a boat, blue on blue, the original plans for the *Star*. I have been living with the ghost of this boat for months now. Ghosts of boats and of people I will never meet. I cannot believe Henry did not tell me this thing everyone in town clearly knows and resents me for. He is doing the opposite of helping us live here.

I pour a large whiskey and head into the attic through a trapdoor in the ceiling. Detritus is piled in stacks: a mustard-colored velvet armchair, several empty aquariums, a pair of wheelless roller skates, a rifle, blackly marred bottles that once contained ink. There are fishing poles and lures: rubbery, squidlike baubles that glint and wiggle so that even I want to put my mouth around them. There is a mirror so thick with dust that it reflects nothing but the time that has laid its ashes there. There is something that looks like a coffin, but of course it's only an old storage box, made of cheap pine. Not for the dead but for their trappings: documents, photos, and files.

I flip through documents until I find what I am looking for: the registration papers. The *Menamon Star* had been a functional lobstering rig since 1935. There was a brief hiatus in function (though not in license) during the Second World War when Henry's great-grandfather served. The *Star* resumed function after the war with Henry's grandfather at the helm. It continued on that way until his father died. Until Henry met me.

He *made it work,* he said. The photos, the keys. He was so happy and so was I. But he lied, Henry. A lie of omission, but still a lie. How many times do you lie to someone when you are married? I think the answer might be: a lot of times. *No, I don't mind, I am not in the mood, you look wonderful.* But big lies, lies like this one? Certainly you can only have so many of those.

Does Henry think I am the sort of woman who he can keep things from? Is this the sort of guy he is: a secret keeper? A glosser-over? No, he is not. I don't think so. I did not marry a fisherman or a secret keeper, I do not think.

It is, however, possible that I was underinformed about who Henry was and was not when we got married.

There is a chance that in our few months of courtship we did not really take the time to do our due diligence. But who slows down for such a thing when they are in love?

I leave the attic and run outside. I am going to show Henry that I know things. That he should not keep secrets from me. That he too may have been underinformed about who *I* was and was not. Outside the one-lane road is wet and black. I start running and I do not stop until I get to town, my wet hair slapping around my ears.

The bells chime a frozen tinkle as I walk into the hardware store, which smells like rubber piping and rat poison. The neon hammer sign is pulsing pink and blue in the window. The tumbler of Red Hots is near the checkout and an old man squinting at the rain asks if he can help me.

"I need some paint," I say.

"What kind?"

"The kind that sticks to a car," I say, and hand him part of the file I've taken with me, a photo of the Lynch family lobster buoy. "These colors." He collects a series of paint chips and splays them like a winning hand of cards. He has a pair of glasses on a dingy braid of string around his neck and he puts these on.

He says, "I suspect what you want is some tadpole green, honeysuckle orange, and walking-on-eggshells white. Will that be all, Mrs. Lynch?"

"That will be all," I say. I scoop some of the Red Hots out of the jar. I let them clack against my teeth and then I crunch them. Sugar and spice. Mrs. Lynch.

IT'S STILL RAINING, so I keep the car in the garage, but open the door so I don't asphyxiate myself. The garage lights are a warm orange color and I clonk the open bottle of whiskey on a plywood shelf next to a drum of gasoline. I have a portable radio, so besides the sound of the rain there is also the sound of Motown. Squeaky-voiced men harmonize with other squeaky-voiced men in a way that is beautiful. *I'm moonin' over you* and *I'm thinking about my baby* and *ain't that peculiar.*

I'm singing and painting and drinking and painting and singing and outside it is getting dark. The foliage is deep green, like in that Rousseau painting at the Met I would sleep under if given the chance: gorillas with faces sweeter than the virgins' and moons like tangerines and all that nighttime black vegetation. When I was small I thought that painting was of capital *n* Nature. That somewhere outside the city limits, past the Spanish groceries that sold dried fishes, past Co-op City, which still smells like burning, past all the storage facilities where people keep the stuff they can't stand to look at but can't throw away . . . I thought the city dropped off, and that Rousseau painting is what I thought the world looked like beyond it. A midnight-dense jungle.

That deep green elsewhere is where I live these days, and tonight I feel at home in it. I will show Henry what kind of native creature I am becoming and then he will know that I can handle anything he has to tell me. Did he really think he could keep these truths from me? I am an investigative journalist! Though apparently I have not been a very good one these past few months.

I am finished. I have clumps of paint stuck in the down of my arms and my jeans are soggy, but the car looks pretty good. In fact, the car looks phenomenal.

Henry's family's lobster buoy was cream-colored. It had two orange stripes circling the middle, where the form begins to taper. It had a light green nose. I step outside. The rain has stopped. The best way to dry a fresh coat of paint, the way I understand it, is a swift breeze.

14

Quinn

I drive the living, mewling Derek Jeter back home and exchange him for his stuffed double with as little explanation as possible. I head to the Uncle, taxidermied mystery cat under my arm.

I'm barely in the door when I hear Jethro calling, "A beer for my friend!"

I put the taxi-cat on the bar. "Who is this?" I say.

"My mother had many tabbies," Jethro says. "But I believe this is Agatha. She passed in '76."

"You taxidermied your mother's cats?"

"She loved them," he says. "And it helped her remember. It's a highly respected science and pastime."

I moan. My grandfather was a taxidermist and my father is an asshole and I've fucked up my article so badly I can't even claim to have moved the family interest along to journalism. What happened to my plan, the screed and the guitar? It was such a good plan and then . . . what did I say I was Leah for? The way Carter looked at me like he knew me from somewhere. His bare feet. His small, clean house. Forget about it. Think about anything else.

I think of all the things neither Woodward nor Bernstein would have done:

1. Forget to write anything down
2. Say "cat slaughter"
3. Accept gifts from an interviewee suspected of a crime
4. Touch an interviewee (unless she was pretty and withholding information)

I'm lousy at this, is the truth. I keep on telling myself that if I stick with writing articles, one of these days I'll just become a good journalist. But maybe it doesn't work that way. Maybe I don't know what the fuck I'm doing.

The summer I was eighteen my mom was in the hospital for the first time. We didn't know it was cancer for the first month. A nervous breakdown, is what they called it. To do with being a single parent and Carter abandoning her when I was so small. *Raising a teenager all alone? No wonder the issues have come to a head now,* the nurses said.

I was angry, and we thought she was going crazy, so we had her in the crazy wing. She slept most of the day, so there wasn't shit to do except sit in the lounge and watch the TV attached to the wall. I sat there and stewed over all the ways this was probably Carter's fault. If he'd only married Marta in some flowery ceremony instead of all that free love crap, maybe he'd have stayed. If only that damn song, the song about her, hadn't done quite so well. Maybe then he'd have lived with Marta instead of singing about her on a nationwide tour and never phoning. If anything else had happened, I thought, and he was here, then at least there would be someone who knew what to do. How to fix her.

In the lounge, I watched game shows. *Password* was my favorite. I loved how ridiculous the clues were and how the announcer would whisper the words to the viewer so the contestants couldn't hear. *The password is,* he would say, *automobile. The password is Alka-Seltzer.* God, I loved that whisper. I was convinced the whisper would tell me what was wrong with my mother if I listened carefully enough. Shared it quietly, just between the two of us.

Then one day a nurse brought in this old geezer in a wheelchair. She rolled his chair right next to mine. She shut off the game show.

Hey, I said. *Don't you wanna know if Carol Burnett can get him to say "carnival"?*

He'll never get it, the guy said. *And it's time for my movie.*

The nurse popped a cassette into the VCR.

Man, I said.

Dim the lights, Lucille, he told the nurse, and she did.

If you stay, there is to be no idle chatter, he said. He was a hell of a guy. He was strong-looking in the chest and arms, but his legs looked skinny in his hospital pants. He wore a hospital top, but over it a tweed sport coat with elbow patches.

What are we watching? I said.

All the President's Men, he said. *It's my film. I have a cameo.*

Are you an actor? I said

As I mentioned, he said. *I have a cameo.*

We started watching the movie and I was thinking it was pretty good. Better than game shows, for sure. By the last scenes I was so into it, all I could see were Woodward and Bernstein scurrying around trying to get their backup by phone. The guy spoke up.

There, he said.

What? I said.

He pointed at the screen. *Fourth cubicle from the back,* he said. I looked. In that cubicle was another newspaperman. Yammering silently into his phone. Writing things down and touching his temple in distress.

That's you? I said.

That's me, he said.

When the movie was over the nurse came back and pressed rewind. She stood there looking at the cassette the whole time. She popped it out, stuck it in the case, and wheeled him out.

The next day she rolled him in again. *It's time for my movie,* he said. And Lucille went through the whole thing again.

Alzheimer's, she said.

We watched the movie.

The thing is, the more I watched it, the better it got. The more I realized it was actually the best movie of all time. It was a month later, when I had seen *All the President's Men* two dozen times, that they realized there was something wrong with my mother other than being tired. That it wasn't just a nervous breakdown set off by my hormones, and that probably she had cancer instead. So they moved her to a different hospital. And I went too.

When Marta's hair started falling out, she insisted on brushing it anyway. *Let's just get this over with,* she said. The losing, I think she meant. She brushed until she had just a few whorls left, curled against her head in patterns like a galaxy map. The tangles that came away in her brush she would pluck from the bristles and let go out the window. She'd drop them, soft knots of hair drifting out across the lawn. *A bird will use this to make a nest,* she'd say. I wasn't sure if that was true.

In the new hospital lounge I watched game shows again, but, man, did I miss that movie. I missed Mr. Fourth-Cubicle-from-the-Back and Woodward and Bernstein too. I missed thinking that my mom was just a little tired, a little crazy. That I could watch my film and wait it out and then it would be time for Marta and me to go home.

When they finally did send us home, it was because they had run out of ideas. When college started in the fall, and they asked me what I was majoring in, I said journalism. Investigative reporting. And that was it. I was a journalist, just like the boys in the film.

I WISH LEAH were here because I have a masochistic urge to tell her how badly I fucked up the interview, even though it would only confirm all her worst professional suspicions about me.

"You're a pretty girl," Jethro says. "You look just like an Irish setter I used to have." He twirls the end of my hair around his finger.

"You make a girl feel special, Jethro," I say, batting his hand away.

This is when the bartender, Sara Riley, tells me she thinks I'd better go outside. Leah is driving around the parking lot in circles. The woody used to be a red car. Now it's old-lady-lace-colored. There are orange stripes, like rings around an Easter egg, circling the passenger door, roof, wood panels, and driver door. The best part is the hood, which is a cheerful springtime green. In sloppy green script, on the driver's-side door, is inscribed: THE MENAMON STAR.

"This is my lobster pot!" Leah drunkenly yells as she passes me, black hair flapping out the window. "It is Henry's family boat returned unto him!"

I weigh my tactical options. "Let me buy you a drink, Captain!" I yell through cupped hands. Leah stops the car, straddling two spaces, and says okay. She leaves her car door open and heads for the bar. I slam her door shut. My palm comes away painted, a red negative space in the shape of a hand on the door.

Settled at a table, Leah tells me that she's probably been fired from the *Star* and also her house. She says Henry was supposed to be a lobsterman and he sold his family history so she could have a home but did not tell her about it because she and Henry are hasty and underinformed.

"I see," I say. "Sorry for ditching you."

"Ohhhhhhh," Leah moans. "I didn't understand that it was for your life, not for a story."

"It *was* for a story," I say. I don't know why I say it. It just seems so much easier to slip across the surface of things, to avoid the sucking mud below.

"It was for your father," Leah says. "Fathers are not stories."

"Mine is," I say. I explain about the cats. I point at Jethro, who is drinking a beer with one hand while petting taxidermied Agatha with the other. I try to get Leah to fight with me about the story, the way we usually do.

"You never told me about your father," she says. "And then I was in trouble with Charley. For not knowing my famous Menamonians."

"I'll be sure to give you the scoop next time," I say.

"No!" Leah says, and slams down her glass. She spatters beer all over the table. She closes her eyes and shakes her head back and forth. "That's not what I mean. I mean you should tell me things. I bet you tell zero people zero things. And not telling people things is not a favor! If you try to not bother people by not telling them important things, all you do is put fluffy unknowable stuff between you, and that is sad and also dangerous."

"You have paint all through your hair, you know that?" I reach across the table and pinch out a piece of green that's dried there.

"Quinn," she says. "I am being very serious. What about your mother? Is your mother a famous Menamonian too?"

My mother is buried in the ground with a fucking weeping willow growing roots through her pelvis. My mother is a song I have stuck in my head that will never play on the radio again. A song of memories I'm stuck remembering in a looping, fragmented way, pieces missing. My mother was my only home.

"Marta is gone," I say. And then I say, "I told him I was you. Carter Marks."

"What? Why?" Leah says.

"Because you're good at things, Bernstein! And I've basically never met him before and I had this whole plan, but then things weren't going the way they were supposed to and you're so good at questions and understanding what needs to be said that it just seemed like it would be easier if he met you first. I thought I could meet him later." I suck air in and blow it out of me in a stream. Three long, hissing exhalations. I feel calmer. *Your breathing is like a pressure release valve,* Marta said. *You have to let the stream escape slowly. You've got to let that stuff out, or the whole joint will blow.* "And let me tell you, Leah Lynch," I say. "You really cocked up this story."

Leah looks down at her damp, paint-spattered body. "I am good at things?" she says, and starts laughing so loudly the few people still left in the bar turn to stare. "You can be me whenever you want," she says. "Do you want to be me later when Henry sees his car?"

I laugh. I'm getting a warm and fuzzy pleasure out of rubbing the sorry state of my life up against the sorry state of hers. I go pull a chair up behind Leah, one knee on either side of her waist. I start picking all the paint from her hair, piece by piece, like one of those monkeys on nature television. Grooming, they call this.

"So how will it be," Leah says, "when you meet Carter Marks again later, as you?"

I touch the fox eye in my pocket just to make sure it's still there and the first thing I think is that I want to live in his house. It was just so fucking cozy in there, and right now, drunk as I am, late as it is, if I could go anywhere, I'd go back there, and fall asleep all curled up on his rug like a pet, like a stray dog, and maybe he would just let me stay, no questions asked. But this is an absurd fantasy and the total opposite of what I'm meant to be doing. *Please,* Marta said. *Please.*

"I just want him to be sorry," I say. "And to be sad. He left my mother and she missed him for years and then she died and I just want him to know how shitty that is." I pull my chair closer to Leah so I can reach more bits of paint. It's easy to talk to the back of her head. "So I guess my plan is just to blaze in there, you know? And haunt him, for Marta. To make him sorry, and then to leave. That's my plan."

Leah pulls a red ballpoint from nowhere and scribbles on a cocktail napkin. She passes it back to me. It reads: *Vague.*

"I guess you'd suggest I destroy his car?"

"I suggest you do not 'blaze in there,'" she says. "I suggest you talk to him and tell him your feelings. About your Marta and your genes." She settles her head onto crossed arms and closes her eyes while I groom. "But you are not taking me seriously," she says, muffled. I watch her eyes relax and see the ghosts of her retinas pulse through her eyelids. I feel like reaching out and touching her there, on her closed eyes, like resting my fingertips on the strange grape of it. She falls asleep on the table. I shake the remaining paint from her hair, clutching the end of it in my fist like a rope.

AT HOME, I try to be quiet as I turn the key in the lock. I creep in, eyes adjusting to the darkness, and I'm about to throw myself on the couch when I see it's occupied. Rosie is sleeping there, all rolled up in this ugly-ass quilt, mustard calico ripped to the batting.

I'm wondering whether I should wake her or just sleep in the bed when her eyes come open. She squints, then screams, a piercing squeak.

"Hey," I say. "It's okay." I hug on to her. Rosie's breathing fast. She gets her arms out of the blanket and grabs on to me. "Hey. Hey," I say into her hair. I rub her back. "Who did you think it was?"

Rosie shakes her head against me. "I don't know," she says. "Not you."

She sits up. Flips on the light. "Where *were* you?" she says.

"The bar," I say. I tell her about Leah's car.

"I wanted to talk to you," she says. "I think we should start a band."

I laugh. "Who?" I say. "You and me?"

"Don't laugh," Rosie says. "You can play guitar and I can sing. The two of us."

"No fucking way," I say. I stretch out on the couch, so she's stuck at the end and I'm taking up most of it. She clambers over and sits on my legs. "You don't want to?" she says.

I close my eyes. "I'm going to sleep, and we're not starting a band."

"Just think about it," Rosie says. I feel her stand up, and I wish she wouldn't go. I open my eyes. She's looming over me, looking down at my face. She looks like a chieftain in her quilt.

"What?" I say.

"I saw Carter Marks today," Rosie says. "Breakfast shift."

I just can't catch a break from this man today. He's everywhere. It's not even his normal day to come by the Stationhouse.

He usually goes on Sundays. Orders huevos rancheros, like me. Not that I'm keeping track.

"What'd he order?" I say.

"He looks just like you," Rosie says, and pulls the quilt around her tighter. She looks at me real hard.

I'd scramble for a lie so that I could keep skimming the surface and avoiding the muck, but I'm tired, and what's the use. "Family resemblance," I say. "Must be the Penobscot. All .0001 percent of it."

"I just wanted to know," Rosie says.

"Well, now you know," I say. Maybe Leah is right and all these things we keep from each other are dangerous. Maybe sometimes you just have to tell. And I don't know how I found myself in this situation. Suddenly surrounded by people ragging me about my life. Friends, I mean. Friends were not part of the plan.

15

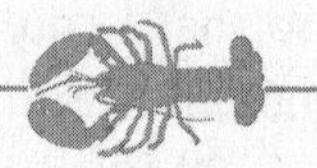

Leah

Outside, Henry is wearing his stripy Samba sneakers, the ones that make him look like a boy. Even though it is freezing, he is wearing shorts, and he is staring at the car, and in the parking-lot light I see that all his leg hairs are standing up. I imagine it's not from the cold but from the horror of the spectacle before him. I tap his shoulder.

"Christ, Leah, what do you want me to say?" His accent gets stronger when he is angry. What. Want. Crows cawing.

"Nothing."

"I'm gonna have to say something," he says.

"Then say it, Henry!" I yell. I jog in place, in anger.

"Leah," Henry says, "is this about the boat?"

And is it ever about the boat. But it is about more than that too.

AS HENRY DRIVES home we are silent. I hunch in my seat, cursing Quinn for being a miserable traitor. She called Henry to come get me. On her way out she fed the jukebox a quarter, punched the keypad. She solemnly watched the bubbles racing through the golden Wurlitzer tubes. Then, all the mechanical guts, all the records and needles, and all the magic, grumbled to life.

J42, she said. *Carter's best. Good luck.*

I listened to the song all the way through before I went outside. A Marks song. The one about the boy who takes the girl someplace she's never been before.

IN THE CAR, I'm shivering, but the paint fumes are strong enough that we'd die if we didn't keep the windows down. We pass a few trucks, drunken teenagers who lean on their horns when they see us coming.

"Wicked awesome ride!" one of them shouts.

It is quiet inside the car. Henry's jaw is quivering. Finally he says, "What were you thinking? Leah, this is not your fucking car! This is my car. I brought this fucking car back from the fucking dead!" He leans on the horn, like he's trying to prove the car is angry too.

"Why didn't you tell me?" I say. "About the boat. And the *house.* And your goddamned destiny at sea?" Because that's what's driving me crazy. It's bad enough that I've unknowingly humiliated myself by traipsing around town in a cone of silence, grinning at people and waving, trying to be friendly. Friendly to people who probably think, like Charley did, that I've forced Henry out of the family business for some controlling, henpecking reason. But worse than that is that Henry is the one who kept this information from me. Who didn't want me to know *all* of him. Worse: not even as much of him as the guy at the hardware store knows.

"Why?" I say again.

"Because it doesn't matter!" Henry waves his hands around

then grabs the wheel again. "We got the house, what does it matter where the money came from? I was never gonna be a lobsterman, so it doesn't matter what Charley or anyone else thinks. And you ruined my car, Leah. You destroyed this fucking car!"

The paint fumes are strong and the booze is still in my veins. I feel dizzy. "So the money for the house. It came from you selling the boat."

"Yeah."

"Why didn't you just *say so*?" I say.

"It seemed too complicated," Henry says. "And you were so happy about the house. I just wanted it to be a good thing. Simple and good. I thought if you heard the whole stupid story, you might change your mind."

"About moving?" I say.

"Sure, about moving," Henry says. "About me."

I think about this.

"How stupid are you?" I say. Because it hurts my heart that Henry thinks I could leave him ever, but he isn't getting himself off the hook this easily.

"Why did you come to New York?" I say. "Were you running away from all this? Charley and everyone?"

Henry sighs a long and angry sigh. "It was for the jobs. I needed more work under my belt so I could get a better gig up here. And I needed to go away so they would stop asking when I was gonna take Pop's boat out."

"And you didn't want to take it out because?" I feel ill. It's as if I've just discovered an extra doorway in my own home. One that opens up to a whole wing of the house I've never seen before.

"I get seasick."

"Bullshit."

"It's true."

"Bullshit!"

Henry measures his words. "I used to puke overboard. And I don't see why I should have to do it just because my father did. He was miserable most of the time and he wasn't around for Mom enough and it was never gonna happen, so it doesn't matter that I sold the fucking boat, okay?"

And of course *this* is what it's really about.

Henry's mama: June.

June collected shells. She knew the names of all the different kinds, and when Hank was out on the boat she used to wake up Henry and Charley early, before they went to school, to go out on the beach. The tide would have washed in all the best ones and it would still be dark out, so they brought flashlights, and net bags, and in the dark June's beam would jump from spot to spot and the water would be aching cold around their feet. Charley was the best at finding pearly ones and Henry was best at spotting big ones that tumbled in the surf.

June taught them how to tie knots with bits of ropes you could still find scattered about the house. An angler's loop under the couch, a buntline hitch in the kitchen drawer. An egg loop, a stopper knot, an alpine coil. Knots holding nothing on to anything. Henry knew them all. June taught them how to hum to a snail on your palm to make him come out of his shell. She taught them birdcalls. She taught them how to count to ten in French. She always knew when they were crying for real and when they were faking it, and if it was the latter she said things like, *Oh come on, enough of that.*

She taught them that when Hank came home the first kiss was hers. She showed them how hers went in the middle of his face, on the mouth, but how the next two were theirs, and how they should plant them, one on each check. How there was a perfect balance of kisses this way. She taught them not to say, *Your beard prickles,* or *You smell like fish.* She taught them the right ways to lure Hank into telling them a story. The right questions to ask, the offhand way to do it. She taught them to read the signs that meant he was in a good mood, and would sing a song or dance a jig if they asked him right.

She could cook anything that came out of the sea but mostly June loved to bake. She was a messy baker, Henry said, and dreamy. The kind who wore an apron tied tight but got flour and egg all over herself anyway. If you tried to talk to June while she was using the mixer, she might turn to answer you, the blades still spinning, spitting off batter all over the room as she delivered a thoughtful answer, paying no mind to what she had been doing a moment before. She wore blue jeans and blouses and scarves in her hair. She used lemon soap and mint shampoo. She had coarse blond hair that she let Charley braid for her in the mornings. She read Henry Greek myths and taught Charley to throw a baseball properly.

One morning June climbed up on an old ladder to clean the gutters, which she had asked Hank to take care of three times already. She thought she might as well do it herself. She was doing a good job, halfway through, when she heard a neighbor calling hello and so turned around to greet him, forgetting all about the gutters, the height. She turned and the ladder lost its hold, and she fell backward and down, landing in the grass. Henry and Charley found her there, the neighbor crouching over her.

Henry is full of stories about his parents that he tells so easily it makes me think he doesn't realize he is breaking my heart.

Henry's mama was the most beautiful woman in the world and I never even met her. I could never be as good as she was, this I know for sure.

But Henry thinks I could be. He believes in the possibility that I am that sort of good woman, and that is why I love him.

That is also why I destroyed his car. Why I crinkle his papers.

Why I set his dinner free. So he'll remember that probably I can't. He wants to be around for me? How about now? And now? And now?

"So this is about me," I say, and smack the console.

"Not really, Leah, no," Henry says.

"Charley thinks it's my fault you sold the boat and let the license lapse."

"It's not."

"Then tell her that!" I yell, because the wind is noisy, though probably not that noisy.

"Okay," he says. "Okay, I'll tell her."

And then there's nothing to say, so we sit and drive and stew. I let my hand coast on the currents outside the window, scooping the graspable mass of the night air.

Henry turns left, onto a one-way street that angles steeply upward. As we climb the grade something large and bright appears in our path. It seems to be blocking our progress, balancing roundly on the crest of the hill. Henry lets up off the gas, allows us to drift back a little bit. He plants his foot on the brake.

"Is that the moon?" I say, which is a stupid question because it is clearly evident that this is the moon in front of us. By some trick of the angle of the street and the position of the skies, it seems to have dipped down. It is fat, eroded only by an eighth on one side, and the deep orange color of wild honey.

"It is." Henry blinks and presses lightly on the pedal, creeping the car over the hill so that the moon springs up. Though shining furiously, it is now comfortably distant from us, and the vehicle, once more. I watch Henry's face. "I thought we were gonna hit it," Henry says. "I braked."

I think that in this moment of improbability I might be able to get away with what needs to be said. I say, "Your mom wouldn't have wanted you to sell the boat."

"How would you know?" Henry says. "For Christ sake, Leah. Don't say dumb shit about things you don't know about, all right?" He is staring at the moon.

This feels like my insides have been carved out. Everything about tonight hurts. Here is this man in the car beside me, who I am married to, who did not tell me the first thing about his life here until he had to. Who tried to keep a whole wing of himself from me.

"Henry," I say, "you need to tell me these things. About your family, and the town, and YOU and *Carter Marks* and, just, everything. So I can understand you. So I can be ready."

"Ready for what?"

"For them!" I say.

For loving you properly, inclusively, cumulatively, I think.

"For Charley and everyone in this town who smiles at you for coming back and gives me looks like I'm the reason it didn't happen sooner and the *Star* is rotting on the Deeps' wharf."

Henry's face twists at my mention of the rotting boat. "I'm ready." He sighs. "You don't need to worry about them. I'm ready enough for both of us."

This has obviously been working splendidly so far.

"But we need to be ready together, that's the whole point!" I say. "It's like those guys in the action movies, where they're handcuffed together, or to the suitcase or whatever? And they have to jump out of the plane with the parachute and they say 'one two three go'?"

I've lost the thread of what I was trying to say. How can I explain it? The way we need to be a team, to know each other completely, for this to work and for me not to feel alone—but I can't find the right words. "You know," I say, "and sometimes the first guy's not ready and so they say 'one two three go' again. And then the second guy's not ready and so they have to wait, until both of them are ready to jump. *You* have to wait. To jump."

Henry gives me a look. "You're pretty crazy, you know that?"

"Are you only realizing this now?" I say. "Vows were made! You promised to love my crazy ass until death! What did you think you were signing on for?"

"I don't know," Henry says. I am horrified to see on his face that he really did not consider this question until now. "Eating together. Sleeping together. Maybe kids? I don't know. What did you?"

"I don't know," I say.

Henry eases his foot off the brake and we climb the rest of the way over the hill. We drive on.

Henry says, "What is it you wanna know about Carter Marks, exactly?"

ON MONDAY, HENRY drops me off at work in his newly redecorated car. Charley comes out of the office. She stands in the doorway as I get out of the lobster pot. Henry waves from the driver's seat. I hold my breath as Charley takes the spectacle in. I'm sure destroying her father's car is just one more thing she can add to my rap sheet. She circles the woody. Her lips are pinched together and it looks like she's trying not to throw up. When she reads THE MENAMON STAR, she guffaws in a wicked way. She is not mad, I realize. Charley thinks this is hilarious.

"How do you like taking this out, Hen?" she says. "The guys at the docks appreciate her?" Henry glares. Because they do. Over the weekend his dad's old friends spotted the car and they think it's the funniest thing they've ever seen. New Englanders believe in comeuppance.

"I don't wanna hear it," says Henry. "Not from you."

Charley turns to me. "It's some nice work," she says, and offers me the flat of her hand, raised high.

"What's that?" I say, wary, not trusting the gesture.

"That, Leah, is an up-top," says Charley.

I smack her hand and enjoy the look on Henry's face.

Winter

16

Quinn

I haven't heard a word from that rat bastard. I left the bait of my name on the article about the cats and now it's December, a month for the lonely to slit their wrists to the tune of "Hark! The Herald Angels Sing," and he hasn't said a word.

Yesterday, it snowed.

Our one-pipe heating system groans like a ghost in Rosie's room, and the rest of the apartment is freezing. I'm rolled up in my blanket like a damn caterpillar cocoon, trying to accumulate body heat. I tried to walk in quietly tonight; Rosie says when I come home late it *disturbs her slumber*. But I've been lying here shivering for half an hour and it's too quiet for her to be anything but wide-awake. Then I hear Rosie in the next room, praying. Her door is cracked just wide enough for me to hear.

"Dear Jesus," Rosie says, like she's writing Him a fucking letter. "Dear Jesus, please keep my father safe from alligators and watch over my mother, who seldom applies a strong enough SPF. May they not meet their end in a retirement home, and if they do may it not be in the accursed state of Florida, which I hope You don't mind me saying, as it was Your Father's doing, though of course some of God's creation is meant to try us."

I wriggle onto my back and stare at the ceiling. I exhale out my nose, trying to warm it. I'd tell her to pipe down, but it's three A.M. and I just got in and I'm afraid that she's awake now because I have *disturbed her slumber*.

"Dear Jesus, please forgive me for my sins such as not charging the full dollar amount on some customers' fried eggs and giving them extra hollandaise for free even though it's supposed to be fifty cents. These are trying economic times and a lot of that sauce gets thrown out anyway."

Saint Rosalind, crazy as a loon.

"Also, please look out for Carter Marks, even though Quinn hates his guts. He might make a good man yet, as he's already a good tipper and a good musician."

That's it. I'm sick of Rosie talking about Carter like some kind of local hero. She's supposed to be on my side here, God knows no one else is, so I'm going to bust in there and tell her exactly what a jerk he is. But before I can get free from the blanket, she goes on.

"Also, Jesus, please take care of Quinn Winters. Let her see the light and understand that we must form a band. She is blinded to the way because she suffers much and says nothing, in the cold, the cold from which, if it is too much to bear, I hope she will seek refuge in my bed."

I hear her get up off her knees and slide under the covers.

For a moment I lie very still, because if I make the slightest noise I won't be able to hear and I'm suddenly awfully interested in prayer. But Rosie's done now.

I wait, but I've never been very good at waiting, so then I crawl out of my blanket cocoon. I am shaking all over, and before I can think about it any more I run into Rosie's room and jump under the covers.

Rosie is lying with her back to me. Her eyes are closed. She says, "Can we start a band?"

"Rosie—"

"Band!"

"To Whom It May Concern," I say, "I will help Rosie start a band."

"Amen," she says. "Now get closer. We need to conserve body heat."

"Amen," I say, and make myself the big spoon, wrapping my arm around her waist.

We lie there. At first, I barely move. I'm terrified Rosie's actually going to fall asleep with me in her damn bed. Could this really be about the heat? My arm starts to ache, the way it's draped over her, dead still, so I give in. I run my hand over her stomach, which is soft. I slide over her hips. Then I skim down to her waist again, as if down a half-pipe, and my hand gains momentum and runs up the other side to her rib cage, over her T-shirt, so my fingers rest against the soft bulge of her breast. I press my nose into Rosie hair and I smell the back of her head and her neck and I kiss her there, my one arm squeezing around her shoulders, the other moving down to cup her belly. As I noisily breathe in her smell, she arches back, pressing her ass up against me, getting closer.

I feel like my heart is running too fast, like it might burn out at any moment, but I just keep smelling her hair, and hoping I won't spook her, like some rabbit in the brush, who will let me keep being this near if I just stay still enough. I keep rubbing my hands all over her belly and up to her breasts, not so slowly anymore, not so gently, until I can't take it anymore and I tug at the waistband of her underwear, feeling it ping against her as I let it go. I'm still wearing shorts but Rosie reaches a hand behind her back so it's flat between my legs. She doesn't move it, just wedges it there, and as I press my body against her I'm bumping up against her palm and fingers and I rock my hips a little to do it more on purpose. And still Rosie's there. She's not going anywhere, I realize.

She shifts her hips forward a little, and I slide my fingers down past the elastic and around the curve of her. Rosie is wet and it feels like she's about a million degrees inside. I don't move at first, because I just want to feel that heat. And then, even then, as I slide up to rub her, I try to move slowly, like I'm not even doing anything on purpose. Like who knows how my hand got down there rubbing her up and down. Rosie makes little noises, sounds deeper than her normal voice but quiet too, and she twists her head to push her face into the pillow to muffle them. But I hear her. And I keep rubbing her like that until she shudders and she grabs my wrist to hold it there. Her grip is serious, telling me not to move anymore, and I don't. I stay entirely still until Rosie is no longer shuddering, and her body goes from arched to loose, and only then do I slowly slide my hand out of her underwear and trail it, fingers damp, up and down her back.

We lie like that for a while, still not facing each other. Rosie frees her hand and squeezes my leg. I could lie like this with her a long time, but there is one thing I am desperately curious about. I lift the covers up over us like a tent and peek underneath, and as I do so cold air rushes in and Rosie starts and yelps, "Hey!"

But I'm already laughing and once I'm started I can't stop.

Rosie sits up and turns to face me, sitting cross-legged on the bed. She is flushed in the cheeks still, and as she watches me laughing and laughing she frowns. "What's so funny? What?" She claps a hand over my mouth to stop me laughing. "This is serious, don't spoil it!" she says, but I lick her palm and she lets go. And that's when I kiss her, and it's a real, true kiss with a lot of emotional wattage going behind it, but if I'm honest, it's probably lousy in the way of kissing because even as I do it I'm still laughing.

Because Saint Rosalind wears plain white underwear, pure as the driven snow, and it's just too good, too good, too good.

IT'S THE THIRD week of December that Carter Marks sends a letter to the fucking editor. It's addressed to Charley, not me, so she's in her office reading it because she's keen on torturing people.

I open the door a crack just wide enough for me to fit my lips in. "I got you that interview with him, didn't I?"

Charley doesn't even look up. "Out, Winters. I'm reading."

I slam the door and go sit on Leah's desk. "How long can it take to read a fucking letter?" I say. She pats my knee but keeps editing.

Charley comes out of her office. "He's giving us tips," she says. "Which is presumptuous and obviously runs along bloodlines."

She hands me the letter. It's handwritten and the gist of it is that Carter thinks that I, that *Quinn Winters,* as he writes, should do a piece about the injustice of a recent town sanction and corresponding fine received by Cliff Frame of Derby Run Road for his inflatable Christmas display. Carter writes that certain thematic similarities between this story and my previous piece lead him to believe a continuity of reporting style, his fucking words, is in order.

This week the town ordered Frame to take down his display or pay a hefty fine. The town said it had to do with not properly housing the electrical apparatus for a semipermanent structure, but Carter suspects, and he's probably right, that it had more to do with his proximity to Elm Park and the quote unquote taste level of the display. *At my urging,* writes Carter, *Frame is refusing to take down the display and will thusly incur a fine, which I will pay.*

"He's got this big heart, you know?" I say to Charley, shaking the letter in the air. "Big fucking heart."

"So you'll write it, right?" Charley says.

"Of course I'll write it, but we're getting the story from Cliff on Monday. Right now I have to go. It's Friday fucking night and I have band practice."

OUR BAND IS called Cassandra Galápagos and the Aged Tortoise, and while we didn't spell out particular roles, I'm pretty sure I know who's who. Rosie's glammed up. Her hair is crimped, which means she wore braids to work, and she's got on eyeliner, which I've never seen before. "Hey, lady, we're not a band yet," I say.

"Notebook," Rosie says.

I've brought out the slim green notebook with my songs in it. I try, fail, try, to hand it to Rosie, the way you work up the nerve to jump off a cliff.

Rosie snatches the notebook from me and pages through breezily, which is excruciating. She meditates on some songs and dismisses others entirely. I hold my breath. I wonder what Carter would think if he knew I was writing songs. Did he ever have an embarrassing notebook, one he had to work up the nerve to show Marta, his song for her tucked away in there? That must have been worse, now that I think about it, because Marta never spared a word for the sake of someone's feelings ever. Sharing anything personal and possibly inadequate with Marta was stone terrifying.

Rosie snaps my notebook shut. "I can't read music," she says. "You're going to have to sing them to me."

Once I've taught her the melodies and strummed through the music a few times, Rosie starts singing. She has a breathy little voice, and though sometimes it's flat or sharp, she always sounds haunting. She makes songs I thought were half-assed sound big, and when she sings her face contorts into fantastic ugly shapes. My fingers hurt because I don't normally play this much, but I keep going so I can watch Rosie.

And just like that, she stops singing, and looks at me. I stop strumming. I would have played all night, I realize, if she didn't stop me.

I shake my hand loose. "You sound like a fucking beautiful little bird, Rosie. You know that?"

She rubs her eyes like she's just waking up and smudges her eyeliner. "I've always wanted to be in a band," she says.

ROSIE SAYS THE season demands a tree. December, so fucking pushy! We're at Arden Nursery to pick one out. A ferret-faced boy in a Santa cap gives us cocoa in wax-paper cups. A man's footsteps creak in the snow. As we sip our cocoa Henry approaches. He's a little bowlegged, and wearing a red hoodie that says MR. LYNCH on the breast. The hood is up. His smile is a good one, no less good for being snaggletoothed. He grasps a saw in his left hand. I wonder if he saw my handprint on his car.

"Quinn Winters," I say. "I work with your sister and drink with your wife."

"I remember," he says.

"This is Rosie," I say.

Rosie says, "We know each other. From school." Then she curtsies. Rosie was in junior high when Henry was a senior.

Henry vigorously rubs his ears through his hood. "How big a tree you looking for?" he asks.

"Our room is not capacious," Rosie says.

He gestures and we follow him into the forest. It's dark out, but strung across the rows are wires hung with steel-caged lanterns, illuminating spots on the snowy ground. Rosie leaps from one light spot to another. I do a big double foot hop onto a patch, which surfaces on my sneakers. Henry looks over his shoulder to see what we're up to and I feel ashamed, like he might roll his eyes at our silliness.

"Never can squash them out, can you?" He concedes a snaggle smile. He points at a tree. "This your size?"

"I think so," I say, but Rosie is walking the aisle now, appraising the trees' relative virtues.

Henry scans the row of firs. "Last year," he says to me, "in New York, I tried to talk Leah into getting one of these." He gestures at the little trees. "They were selling them in front of the drugstore. It had snowed, so they were sopping wet, but lit up nice. So we go look at them but Leah keeps shaking her head and saying they're too tiny."

I laugh, because I can imagine Leah scoffing at these four-foot shrubs. "How'd things work out for you?" I say.

"She said she wanted to be able to stare up at it. For it to feel big like the tree in that *Nutcracker* ballet. So she goes ahead and pays for a ten-footer." Henry has this look on his face like he's marveling at the idea even now. The audacity. The stubbornness. How much he loved it, in spite of himself.

I say, "How tall were her ceilings?"

"Eight fucking feet," Henry says, shaking his head and grinning. "I spent an hour sawing off the top of it, getting it straight, and she was crying and saying it wasn't going to look the way she wanted, but in the end it was all right. You know, with the top sawed off it looked like that tree was growing right through the ceiling. She liked that. Said it was magical."

"You picked a crazy one," I say.

"It's not that she's *crazy*," Henry says, carefully. He swipes his hood off. "She just imagines things better than they actually are. And it rubs off. That's what gets me about her. Things usually look pretty shitty, the way I see them. Boring, at least. But hanging around Leah, you get to see things her way. I wanted to keep that up, and to help her keep imagining things the way she wanted."

"So you *married* her?" I say.

"No regrets," Henry says, smiling.

"I found the one!" Rosie yells. We tromp over. "This one," she says, "is perfectly imperfect." Henry raises his saw to cut it down but Rosie says, "Wait!"

She spills some cocoa on the ground. "For the gods," she says.

17

Leah

I call my parents.

There's snow here, I say. Is there snow there?

Yes, they say, but it's mostly brown.

Henry's out selling Christmas trees, I say. It's very festive.

We almost went ice-skating, they say. We looked at everyone going around and we said to each other, Let's go!

But you didn't?

The line was very long.

Have you ever done anything terrible to each other? I say.

What kind of question is that? they say.

So no, I say.

Of course we have, they say. We're married.

Are you okay? they say.

Everything is very good here, I say.

WE ARE WAITING for the lights to go on.

Parked in Quinn's car, outside Frame's house, a bulging shadow hulks some yards off, the reason for Frame's fine and Marks's letter. The woods are quiet because it's winter and there is nothing left alive out there. The blast of ship's horn punctuates the silence. Quinn is shivering because she's cut the engine and thus the heat, citing good investigative practice. She says an idling car would look suspicious if someone spotted us. I tell her I'm pretty sure Watergate is over and no one is on our tail but she pretends not to hear me. She's already had one cup of coffee and is now drinking the one she got for me, which I'm not drinking because it's only six o'clock at night and we've only been here half an hour. This whole thing is ridiculous, but I have to admit, a little fun too. Quinn has a way of turning everything into an event.

"Uncle later?" I say.

"Can't," Quinn says. "I have band practice."

"*Band* practice?"

"It was Rosie's idea. I'm humoring her."

"Humoring her?"

"Dating her?" Quinn says. She gets the kind of sneaky smile a person has when they're thinking about how wonderful something is. She's trying not to let it spread, but she fails, and when she turns to me her face is a sloppy grinning revelation of helpless joy.

"You are in so much trouble!" I say, and point at her face. "Look at you! You are so far gone!"

Quinn shakes her head. "So much trouble," she says, still grinning.

"What do you mean dating?" I say. "Have you been on *a date* somewhere?"

"Sure we have," Quinn says. "We've been to the Uncle, the waterfront, our house."

"You absolutely cannot go on a date with your roommate to your own house," I say.

"We're just—*together,*" Quinn says.

"I see," I say. I consider this. "Would you characterize Rosie as . . . *solid*?"

Quinn laughs. "Not by a long shot," she says. "That girl is crazy for miles."

"Give me a sip of coffee."

"Nope. Mine now," she says. "Too late."

A car comes around the bend. Its high beams project a waxy yellow triangle on Quinn's forehead. She sinks her teeth, softly, into the rim of her Styrofoam cup.

"Halogen-lamp fuckers," she says.

I make out someone coming through the yard. "Frame's here," I say.

"Shhh," Quinn says.

"Don't we need to interview him anyway?"

"Shhh!"

"I think it's great about Rosie."

"Shhh."

A man's form, blue against blue in the night, stalks over to the phantom display. His shadow hands stretch wide and come together. He is plugging one thing into another.

And then I can't see for all the holy brightness.

When my sight returns I see the inflatable Christmas decorations growing, like the wicked witch's feet in reverse. Blown up and shivering from the influx of light and air and life, a panoply of hideous creatures are thronged on a wooden platform. Wobbling in the inflatable tableau are: Rudolph, a trumpet-horned monster, a New England Patriot, Snoopy, a snowman with a toothy grin, which is confusing, a yellow japanimation mouse, Mickey Mouse, Mighty Mouse, Snoopy again, but dressed up as Santa Claus, a bloated woman in a veil, maybe the Virgin, Rudolph dressed up as Santa Claus, a New England Patriot dressed up as Santa Claus, Elmo, Elmo dressed up as Santa Claus, and a five-foot snow globe with shiny Mylar flakes blowing around inside like it's a glitter nor'easter.

Frame's illuminated back is all we see as he slowly returns to his house.

"It's glorious," Quinn says. She hand-rolls down the window. All that light is kicking up glare.

"It's the tackiest thing I've ever seen," I say. "Though remarkable."

Quinn says, "This is some grade-A revolutionary shit."

"Revolutionary?" I say.

When we get back to the office, the windows are dark even though it's only six.

"Maybe she's dead," Quinn says. But there's a letter on the editing desk with a note from Charley. *Town hall meeting tonight. See you there.*

BY THE TIME we get to the middle school, I have two voice mails from Henry about the meeting. Quinn, who is driving, gets on the phone with Charley. "Write this down," she says to me.

"Oh," I say, "you mean in my *notebook*?" It is immensely satisfying to pull it from my pocket and wave it around.

"Just write it down, Leah!"

Here is the news: Yesterday, Mikey Eubanks from the bait shop received a citation for trespassing on the *casa grande* property, officially known as the Dorian property. The thing was,

Mikey didn't know he was on the property at all. He was just sitting on the carousel in Neversink Park, looking out at the water. He was also listening to the Stones' *Exile on Main* at full volume on his radio and sipping from a fifth of whiskey, so he'd thought *that* was the problem. But it wasn't. Use of the area commonly known as Neversink Park, Eubanks was told by the officer who gave him the citation, was no longer permitted. The park was part of what used to be the Sanfords' property. While the Sanford family put up a sign that said NEVERSINK PARK, and permitted use of the land by the public, carousel included, they never officially gave the land to the town. Even the carousel, which was built by some original Sanford many years ago, was technically privately owned. As such, when the Dorians bought the Sanfords' land, they bought the rights to the park and the carousel too, and they were making them private.

By the time we get there, the parking lot is packed and people are streaming into the gym. There's hardly room to drive between the rows and Quinn almost mows down a man who spits retaliatory tobacco juice in our wake. I spot Henry pacing in front of his nursery truck. He's stopped driving the lobster pot to avoid being teased.

"I'll see you in there," I tell Quinn. "Save seats."

I slam the car door and head for Henry.

I say, "I got your messages. What's—" But before I can ask, he grabs my hand and shakes his head. He stares nervously at the gym doors. "It's gonna be a madhouse in there," he says, squeezing my hand. "Stick close, okay?"

"I'll stick," I say, and squeeze back.

We head inside and Quinn waves us to the front. I sit, Henry to my right, Charley, Quinn, and Rosie to my left. The meeting was moved from the town hall to the school to accommodate overflow attendance. I estimate fifty people. The gym smells like rubber flooring and damp overcoats. There is a general din of squeaking sneakers as people get settled and I, impatient, nervous, count the eight basketballs trapped in an overhead net that hangs between the ceiling and us. Henry is as jittery as I've ever seen him. What have you got yourself into, Henry? I think. And then realize that when you are married, you have been gotten into things too.

The town clerk, Maude Gunthrop, is wearing a peach skirt suit with flesh-colored tights and blue snow boots. She calls the meeting to order and asks that the second chair, whoever that is, read the minutes from the last meeting. "As first chair, I call this meeting to order at six twenty-two P.M. Will the second chair please read the minutes from last meeting?"

"Forget the minutes!" someone shouts. "We've got stuff to talk about." There is sympathetic muttering.

"Mr. Dawson?" says Gunthrop. "Yes, hello, Mr. Dawson, welcome. Mr. Dawson, if you'd ever come to one of these meetings before . . ." With this, she scans the crowd. "In fact, if any of you had *ever* come to one of these meetings before, you would know that this is how we begin. Protocol does not drop out all of a sudden just because we have a few additional constituents in attendance, does it, second chair?"

"No, ma'am," says the second chair, a thin man with a head of hair like a pelt, whom I suspect of being married to the first chair, or, at least, of sleeping with her.

"Damn, Gunthrop!" Quinn says admiringly. She leans across to hiss at Charley and me, "Let's get *her* on staff!"

The second chair then proceeds to read the minutes from the last town hall meeting. Then Gunthrop asks if there are issues from the floor.

A man with chestnut hair swept back like a lion's stands up. "I motion that we discuss the legal limitations of Neversink Park and the Dorian property." His voice rings like a bronze bell.

Henry turns pale. Charley nudges me and says, "You know who that is by now, I hope?"

Carter and Quinn look so much alike I can't help but stare.

18

Quinn

Not only does Carter now appear properly fucking shod but Rosie's face lights up the moment he stands. "Cut it out," I say.

"What?"

"Glowing."

"He's wonderful," she says, her *wonderful* three syllables long and she's not the only one. Half the place has faces glowing like Rosie's. It's not just that Carter is a semifamous musician. It's that something about his bigness draws people in. I could pretend I don't get it, but I have a fox eye in my pocket. Rosie whispers, "The other day, when I brought him his eggs? He said it was vital we preserve the historical traditions and character of Menamon. Did you know the Stationhouse has been around for over eighty years?"

"Is that why our utilities blow?"

"Would you shut up?" Charley hisses. "I'm trying to get quotes."

Carter says, "But, Ms. Gunthrop, isn't it the benefit of governing a small town that tradition may prevail over power? Logic over bureaucracy?"

I sink low in my seat, but also hope maybe he'll see me.

Gunthrop reiterates that the area we know as Neversink Park is not actually public property and that if the Dorians want to fence their land and get rid of the carousel, they can.

It only takes a moment for this to sink in, and then half the room is on its feet and talking at once. Billy Deep trips all over himself standing up and says, "Who said anything about getting rid of the carousel?"

"My kids grew up riding that carousel," a woman in a wool sweater says. "It's a historical landmark."

A man with a red beard says, "What are they gonna do, mail out special invitations to the kids who want to ride it? Make them RSVP to get in past the gates?"

"No way, Frank," Cliff Frame says. "They'll tear it down. They probably think the thing is tacky. Probably it's a semipermanent structure."

"Ms. Gunthrop," Carter says, and everyone gets quiet for a moment. "I wonder if you might let us know exactly what the Dorians' plans are in regard to the carousel. Are they open to discussion with the town? Perhaps an arrangement could be made to preserve just that section of the park so that—"

"You don't get it," Gunthrop says. She shakes her head and smiles joylessly. "There's no discussion to be had. The park is their land, and the carousel is their property. So whether they want to use it, or share it, or pay a bunch of wreckers to take the thing down, stick by stick, it's up to them."

From the back, someone shouts, "Don't kill the carousel!"

There's a new uproar, but Gunthrop waves her hands around

and shouts, "Meeting over! Meeting over!" When it becomes clear that no one is leaving, she and the second chair pack up their papers and scurry out the back entrance, people shouting after them: "Don't kill the carousel!" Everyone stands around arguing for a while, until it's clear she isn't coming back. Muttering, they start filing out into the parking lot. Henry and Leah move fast, and by the time we've made it to the aisle, they're gone. I'd hoped we'd compare notes—I wanted to know what she thought of Carter. If anyone could be invulnerable to his speechifying, I think it would be Leah, and I love her for that.

OUTSIDE, ROSIE, A gleam of purpose in her eyes, says, "They can't get rid of the carousel. We need to *do* something." People are milling around the parking lot.

"Rosie, be serious," I say. "When was the last time you rode that rusty old trap?" Because, sure, she probably rode the thing every weekend of her childhood. It has sentimental value. I understand. But this new stance is about more than that. Rosie loves this sort of thing, sweeping generalities about justice and love. She's the sort of girl who dreams of participating in something big. I was maybe like that once, for a second, before Marta, before everything.

I light up a cigarette and sit on the hood of my car. I see Billy leaving the meeting with his angry-young-man face on. His hands are shoved deep in his jacket pockets and his chin is tucked to his chest. "Hey, Billy," I say. "Come here, what's up?"

"Quinn, I have serious things on my mind today," Billy says. He hasn't yet forgiven me for putting an end to his lucrative cat-bagging. But he perks up at the sight of Rosie. Everyone does.

"We're going to get a few drinks," I say. "You want to come?"

"Can't," he says. "My dad just headed to the Uncle." It's not that they wouldn't serve him, I know, but that Joseph wouldn't stand for it.

"I'm a proficient bartender," Rosie says.

I say, "Where do you think we're entertaining, lady?"

"I have a key to the Stationhouse," Rosie says.

"Billy," Carter calls from the gymnasium. A triangular window illuminates a basketball hoop in its frame and the bickering voices come loud and then soft as the gym doors swing on their hinges. I think about booking it before he sees me but Carter lopes over to us fast. I hop off the hood.

"Billy," he says again, but then he sees me. He's short on air and braces himself, hands on his knees. "Ms. Winters," he says. Winters. He's read my piece, and he knows, and I understand he's crouched down like that to catch his breath, but I think about the way a father is supposed to bend at the knees when he talks to a child. To get down to her level.

I exhale. I feel a little shaky. A little mad. It's unfair that he spends even this sliver of time with other people. There is such a deficit, a negative amount of time he's not spent with me.

"The *Star* appreciated your letter," I say in a way that I hope conveys my deep and abiding sarcasm. "We stopped by Cliff's tonight."

"I look forward to your piece," Carter says. He's looking at me now, not rattled but not easy either. *Really* looking at me like he didn't last time and I hope he's seeing a ghost. I hope it's clear that this is a haunting going down right now. *Please go see your father,* Marta said. *Please.*

Carter stands up and says, "Rosalind." He dips his head, a cowboy bow.

"Hey, Carter," she says. Then, "I want to help. How can I help?"

"Rosie," I say, louder than I should.

"Whatever you're here to talk to Billy about, I want to help with it too," she says. Billy grins, like he's somehow responsible for bringing her into the fold.

"Rosalind, I'm only here to offer Billy a ride home," Carter deflects.

"Bullshit," I say. I can tell by his face he's surprised. I get a rush of fear like I have one foot off a ledge. I squint at the sky because I'm unable to back up my gall with my face. The night is clear. I focus on the center star in Orion's belt.

"I'm all right," Billy says. "I'm going to get a drink with these ladies." He puts a hand on each of our backs and I grind some sand from my teeth. "I'll come see you tomorrow."

"Me too," says Rosie.

Carter smiles but shakes his head. "As much as I'd enjoy your company, Rosalind, there's really no need. I'm just showing Billy some old instruments he's interested in."

"That would interest me too," Rosie says. "Quinn and I are in a band."

I could kill her, but instead I keep staring at the sky. I can feel Carter looking at me. One two three stars in Orion's belt. One two three in the sword. Elsewhere in the lot someone tries to start his engine. It sputters, screeches, turns over on the third try.

"Well then, by all means, come by," he says. He clears his throat, making his voice even deeper and more fucking mellifluous, as impossible as that seems. "Ms. Winters, you should feel free to stop by as well. An important cause always has at least one journalist in its pocket."

"I'm not pocket-sized," I say.

"Quinn," Rosie says, but what the hell does she want me to do?

"Well then, see you around," Carter says. He leaves.

I HAVE WHAT I think is a memory but if I'm honest might only be a dream, of Carter singing to me as a baby. If I try not to think too hard, remembering around its edges, it'll develop. I remember him whistling the melody line of "Thick as a Brick," the part

Anderson plays on his flute, and then singing me the rest. That's it, the whole damn memory. But I've held on to that a long time. Now, however, that I've actually met him? I feel like that memory can't have been true. It must have been just a lonely-ass dream.

ROSIE LETS US into the Stationhouse even though it's after-hours. I'm pissed at her and she knows it. I get a bottle of whiskey and my guitar from upstairs, and when I pour the drinks I pump Billy's full of ginger ale so I don't get him into too much trouble.

Rosie is in the kitchen cooking us a griddleful of home fries. "You never let *me* in here after-hours," I shout in. And believe me I have asked. Many a night at one in the morning I have dreamed of those industrial-sized ice cream buckets they keep in the walk-in. But Rosie was always firm. *That wouldn't be professional,* she'd say.

I mess around with some finger picking. Play a few chords.

"It's for the cause," she calls back now. "Billy is working to preserve Menamon's historic character."

"There's no fucking cause," I say. "There's just Carter bitching about that shitty park and Billy catnapping people's pets. Which, by the way, I think is reprehensible."

"You're just pissed because your old man likes spending time with me," Billy says, all of a sudden a big man, an appeaser.

"That is not true," I say. Through the crisscrossed windowpanes I see the moon cut up in four pieces. "How the fuck did you know that?"

"He told me," Billy says, and reaches for his drink like it'll save him. He vigorously chews ice. "Besides, you're his spitting image. Doesn't take a DNA test." He looks out the window. *"Moon river,"* he sings.

And *this* is the thing that's knuckling down on my heart: everyone fucking knows, including Carter, and it doesn't change anything. That scrap of please Marta left me, it felt like the first direction in a scavenger hunt. I thought if I did like she asked, the next step would just become obvious, one clue leading to another waiting on Carter's doorstep or something. Marta, did you have any plan at all? I whistle Jethro Tull. I try to pick out the chords for "Moon River."

"Where'd you pick up a dusty old song like that?" I say.

Billy tilts back in his chair so a square of moonlight falls on his buttoned-up belly. "They listen to WKML while they shuck the oysters in the back," he says. "I hang out in there sometimes."

"Sing it again," I say.

"Moon river!" he croons, his voice filling the empty room.

"Motherfucker," I say. "Billy, you can sing."

Rosie comes out with a plate of potatoes all browned up with onions and peppers mixed in. She takes a seat and pours the Stationhouse's cranberry chipotle sauce all over them. Billy is ready with a fork, starts shoveling it in.

"Want to be in our band?" Rosie says.

His mouth full of food, Billy says, "What band?"

"Cassandra Galápagos and the Aged Tortoise," Rosie says.

Billy rolls his eyes. "I'm not being in any band called Cally Hoo-Ha and the Fuckin' Turtles," Billy says. "That's gay."

I give him the hairy eyeball.

"You know what I mean," he says.

19

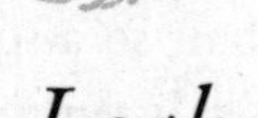

Leah

I make sandwiches. I feel wound up from the meeting. When people argue I get a little bump in my heart and can't help wanting to cheer along. I wash a sharp knife in the sink and see that the moon is big tonight. Henry rails about the meeting and people's shortsightedness. "A run-down old carousel. They're crazy. It's not even their property. The land *belongs* to the Dorians."

Shut up, I find I want to say, even though I realize that it is, perhaps, a little childish for everyone to make such a fuss about a few run-down carousel horses.

"Leah," Henry says, "I've got to show you something." He goes out to his truck and comes back with a large paper tube.

Henry spreads the blueprint out on the counter. I look over his shoulder. It's the plans for the Dorians' house and the different sections of landscaping that will surround it. The ones he's been working on for months.

"Look here." Henry pulls me close. He holds my hand as he shows me where the orchard is going to be. The rose garden. Where Neversink Park used to be but will be no longer.

"This is why?" I say.

"This is why," Henry says, and traces the property border with his finger, rows of little symbols there. And I get it. In Henry's sketches? There is deer fencing, eight feet tall, blocking the whole property off from the rest of town.

This is bad news.

Henry may well be the only person in this town who knows why the park is going. He is definitely the only one who wants it to go.

"It's better than a busted old carousel, isn't it?" Henry asks.

I let go of his hand. I lean back, my hands pressing against the cabinets, bouncing my body forward and back. I haven't earned the right to argue like a local yet, but that's exactly what I want to do.

"It's about more than the carousel, Hen. That house looks like nothing else around here. I heard it's going to have a red-tiled roof!" I don't really want to pick a fight but already I'm imagining the article about the meeting: public dissent, impotent local officials, Marks with his country preacher's voice. I feel it, the mental swirl of a story coming together. I live for this feeling, am usually delighted by its arrival. But now I don't know if I can have it. Because with this story, of course, there is the issue of Henry.

Henry says, "You've got a problem with red roofs all of a sudden?"

"No, not really, but it's not exactly in keeping with the local aesthetic, the local culture," I say.

Henry looks at me, latently angry. He mushes his hands all over his face as he says, "For Christ sake, Leah. Who cares?"

"Charley hates that house," I say. "She hates Elm Park too." I already have it in my head, the story, and I'm protective of its little spark, my right to write it. Maybe this whole thing will blow over. Maybe in a few weeks people won't even remember who the Dorians are.

Henry says, "*I* hate Elm Park. I hate their gates and their stupid Home Depot ground cover. But the Dorians' property is gonna be beautiful. Leah, it's really gonna be *something*." He smoothes out the plans and tries to get me to look again, but I don't want to see them. Why is Henry saying these things? He should be angry like the rest of Menamon. The Henry who told me a million stories of Maine would definitely be angry, wouldn't he? I want to yell at Henry, *You have changed! Change back!*

"What if I showed people the plans?" Henry says, and leans forward on the counter, hovering over his pages. His hoodie rides up in the back, exposing a slash of skin.

"Henry, you're deluded," I say. "People aren't going to feel better about losing their park just because one family's backyard is going to be beautiful."

"But it's *in* Menamon. Just look, Leah." He starts tracing the paths through the property and explaining where everything goes. The plantings, the structures. And I'm trying to see what he's seeing so I can understand how important this green world is to him. But it's already too late. Because this time, when I look? My newspaper brain is awake and ticking away. It is remembering measurements, specifics, filing details away and figuring out what it all means. I shut my eyes.

"Hen, you shouldn't be showing me this."

"Why?" he says. I open them again and Henry looks so hurt and confused that I feel a rush of love. I love Henry for not being able to imagine a single reason why showing me something like this, me, his wife, but also a local journalist, might be a bad idea. It's total trust, and I hope I am worthy of it. Before I do or say anything I'll regret, I kiss Henry on the cheek, and tell him I am going to bed.

As I climb the stairs I realize that sometimes the way you love someone best is by saying nothing. This is a terrible kind of thing to have to know, and I wish I could go back to when everything was simple and romantic.

Upstairs, I wash my face. I turn off the lights and climb into bed, though I don't feel sleepy. When I was sixteen, I had it bad for a boy who was nothing like Henry: a New York City prep school kid with long eyelashes, born of rich Oklahomans. He lived to cut up. His mother let us close the door to his bedroom after school as long as we went to the museums with her every month. She called these trips *our dates.* Once we went to a Chelsea skyscraper full of art studios, someone different on every floor. There was a gallery of enormous abstract paintings based on a Roman naval battle where they set a whole fleet of ships on fire. She kept us in that room for almost an hour. Every painting looked the same to us: messy swaths of color with little black sticks floating in the middle of them. My boyfriend wandered off to pretend to be the elevator operator.

What sort of art do you like? his mother said to me. I told her Chagall. He was my favorite back then. I loved those flying goats and mermaids and fiddles.

I liked Chagall when I was young too, she said. *But when you're older you'll like this instead.* I thought she was terrible for saying that. I thought there was something very wrong with her if this was the kind of art she liked, or else she was a fake. There wasn't anything happening in those paintings, it was just shapes: messy swaths of color with little black sticks floating in the middle of them. She explained that the color was the fire, the sticks were the ships. The fire was blue and the fire was orange and sometimes there were a lot of sticks and sometimes there was only one. I nodded and hoped my boyfriend would come back soon.

I don't really like Chagall anymore, it's true. Sometimes, goats are just goats. Sometimes I remember my boyfriend's mother staring at all those flaming ships, and I think that she really did like them. That once you get older you see that there's an indefinable fire and that everything else is just little black sticks.

Yes, some of the ways you have to love someone are not very glamorous and I will say no more stubborn things tonight. I will be worthy of Henry's trust, and I will love him better in the brightness of morning.

I WALK INTO the *Star* the next morning and Charley says, "I hope you have a lot of ideas for this article, because there's no way we're letting those people take Neversink."

"I was thinking of something more impartial," I say, though of course I do have a lot of ideas. I have the whole story laid out in my head, not a ripple in it, lead to closing line.

"Forget that. If Carter Marks says the benefit of small-town government is that you can defy bureaucracy and be logical, the benefit of a small-town newspaper is that we can take a stand and I won't have anyone to answer to."

"Except Henry," I say, though this is obvious.

I had hoped that Charley, with her fierce family pride, would be the one to rein me in, but she says, "Henry's in the weeds and he knows it."

Is that a pun-filled headline? Sisterly confidence? Charley is wearing a Red Sox baseball cap and knee-high blue rubber boots. As she digs through drawers of files I've never seen anyone open before, her ponytail swings. It's nine A.M. She should be chain-smoking and beating advertising money out of broke local vendors by now.

"What are you looking for?" I ask. Is it really this article that has her back in gear?

"The story we ran on those lots going up for sale," Charley says. She points a finger at me. "We'll run it again alongside the piece on the meeting. Then we'll start working the tick-tock for this mess. Back-burner any human-interest stuff until this is done."

"Yes," I say. Yes, yes, yes. Because when people are riled about something, and you write about it, it gets them more riled. Because Charley doesn't usually give a damn about anything except selling ad space and not pissing anyone off, but now she's come into the newsroom proper, and it's on.

I boot up my computer and think about everything I want to make sure I include about last night's meeting: the tobacco spitter, the size of the crowd, the deer fencing. I look up the town clerk's e-mail and think I'll request a copy of the minutes, because they've got to be public record.

I'm about to start writing, but I pause, because I know that this won't be great for Henry. In fact, the best thing I could do for him would be to try to talk Charley out of giving this story so much attention. If we didn't fan the flames this whole thing could die and the Dorians might be old news by Tuesday. Henry would be free to go forward with his plans as is. I think of Henry with his face all beaming and wrapped up in his imaginary green world, his dream project. I should kill this piece, for him.

But then I hear Charley cursing as she bangs around in the filing cabinets, and I think about how I can't wait for Quinn to get here and see her this way. I have a chance to do some actual writing again, and to show Quinn how it's done. We finally have a chance to play at Woodward and Bernstein for real. And so I stop thinking about Henry, and let the eager gears of my newspaper brain take over.

I open the piece with a description of Carter Marks, rising above the crowd to speak.

20

Quinn

I sit in a wobbly chair and watch Rosie marry the ketchups. I'm helping with her side work so she'll make her meeting on time. It's the last day of February, that blip of a month, which means that a bunch of bums who got riled up at the town hall meeting are going to get together and groan about the Dorians and Elm Park at Carter's house. This is their third monthly meeting, and Rosie says, this time, they're going to plan their next move. To save Neversink and the carousel they must, Rosie tells me, be unified in action.

Rosie lines up the more-full ketchups then balances their less-full partners on top, bottles mouth to mouth. Her forearm is dented in a line near the inner elbow, the fold a ghost of baby fat. She's written *Carter's @ 7!* in blue Bic on the underflesh of her arm. Through her ears are two sets of twinkly studs, and enormous hoops.

"Will you help me with something?" Rosie says. I don't so much agree to help her as follow her to the walk-in freezer. Rosie points at an industrial tub of ice cream. "Could you put that in your car?" The thing must be ten gallons.

"Why would I put that much strawberry ice cream in my car?" I say. For a moment I think, stupidly, she might be planning something for us. A picnic.

We'll take these ten gallons of ice cream somewhere beyond town limits. We'll spread a blanket under an elsewhere-bound overpass. We'll eat the frozen strawberries and cream out of the drum with plastic cutlery.

"I won't be able to get it to the meeting otherwise," she says. "Can I have the keys, please?"

"Rosie, that's, like, stealing," I say, and she looks at me like that's the lamest thing she's ever heard. Like all of a sudden I'm the naive one. But this is not like her. "I'm not giving you the car so you can steal strawberry ice cream for Carter Marks," I say. The freezer's cooling mechanism circulating air sounds like the inside of a seashell.

"You can or cannot be involved, but I'm going," Rosie says. She gives me the Stationhouse keys. "Lock up."

Rosie sets the ice cream drum on its side and begins rolling. I stand in the walk-in, not wanting to follow her. My sweater is in the other room and all I have on is a red baseball tee with a peeling #9 decal on the chest.

I cave. I grab my sweater and jog to the porch and see Rosie rolling the drum across the parking lot. The condensation on its sides picks up grit and ice-melt salt as she rolls. "Rosie," I shout after her. "That isn't going to work, come on."

"This is my part," she says, or something like it. It's hard to tell, because she doesn't turn around. All I see is her ass bumping up and down as she spins the drum forward.

I get the car and drive up beside her. "Get in the car," I tell her.

Rosie stands up and catches her breath. "It's heavy," she says. She hoists it into the way back. She takes a seat in the passenger side and buckles up. As her buckle clicks I realize she knew it was only a matter of time before I came after her. I feel like laughing. I imagine if Sam, if any of my exes, saw me now, they would laugh too. Because I didn't used to be this kind of lady. I used to be the one who went off to sulk when things didn't go my way.

Marta used to watch the horse races. She loved the Derby, always bet a few dollars on some hopeless long shot. For fun, and because Marta was the patron saint of lost causes. She never won a thing but once. The 2009 Derby, she bet ten bucks on a fifty-to-one horse no one had ever heard of called Mine That Bird. You should have seen us screaming our heads off and jumping up and down in our living room, knocking over bags of chips and bottles of beer, making a terrible mess as that horse streaked up and won the whole damn thing. We laughed hard and celebrated Marta's win the rest of the afternoon. We couldn't believe it. No one on TV could believe it either, and when they interviewed the jockey all anyone could say was *How? How had he done it?* The jockey said, *I rode him like a* good *horse.*

Rosie's settled in the seat now and peeks over her shoulder to make sure the ice cream is still back there. Her arms are goose-bumped. I toss her my sweater.

THERE ARE TRUCKS and cars in Carter's driveway, which reeks of exhaust. Probably dockworkers inside, the kind of men who think emissions testing is a government conspiracy. Rosie leads the way to the door and I follow, carrying the ice cream, my back threatening to give out the whole way.

Sara Riley from the bar is the only other woman there. Her silvery hair is brushed neatly and her sleeves are rolled up. The rest are men: Joseph Deep, Jethro Newkirk, Cliff Frame, Mikey Eubanks, Billy, and three more boys his age. There aren't enough chairs, so some of them are sitting on the floor. They've tracked dead leaves, crushed up, onto the rug. Should've taken off their shoes, but what do I care.

"We have ice cream!" Rosie says. She gestures at me, like I too am a surprise.

"Nosing around trouble, Winters?" Riley says. "You shouldn't be here."

"We have ice cream, Riley," I say. I set the tub down in the middle of the circle. "You got a spoon?"

"Carter!" she says. "No journalists."

Billy produces a plastic spoon from nowhere and starts in on the ice cream. "Strawberry is the worst flavor," he says. The other boys root through the kitchen for spoons.

Carter comes in, wearing boots and a worn gray T-shirt. He has not shaved. He appraises us and the ice cream. The copper pots hanging behind him sway.

"We might need a journalist," he says. "Pull up some rug."

"I don't know, Carter," Jethro says.

"Seriously, Jethro?" I say. This is ridiculous.

"We're wasting time," Carter says. "Some of the boys have school tomorrow. Let's talk." Two of the boys, mouths full, look embarrassed, swallow.

"The fences have started going up already," Riley says. And I swear to God she's brought fucking snapshots. She spreads them on the rug. I snort. Rosie gives me the fisheye.

"Have they done the whole perimeter?" Carter asks.

"That's a ways off," pipes one of Billy's friends.

"Who asked you?" says Jethro.

"He's working construction on the job," Billy says. He looks extra pale tonight.

"Don't say that in front of Quinn," Jethro says.

"What the fuck, Jethro?" I say.

"You might weasel," says Riley.

"I've never blown a secret in my life and don't act like you know me well enough to say different," I say, standing up.

Riley sets her jaw. "I might know you better if you'd lived here more than a minute," Riley says.

And I'm so sick of this. I feel like I've been living here for ages and forget it doesn't look that way to other people. How long before my dues are paid? "It always comes back to the credit with you, doesn't it, Riley?" I say.

"Quinn won't tell," Rosie says. "I know she won't."

"Thanks a fucking lot, Rosie," I say.

Rosie twirls an earring around in its hole. Everyone is quiet.

"Can I talk to you a minute?" Carter says.

No fucking way, I want to say. But he walks into the other room and I guess I'm supposed to follow him because everyone is looking at me, though maybe just because I've embarrassed myself. Rosie isn't looking at me. Her face is bright red and her hands are still. Her position here, I see now, is tenuous. Everyone watches as I try to meet her eyes, but she's fixed on the rug pattern.

I have no choice but to agree, so I follow Carter down the hallway, his boot steps too loud in the wood-planked hall. "I need your help with something," Carter says over his shoulder. He opens the door to a roomful of taxidermied animals. My grandfather's studio. It smells odd. There's something too warm and chemical about the air. Wires, drills, a sewing kit are all strewn over a large worktable. Molding clay sits in damp, plastic-shrouded lumps. There are more boxes like the one he showed me with the eyes. Big crates stamped WASCO. We are watched by yellow molds of deer heads and fox bodies that have the blank expressiveness of Greek masks. In the corner is a stack of old tapes: *Advanced Squirrel Mounting Techniques* and *Carcass Casting a Bobcat.*

On various mounts the animals are posed in creepy tableaux. A raccoon is reared up on his weird feet, tail defensively slung to the side. He's poised for battle with a copperhead snake who is coiled at the base, his scales more visible for being shellacked. The plaque has the date and, in quotes, *Raccoon vs. Copperhead.*

Carter lets me look around. "Quietest place in the house," he says. "I'm taking you aside because I think you should go, but I don't want to tell you what you have to do, and I didn't want them to hear me say so."

"Why the hell should *I* go?" I say. "I didn't start yelling like crazy Riley." I can't believe he actually thinks he's going to kick me out of his house right now. That he can get away with this.

Carter shuffles and moves some nose-shaped and wet-looking glass pieces around the table. "I'm saying you can do what you want, but that I think you should go because they're just starting to let Rosie be a part of things," he says. "And I know you care about her. And I know you know she wants to be part of this."

Behind Carter I spot a barred owl. It looks just like the one Mom called down. I wonder if they all look like this, being the same species, or whether these two are actually more kin than others. She looks pissed off, this owl. Her feathers don't lie straight, they're ruffled, and one of her wings is crooked.

"Your father made these?" I say.

Carter nods. "Jethro's done a few, but mostly they're my father's, yes."

"Your father, my grandfather," I say slowly.

Carter looks like he wants to say something. He opens his mouth and his eyes get big and panicked. It's not that he's speechless, I think, he just doesn't know which thing of many bullshit things to say first.

"Quinn," he says.

"You tell me you think I should go, because you're looking out for *Rosie*? I didn't even want to come today, okay? I *never* wanted to come here at all, except she asked me to. Fucking Marta asked me."

"You don't have to go," he says. "I'm sorry. Just—"

"Don't say sorry. She's dead," I say. "Marta is. And don't tell me she lived a full life because you don't even fucking know. You missed it. The whole long excruciating thing."

He stands there hopelessly, his body open like he'll take whatever it is I've got. "I read about it in the paper," he says.

"The obituary?" I say, before I can stop myself. Then he moves likes he's going to say something, and before he tries to fucking explain everything or show me a boxful of never-posted birthday cards, or explain why he never could love my mother at all, I get the hell out of there, angry at how stupid I was to think that scrap of *please* was the first step in a scavenger hunt. That Marta was just waiting for me somewhere, wondering why it was taking me so damn long to piece together the clues.

I stomp out past the dead animals, past Rosie calling after me, past the seven fucking rebels eating ice cream.

I WAIT UP for her, back at the apartment. I lie in the bed, with its pink sheets, and look at the postcards on the walls from Rosie's parents, pictures of oranges and alligators and big greasy women in bikinis. Two hours later I hear her thumping around the Stationhouse. I creep down in sock feet.

Billy's at a table drinking ginger beer. His nose twitches from the bubbles. "Heya," he says. "Hungry?" I don't say a thing, just push through the swinging kitchen door.

Rosie is at the griddle. She's got her black pocket apron on, the tie in the back catching her T-shirt, hiking it up in a bunch. Her hips spill over her jeans in the back. On the griddle there is one giant sunny-side-up egg puddle with six orange eyes. She speckles it with pepper.

"How was the rest of the meeting?" I ask.

"Good," she says. She flips the giant egg over. One of the yolks breaks and dribbles.

"Just good?" I say, because if she's not regurgitating details it means she's still mad at me. And I don't blame her. "Rosie, I'm sorry," I say. "About earlier."

"I'm probably never going to be a singer," Rosie says. She pokes at the eggs.

"What? What are you talking about?" I say. "Of course you are. Someday you're going to be so famous I'll need to buy tickets just to see you."

"Don't tease me, Quinn," she says. Her cheeks are pink and the hair around her forehead is damp from hovering over the grill. She sighs and leans against the counter, arms crossed. "I'm young but I'm not stupid. I'm not leaving this place anytime soon or probably ever. I'm never going to live in a big house like that. So I might as well do one thing that actually matters. The park? The carousel? That's something I can do."

"Hey," I say. "That's not true. You can do whatever you want. You just have to work at it. You and me, we're going to practice more. You'll see." The truth is that I feel like I'm trying to convince a kid that Santa's real. Like I know he's not real, and the kid knows he's not real, and really it's *me* that needs the kid to keep believing.

"I know what's possible," Rosie says. "Stopping things with the park is possible and I can do it. Don't try to tell me the rest of it is. You don't even believe it yourself."

She's right, of course. People love to tell you that in America everything is possible and all you have to do is want it enough.

Work hard. Keep trying. But those people never knew Marta. Never saw how whole long stretches of your young life can just disappear into sick-smelling bedrooms and hospital lounges. How one day you're suddenly twenty-four, hard in the heart and utterly alone with no idea of what to do with yourself, much less ready to work hard for your fucking dreams. Those people don't know what they're talking about.

Still, it's a lie I wish I believed. It's nothing I want Rosie to know. "You're so young, Rosie," I say. "You can do anything you want."

"I just don't think that's true," Rosie says.

"Rosie, what happened at that meeting tonight? I'm sorry I left like that. What are you guys up to?"

"Nothing," she says. "I mean a lot." And there's a look on her face I don't like. Like part of her mind is all wrapped up in this spinning thing inside her I can't get to. I feel her slipping out of my family portrait, leaving me alone. Just the tip of Rosie's sneaker visible as she runs from my perfect frame, ruining everything.

"You don't owe Carter anything," I say. "He doesn't know shit, Rosie."

"Don't talk to me like a child," she says. "I take care of myself."

And it's not that I don't think she can; it's that I don't want her to. I want to do it, the caretaking. I did it for my mom, after all. I know no one would believe this but it's something I'm good at, really. *Let me.*

21

Leah

In April, the Dorians decide to come see how the construction and landscaping plans are going. Henry tells me and then reminds me every day for a week. When he's not reminding me, he's asking me about nasturtiums. He hates nasturtiums, he says, will they really want nasturtiums? This is the only request the Dorians have made throughout the entire project.

I say, "Sure they will," because I'm reading the *Gazette,* which features a small but front-page story by a woman I was interns with. It's about a UN delegates meeting taking place in the city. It seems pretty thin to me. For front page? Come on.

"Why! Why will they want nasturtiums?" Henry says. He throws up his hands and stares at me, boggle-eyed. I imagine a *Menamon Star* front pager: LOCAL MAN DRIVEN TO MADNESS BY NASTURTIUMS.

I AM HAVING a dream in which Henry shows his landscaping plans to the Dorians, who in the dream are played by my parents. The sound of ironing wakes me, the hiss of its pass. I open my eyes. The light is dim and blue, and Henry, showered already, is wearing nice pants and gold-toe socks and a sleeveless undershirt, his face too close to a white button-down shirt as he passes the iron over it. He has shaved, and I can smell the almond cream that will make his cheeks smooth for all of an hour. His jaw is squarely set with a determination that is sweet: he uses the iron like it's a spade. Like he can dig the wrinkles from his shirt. I wish he wouldn't have to put the button-down over his undershirt. He looks so nice as he is.

I close my eyes. The dream blips, trying and failing to come back. No, the Dorians will not be my parents masquerading under another name. *Surprise! Here we are; we've bought a summer house to be near you!* No. They would not do that. It is six o'clock on a Sunday in New York right now. My mother is sleeping, shiny under the eyes with cream, her décolletage smelling of lilacs. She's a nighttime moisturizer. She has a miniature radio near her bed and listens to it through one earpiece as she sleeps. Never music, usually late-night talk radio. In the darkness, all these late-night callers are phoning in and whispering in my mother's ear. She says it helps her sleep. I asked her once, *Doesn't that give you strange dreams?* She said, *What dreams*?

My father is likely awake and looking through the paper right now. He'll be wearing a bright African-print robe purchased at one safari resort or another, the waist cinched around his stomach, no longer as flat as it was in his tennis-playing days. He'll be quietly exclaiming over the idiocy of the paper, both the events that have transpired and the people who have chronicled them. *Are you kidding me*? he'll be saying, looking around to see if there's anyone to elaborate for. Then, returning to his paper, *You've got to be kidding me.*

I open my eyes again. "Morning," Henry says. "The Dorians come today." As if I didn't know.

"I had a dream about nasturtiums," I lie. "The Dorians said they wanted you to rip them all up."

AT THE SITE I try hard to remember that I must not call the house the *casa grande* while the Dorians are here. The property map lies on Henry's truck hood and he traces the route he will take the Dorians along to view the landscaping plans. It is hard to imagine what the Dorians will see when they arrive. What I see is a hulking monstrosity of wood beams on a dirty concrete foundation. The builder is inspecting his building. The electricians are taping wires that seemed conspicuously exposed to the spring damp. Everyone is doing his job. I pace about. Today my job is to wait and then to smile and be kind so the Dorians see that a city person can live in Menamon too.

"Hey, Leah," Batman calls. He is sitting on some lumber, his hair lying neat over his blue anorak, his hands perfectly still. Batman knows how to wait. "Leah," he says, "if you keep pacing we won't have to till that land."

"I'm sorry," I say.

"Leah, it's okay." He smiles, and it is such a good smile. I wonder who the person is that Batman loves the best.

There is murmuring from the men, and when I turn an enormous black car is wending its way toward us. Henry's body goes rigid, tall, like a soldier's, and again I anticipate my parents climbing out of the car. Of course this is ridiculous, but I feel a slow-creeping panic all the same. What would they think, seeing me like this? Here I am with my pant cuffs dragging in the mud, on a small-town beat where taxidermy constitutes big news, my hair going wild, the little pieces around my forehead astray.

The SUV parks and the car door opens. A man steps down, gives a quick wave and walks around to the other side of the car. He opens the door for his wife. No, these are not my parents. The Dorians are not like my parents at all. In fact, they are young. They are my and Henry's age.

As if rehearsed, Alex Dorian goes to speak with Henry and the builder and Elena Dorian walks over and kisses me on both cheeks. She smells womanly, her perfume better suited for someone two generations older than her. Than us. "Hello," Elena Dorian says. "You must be Leah."

"Yes," I say. "So nice to finally meet you."

Mr. Dorian is clapping Henry on the back. He is a peer I never could have dreamed for Henry. When I first met Henry I knew he was not like the boys in New York with their vodka tonics and smartphones and cologne, but the way he is with Alex Dorian troubles me. Before, he was Henry, by a bonfire at my parents' country house, laughing, baring his snaggletooth, falling off a log over something someone had said. Henry, eating a breakfast sandwich so intently you'd think it'd save his life. Henry in soft pajamas, grumbling in his sleep and radiating heat like a furnace. I sensed it when I first met him, and knew it later, when he grabbed my ass and pulled me to him, what kind of man he was. That his were hands that really knew how to do things. They were decisive and hard and for once I knew it would stick, my love. It had been a too slippery a thing for so long, with other men. But Henry was the sort of man who had nooks and spaces all through him where I could squirrel my love away. And I didn't bother remembering any of the hiding spots. I just stashed it there, in him, again and again.

Alex Dorian laughs at something Henry has said, smacks his thigh, and Henry winks at him. I wonder about the reserves I'd tucked away. I suddenly feel that I would like to open up a few. Just to get us through this dark season, with the days still short and Henry getting more or less like himself, I am not sure which. Henry laughs a laugh deeper than normal and points a finger at Mr. Dorian, saying something about his car. Mr. Dorian puts his hands up in the air and chuckles. *Mea culpa! Mea culpa!*

As Henry is chuckling next to Alex Dorian I know he is imagining them going out for drinks together, talking about additions and upkeep, being friends. Henry does not want to drink beers with the guys from the docks, the boys he grew up with. Henry's mind is full of this new Menamon with nice houses and stable jobs for everyone. He wants people to see how much better things could be. Better than snooping neighbors and crumbling barns and drunk cousins and dangerous jobs that barely pay the bills.

But this thing that Henry is trying for? It's impossible. I say this not as his wife, but as a newspaperwoman. If people let it, this town will change, and not in the ways Henry wants it to. When I wrote for the city section, I saw it happen again and again. The Lower East Side, Williamsburg, Bed-Stuy. Places don't get better for the people already in them; they change so new people want to live there and then the old people have to scatter. It's just the truth. And, because I am my parents' daughter, I also have this gruesome understanding: no matter how many attaboys pass between the Dorians and Henry, he will always be their employee and not their friend.

Of course, there's no way to tell Henry any of this without sounding like a condescending, know-nothing From-Away. So I don't. So here is Henry, changing before my eyes.

Where is that love I tucked behind your ear last winter? Where is the store I left between your ribs?

Elena Dorian comes over to chat with me. "Look at it! It will be so wonderful," she says as she gestures at the skeleton of the house. I know she is seeing something there but it is beyond my imagination what it might be. I think of my own house, worn smooth from care and rubbing. It is nothing like the *casa grande.* I wonder, if Henry had the option of swapping this house for our own, would he do it?

"It will be stunning," I say. *Stunning.* A word I have not used since I left New York.

Henry says, "Mind if I drive your car, Alex? I'd like to take you on a tour of the grounds."

We bump along the road and it is dim inside this large dark car. The leather seats are so smooth I fear I will slide along the bench to Elena. She is petite and compact. She has long dark hair slicked neatly back and fastened with a tortoiseshell barrette. She has on a black sweater over dark and tailored jeans, large gold earrings, and a string of red beads. My legs do not neatly cross behind the passenger seat. Instead I am folded up at all angles, trapped in this close space, the smell of Elena's perfume heady and intimate.

"I'm thinking that this section will be perennials and vegetables," Henry says. His phone buzzes. I see him look at the screen, then silence it. "Closest to the house so you can pick flowers and vegetables easily," he continues.

"Good, good," Alex says.

Henry points. He describes the rings of shrubberies that will reach your elbows in five years' time, rows of flowering trees that will bloom on and off with each season, an alley of grass between them, for children to run down, Henry says, of all things. I feel a catch in my throat as I see all these imaginary things rise up from the dust. Will Henry someday imagine grassy corridors for our own children to run down? He goes on: Here is where I will plant your imaginary cherry tree. Imaginary daffodils in the spring and imaginary cabbages in fall. As the foliage gets deeper, imaginary hellebores and shade-loving plants.

"Alex," Elena says. "Move your seat up, you're squashing poor Leah back here." Alex mumbles something and his seat moves forward on its electric track, releasing my legs.

"Thank you," I say. Oh, thank God, thank you. Elena wears the same perfume as my mother. Volupté. She smiles at me so kindly, and has freed my legs from the seat. I want this woman to tell me I am good, I realize, that she likes me and that it is okay that my local beat is taxidermy and that the little pieces of hair around my forehead are astray.

"You know, Henry," Alex begins awkwardly, "this sounds fantastic. Really fantastic but—" My stomach drops. Are they going to quash Henry's hopes, after all this? "We were thinking—" Alex stares back at Elena. *Help me,* his face says.

"Well, we know you're primarily a designer, not some kind of a *fieldworker,*" Elena says.

"We were wondering whether we might hire you on sort of a permanent basis," Alex says. "To maintain the property."

"It's just such a big job," Elena says. "We won't be here much of the year and we couldn't possibly maintain the whole thing ourselves."

"We would make it worth your while, of course," Alex says, rubbing his fingers together. Imaginary coins. Imaginary dollars.

Henry looks back at me now, and he is beaming. "Of course," he says. "Let's talk about it, but yes. I'd love to."

"Excellent!" Alex says. He reaches over and they shake. Henry steers us over the dirt road and I reach over and put my hand on his shoulder to let him know that I am happy he has scored his dream job. He will be proud about the money, I know. We make enough, he and I, as we are now. But this job, on top of his Arden pay, will make Henry our breadwinner, like I used to be when we lived in the city. He will enjoy this reversal of roles.

Henry's phone starts buzzing in its holster. He silences it again.

"It will be so nice to get out of the city," Elena says.

Henry and Alex talk about finances. Elena and I peep from the windows.

Quietly, she says, "I think you're quite brave."

"Brave?" I say.

"It must be frightening at night," she says. "With all the wildlife and quiet." Her eyes are dark and very big. She seems less like a grown-up than she did a moment ago.

"Oh, you'll be fine," I say. "It's a small place. Cozy. There's nothing too wild." She squeezes my knee, but it is I who feel grateful. She is worrying about God knows what kind of animal, wolves or bears, and she has let me comfort her. For the first time I have gotten to be a local, someone who knows the ropes.

I am still smiling at Elena as we round the corner to the eastern part of the property, the beach and the park and the carousel. There, stretched across the road, is a long line of cars and people. People I know. They are standing there with their arms spread wide. They are blocking our way.

22

Quinn

Carter's gang gets the tip-off that the Dorians are coming to inspect their monster-estate-in-progress because Jake Hanley from the construction crew was running his mouth at the bar. He was there, whining about how they were killing him with more overtime than he could handle leading up to the visit, which Jethro, on a bar stool down the way, heard and had a lucid moment. He convinced Hanley they should go tell Carter immediately. Jethro wasn't up for driving, so he made Hanley give him a lift in his truck. They rolled up to Carter's house at one A.M. leaning on the horn and flashing their high beams in his windows. Jethro was half falling out the window, shouting: *It's an emergency, Marks! An emergency!*

Plans were made, and Rosie is so excited about it all that she's forgotten to be mad at me. So I'm tagging along, as a representative of the press, of course.

From where I've parked, I can see Carter's gang, all huddled together. It's cold out. The snow has melted but the ground is still rock hard, glittering with little crystals of frost. In the huddle is Mikey from the bait shop, Sara-Riley-who-hates-me from the bar, Joseph Deep and Billy, Jethro, some of the guys from the docks, and some schoolteachers too. They're milling around in the park. Jethro sits on the carousel base with a cup of coffee in his hands. Billy's bent upside down trying to inspect a horse's wooden teeth. Everyone has parked their trucks and cars in a line across the Sanfords' old property. The line is at the juncture where it was commonly understood their pine-sheltered backyard ended and the rocky, sandy stretch of oceanfront park began.

The blockade, cars fender to bumper, separates the rest of the Dorian property from Neversink Park. Jethro's F-150 is parked at the far end of the line at a challenging angle, flush against a station wagon on one side and near an enormous pine tree on the other. A lot of these guys' cars have gun racks. When Rosie said they were going to have a protest, I pictured hippie song-singing with organized chants. This is way more serious than I thought and a look at Rosie's face shows she's trying real hard to be brave, but she wasn't expecting it either.

Rosie is all dressed up as only Rosie can be. She's wearing a dress, red with little white dots. The hem hits around her blue-jean knees and she's got her waitress-white no-slip sneakers on, so she means business. She is clean-faced today, no makeup, and her skin is almost glowing it's so pale. While girls in bands wear many earrings, small-town political renegades don't, it seems. She's wearing a single pair of silver studs.

"Rosie," I say, "where's your jacket?" I sound like someone's terrible boring mother, but April in Maine could freeze a person dead.

Rosie says, "It will ruin the effect."

I spot Carter drinking coffee from a plastic mug. I have promised myself we won't reprise last time's performance. Not today with Rosie all worked up. He's wearing a green sweater, jeans, and work boots. His face is colorful in the cold and he's looking at Rosie in her red dress like she is the sweetest thing he's ever seen. I start worrying that he might be writing a song about her in his head. Composing some stupid folk ballad that'll make its way to J43 in the Uncle's jukebox.

Carter tugs his collar closer to his jaw and says, "Good morning, Quinn." I give him the salute. "Good morning, Rosalind. You look nice," he says. The other men laugh a little.

Sara Riley, wearing a thermal shirt, her fierce little breasts perked up in the chill, shakes her head. She pushes her enormous tortoiseshell glasses that may or may not be for her vision up on her silver head. She's staring, not at Rosie, but at me. Like, *Don't you know you're ruining everything?* Sara may hate me but I know for a fact that she lives in a nice little clapboard house on the other side of town with the branch librarian, a plain, quiet woman almost as tall as Leah who sometimes goes jogging down by the boardwalk in a full wind suit. I know they have three dogs. I know this and I know that there are a lot of women like Sara in hard little towns like these. A lot of women like me too, I guess. Women who don't want to have to talk about things all the time, for Christ sake. Luckily, in Menamon, no man, woman, fisherman, or child wants to talk about a goddamn thing. New Englanders know that some things can just be understood and left be. That is, unless you show up to the motorcade with your girlfriend in a red dress.

Carter stands next to me, still looking at the men. He speaks out of the side of his mouth, in a low voice. "You shouldn't let your girl walk around in the cold like that." I wheel around to ask him what the hell he knows about anything, but once I've turned,

I can see in Carter's face that he's not ribbing me. He doesn't want Rosie to be cold either.

I fold my arms and settle into place beside him and say, "She left her sweater at home. On purpose."

"Ah," Carter says. He crosses his arms. "You going to join the line today?"

"I can't do that," I say. "But I'll write it up."

"That'll be good," he says. "Get Rosie in the picture."

Carter walks off to join the huddle, and I find a stump to sit on. I get my notebook out. I tell myself this is an important role I'm playing. Leah and Charley have no idea I'm here, because I decided not to tell them, keeping Rosie's tip-off to myself. When I show up with this story Monday, I'll be a hero.

Everyone stands in front of the car line. Rosie too. She's not making any small talk, showing these guys she belongs. Jethro is standing next to her, dead sober. There's something tight-wound about his features that must come unspooled when he's drinking. The wind picks up and I'm wondering whether it will rain when I hear the car. All along the line the protesters stand tall, their bodies and their cars between the Dorians and the park.

Holy shit, I think as I crouch there on the sidelines, worried and excited: it was me who started this. No one will ever know it but it was. I know it was just some gravel I threw, just an imaginary window I shattered. But all that time ago, with Rosie at the substation? It was me who cast the first stone.

23

Leah

As we approach, I piece together the missed calls: they must have been from Batman. Cars form a barrier between us and the park, a Volvo with a gun rack on one end and Jethro Newkirk's truck on the other. At first I think, What are they doing here? Carter, Billy, Jethro, Rosie—but then I understand. Not only that this is some sort of protest, but that I am going to be busted, sitting in this car with these New Yorkers, confirming everyone's worst suspicions.

Batman is squatting, smoking a cigarette. He stands up and nods as if to say to Henry, *Yes, what you are thinking is true. This is why I called you the three times you didn't pick up, you fucker.* He tosses his hair over his shoulder. There it is, the Batman move.

"Goddammit!" Henry says, and throws the car in park. We have come to a stop not fifteen feet from the line.

Carter waves. "Welcome," I see him mouthing. The word rolls hugely off his lips.

"Well, is this a little early-spring planting?" Elena says hopefully, still smiling at me.

Henry slams out of the car. Outside, he drops the kindly-rural-landscaper routine and rages at the line of people, pointing desperately away from the park and out of his imaginary orchard. I can see it happen down the line of people as they look at my husband. I watch them realize that Henry is complicit in this: the theft of the park and the carousel, the advent of city people. I watch one face after another look at this man they have known since he was a kid and think, Not Henry? Hank? A Lynch? Joseph Deep is the worst. When he sees Henry it's as if some vital part him goes dim. His face is like a movie screen with no picture showing.

Jethro is the first to start shouting back. From inside the car everything is a murmur. Henry yells and then he's pointing at Carter Marks, really getting his finger up near his face and Carter is no longer smiling. Instead he gestures for everyone to stay calm. Henry is still shouting and waving his arms when Rosie Salem shakes her head back and forth as if to say, *No, no no.* Then she shouts something. Whatever she's said freezes Henry in his tracks. He stops waving his arms and stands very still. He says something, calmly, to Rosie. Something that makes her raise right up on her toes like she wants to rush at him. But she does not break the line. None of them do.

And then a figure rushes in at Henry, rabbitlike, from the bushes, and I realize it is Quinn. Her hair is loose and down and all her sharp angles are in motion, moving with angry energy as she yells at my husband.

"Leah, what's the matter?" Elena says. And I can tell that she is frightened. Like she would be of the bears or wolves. "Alex, I think maybe we should go." She grasps her husband's shoulder firmly as she says this.

"I'm sure it's nothing," Alex says.

"Everything will be fine," I say, which is absolutely a lie. "Just give us one minute." I jump out of the car. I tell myself that I am going to stand beside Henry, but then I feel the gravitational pull of everyone in the line and I want nothing more than to be one of them, a local, like I got to be with Elena in the car. Henry is wrong. He should be in the line too. This is what real Menamonians do. What we need to do, to live here.

"Quinn!" I yell. Quinn snaps around to look at me. Everyone in the line looks at me. Most of all, Henry looks at me.

Quinn says, "What the fuck are you doing in that car, Leah?" And I don't know what I thought she would think, my climbing out of this black SUV. The Dorians slam the car door and I hear the locks click.

"I can explain," I say, to everyone.

Henry is the first to understand that I am defecting. His face says, *Don't.*

"Get back in the car," he says quietly.

"I'm sorry," I say, and go join the line. I take Rosie's hand in my hand. I take Jethro's hand too. He looks angry or confused that I have broken their grip, so I say, "Move over, Jethro. Make room for me."

Carter's face is stony. This is not happening the way he thought. But he says, "Hello, Leah Lynch. Welcome."

Quinn comes and yanks me away. "What in the hell do you think you're doing?"

I shout back at her, "You're pissed when you see me over there and you're pissed when I'm over here too! Where do you want me to go?"

Quinn breathes heavily and drags me over to the tree line,

where she sits on a log and pulls me down next to her. "You go here," she says. "Don't you have that goddamn notebook? Pull that out right about now, huh?" That Quinn thinks objectivity is possible at this point is crazy; even I can feel the wattage crackling in these people, Henry and the Dorians and Carter and the others. But she's right. This is what I'm meant to be doing. I can help better by reporting than by standing in a line. So I take out my notebook, and Quinn takes out hers, and we realize that it's gone quiet, so we look up to see everyone staring at us.

"Has the peanut gallery been settled?" Carter says.

Henry looks at me, angry and injured, the same way he did when I turned his father's car into a lobster pot. I know he's still hoping I'll get back in the car, but once opened, some boxes can't be closed, and I'm not even sure I want to close this one. Guilt and anxiety squeeze my throat tight. My brain vaults forward to how I'll have to explain and apologize and smooth this over later. I shake my head to dislodge the thought. Later. Right now the only thing I can do is what I was meant to be doing all along, so I start writing things down, taking notes for the story.

"Listen, Hank," Carter says. "I don't know what you have to do with those people but you've got to tell them they can't go through here today. You have to tell them they own all of that, but the park and the carousel, it's ours."

Henry shakes his head. "This is their property, Carter." He looks around at the line. "They paid some of you for this property, in case you don't remember."

"They're going to kick us out of our shops and raise our rent!" Billy yells, and a wave of affirmative shouts rises behind his words.

"Shit," Quinn says, looking at my notebook. "How have you taken all that down already?"

Henry yells at Billy, "These people have nothing to do with

Deep's. You have no idea who those people in the car even are." He points at the black-tinted windows.

Rosie pipes up. "Hank," she says. "Hank, you've got to know your father wouldn't have wanted to see a house like this in town. Your mother neither."

And I remember now that they had gone to school together. That Rosie was a small blond thing in the junior high when Henry was a senior. That to her he must be something very different than he is to me. A Lynch. Hank. From an old family with a wicked older sister you knew better than to mess with. Maybe this is why Rosie thinks she can get away with saying what I never could.

"My father," Henry says, "would have let this town rot away until it was the worst pit in Maine. He would have driven in the last coffin nail himself just to be sure nothing changed. And my mother, if this place wasn't what it was, might be here still. So you should probably just shut up, Rosalind."

Rosie is quivering in place. "You're not the only one who has family from this town, you know, Hank? You act like you're the only person who wants to make anything better or cares, but what do you think we're doing here?"

"I think you're a bunch of ignorant fools," Henry says. "Fishing is dying. The ironworks is dying. The local businesses are dying and have been for years now. We've got to come up with a plan B or we'll just be a town full of drunks telling sad old stories in our junky yards who no one gives a *damn* about."

In the middle of this proselytizing, Jethro has broken the line. He charges at Henry. Carter moves to stop him but not before Jethro's clocked Henry in the jaw. A sucker punch.

My stomach drops out. I want to rush to Henry, but I freeze—because what *was* that he said? And the *way* he said it, all shot through with bitterness and anger, I didn't know Henry had that inside him. Sad old stories? Those stories are what I fell in love with. And so I look at this man, who has said these things, who is bleeding from his nose, and the truth is he looks like a stranger to me. So I stay where I am. I don't go to him, this man who cannot possibly be Henry.

Jethro is standing there, heaving, his shoulders moving up and down, in a rage, ready to swing again. And then, in the greatest act of beauty I've ever seen from Henry, his body turns on its axis like a discus thrower's and he hits Jethro back. Like his body has always been made and built to do this.

After that it is too hard to tell what is happening. Carter tries to find a way between them to stop them and the line is yelling and the black-windowed SUV stares dumbly on. I hear a whoop then, like a boy playing Indian, and Billy has charged into the fray, arms swinging. He charges between Jethro and Henry, who are too busy swinging to notice. I hear Joseph Deep say, "Billy, no!" But it's too late and there, between the two men, Billy intercepts a swing, and maybe it's Jethro's and maybe it's Henry's, but Billy is down on the ground.

There is a shuffling of feet as the men back away from each other, confused by what has happened. Billy is a heap of bird bones in too-big clothes. Henry and Jethro stand with their arms held out, as if by keeping their hands away from their bodies, they will be made blameless for what has happened.

"BILLY!" Rosie shouts. She runs and falls onto Billy and he's awake again. One socket is red and his lip is split and his eyes are squinched shut as if Billy knows that to open them will only usher in a whole long experience of pain he's not ready to greet yet. "Motherfuckinggoddamnsonsofwhores," he says.

Rosie wraps her arms around him. She tries to lift him up. Henry reaches down to help because Billy's just too heavy for her. "Here," he says, and Rosie says, loud but not a shout, "You leave him alone, Mr. Lynch." The way she calls him Mr. Lynch . . . it sounds like an invocation of the Father and the Holy Ghost and the Son who is Henry all at once. It stops Henry. He lets go.

Rosie heaves Billy up herself. Billy says, "All right, I'm all right, okay," and he leans on her as they shuffle back to the car line.

Henry wipes his sleeve across his face, and when he drops his arm to his side, there is a long rusty stain streaked across it. He looks at me, holding his arms out a little, like, *Yeah, here I am.* A jolt of fear spikes in my chest. I am terrified. Terrified for Henry, who is hurt, and in trouble. But also terrified, because how did I not know that Henry could fight like that? That he felt this miserable way about Menamon? What other secret parts of my husband are still waiting, unexploded?

Quinn looks at me with her teeth bared and says, "Are we remaining fucking impartial now?"

A joke, I think. Everything will be okay if I can just make a joke. So I say, "Oh, I just thought you were a yellow coward."

"Fuck you," Quinn says, and drags me with her to the car line, going after Rosie. I let her take me, turning away from Henry.

The SUV windows are dark enough that I can't see the Dorians except for their silhouettes. There is a sort of dumb show happening inside and I think perhaps Elena is pleading with her husband or yelling at him. She has realized that we are the thing she was so afraid of. Knows she will not be able to keep us out of her house. Not with deer fencing even. We are trickier sorts of animals than that.

"Leah," Henry says, calling me back. And when he says my name like that, I love him so much it hurts. At our wedding, at city hall, he said he would love me until I died, and I said I would do the same, and I meant it. I want to be the woman who's going to make him feel like a man and not a fool. That is what he needs right now and so I think that I will go to him and slip my arms around his stomach like a sailor's knot and grasp him and cry onto his dress shirt and say I am sorry and I love you and I am so, so sorry, just please take me home right now.

But then I hear the two blasts. The train whistle.

"Eleven forty-two," Rosie says, because that's a girl who has the train tables ticking away inside her. A girl who wears no watch because she's never been out of the range of the regular blow of it.

Not so far in the distance the engine is wheeling through Menamon. I hear the bells clanging at the crossing. I imagine elderly diners at the Stationhouse squinting against the dust kicked up, children covering their ears and looking big-eyed at the bright pieces of silverware hopping across the table, everyone pausing together for a moment as the train, headed south, headed anywhere but here, rattles the building down to its foundation.

And here, in our own pause, I see that Henry's jaw is swollen and there is blood on his neck. Actual blood. Because he is real, this Henry. He is here on *business*. There is a large black car full of clients behind him. He is trying to improve his hometown in the most practical way he knows, and is willing to dismantle his father's legacy to do it. He is trying to support his wife and establish his landscape-design reputation and he has struck the fisherman's son by mistake. He knows how to throw a punch, and now he is bleeding, and he *needs* me, but who *is* this man? I am frightened by my own ignorance, and cowardice, and I cannot make myself go to him.

So I do what is easy. What is so very much the wrong thing to do it is almost a joke. I go to Billy. I say, "Come on, we should get you cleaned up." I smack him on the back in a way I'm sure hurts but spares his pride. This is what I should be doing for Henry. He is my job to take care of. Someone else will deal with this boy and no one else will take care of Henry.

Everyone is silent, watching Henry in his shame and me in my wrongdoing, and when I can't stand their anticipation another second, I shout out, "MARKS! Are you going to give us a ride somewhere or what?"

There is a commotion. At first I think everyone is yelling at me for betraying my husband and I cover my face with my hands. But then Quinn grabs on to my arm and yanks me away and I open my eyes and see that it is the Dorians causing everyone to run and shout.

They are driving toward the line of cars.

As we run away from the car line I see what they are trying to do. At the end of the barricade, between Jethro's truck and a pine tree, there is a gap just wide enough that a car *might* be able to get through. Indeed, someone *might* be able to leave through that gap, and cut over to the harbor road, and drive away from all us crazy people.

While everyone else is yelling and scrambling away from the accelerating SUV, Jethro runs toward it. The Dorians drive their car, faster and faster, and as they try to fit the SUV through the too-small gap there is a screeching, crunching sound. They push the car forward and through, scraping and caving in the cab of Jethro's truck as they go. And then they pull out on the other side of the line, and we watch them drive away, down the harbor road. Jethro reaches the line too late. He bangs on his ruined truck and yells after them. Yells and bangs. Yells and bangs.

24

Quinn

Everyone in the line received a two-hundred-dollar fine for disrupting the peace. We were just standing around by then, tending to dumb-ass Billy, trying to steer clear of Jethro, mumbling to each other about *those fucking people. What kind of fucking people think they can do a thing like that?* Then some pissy little state trooper drove up in a Victoria with his siren on. I didn't get a fine because I was reporting, not protesting, but I wanted a fine so bad I almost begged the guy to give me one. Even fucking Leah got a ticket. Jethro all but dragged the officer over to his truck. The officer took down his report, Jethro screaming his head off and pointing at his busted truck like it was a dead child, the officer nodding and jotting like he couldn't get out of there fast enough.

Leah was standing there like she didn't know whether to run

or fall down dead. Rosie elbowed me. I shouted, "Hey, Leah. Come with us."

I'M SPLAYED ON Rosie's bed like one of our gravel angels from months ago and she's sitting at her desk, looking in a mirror just big enough to shine her face back at her. She's taking a zillion bobby pins out. Her hands flutter about her head, materializing pins, which, when she drops them on the desk, make a plinking sound so soft I shouldn't be able to hear it. As more and more pins come out of her hair I start to fear that Rosie might just come apart at the seams like a rag doll. She might crumple over in her chair, a bunch of calico and stuffing, leaving me all alone in the apartment, swearing she was real just a second ago.

I may be losing it.

Leah's waiting for us in the living room, but I just want to stay here, watching Rosie, for as long as I can.

"So Billy's gonna have a shiner, huh?" I say.

"Yes," Rosie says. "It's unfortunate. But maybe it will be good too. Make people see." What if it had been her, I can't help but think, who got hit instead? On the way home in the car I kept squeezing her hand until she said, "Everything's fine, Quinn. Nothing bad happened." And she was right. But when she got yelled at, and when she ran to Billy, and when the SUV crushed past Jethro's truck, all those things were carving out a space in my mind, the way a river moves through mud. The space is the story of how something bad *could* have happened. And when you're in love, once you believe in the possibility that something bad might have happened, it's almost just as bad as if it actually did.

"Rosie," I say, "if someone ever punched you in the face, I would kill them."

She laughs a tinkly little laugh that means she's not taking me seriously. She obviously wishes she could take it back as soon as it's out because she claps her hand over her mouth. After a moment she lets her hand drop. She shuts her eyes. "How?"

"What?" I say.

"How would you kill them?"

Rosie's got most of us fooled into thinking she's America's sweetheart, but this is a girl with a morbid streak a mile wide. And maybe she's not the one doing the fooling. If I, if everyone, looked closer, maybe we'd understand that Rosie, abandoned by her parents, working regular double shifts, living in a shitty hometown she won't be able to afford much longer, might not be all sunshine and light after all. But no one wants to look close.

I say, "Oh, you know, I would kill him with a sword, I guess."

Rosie laughs a dark lady's laugh. She tackles me on the bed.

"How very chivalrous," she says. "Now come on, we have a guest."

25

Leah

Quinn is intent on her guitar. She sounds good. She is not good at the news, but this is something she knows about. Rosie hands out cups of whiskey and sits on the couch, leaning forward onto her knees. Her arms are plump like a child's and her stomach has a soft curve to it.

Rosie sings along with Quinn's playing: *"What bird is at the window? A sparrow or a lark? Not an owl for sure, no. It's hours past the dark."*

"You don't have any harmonies in you, Leah Lynch?" Quinn says. She slugs some whiskey. "Tell me a song, Leah, and I'll play it for you."

I look at Rosie and she nods at me. I am trying to come up with a song but all I can think of is what tonight would have been like if I'd just stayed in the car with the Dorians. I think about how Quinn came raging from the sidelines when Rosie was in trouble and wonder why *I* didn't have that much loving snarl in me. I failed to rush to Henry. Didn't want to know that ugly, difficult part of him I'd never seen before. I don't know what I can do to fix myself so that when I go back and tell Henry I won't ever hurt him like that again, it will be the truth.

"Leah?" Rosie says. "Can't you think of a song?"

"Play anything," I say. "I'll sing. Just play and I'll make it up as I go along."

LATER, I AM full of whiskey and my voice is hoarse from singing, loudly and badly. Quinn sets up the couch for me to sleep on. I wash my face and take my jeans and bra off and get under the blanket. Quinn pops out of the bathroom. She has toothpaste on her red T-shirt.

"You need anything?" she says.

"No," I say. But there is something. I'm not sure whether I really want to hear it, but I have to. I say, "Quinn, what was it Rosie and Henry said to each other? That got everyone so mad, just before you came running out of the woods?"

"Nothing," Quinn says, rubbing her eyes, deflecting. "People were just all riled up."

I am good and drunk and I don't like being protected from information. I have had quite enough of this from Henry already. I stand up on the couch. I am wobbly on the cushions and the frame groans beneath me. I say, "Don't you dare lie to me, Quinn Winters!"

"For Christ sake, get down, Leah," Quinn says. I sit down and fold all my limbs up appropriately. Quinn leans back against the stove and crosses her arms. "She said his mother would be ashamed if she could see what he was doing."

"And what was it he said back?"

Quinn sighs. "He said trash like her wouldn't know the first thing about his mother."

There is too much, too awful, to know about a person.

"Rosie might have been right, you know," I say. "About June. Henry's mother."

"Yeah," Quinn says. "But you just don't say a thing like that to a person." She springs up off the stove and palms my head. "Good night, Leah."

After she closes the door I pull up the covers and try to sleep but my brain is going around and around. I think about the deer fencing that has already begun circling the Dorians' estate. I think that my own yard will be next. And then the house. And around the bed, and around my body and my heart until everything is deer-fenced and I will be safe and unable to move at all.

I take out my notebook and I write down everything I saw or heard, remembered or pieced together today. I write clearly, not in shorthand. I leave the notebook on the floor for Quinn to find, because at least I know I took down enough material for a good article in those pages.

The light under Quinn and Rosie's door goes out and it is quiet. I get dressed.

I trip down Quinn's stairs and then I am walking away from the Stationhouse, away from the tracks. I walk past the cemetery, which is not quite as spooky at night as you might think. A million peeping insects and frogs are all talking at once. And then there is that chortle and wail. That stupid loon call you cannot escape around here. I hear first the four-note chortle, like an insane nervous laugh, and then the long blow of birdsadness that follows. That's the sound that gets me. Like someone calling hello in the night. *Hello. Hello. Hello.* Like mourning so terrible it sounds maudlin.

I give a chortle. I let out a wail. I honk again and again until I am short on breath. Leah Loon.

26

Quinn

In the morning Leah's gone and she's forgotten her notebook. She's got problems, I know that, but I'm annoyed she couldn't wait a damn minute so we could go to work together. I'd wanted to ask about her and Henry. I'd have done it politely: *Hey, how did it all go down the tubes and could you please provide me with a list of warning signs?* I grab Leah's notebook and go.

At the *Star,* Charley is all kinds of worked up. I can tell because she's chain-smoking in the main office, which she knows I hate.

"It smells like a fucking Winston-Salem in here, Charley, what's going on?"

"Nice of you to show up, Winters. It's almost ten and we have shit to do today." It's going to be a bad day; you can tell with a boss like Charley. One thing out of her mouth in the morning and that's all the weather report you need.

"Leah's not here?" I say.

"No, she's not, and when I called my brother he informed me she was staying the night at your place." Charley looks at her cigarette to see how much is left. It disappoints her. "We've got to get this story in, *now*."

"She was gone when I woke up," I say. Where could she have gone if not back to Henry's? "Charley, are we really going to run this? I don't think you're going to like this story very much."

"I know the gist already. I went to the bar last night," Charley says. "But give me your notes."

I think about it, then I hand over Leah's notebook. Charley sits down on my desk, her ass in a pile of papers. Her hair is all bed-rumpled and it looks good on her. Good old rumpled Charley, sexy as a fishwife.

Charley smashes her cigarette out in a SLOOP RACE 1999! mug. Then she rubs her hands all over her face. "These are good, Winters. They're good notes."

"Thanks," I say. I consider taking the credit. "But they're Leah's. I sort of froze up out there." I can't take credit for Leah's work when she's not even here to elbow me for it. Leah! Gone where?

"They're good, they're good," Charley repeats. "I was afraid they'd be good."

"What do you want me to do with them, Charley?" I say, hoping she gets what I'm saying—that I'm offering her an out. Would Woodward ever do this? Offer to suppress information to protect a party? No, I don't think he would. But I'm the reason we're in position to cover this story in the first place, and Henry is Charley's brother, and this can't be easy.

She shakes her head. "No, write it up, Winters. Take your good notes and write up the story." She's shaking the notebook in her hand like a developing photo. She looks for another cigarette, spots her pack across the room, and slumps.

And I love Charley for this. Unwavering, is fucking Charley. "If we run this," I say, "they're gonna show up to your brother's house with pitchforks and torches."

Charley doesn't say anything. Just keeps shaking Leah's notes. "They're good notes," she says again. "Did Hank really say that? Henry? Did he really say what she says he did?"

"Yeah," I say. "He did."

She puts her finger on a spot in the journal. "I assume your story will elide the part where Leah tried to join the line?"

"That is correct," I say.

WE'RE ALL SITTING around at Carter's house, on the lawn. The men are in wooden Adirondacks and a few busted armchairs hauled from under the deck. I sit cross-legged on the ground. Carter does the same, across the circle. Spring is toying with us. It's almost sixty-five degrees.

"So you all know we got fined," Carter starts.

People groan. "Fucking bullshit," someone says.

"We have the right to demonstrate," Billy Deep says.

Carter says, "They say we were trespassing on private property. And we were." He glances around the circle. "All of you have got to realize that there are going to be real consequences to our actions here. If there weren't, it would mean we weren't doing the right sort of things."

Rosie's ready to bust a seam she's so excited. Real is just how she wants it.

Carter pulls a folded paper from his pocket. "This is our list of fines," he says, and reads from the list: " 'Carter Marks, two hundred dollars. Jethro Newkirk, two hundred dollars . . .' "

"Good luck to them getting that out of me," Jethro says. Jethro received a large check from the Dorians to cover the damage to his truck, but refused to cash it. He made a big show of it at the Uncle the other night, standing on his stool and burning the check with a lighter while a bunch of other guys clapped and yelled.

" 'Sara Riley, two hundred dollars. Billy and Joseph Deep, two hundred dollars each.' "

"Billy's a minor," Joseph says. "Do they really have the right to fine him?"

"It won't go on any record," Carter says, "but you get fined as his guardian." Billy looks green in the face.

The list goes on and on. White, Keneally, Foehr, Robinson, Slane, Kraut, Gandossy, Birch, Palmer, Davis, Dickinson, Warner, Burritt, Sabia, Corti, Kenefick, Klufas, Sokolowski. The whole lot of those guys who were at the tracks. As their names are read off the guys from the docks sit farther forward, leaning over their hands.

" 'Cliff Frame, two hundred dollars. Rosalind Salem, two hundred dollars.' "

Everyone but me owes the stinking town. You can feel the air going out of people. Even Rosie is looking weary.

"And Leah Lynch," Carter says. He looks around but of course Leah's not there. Everyone is looking at their feet, kicking at the baby grass shoots. Carter slowly puts the list back in his pocket. "Here's the thing," he says. "You are not paying these fines."

Everyone looks up.

"Wait a second, Carter," Joseph says. "I'm sorry but I can't just not pay it. If I get on bad standing with the town, I'll have no chance of renewing my permits next year."

Carter waves his hand. "The fines will get paid," he says. "But we're not going to pay them. We'll raise the money."

"How in the hell are we gonna raise that much money?" Jethro says.

Carter rubs his neck. He looks embarrassed. "Well," he says, "I was thinking we'd have a show. A benefit concert."

"Yes!" Rosie says.

All the guys are grinning now and nodding.

"Who's playing?" asks Billy, slow as always. And everyone starts laughing.

"That guy right there," Joseph says, pointing at Carter. "I'd bet you Mr. Marks knows a thing or two about how to put on a show."

Billy turns red and everyone claps him on the back and then they all start clapping Carter on the back. Carter looks sheepish and pleased.

Jethro shakes his head. "A concert's not going to fix anything," he says. "We have to do something else. So our fines get paid. That's not going to stop them from bulldozing the park. It's not going to stop the town from letting a dozen more houses like that go up till there isn't a scrap of waterfront left that isn't some asshole's backyard."

The guys all look at Carter. He lays a hand on Jethro's shoulder and says, "One step at a time, huh, Jethro?"

Everyone goes back to talking, speculating about the concert. To be honest, I've always wanted to see Carter play a show, ever since I was little. Even when I was hating him, I searched for footage of his gigs. I bought every live recording. I lay on the floor of my bedroom with the door locked, listening to live albums with my eyes closed, pretending I was there, imagining all the details and clapping along when the audience did. *What are you up to in there?* Marta would ask through the door. *Nothing,* I would say. *Definitely nothing.*

Marta says they met in a restaurant. She was there with some girls she knew from art school, pottery class. Carter came over and asked her out and she said she thought he was good-looking but seemed down on his luck. Raggedy, and definitely not a student. *He looked like trouble,* she said. But she said yes because Marta went after trouble always.

He came to pick her up at the dorms that Friday, showed up in denim. She and her roommates watched him from their window as he strode across the parking lot. He was carrying a melon-sized rock in his hand. Marta went down to meet him. He was standing there in the doorway, hefting the rock between his hands. *So where are we going?* she said. He said, *The parking lot. I got this for you.*

Marta said it was one heavy rock. *It's a geode,* he said. *It's got crystals inside.* Marta carried the rock in both hands and followed him. He got a hammer from the trunk of a car she was not impressed by. *Put it down right there,* he said. *Now take this and hit it right where there's that white spot.* Marta looked at the hammer he was holding. *What color are the crystals inside?* she said. And Carter said he didn't know, there was no way of knowing until you opened it. They could be silvery or brown or blue or purple. She pointed to his hammer. *You swing it,* she said. *And I sure hope those crystals aren't mud brown.*

Marta stood there with her arms crossed as Carter crouched down. He took a big round-armed swing at the rock. He swung the hammer three times before it cracked open in two uneven halves on the asphalt. Inside, the walls of the geode were a deep amethyst purple. *Well, that is nice,* Marta said. She brushed some of the stone dust from his hair and let him take her out to a bar in a part of town she would never have gone to with anyone else.

When he brought her home later they paused in the parking lot, thinking about kissing. They heard giggling. *Geode man!* her roommates called from the window, swooning and giggling. *Come back and bring* me *a rock, geode man!*

That was the story. Sometimes I wonder, if that geode had been mud brown inside whether I would have made it into this world at all.

27

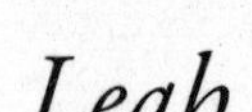

Leah

I wake up with the a/c thrumming loud and a scratchy motel comforter pulled over my head. I can hear someone's kids, happy and screeching in the parking lot outside. I get up and open the blinds. The kids are chasing each other around the motel sign. The pink neon is faintly flashing:

VACANT. VACANT. VACANT.

Last night a girl named Bethany checked me in under the name Leah Loon. I'm supposed to check out at eleven.

Things look misty and a little green out the window. If I went home, returned to Henry on an almost-spring morning, we might be able to go back to what it was like before. He could pretend I'd never heard him say those things or seen him hit Billy and I could pretend to be a good wife who didn't abandon her husband when he needed her or wrote articles that hurt his job.

I am good at many things, really, I am.

I get back in bed, pull the covers up, and turn on the television.

I try to focus on the nature show, flickering on the screen, but then I start thinking about Henry at home and how he is probably pretty upset. And I don't want him to be upset, but I need a little time. Time to understand who Henry *actually is*. Because who was that person at the tracks who said such terrible things and threw such beautiful punches? Could that possibly have been Henry?

I have a sneaking terrible feeling that all these surprises are actually just glimpses of Henry's Henryness. That these are things I might have learned about him before we got married if we had not done things so quickly. And back at the house, he may be thinking the same thing about me. I can't bear to go home and find Henry, looking at me, head cocked, disbelieving, thinking: Who are you?

I flip through channels, looking for anything that will hold my attention.

Because if this new Henry is the real one, then I'll have to say good-bye to *my* Henry and all the old ways I thought about him. I'm not ready to do this. I love my Henry, after all. I married my Henry. This new, real person? He's an interloper.

I turn off the television and open the drawer next to the bed. The Twilite Motel has room service. I'm about to order some eggs, bacon, juice, when I see they have a drink menu. I can order room-service beer. I can even order room-service cocktails! I order my small feast plus a Bloody Mary. The omelet full of cheddar and apples is good but the Bloody Mary full of horseradish and gin is even better. I phone up Bethany and I order another.

Two Henrys is too much, this room is thirty bucks a night, and Bethany has my credit-card number on file.

I have always wanted to go on a bender.

28

Quinn

It's been three days and no one has seen Leah. Especially not Henry, who's sitting at *her* desk right now ticking off all the places she's not. Namely: here, the bar, and my place. *She could only be,* he keeps on saying. *She could only be.*

But what the fuck does that mean? *She could only be.* She's almost six feet tall and capable of taking down dictation at fifty words a minute. She can hold a half bottle of whiskey and still drive a station wagon. You never know what she's going to do until she does it, so why the hell does this guy, married to her for life, think she could only be in one of three places?

I almost feel bad for him. In the past days signs have been springing up in front of Henry's house, Leah's house, like mushrooms. Big poster boards on stakes that say things like SAVE NEVERSINK PARK! and DON'T KILL THE CAROUSEL! and DON'T FENCE ME OUT!

Office. Bar. Quinn's. Henry keeps ticking these three places off like he's the fucking Rain Man. He's poking through Leah's papers, looking for clues.

"When I was a kid," Henry says, "my father would bring us here after taking us out on the boat. My grandfather was editor." Charley comes out of her office, where she's been on the phone calling around to see where Leah might be. She hands Henry a frame she's taken off her office wall. It's an article from the eighties with a picture of her (so small!) and Henry (even smaller!) holding this long fish in their two sets of hands. The lead says, THE BLUES ARE RUNNING! The caption: *Pictured above, Charley and Hank Lynch Jr. with their first catch of the season.*

I point to the picture of Charley. "Such a cute kid. Can you believe that's you?"

"Of course I can, Winters, what sort of dumb-ass question is that?"

"Anything?" Henry says.

Charley says no, and lays a hand on his shoulder. "No one's seen her, Hen."

"Maybe she's in New York," I say. "I mean, doesn't she have parents and all?"

"I doubt it," Henry says, "but I'll call them later." He holds his head in his hands.

I get that. Who wants to say, *Hey, your daughter who I married seems to be missing and do you have any idea where I could find her*?

"Just try not to worry so much. I'm sure she's fine," Charley says. She clears her throat with a nicotine rattle. "Maybe she just needed some space."

Needed some space? I give Charley the fisheye. I've never heard such tenderhearted bullshit out of her before. Something is up.

"What were you doing there anyway?" Henry says to me.

"The park protest?" I shrug. "Covering a story. Went on an anonymous tip-off."

"A tip-off," Henry repeats. "You mean Rosie. You should tell Carter he'll never change anything if his front line is full of high school space cadets."

"Hen," Charley says.

"Are you talking about Rosie?" I say, and I'm on my feet. "You kiss those rich clowns' asses for a paycheck while they build a mansion on Rosie's childhood home and you make fun of her for doing something about it?"

Henry shakes his head. "What do you know about any of this?"

"I've been living here for almost a year now and my—"

"Exactly," Henry says. "You're a fucking flatlander, and if you knew a thing about this town, you'd know houses like these are the only way to get people around here decent jobs. It might," he says to Charley, "even make it so you don't have to freeze your ass off on a boat every day of your life just to take care of your family."

Charley shakes her head. "When you tear down one thing so you can build another, you change a place. You make it new, so it's not ours anymore. Sure, it's only a little change, but if Elm Park does it, and the Dorians do it, and you help them . . . I'm saying, all the little pieces of home you're giving away, they start to add up. And then someday, we'll look around and think, Whose town is this? None of it will be ours anymore." Charley pauses. "Hen, you've got to stop. I know it's a good job, but you've got to stop."

Henry sits there looking at his hands for a while. Then he stands up. "I'm going to find Leah," he says. "I don't know how you can just sit around like this." He gets up and slams out the office door.

Charley watches the hinges settle and then thumps the desk with her hand. "He always fucking leaves in the middle!" she says. "Even when we were kids he did that. Left in the middle of the fight before he ran out of things to say." She picks up a cigarette from her pack and lights it. Mouth full of Marlboro, she says, "I never run out of things to say, and he knows it."

"Give me one of those," I say.

"You quit," Charley says. "I hate mooching quitters."

"Just one," I say. "Just one for a lonesome flatlander?"

She snorts, and hands me one. I knock on the glass of the framed article. "You fished?" I say. "I can't imagine you fishing."

"Bring me a bluefish and I'll clean it for you faster than any Deep," Charley says.

"Is that a rivalry dating back to the days of the 'lobster wars'?" I say.

"You *sound* like a flatlander when you talk like that," Charley says. She stubs out her cigarette, looks at the pack, tosses it to me. "Take these with you," she says. "It might help."

"Help with what?" I say.

"Leah's at the Twilite Motel," Charley says. "The woman at the desk said a tall lady named Loon checked in two days ago."

WHAT A DUMP. The Twilite Motel's neon sign is on in the daylight and it hurts to look at it. Rosie has left her yellow plastic sunglasses in the cup holder. I put them on and everything looks a little less April-bright and ugly.

I head for the squat hovel labeled OFFICE. There's a stocky blond girl in a motel-logo shirt leaning on the counter at the desk. The collar of her shirt is half flipped up and there's a stain on her sleeve. She is drinking a Diet Coke and reading an enormous book. She looks up. She has dark circles under her eyes.

"What are you reading?" I ask.

She flips the pages so they run through her fingers, like it could be anything. *"Anna Karenina,"* she says. "It's pretty good."

There are just too many girls to love in this world. "Do you know where I might find a guest of yours, a tall lady with dark hair?" I say.

"Miss Loon? You'll find her poolside," she says.

Outside I round the parking lot, pass the motel rooms, and then I see a concrete square surrounded by a chain-link fence. Here is the in-ground pool, absolutely green and surrounded by an optimistic number of chaise longues.

In one of them is Leah. She is dressed in the same muddy jeans I saw her in last as well as an enormous brick-red sweatshirt that says DOWN EAST on it. She has the hood up and is wearing a pair of large black sunglasses, the price tag still dangling from one of the arms. In her hands she's holding a copy of the *Boothbay Register,* which she seems to be reading, or at least flipping through. In her lap is a box of taffy and on the ground is a quarter-empty bottle of White Horse whiskey.

Apparently the Twilite Motel has a gift shop.

"Hey, Loon!" I shout. Leah looks up at me. She doesn't seem pleased. She goes back to reading the paper. I open the fence gate and take a chaise next to her. I push up my sunglasses. I'm wearing my mother's old Irish sweater and I pull my hands into the arms and hold the openings shut. I wiggle down into the chaise and still it's not comfortable at all. "Are you having a breakdown?" I say. "Or just a bender?"

"Do you know that this establishment does not offer the *Menamon Star*? I gave them a piece of my mind, let me tell you." She flips the page again. Either she's not really reading or booze counts as a performance-enhancing drug for journalists. "So I got the *Register* instead, and now I'm thinking I'll have to go apologize. Because this paper is vastly better than ours. Look at this, they have a world news section. Boothbay is reporting on the economy in China, for Christ sake."

"But you don't want to write about stuff like that anyway, do you?" I say.

"I don't want to write about anything at all," Leah says. "I quit. My notebook I bequeath to you."

"Please don't start bequeathing anything just yet," I say. "It's premature and fucking creepy."

Leah finishes what's in her glass of whiskey. "You're right," she says. "Let's just say I'm on vacation."

A car drives by the motel and the chain-link fence around the pool rattles. The concrete is bumpy and stained in spots and the chaises are yellowing and brittle. The bare branches of the trees all around us wave back and forth as a wind blows hard; leaves from the parking lot blow through the fence. They land on the surface of the pool, which, despite its color, still smells of chlorine.

"This is some pleasure spot," I say. "When are you coming back?"

"Oh, I don't think I will," Leah says.

"I think you're out of vacation days."

"Has Henry been by the office?"

"Yes."

She crosses her arms, like I'm trying to trick her into seeing him.

I cross my arms too. "He's worried about you. He doesn't know where you are. He just wants to talk to you. How bad could it be?"

"You are a black kettle," Leah says.

"You are drunk and conflict-averse," I say. "What's a kettle?"

"Have you talked to Carter yet?"

"We've talked plenty," I say.

"I mean about your geeeeeeeenes," Leah says as she pours some more White Horse into her cup. "Do you want some of this?"

"No thanks," I say. I lean back in my chaise. "I don't really know what to say to Carter anymore. I had that whole plan and then I messed it up. Now I have no plan."

Leah reaches over and squeezes my hand. "You are winging it," she says. "I am also winging it."

There is a terrible sucking sound from the pool.

"There's a squid in there," Leah says.

I get up and look over the edge. There's a turquoise plastic hose attached to a rubbery contraption, quite squidlike, that is presumably cleaning the pool. The squid vacuum suctions on to the walls with its mouth and scoots around. It gets stuck in the corner, where it clicks frantically before falling off the wall and floating in slow motion to the bottom. It makes no sound when it hits, but once it rights itself, it begins to whir again, blazing a small, marginally less slimy trail across the concrete of the deep end.

"Give me some taffy," I say to Leah. She hands me a piece. It's rock hard. "For fuck's sake, Leah, let me take you home." I chuck the candy over the fence.

"I can't yet," she says.

"Well, you can't just stay here and drink White Horse forever," I say.

"Then I won't," Leah says. She picks up her cocktail glass and tosses it into the pool. It plonks nicely as the glass fills with water and submerges. She lies back down. "There's free Wi-Fi here. Will you bring me my laptop?"

"No! No, I will not. Besides, I thought you quit."

"I did," Leah says. "Now that I'm retired maybe I'll become a novelist. I'll write something a million pages long about crooked cops and public transit fraud. It will be one of those rectangle books you get at the supermarket."

A ship's whistle blasts from not so far off. It's five thirty and already it is getting dim.

"Do you want to stay with Rosie and me?" I say. "You can."

She shakes her head. No.

"We ran the piece, you know," I say. "I wrote it from your notes. It was Charley who said to."

"I figured you would," Leah says. "What did people say?"

"They're pretty pissed," I say. "Henry's taking the brunt of it. There are angry signs in your yard."

She nods. "I just feel too tired. I'm too old and weary to fix everything I need to fix. I feel about a million years old."

"Leah," I say, "you are not old. We are not old. You're a newlywed and you're not even twenty-five. You're eating rock-hard candy and drinking whiskey from the bottle."

She looks around, as if cataloging evidence. "That seems like an accurate assessment," she says. "Good analysis, Woodward."

"Give me that whiskey," I say.

She hands me the White Horse and I take a slug. Then I break out the cigarettes. "From Charley, with love," I say. "She said your notes were good." I put two cigs in my mouth, light them, and then pass one to Leah.

She inspects it, and then drags deep and natural. I should have known she was a pro. She stretches in her chair. "I am not old," she says.

"You certainly don't look very old right now," I say. I twist my head on the chaise to look at her sideways. I stand and hold my cigarette in my mouth, smoke getting in my face. I lean over Leah, pull up her hood, and tie the two red cords of her sweatshirt in a bow under her chin. "There," I say. "You're fucking

Shirley Temple. C'mon, get in the car. We'll get something to eat and then we'll decide where we're going."

Leah sighs and undoes the sweatshirt bow beneath her chin with a single tug. She pulls down the hood and takes off her sunglasses.

"This place is a dump," she says.

29

Leah

We round the corner and it's blue outside, almost dark. The clamshell driveway crunches under the tires in a way so familiar I feel like crying. The front lights illuminate the yard in overlapping circles. There's baby grass there. *Try not to walk on it if you can*, Henry said when he seeded it. I've seen him pull ridiculous stunts to get from the front door to the drive, scooting around the perimeter of the house, back to the wall and arms wide like a cat burglar, just to protect those seeds.

But here is Henry now, in the grass, and here is Batman too. They are walking all over the front yard, drinking beers from cans. Everything is lit up: papers and signs and buoys. It looks like there's been a party. I think, What the hell is wrong with Henry that he has thrown a party?

"Hey!" Quinn shouts. She leans on the horn twice. They both look at Quinn. Then they look at me.

It is not a party. The signs say DON'T KILL THE CAROUSEL and JUNKYARD. They have been rammed into the ground where Henry's grass was growing. The buoys are rotted and rope-strung from the trees. I watch them swaying overhead in the blue dark. I imagine this is what the surface of the ocean looks like if you are a fish. I did this. The article Quinn wrote from my notes. Or is that not true? Did Henry do this to himself?

Quinn rolls down her window and I smell smoke. I roll down my window.

"What's burning?" I say to Henry.

He is standing very straight, holding a sign in his hands. "Some signs is all," he says. The last time I saw him he was dressed up so nice and clean. In his pressed shirt. His good pants. But now Henry is the way I like him best: in jeans worn white in spots and stained from fence paint, loose so they move about his legs as he walks. He is wearing his work boots and it is cold outside but he is wearing a T-shirt. He does not seem cold. He may not be who I thought he was but he is like a goddamn bear, my Henry. His face has not been shaved and his scruff makes him look more grown up. He is familiar and he is strange too, this man I am returning to.

"Leah," says Batman. "Do you want to help us?" He holds up a beer, like he might throw it. His hair is pulled back in a shiny black knot. He is wearing the same blue anorak I saw him in the other day and I do not think that he is here because Henry has paid him. I think he is here because he is the kind of friend who comes over when there are signs in your yard calling you a traitor and someone needs to burn them.

Quinn gets out, so I have no choice but to get out too. I feel like a jerk standing there in my Down East motel sweatshirt but Henry doesn't say anything.

"We built a fire pit in the back," Henry says.

"She wasn't at my house. Just for the record," Quinn says. She offers her hand to Batman. "Winters," she says. "I saw you at the tracks."

Batman grins. "Bertilio," he says, and shakes her hand. "I saw you too. You're a fast runner."

Quinn points to the car. "Can I give you a ride somewhere? I was about to head home."

"Sure," Batman says. He comes over and hands me the beer. "Welcome back, Leah," he says.

They reverse out of the driveway and Quinn toots the horn twice to say good-bye. I think, Please do not leave us alone here in our own house like strangers.

Henry and I stare at where the car has left. His bare arms are red in the cold. Footprints indent the still-soft earth where the grass seedlings have been trampled.

"Come here?" Henry says, very quietly so it is a question. I step toward him. He puts his arms around me, wraps me up, my arms at my sides, and he clutches me to him.

I squash my face against his chest and I smell him. That same piney smell. Even out here I feel him warming me up. I am still clutching Batman's beer in my hand.

I keep my face close against Henry's chest because I know that if I look up I will kiss him and it cannot be this easy. I press my sharp chin against his chest and I say, "Do you need help? Burning things?"

He says, "Yeah, I do." So I squeeze him and then I let go. I pick up a big pile of signs from the driveway, and so does Henry. We walk around our house and there, in the backyard, near to the beachfront, is a real bonfire. I see that Henry and Batman have dug a hole, and in it they have built a fire of driftwood.

I heave signs into the bonfire. The flames come up the sides and the signs warp and burn, the edges being eaten inward.

Henry throws his on too. The sound of the wood popping, and the beach, and the bell buoys not so far away, makes me sleepy. I stand in front of Henry and lean back into him. He grabs on to me and we watch the fire. Now I open my beer. We wait until the fire is small, glowing but no longer roaring. Then we go inside.

In the dark kitchen, Henry says, "Nice sweatshirt."

"Ugh," I say. I pull it over my head.

Henry smiles, and I feel a nervous spasm in my chest. Here we are. Real me. Real Henry. He leans against the counter, waiting. And I want to go to him. To cross the space of the kitchen and fix this.

I feel dizzy, because does that mean I still love Henry? Even if Henry is not *Henry*?

We fell in love so quickly. It was recognition in the bar that day: *You, you are the one I can love best.* But we didn't know why. We didn't know the first thing about each other. Just that this was what the lightning strike was meant to feel like.

We've been married almost a year and finally, now, I think I see who Henry is. The idea of him I had, that carefree, wisecracking, earth-working Mainer? That was a fantasy. Someone from his tall tales. A romantic idea I loved so much I didn't want to let it go. But he is more than that. He is funny, yes, but he worries about things too. He is strong, but I am capable of hurting him. He tells magic stories, but he also takes out the garbage. He is responsible, a man in a house with a wife. He is ready for this, our grown-up life together. More ready than I am, for sure.

We fell in love with the people we thought we were. And we were wrong about those people. But we were right, I think, about the love.

I wonder if Henry feels the same.

After all, I am certainly not who Henry thought I was. Which was what? The tall newspaper lady who drank as much as he did?

The girl who hung on his stories and begged for more? The New York journalist who would throw it all away and spend her days loving him by the sea?

I wish I could be her. Whoever that girl was that he thought he was marrying. I bet that girl is wonderful. I bet I would marry her too, if I could.

Sadly, he is stuck with me instead.

"Come on," I say. "Can we go upstairs?"

"Sure," Henry says.

We climb, a procession of two, me following him up the steep and narrow stairway. He opens the door to our room. It is just so large, the bed. The dresser is big and hollow as a boat. The so-high peak of the ceiling and the shaky ceiling fan and the amount of space to be filled, I cannot do it.

"Come here," I say. I take Henry's hand and lead him across the hall. Here is a room we do not normally go into. Henry's room. It looks exactly like I imagine it did when he was small. It wasn't Henry who preserved it, of course, it was June. "Here," I say to Henry. The bed is made with a red starred quilt. It is small, but big enough for both of us if we press together. "Lie down with me."

Henry looks around the room. The walls are pale yellow and one whole wall is a bookshelf full of hardbacks: *The Hardy Boys* and *Greek Myths* and *Edible Plants of New England* and *A History of the Maine Coast for Young Men*. There is a mobile of boats hanging over the bed: small carved-wooden skiffs, dinghies, and sailboats. Henry pushes a sailboat with his finger. The mobile sways.

Henry takes off his boots and lies down on the bed. The boats go slowly round and round. He pulls a book off the shelf, *American Heroes*. Says, "Do you want to hear about Johnny Appleseed or Paul Bunyan?"

I take off my sneakers, my socks, my jeans. I unbutton my bra under my shirt and pull it out one armhole. "Paul Bunyan," I say. I lie down and press up close to Henry. I take a sip of my beer and then I put it on the windowsill behind the headboard, which has a spyglass on it. A fossil of a seashell. Some brown shards of beach glass Henry probably collected as a child. Shards that were probably once pieces of beers drunk and thrown overboard.

Henry flips the pages. The book smells old, like children's books always smelled when you were small and the librarian read to you. Or June. I imagine that June read to Henry. I imagine she chose Johnny Appleseed and not Paul Bunyan. I take the book from Henry's hands and put it on the floor. I pull the covers over both of us. We watch the little boats. I feel so much better here, in this child's room, than I ever did in the master bedroom. Here, I think, maybe, Henry and I can be more like ourselves. Here, I will be able to work out the way to love the man he actually is instead of the man I thought he was. Here we will be the way we are supposed to be instead of pretending that we are grown-ups who sleep in a master bedroom and have it all figured out.

"I like this room," I say. "We should sleep here more often."

"Okay," Henry says. "We can do that. Listen—"

I cut him off. "Hen, I don't want to . . ." Because maybe everything can be this easy. We can start over and sleep in this child's room and not have to hash through the mess we've made. Maybe Henry won't have to realize just quite how strange I am.

"We've got to talk some," he says. "This is what grown-ups do, Leah. They talk."

"Talk about what?" I say, like an idiot.

"Do you think we made a mistake?" Henry says. "Moving up here and everything? We can go back to New York if you want. You might be happier at home."

"I am at home," I say. "I feel very much at home."

"Well, I don't know if I do," Henry says. He strokes my hair. We lie there for a while. "It's okay if you don't like it here. I know it isn't all it's cracked up to be."

I think about this. Sometimes when Henry is talking about his hometown he is talking about himself too.

"Sometimes *I'm* not all I'm cracked up to be," I tell him.

Henry gets up on his elbow so he can look at me properly. He squeezes my hand. "Me too," he says.

I pick the book up off the floor and hand it to Henry, the pages opened to Johnny Appleseed.

"Read," I say.

Spring

30

Quinn

When Leah walks into the *Star* office for the first time in weeks, it's a warm May day. Up here, a warm day gets people batshit-crazy excited.

Posing in the entrance to her office, Charley grips the top of the doorframe, practically hangs from it. "A full staff to kick around!" she says, delighted.

"Hi, Charley," Leah says.

"You had a good vacation?"

"You bet," Leah says. "So, what's the story?"

Charley smacks the doorframe. "Winters!" she says. "Fill Leah in."

I catch her up. Since we ran the piece about the protest, we've been running a story in every issue about the ongoing debate over Neversink Park and the Dorian property. Interviewing people about what they think. Publishing minutes from town committee meetings about zoning. We haven't officially taken sides, but our full-page historical retrospective on the long-standing local love and lore of the carousel? It brought a tear to many an eye.

"Tell me that wasn't the headline," Leah interrupts. I pull last week's paper from the shelf and hand it to her. The headline: A LOOK AT THE LONG-STANDING LOCAL LOVE AND LORE OF THE NEVERSINK CAROUSEL. Leah moans, as if in real physical distress.

This week, we're publishing a piece about the Sanford family and their generous creation and maintenance of the park.

We work for a few hours before Charley comes out of her office again and says, "Don't you have some business at town hall?"

"Yes, ma'am," I say.

"Take Lynch with you." Charley closes the door behind her.

"She called you Lynch," I say.

"She's hoping it hasn't worn off," Leah says. "Where are we going?"

I explain about the benefit. Leah reaches into her bag. She's got an envelope all stamped and addressed to town hall.

"So you're saying I shouldn't pay this?"

"Not until the benefit," I say. "And about that. Carter doesn't think he needs a permit, but if he doesn't get one, the cops will have an excuse to barge in. And wouldn't it be nice if there were just some music and there was no chance of trouble? If no one had to be worrying about anyone?"

"You mean Henry," Leah says.

"I was thinking about me," I say. I was thinking about Rosie.

TOWN HALL IS a dreary little building next to the post office. Leah stoops as she walks down the hall. The bureaucrat behind the desk in the clerk's office is wearing a too-large pink T-shirt with paisleys on it and a pair of eyeglasses around her neck on a long fake-gold chain. The glasses sit on her enormous shelflike bosom, and when we ask her for the necessary forms for the permits we need, she wheels her office chair over to the appropriate filing cabinets to get them for us without standing up. She visits several different cabinets, collecting forms, and then she wheels back, licks a finger, and flips through. Permission to hold a public gathering on town property. Permission to hold a gathering on the town green in particular. Permission to play music and set up electronics. Permission to grill in the open.

"A party?" she says. "How nice."

Leah and I take turns filling out every damn form there is in this town. We hand them back to the bureaucrat, who retrieves her giant glasses from their leash. "I'll get her to sign them right now," she says. "Save you a trip."

I drum gleefully on the counter and Leah looks around the office, at all those filing cabinets. Then the bureaucrat trudges back from the back room, frowning at the papers. She hands them to us. "I'm afraid your request to use the town green has been denied," she says.

"On what grounds?" Leah says.

"Ms. Gunthrop says you've failed to give proper notice. The green is already all booked for the spring."

"Gunthrop?" I say. "She's in charge of stuff like this?"

"I'm in charge of everything," Gunthrop says as she emerges from the back room. She is wearing a lavender skirt suit. "The town will be spraying pesticides all week."

"What kind of pesticides?" Leah asks, calling Gunthrop on her obvious lie. "Could you refer me to the company that will be spraying? I've been looking for someone to care for my own yard and—"

"This is bullshit!" I say. "Tell the bugmen to come another day!"

"I'm afraid it would be very expensive to reschedule," Gunthrop says.

Leah asks, "If we file for a permit today, what's the earliest we can use the green?"

"I'd have to check the town calendar," Gunthrop says. "It could be months. We're actually just closing for lunch right now, and I have meetings all afternoon, so I'm afraid if you'd like me to check the calendar, I'll have to ask you to come back tomorrow." She strides out of the office, waving to us as she goes, a little kid's wiggling-fingers good-bye over her shoulder.

The paisley bureaucrat is still holding our forms. She ducks under her desk and we hear an awful whir.

"Are you shredding our forms?" I say.

"You'll have to get going," the bureaucrat says. She shoos us out of the office and hangs a sign on the doorknob that says WE'LL BE BACK IN . . . , with a little clock. She moves the clock's hands to two P.M. An hour from now. "See you tomorrow," she says, and wobbles down the hall.

Leah and I stand in the hallway, the overhead lights flickering orangely. I feel like I might seize.

I say, "This is what you get for trying to do things legally. So I guess we won't have any permits and I guess it will just have to be another fucking mess with more cops and then of course I guess more fines. And then we'll have to have another concert to pay off those fines and then I hope Carter has a really good plan. I mean, I hope John Lennon is going to rise up from the grave for a very special duet because otherwise—"

"They left the door unlocked," Leah says.

"Sure," I say. "Half of Menamon is unlocked."

"So why can't we just get them, then?"

"Them?" Law-abiding Leah Lynch . . . dare I hope?

"The permits. Come on." She pushes the door open. Inside, she blows through the knee-high O.K. Corral door that separates the waiting clientele from the office workers. "Over here," she says, like it's nothing.

I throw my arms around Leah and hug her. This is what I've been waiting for: sneaking around an office and stealing documents! It's Butch and Sundance, Woodward and Bernstein; it has been all along.

Leah shrugs me off and starts opening drawers, looking for the forms. "Here's the one for grilling," she says. "We'll need the others too, plus some sort of stamp or seal. Or a picture of her signature."

I sit on the bureaucrat's desk. The top flexes in with an aluminum bang. "You know, Mrs. Lynch, this is hardly professional behavior," I say. "Would you care to comment on the effect a whiskey bender has had on your career?"

Leah makes a face. "Are you going to help me or are you just going to make suspicious noises?" she says. Bossy Leah is back. I hop up and the desk bangs out.

As we're rifling, we're careful to leave everything as we found it, though it's hard to remember what things looked like because this is actually the most boring office of all time. The drawers are full of voting records, receipts for ordering office supplies, copies of people's liquor-license applications, paperwork paperwork paperwork.

Leah starts going through a filing cabinet in the back room, in search of old permits that might have Gunthrop's signature on them. "So we can make a viable facsimile," she says.

I find the form that allows us to have amps, to plug in and jam hard, but after half an hour of searching we still haven't found those that actually allow us to hold a gathering on the green.

I pull open a cabinet in the rear of the room and flip through the manila folders. More boring shit. Land deeds. Construction permits. I see a file that says *29 Penobscot Road.* This is Rosie's street. I think maybe I'll find a picture of her house in the file.

I open the file and there it is. A small house with gray shingles and blue trim. There's a second-story deck and all sorts of crazy shells and buoys hanging off it. There are three chairs on the deck and a tidy garden below. There's a dogwood tree. It's just a house, but it's a nice house, and I imagine if it were mine I wouldn't want it razed.

The photo is clipped to a bunch of papers and I slip it off the stack and into my pocket. I look at the stack of papers in my hand, mostly inspection documents. Papers evaluating the condition of the roof and the age and viability of the heating system. The deed for the sale between the Salems and the Dorians. It's a good deal. Way more than a house like that could be worth and definitely enough for them to live comfortably for a very long time. I slip the folder back into the filing cabinet.

And then I notice that the next folder is a Penobscot Road deal too. And the next. All the deeds of sale for the Penobscot properties to the Dorians are grouped together in this cabinet. Behind them there's another folder, a thicker one. I look at Leah across the room but I don't say anything because I don't want her to know I've filched the photo of Rosie's house. I look at the clock. Another ten minutes have passed. Bureaucrat will be back in twenty.

I pull the thick folder out. Inside is all the paperwork that was necessary for the Dorians to demolish the Penobscot houses. The paperwork needed for them to fuse the properties together so they might be treated as a single-value entity for tax purposes. The building inspector's report and their building permits.

The next folder has a series of amendments and waivers to the standard building permits issued in the last folder, orders from

Maude Gunthrop and even George Barker, the first selectman. Their signatures are all over the papers.

"Yes!" I say. "Leah, I've got a copy of her signature. A copy of the first selectman's too."

"Great," she says. "Now we just need that last permit. It's not a copy of the permit you've got there, is it?"

"No," I say, "it's—" And I look at it and the bureaucratic legalese makes my brain bleed.

It's a document that says the town's Scenic Easement Policy restricting building rights on Penobscot Lot Six has been waived. It's signed by Barker and Gunthrop. The next has to do with a designated nesting habitat for loons on Penobscot Lot Two. It's also a waiver. There's a manila envelope in the back of the file. I open it up and it isn't a waiver or a document of any kind. It's a stack of photocopies. Of checks. Made out to the town from the Dorians. Each check is attached to a payment advice showing where the money was allocated. They say things like *Menamon Tourism Initiative* and *Business District Development Fund.*

"Leah," I say. "Come look at this."

"Did you find the permits?" she asks, standing up and stretching.

"No," I say. They couldn't actually have been dumb enough to just file these here, could they? I must be wrong. But I look at the file again, and then I think of the paisley bureaucrat and every other local official I've met in this town. Yes, yes, they could be. Yes, they are. "No," I say to Leah. "I found something better."

Leah comes over and takes the files from me. "They're letting them break all sorts of rules," she says. "Building laws. Environmental laws."

"Yeah," I say. "And in return they're funneling money into pet projects."

"Business District Development Fund," Leah says. She walks over to a cabinet she was looking through a few minutes ago. She pulls files for each of the programs listed in the payment advices.

"We've got twenty minutes," she says. "We've got to make copies of all of this and get the hell out of here."

"Isn't that kind of illegal?" I say.

Leah grins. "What would Woodward and Bernstein do?" she says.

31

Leah

When we show Charley the files she immediately heads for her office, shouting over her shoulder, "I'm calling the printers. Our account maxes out at three hundred copies and I think we'll need more than that."

"Our circulation is three hundred copies?" I say.

Charley throws her hands up. "We print that many and I know for a fact half of them get used as wrapping at Deep's," she says. "But if you write me this goddamn story next week, we'll increase the run."

She slams the door.

I sit down on my desk.

Charley opens the door again. She's cradling the phone to her ear and fumbling with a cigarette. "I'm supposed to say 'good work,' right?" She lights the Marlboro and says, "Hello?" Someone has picked up at the printers. She closes the door.

"This means we're running it," I say. It means a lot of things, because if we run this piece I can't say for sure what will happen with the Dorians but I am pretty sure they won't be looking for a full-time landscaper. We'd be fine, Henry and I, on just our two paychecks, but that's not how Henry will see it. Not if I'm the one who wrote the article.

Something else has been bothering me too. All those files. The easements. The fencing exceptions. How could Henry not have known? Could he really have been breaking that many rules with this project and not at least suspected something seriously illegal was going on?

"Hell yes, we're running it," Quinn says. She puts her chin on the desk. "But first we've got to tell Carter," she says.

"So call him," I say.

"It will sound better coming from you," Quinn says.

I shrug and pick up the line. Charley has already established that we'll need to run more copies with the printer and now the guy is telling her all about last night's Sox game. "Oh really," Charley says, which is odd because I've never heard her encourage anyone to talk longer before. Is Charley flirting?

"Sorry, I need the line," I say, and press the button to disconnect them.

"Hey!" I hear Charley yelp from her office.

Quinn looks green as I dial Carter. The phone rings twice.

"What's happening?" she says.

"It's ringing, what do you think is happening?" I say.

"Hello," Carter says, his voice so deep I feel like I'm phoning in a request to the radio station.

"Carter, this is Leah Lynch at the *Menamon Star*. Quinn Winters and I have some documents we'd like to discuss with you."

"Certainly," he says. I get the impression he's humoring me.

"Could we meet you somewhere?" I say.

"The Stationhouse?" he suggests.

"We could be at the Stationhouse in . . . fifteen minutes?" I say.

"No! No!" Quinn is hissing right next to my face. "It's too public. Tell him he doesn't understand how sensitive these documents are."

"Do you want to get on the phone?" I say. "Or do you want to let me do this?"

Carter is laughing on the line.

Quinn looks at me expectantly. Her eyes are enormous and her mouth is half open. "What's he saying?" she says.

I hold the telephone away from my face so she can hear. "He's laughing," I say.

Quinn bangs on the desk.

"Carter?" I say into the phone.

Carter laughs once more. "She's just like her mother, is the truth," he says. "But don't tell her that. We can meet at my place."

"See you in fifteen," I say, and hang up.

"What? What is it?" Quinn says. She's wearing these thin old jeans, holey at the knee, and a yellow T-shirt so faded it's almost white. Her hair has grown long; it is snarled but almost down to her waist. She is full of all this anxious, angry energy. I've never known anyone else like her.

"You've saved my ass a couple of times, you know that, Winters?" I say.

"You looked like you might drown yourself in that pool," Quinn says.

WHEN WE GET out of the lobster pot at Marks's house, we hear him shout, "I'm around the back." Quinn and I head toward the other side of the house and unlatch a tall wooden door with a pineapple shape cut out of it. It swings open grandly, and there, reclining in a pink velveteen armchair in a corner of the yard, is Carter. Next to him stand a holey, overstuffed brown chair with enormous arms and a squat blue corduroy chair, stunted legless on the ground.

"Nice patio set," I say as we cross the yard. Quinn shuffles behind me like a hiding child.

"Why don't you girls have a seat," Carter says. Quinn sits in the tattered brown chair with the big arms. She holds her fists in her lap like Alice in Wonderland, small in her seat and trying hard to be well behaved. I hold up the file folder.

"Are these the very sensitive documents?" Carter says.

Quinn blurts, "The town is taking money from the Dorians to bend all the building laws." She leans forward but her body stays rigid.

Carter makes a face, like he's not sure he believes it, but takes the copy of the files I've made. He flips through the pages. When he has examined half the packet he looks up. "They shouldn't be allowed half the stuff they're doing up there," he says.

"Not the serial borders, not the alternate driveway," I say. "They're not supposed to be building a chicken coop on most of that land, much less a house. The parts that used to be the backyards on Lots One and Three? That's scenic easement."

"Their fences," Carter says.

I nod. This is the part I hoped would not have to be a big deal, but of course it is.

"Legally their fences can only go around two-thirds of the property. The fence that's going up on Lots One and Three is technically in the scenic easement. It's illegal."

Carter looks at me. "Deer fencing," he says.

"Yes," I say. "Deer fencing, which— " I hesitate. I don't know whether I should say what I know or keep my mouth shut. I want to find a way to break this story and protect Henry too, but it seems impossible to do both. I *have* the information. I *have* the news. How can I not share it? It would go against every part of who I am to not share news like this.

"Which," I start again, the betrayal rolling, "according to some research I've done, will be eight feet high." These specifics are from Henry's blueprints. The ones he rolled out for me in the kitchen. The ones I told him he shouldn't be showing me. I have retained all the details, and now, it seems, I'm going to use them. "According to town law, they can't go that high. Fences can only be six feet."

"Six feet won't keep a deer out," Quinn says.

"It would seem that's why the town has received about five thousand dollars for the Downtown Business Improvement Initiative," Carter says.

"Five thousand is just for the fences," I say.

Quinn says, "They've paid the town about thirty grand total to bend the rules."

"And screw the loons," I say.

Carter looks up from the file. "You gonna write this up?" he says.

"Yes," Quinn says. In my head I say "maybe." Maybe I will write this up but maybe I'll be a good wife instead. I shouldn't write it, like I shouldn't have told them about the fences, but I'm a newspaperwoman. How can I not?

"If I said to wait until after the benefit, would you do it?" Carter says.

"We can't write it that fast anyway," I say. "It'll take a few days to get everything confirmed."

"Why?" Quinn says.

"I just want the benefit to be a good thing," Carter says. "No mudslinging."

"If you don't want our mud," Quinn says, "then don't take

it, okay? Give us back our files." I see her clench and release her fists.

"I want it," Carter says to Quinn. "Just not until after the benefit." He looks at me next. "Are you going to put your name on it?"

"Charley, our editor, Charlene Lynch, she'll stand behind it. I'm not sure about me."

Carter nods. "Does Hank know about what they're doing?"

This, of course, is the question. Does he? In my stomach I think the answer has to be no, Henry wouldn't. But I saw the drawing. Henry's penciled-in eight-foot fences.

"That's what I'm going to find out now," I say. I point at Quinn. "I'll see you tomorrow. We'll start then."

I'M DRIVING HOME when I see Henry's truck parked at Deep's. I wheel into the lot. The glass storefront is all steamed up and the front door is open. Inside, I see they're laying down a bed of new ice chips in the case. A million little shavings in a heap. There's ice all over the wet floor and a man is sweeping it out the front.

"Hey!" I hear. I walk around the shop and find Billy Deep in a black rubber apron and knee-high rubber boots hosing down the docks. He grabs a bucket and heads for me. His shiner has melted away. "You looking for Hank?"

"What's Henry doing here?" I say.

"He came to apologize for my eye and all," Billy says. "I told him it was fine, but that I didn't have much to say to him. No offense or anything."

"Where is he now?" I ask.

Billy points to a shack down near the docks. "Shucking room," he says. "I told him my eye might feel better if he shucked the rest of my oysters."

The shack's doorframe is open, plastic flaps hanging down. It's a small room. Three long tables are covered in burlap sacks. The smell is briny and every possible thing is wet. Henry stands at the end of one table, next to a transistor radio tuned to the classic-rock station that plays a sea shanty an hour every hour. He is also wearing a black rubber apron. His shirtsleeves are rolled up and his arms are wet to the elbow, the hairs slicked down. His cheeks are red. He is shucking fast, for the sport of it.

"I thought your father was a lobsterman," I say.

He looks up, still shucking. "Hey," he says.

"I saw your truck," I say.

"Doing penance," Henry says. "Two Hail Marys, one Our Father, and ten dozen oysters."

I cross to him and the shells crush and splinter underfoot like a whisper traveling through a crowd. I sit on the table next to the radio. I watch Henry from the side. He may have picked up his pace since he realized I am watching. The Henry I love would want me to see him be good at this. And he is: bits of shell flake off like paper as he digs the knife at the crevice, searching for the sweet spot. He splits the shell open with a hard crack of his knife and the muscle that holds the halves together gives way, exposing the meat.

"So what's up?" he says. "Unless you just came to say hi." He smiles at his hands as he says this.

"The Dorians are having you build in the scenic easement," I say.

"Hrm," Henry says. He keeps shucking, angling the blade into the roof of a shell, popping the top off. "I thought that might be so. Property that big."

"And they're building on a loon nesting ground," I say.

"Oh my," he says.

"It's environmentally protected!"

Henry gives me an *oh please* look but doesn't stop shucking. "You hate the loons," he says.

"Not homicidally. Henry, listen," I say. "The Dorians have paid almost thirty grand in bribes to build that house. The money is being used to turn the waterfront into a shopping district that will drive out the Deeps. And probably make more Elm Parks."

Henry is not asking any questions, or looking surprised. He is focusing on the oyster in his hand and how to crack it. I wait for him to say anything, but he doesn't.

"Did you know?" I say.

"Does it matter?" Henry says. He watches his hands doing their work together, the one holding and the other popping, a perfect efficiency of motion. He stops, and looks up at me. I had not counted on this but I know that he is right.

The question that's important isn't whether or not Henry knew, it's whether or not it matters. To me.

Henry is always thinking about us when he makes choices. And sometimes, I'm just not. Sometimes, I'm thinking about the news, or I'm thinking about what *I* want, and he knows this, because he knows me. He has forgiven this fault before, but now he is showing me the way to do the right thing for us. He is asking me to choose him instead of the news. To choose us, instead of how much I want to write this piece.

I want to rail against the injustice of Henry having asked this of me, but I know that's not really what matters. It's not about anyone *asking* me to do anything. When you're a child people ask you to do things and you balk, or obey, but grown-ups give up things they want of their own accord. They make this sacrifice, not easily, or lightly, but willingly. Because that is how you grow a family.

Did he know and does it matter.

"I have files, Hen. Proving it. We're going to run a story."

If there's a hitch in his movements I am too slow to spot it.

"Is my name in the files?" he asks.

"I don't care what's in the files; I care what you're telling me," I say. "I want you to tell me whether you knew."

Henry shakes his head. "No, you don't." He tosses another oyster in the bucket. "You want me to tell you that I didn't know and that everything is fine and I'm just as much of a sap as the rest of them." He reaches to push his hair out of his face with the back of his wrist. "A noble sap."

"That's not true," I say. "That's not what I want at all." But he's right. That is exactly what I want.

Henry stops shucking and reaches into his back pocket and pulls out a pale blue rag. He tosses it to me. "Here," he says, because I am crying.

I blow my nose. The rag smells like shellfish. "What do you want me to do?" I say.

"Not run the piece," Henry says. "Or at least, not help them write it."

"You know I can't do that."

"Can't or don't want to? What will happen if you don't? For Christ's sake, Leah, this is Menamon. It's not like it's gonna be WikiLeaked."

I shake my head. "I'm writing it," I say. "Your name won't be in there, but I have to write it."

Henry's hands are flat on the shucking table now. "Leah, we're talking about my job," he says. "What are we going to do if I lose my job?"

"It's just part," I say. "You can still work at Arden. We'll be fine."

Henry shakes his head. He doesn't believe it. "Who are you trying to impress, Leah? Them?" He gestures at what must be all of Menamon. Or the Deeps. Or the culpable oysters. "They don't give a shit about anything. They act like they do, making signs and holding protests, but all they want is for things to stay the same, because they're scared. Have you ever heard of that before? A protest to keep things the same? And you, you're trying to help them because, what, you think they'll thank you for it?"

I blow my nose in his handkerchief again. He comes over and takes it back. He wipes his hands on his jeans and then leans into me. I am still sitting on the table and I wrap my legs around him. I hold on to his waist.

"I need the handkerchief back again, please," I say.

He ignores me. "They won't thank you, Leah. I can tell you that right now. You can give your whole life to these people, and the moment you do one thing they don't like, it's over. They'll rag you for it until you die, or you move away. And then they'll say it's because you didn't have it in you to stick it out here."

"So . . . what?" I say. "I don't write it. I forget all about it. Quinn will hate me. Charley will hate me, again. Every man, woman, and seafaring child in this town will hate me. And what am I supposed to do then?"

"You're exaggerating, and besides, *I* won't hate you, Leah. What do you care what they think? It'll just be us. That's why we got married. So it could be us."

I think of my life before Henry. How cold it was. How I had everything I needed and I was good at many things, but how it wasn't until Henry showed up and told his roommate we were both winning at Scrabble, and taught me how to see through sidewalks to the soil, and told me we did not need to go to Niagara Falls if I didn't want to—it wasn't until then that I felt like anything mattered at all. Besides the news, of course. And there will always be news, but those things that Henry showed me, could I lose them? If it were just me and Henry, not needing anyone else, could we live that way?

It sounds romantic, but I know the truth. I know what happens to people like that.

"Can I just think about it?" I say.

I CALL MY parents.

Am I selfish? I say.

Of course not, they say. What's wrong, you sound stuffed up.

Allergies, I say. Spring pollen.

I miss you, I say. Tell me what I'm missing there.

Nothing, they say. We miss you and you're missing absolutely nothing.

Is something wrong? they say. You only say you miss us when something is wrong.

That's not true, I say.

32

Quinn

We both listen to Leah's car pull out. We're alone.

Carter is staring off into the woods, a pleased expression on his face. I point toward the pond. "You swim in there?" I say.

"Naw," he says. "Used to, but then a snapper moved in."

I nod, look up. It's nice back here. Green and cool like one of those places where children get to have adventures in storybooks. One of those places that makes you, the kid being read to, think, Why can't I live someplace like that?

"Used to be they were everywhere," Carter says. "The turtles. Before they put a road through the wetlands in the middle of the night."

That sounds like the sort of story Leah would jump all over and I half want to collect it, bring it back to her, but instead I say, "Well, that's one all-right thing, then. I mean, you don't want fucking snapping turtles roaming all over the place." I feel like a sulky teenager seething at the dinner table with Marta all over again, incredulous that she could not answer all the questions I had. *Why did he leave? What was his favorite dinner? His favorite animal?*

Oh, I don't remember that, she would say. I seethed and seethed.

Carter pushes back his hair, the silver pieces grouping then dispersing. "What do you think about Billy being involved in all this?" he says. "You know him pretty well, don't you?"

"I don't know," I say. "I guess it's all right."

"I worry about him, a kid like that," Carter says. "Getting hit like he did?"

"Yeah," I say, but the thing is, what the fuck is Carter doing worrying about Billy? I mean, sure he's a kid, and maybe someone should worry about him. Even I worry about him from time to time, but he's got a family of his own. I mean, I've been clocked before. No big deal. In field hockey, every game. Girls in tartan plaids are rough, and I was fast and they knew nothing short of blood loss would stop me.

I got clocked again later too, in the prime of my adulthood, when it really counts, if we're counting here. In a bar, the second time. Some guy who was messing with Sam when she was still something like my girlfriend. I talked smart to him and he got me good in the mouth with a fist, like men do. Then again, in the eye.

I ran out of the bar after it happened. The guy was gone by then; Sam was fine, I figured. I was sure I was dying, if you want to know the truth, and I thought I'd spare Sam the scene. Dying for sure, I thought. What the hell did I know? I was just some skinny kid from Mystic barely old enough to drink in the first place. So I ran, and I sat on a park bench by myself, stinging and throbbing and aching until I realized it felt enough like a hundred other things I'd felt before to mean I wasn't dying. I headed home, and when I got there, sitting on my stoop, with her little elf face and fucking tiny nose and tiny ears and overall girliness, was Sam, so different from the other women I'd been with. She was like a real lady in the movies sitting on my front stoop crying with all her mascara running down the face like a mess, and me swooping in to comfort her even though I'd bit into my tongue so bad my mouth was full of blood.

She started hitting me on the arm and saying, *Why did you run away! Why the fuck did you run away like that?* And it didn't hurt much, because she never knew how to make a fist right, but more blows were the last thing I needed.

So I grabbed her wrists and said, *Hey, hey, it's all right. I'm fine see?* And I gave her a big grin, which was probably pretty bloody and horrific, because she just starting crying all over again. *For Christ sake,* I said. I brought her inside and she calmed down then. The colors were starting to run and collect in the space under my eye. It stung and ached at the same time and my cheek was too large. Sam found a half bottle of vodka, real cold, in the freezer and we took turns holding it against my eye socket and taking shots. The shots were cold, and then, as the heat leached out of the shiner, they were warm but we didn't give a fuck. It was six A.M. and Sam kept saying she was sorry. She was so sorry, but hey, it wasn't her fault. She wasn't the one who was supposed to be taking care of me.

Carter is staring off at the tree line again. I can't just sit here with him like we are normal people shooting the shit. "Let's go look at the pond," I say.

"Sure," Carter says. We walk over, me staring at my feet and he at his feet. And then I am staring at his feet and he at mine. I notice the lifting tarsals and the way our toes spread in the new grass. I do not have Marta's feet, her fat little baby toes—no, my feet look like they have about as much rigging in them as a bridge, and about as little flesh. And Carter's are just like them.

The pond is green and murky. It smells like green born but rapidly decaying. Carter's probably about to launch into some sort of talk about ecosystems, but before he can start talking, I start unbuttoning my pants.

"Quinn?" Carter says. But I've got them off now, and I'm in my T-shirt and a pair of Rosie's white underwear, which are really too big on me, but I like sharing clothes, and I don't care, and I get a running start for the water.

"Quinn!" I hear Carter say as I launch out over the pond.

I plunge down. The water is blood warm. I make the mistake of opening my eyes underwater. It's wild in here. Everything looks brown and I feel reeds twisting around my legs. A weird primal terror takes hold of me and I push off the lake bottom, meaning to rocket myself back up to the surface, but the ground is silty, slimy, years of rotten leaves and muck, and I don't push off the way I think I will. Instead I just slip around, dancing on the bottom. I begin to paddle, up and up with my eyes closed, until I break the surface.

Carter is pacing back and forth on the edge of the pond like a dog who can't swim. "What the hell are you doing?" he says. "Get out of there! That snapper could take half your calf off."

I've finally got him to lose his cool. "I'm just swimming, Carter. You know. Swimming." I scissor my legs and kick and churn the water.

"You're nuts, get out of there right now," he says. "I wasn't kidding about the turtle, he's the size of a puppy. Quinn, get out of there."

I am treading water furiously, sputtering and flicking my hair around, and the algae is swirling around me like mad. I kick with my feet and throw my hands up in the air, arms streaming water, and say, "Why don't you save *me,* Carter, huh? I've been treading for *years*. Why don't you come on in and *do* something about it?" I have water in my mouth and in my eyes and I spit and I blink.

"For Christ sake," he says. He's not sure, but he pulls off his shirt.

He stands there, in his pants, thinking, pacing the perimeter. I start doing a backstroke around the pond, dipping down my feet so the turtle will know I mean business. Part of me hopes he does come and fuck me up. Let that turtle clobber me! Let him show Carter what it looks like when someone other than Billy gets sucker-punched.

Carter pulls off his jeans and jumps into the pond wearing just his shorts. He makes a big splash and surfaces sputtering and paddles over to me. For a moment we're just treading water next to each other.

"What the fuck is wrong with you?" he says. His wet hair is dark and slicked back. He's seal-like, bobbing above the water.

I flail. I crash my arms down on the water surface and I splash at him. I say, "With me? What the fuck is wrong with you? You were supposed to save me, Carter, okay? Me and Marta both, and where the fuck were you?" I splash and splash and I'm throwing up algae and muck and I'm not even treading anymore, just flailing. I duck underwater and then come up again and I will swallow as much lake water as I please, I swear I will fucking drown myself right here if that's what it takes.

"Quinn," he says. "Quinn. I'm sorry, okay? Just come over here. Just get out of the pond and we—" He tries to grab me, but I have too many arms all flying around and I'm coughing, and I'm not going peacefully. No way. My teeth are clenched so hard my jaw aches and I flail and then he catches me by the wrist.

"Come here," he says.

"No," I yell. "It's too late. It's too late now, Carter. If I want to wrestle turtles and drown myself, there's nothing you can do about it anymore!"

But he's still got me by the wrist. He pulls on me, and I pull back, but he is stronger. Goddammit, I had not thought he would be so much stronger than me. He pulls me to him by the wrist, and when he gets me that close he swipes all the wet hair out of my face. He drops my wrist and grabs on to me.

He's the only one treading water now. He's holding me. He's got his arms around my back and I am pressed to his chest and somehow he is treading enough for both of us to be afloat. I say, "No!" I say, "No, no, no, no," over and over again, and I struggle to get away from him and slip out of his grasp.

But he has me there, clasped to his furry chest, which is heaving, and he says to me, "Shhhhh." He says, "I've got you. I've got you by the gills."

And I stop flailing against him. Because this is what my mother always said. She would squeeze me close when my thoughts or mouth were running too fast. When I was acting generally crazy or angry. She'd trap me in her arms and she would say that she'd got me by the gills. She wouldn't release me until I was calm.

But Marta was always the crazy one. Crazier than me even. How could I have thought she'd come up with this on her own? How could I not have realized this was something she knew because, once, someone had done it to her?

"Oh, fuck you, Carter," I say, but if I'm honest, all I want is for him to keep pinning me to him here in the water, snapping turtles lurking beneath us in this lake in a yard that feels like home for no goddamn reason at all. And so I just keep still.

Carter clasps the back of my head and presses me closer, my head against his chest so I can hear all his organs bumping around in there.

He says, “I got you. You know that? You might not need it now, but I do, I've got you by the gills. Whether you like it or not.”

33

Leah

We are in our backyard, under one of the large pines, a blanket of needles beneath our feet. Henry is eating a bowl of oatmeal and I am drinking coffee, keeping him company before he heads out to the *casa grande*.

Henry moves his spoon around, stares into his bowl. "How's work?" he says. And I know it's not Charley or the paper he's asking about. It's me. How I'm doing, feeling about all this. Because I told Quinn and Charley I couldn't work on the piece, and since then have been sulking around the house. Sulking around the office. I did the right thing but I am not a good sport. Our peace is uneasy.

Quinn and Charley were pissed. *You realize how idiotic this is?* they said to me. *We're running the story one way or the other. What difference does it make whether you help or not?* But to Henry, it makes a big difference whether it's his wife's name in that byline or not. Its presence, a condemnation. Its absence, a declaration of solidarity.

Henry was so happy when I told him I'd done it. He made dinner. He grilled, and through the screen door I could hear him singing a little as he flipped the blackening vegetables with a metal spatula. As he set the table that night, he laid the plates on the table with such enthusiasm that he shattered one, the white seam of china inside the blue enamel visible as a vein.

But his happiness is wearing thin. Not only because I have been sulking but because he is bracing himself for the article and what it will mean for the construction. He's working long hours to get as many saplings and plantings in as he can. It's as if he thinks he'll be able to keep this job if only he can water in enough boxwoods.

So, how is work? While Quinn and Charley have been researching and fact-checking for the Dorian piece, I've been writing the majority of the paper: LOBSTERMEN PETITION FOR MINIMUM CATCH SIZE DECREASE! LOCAL 4-H TO SPONSOR CAKE WALK! ALBINO DEER SPOTTED NEAR SOUTH FORK, AGAIN! While I find myself cropping photos of lemon meringue pies and coming up with terrible puns to keep myself amused, Quinn and Charley are calling up state offices about land deeds. Calling up banks to confirm the accounts are what we think they are. Looking into the Dorians' past real estate records, and requesting anything that's on file.

"Work is fine," I say. " 'Red Tide: Is It Worse Than Ever?' "

"Is it?" Henry says.

"Experts disagree," I say. "It's highly controversial. How is your work?"

Henry nods. "Good," he says. "We put in three Japanese maples yesterday."

I nod. We sit there quietly. We have never had trouble finding things to say to each other before. I sip my coffee.

A pinecone drops from the branches above us. Henry kicks it over to me. "When I was a kid we used to collect these," he says. "My mother told us there was magic in them, and if we let them dry long enough, we could release it. At Christmas we chucked them in the fire and the flames changed from orange to yellow-green. Mom told us that was the magic being released and we could wish on it." He stirs his oatmeal around with the spoon and it steams.

"So they *were* magic?" I say.

"Definitely," Henry says. "All my wishes came true."

I pick up the pinecone and finger its pieces. This is the kind of story that made me fall in love with Henry. All the haunted carousels and the fishermen's weddings and magic pinecones. "What was it really?" I ask. "That made the fire change colors?"

"What, you don't think it was magic?" Henry says. He thumps me on the leg. "C'mon," he says.

I shrug.

"Borax," he says. "Laundry detergent basically. You have to soak them in it, then let them dry out again. My mother used to soak them when we weren't looking."

Of course she did.

I worry that all the old saints like June are being driven out of this place. The kind mothers, the stoic fathers, the fishermen, and the local legends from Henry's stories—I fear I have showed up just in time to catch their last days. Maybe I'm too romantic. Maybe that's just what a story is. The sort of thing you have to understand on its own terms, a stretched truth and not a real thing at all. Maybe if you believe in the real-bodied truth of such things or places you are a fool.

Everyone needs to grow up sometime. Maybe even towns need to grow up. To stop imagining what they want to be, and just get down to the dirty business of what will keep them alive.

Henry gets up and offers to take my mug to the dishwasher. I give it to him.

"I'm headed out," he says. "You want a ride?"

"Sure," I say, and follow him inside. Even if I did help write the piece, it probably wouldn't be enough for all those old blinking ghosts to stick around.

34

Quinn

Rosie clomps downstairs to meet me, a Polaroid postcard in her hand. "I haven't sent them one in more than a week," she says. "If I stop now they'll think it was a phase." Rosie's hair is brushed out and hanging down. She's wearing one pair of enormous silver hoops. I think she's lost weight these past weeks.

I grab her hips. "You're not eating enough," I say. "Or sleeping enough." She's out late every night with those guys, plotting. Even Jethro has been off and on at the Uncle.

Rosie hikes up her pants. "I'll sleep tonight, after the benefit concert," she says. Her pants slide right back down to where they were. If Rosie's ass starts shrinking I swear I'll cry.

As we walk to the car I say, "Listen, I'm going to park the car over behind the post office so that if a bunch of people try to leave the green at once, we won't be stuck."

"Why would that happen?" Rosie says. She opens the passenger door. Stands there, her chin tucked to her neck, putting up her hair, one wrist flying around, looping the rubber band.

"If the police come," I say. "So if they come, don't do anything stupid. Just book it over there, okay?"

"Quinn," Rosie says. "If the police come I'm letting them take me." Like this is obvious.

I don't think they make arrests for performing folk music without a permit, but it's not the police I'm worried about. It's what the rest of those men might do if the police try to shut the show down. "Rosie," I say, "if the police come, please let the other guys deal with it, okay?"

She looks at me like I'm a moron. "But then what would be the point, Quinn?" We're talking over the hood of the car, each of us on a side. "I've worked just as hard as they have and I'm not going to let them or you keep me cheerleading and painting banners. When this is through I want everyone to know I was a part of this. A big part. So I'm not going to let you whisk me out of there like some kid."

But she is a kid. And I know she's worked hard but sometimes I wish she'd be thinking about me instead of about Carter and his Rebel Seven. Thinking about the two of us instead of a busted old carousel and this shitty town. "Just get out of there if things go wrong," I say. "Okay?"

"Arrrrrr!" She makes a frustrated noise. "Why can't you understand anything ever!" She slams the car door. Why can't I understand anything ever? This is a damn good question. I swear I once yelled that exact same thing at my mother. I think I was nineteen. Yes, I think it was when I was Rosie's age.

So I pull a Marta. "Fine," I say. "Fine. Let's just go."

"No," Rosie says, shaking her finger at me now, like I'm going to be learned a lesson. "No, we're going to walk there. Let's take

Kenamon Road." She waves the stamped Polaroid she was going to mail to her parents out in the air between us. "You'll get it," she says. "I'm going to show you and then you're going to get it."

We start off down Main Street like normal. Wobbly shrubs full of yellow blooms have appeared in people's yards. There is green climbing everywhere, vines sneaking up around telephone posts. The power lines are strung low, sweeping from post to post. It makes me nervous when the breeze picks up and they sway.

Rosie leads me onto Kenamon Road. "Kenamon?" I say. "Is that like a street planner's typo?"

"It's a different version of the same word," Rosie says. "*Menamon* is Penobscot for somebody's son. *Kenamon* means your son."

The whole street is a leafy tunnel of green. The air feels cool, and all the little houses here with their weird slanting porches have the strangest things out on the lawns. Junk, Henry would say.

"It looks just like my street did," Rosie said. I'm looking around and it is clear, yes, this is the sort of place where you can grow a Rosie. Rosie takes my hand. The porches all have columns and the paint peels off them in strips, because sea air, even at a distance, will strip away your best intentions. There are chairs on these porches. Lots of them. Like whole families are prepared to sit together for long stretches of time here.

These houses, they are so sweet. It's not like where I grew up with Marta. Not at all. The road is not paved and Rosie keeps getting pebbles in her sandals. She stops, leans against me, and flicks her ankle around. On one porch there's a well-worn easy chair full of pillows pointing directly at another easy chair across the street, ready for a cross-road conversation. The people who live here are not rich enough to secrete their yards and lives from one another, like they do up in Elm Park, where privacy is part of the pitch. It feels like *Swiss Family Robinson.* I see a row of dead horseshoe crabs lined up on a set of steps. A rusted old oven spills blooms on a lawn. There's one yard so covered in child-sized sports equipment it seems the house's children must have a league, a dozen players at least. A brown rabbit scurries under a bush. I smell a barbecue grill. I hear guitar music from somewhere. Maybe it's Carter, warming up with an amp, broadcasting a pied piper's call to join him on the green.

I wonder what I would have been like if I'd grown up here. Different for sure. After all, Carter did, Rosie did, and they seem to get some things that I just don't. They trust in things I can't imagine.

"How could anyone bulldoze these?" Rosie says. "Do you see?"

She's right, and I think they're bastards. But you've got to think about the truth sometimes too, so I say, as quietly and nicely as I can, "And that sucks. But they paid for them, Rosie. You know? It doesn't make it right, but they paid for those houses."

"Yeah"—Rosie shrugs—"but we thought they were going to live in them." She leans on me again, slipping pebbles from her sandal.

Rosie says, "So this is what it was like. Down on Penobscot, where I grew up. And now they've built that thing and poured concrete all over my magic seashell and my letter to my future self and my lock of hair. And my parents are gone and I wouldn't mind so much if that house was at least still there, even if I couldn't live in it. Then I could at least still walk by and remember how nice things used to be. But it's just gone, and the whole town will be gone soon too. It'll all become something different and the something different will be exactly like everywhere else. And if that happens, I want no part in this."

"I thought you wanted out of here," I say. "To be in a band and tour the world."

"I used to think so," Rosie says. "But it hasn't seemed so bad lately. What with Carter, and you, and all this stuff happening? It's not like before. I want things to stay the way they are right now."

She looks up at me, embarrassed, and I get it. This stuff with the carousel, and town, it's about her, but it's about us too. The two of us, together, is part of the reason why Rosie thinks Menamon is worth fighting for these days. I was just too dumb to understand it, because sometimes I can't understand anything ever. I grab Rosie's face and I kiss her. On her mouth but also on her eyes, her forehead, her chin. It's emotional spillover is what it is. It's like: I love you so much I can't just kiss you here I've got to kiss you there and there and there.

Rosie smiles and kisses me back, only once, only on the mouth, but she means it. We walk to the end of the street and come out on Bayonet Lane, which will take us closer to the town green, to the show.

WHEN WE GET to the green, it seems like every teenage boy in town has showed up and offered himself as an electrician, a grip, a groupie. They've heard that Carter Marks is going to sing. Sure, none of these kids know what folk music is, but this is the biggest thing that's happened to Menamon in so long that Carter might as well be the fucking Beatles.

The boys are snaking wires and carrying black boxes all over the green. We've had three whole days of sun, so the mud is firmed up. It's seventy-two degrees and sunny. People are starting to spread out their quilts and beach towels. Old people are struggling to set up sea-rusted beach chairs that creak. Kids are toddling about, followed by tired-looking but happy mothers. Happy is what everyone looks like, because if this town knows anything, it's to take a spring day when you get it.

The boys unfurl a hand-painted banner above the gazebo's

gables, and I recognize the loopy handwriting immediately. Rosie's. The banner says CONCERT FOR THE THAW.

We sit up front, in the grass, and watch things come together on the wooden platform someone found time to build in front of the gazebo this week. Billy Deep taps a mic, and the sound reverberates. "One two three," he says. "Hey, Rosie! How do I sound?"

"I can hear you all right!" Rosie shouts back, through cupped hands.

More people show up. Joseph Deep is running the grill, making burgers, clams, and corn. All proceeds, says another sign painted in Rosie's handwriting, will go to pay fines unjustly incurred at the Neversink Park Protest. By the time the boys begin carrying instruments onstage, the green is packed. Two hundred, maybe three hundred people. When Carter and his band head up to the bandstand, people applaud.

Carter's wearing jeans and a faded red T-shirt, nothing special, but he walks onstage with some swagger in his step. He's got a smile creeping up on his face he's trying not to let show. His hair is loose and falls almost to his shoulders.

Three men climb onstage. There's a rail-thin guy with a bristly mustache wearing a huge green baseball cap. He picks up a Gibson I'd give my left arm for. A man who looks like a bear—square-jawed, sideburns black and hair thick, enormous hands—picks up a bass. The drummer has silver hair and twinkling eyes. He looks ten years older than the rest of them. He's wearing a black brace on one hand and holding his sticks in the other, and he's got a smile you'd pay a million dollars to see. Carter's checking out the setup and talking to them and they start laughing about something.

Carter loops his guitar strap over his head and plucks a few notes. They ring out and silence the crowd. Then he comes forward and takes the microphone. "Hello," he says. "I'm Carter

Marks and these good men are the Jackson Ramblers. I'd like very much for you all to welcome them to town." The crowd claps and the Ramblers nod and tip their caps.

"Whoo!" Rosie shouts so loud I grimace. She elbows me, and I give a little whoop.

"We'd like to start with a special song for the good folks at town hall," Carter says. He counts off and they launch into "Big Yellow Taxi" by Joni Mitchell. The crowd is cheering and laughing and everyone sings along extra loud at the parts about trees and parking lots. Rosie is singing so hard her eyes are shut.

They go into their own set next, a mix of Carter's stuff plus some blues and trad. The Ramblers and Carter play together perfectly. I watch them shoot each other looks before solos and double up on a chorus on the fly. It's like they've been doing this for years. And then I realize, they probably have. The bass player I recognize from an album of Carter's I used to have. The old drummer too, he just used to be more unkempt and dangerous-looking. Carter's got the old band back together.

They play highlights from their old albums, most of which no one knows. But I know them all. Every damn song I grew up listening to and wondering about. Dissecting the words and imagining what Carter's face looked like when he was singing them. And here he is.

In the grass, Rosie and I are swaying back and forth together as night has come on. It's blue-dark out, and then I see Cliff Frame messing with something out behind the gazebo. He brings his hands together, just like he did with his Christmas display, and a million little twinkling lights go on. They are strung all around the green: in the trees and around the gazebo and over our heads. Carter says, close into the microphone, "Mr. Cliff Frame, everybody," and everyone is on their feet and cheering.

The Rambler with the mustache and the green hat produces

a fiddle, and Carter counts it off for the next song. It has been winter for so long, and finally here we are out of our houses and together. Some of the old-timers get up and start dancing. Rosie pulls me to my feet and we're dancing too. The lobstermen and fishermen dance, because seafarers are always the dancing kind. The guys from the ironworks, though not dancing, are stomping their feet and nodding like they approve. Carter's voice is so low and smooth it carries into the night. I imagine even Maude Gunthrop is able to hear it up at her house.

"Ladies and gentlemen, thank you so much for coming out tonight. Let's hear it for the Ramblers!" Carter says. Everyone gives a big cheer and Rosie and I jump up and down. Then Carter says, "For our next song we'd like to call up a special guest. Miss Rosalind Salem, would you come to the stage?"

Rosie kisses me on the cheek and then cuts through the crowd. She jogs up the steps and is out of breath by the time she gets there. "Hi," she says into the mic, and Billy Deep lets out a whoop that sets the whole crowd laughing and clapping.

"Rosalind is going to help me sing the next number," Carter says. "A song called 'No Medicine.'"

My song. It's my song.

I am so embarrassed I think I should probably die. It's too awful, just a scrap of nothing in my notebook. I played it for Rosie only once. I see Carter and Rosie talking and nodding and they're about to start, so I start pushing my way through the crowd, getting the hell out of there. "Excuse me, excuse me," I say. But then Carter starts playing.

You thought I was a train, come barrelin' down the tracks
I thought your heart was a white, white bird,
but when it flew off it was black

You thought I was a fighter, you thought I was a saint
Your face it looked like broken glass when you realized I ain't
There's nothin' to be done for that, no medicine I can give
Can't patch up what's broke too bad,
some ills you have to live with . . .

When I hear how Carter takes my opening, those first couple chords, and adds all this finger picking to it, I turn around. Because it sounds really good. He drives the intro into a rollicking rolling verse, and Rosie sings, her voice deep. The Ramblers sing the low harmonies behind her. The chorus Carter has brightened, and made faster, so it sounds half like one of his songs and half like one of mine. Rosie belts out the chorus, and I can't believe her up there, in her enormous earrings, with her deep voice. Carter jumps in with the tenor part, and when they harmonize I almost die on the spot. Everyone in the crowd looks like they're a little bit in love with Rosie singing like this, but I don't feel mad or jealous or any other rotten thing. Because it's my words she's singing. They can love her all they want, 'cause it's my song she wants in her mouth.

They hold down the last line of the chorus, long and low, and then everyone cheers. For my song. Just like they would one of Carter's. I'm still frozen there, halfway to the exit, when Rosie comes trotting through the crowd. When she gets to me, she stands facing me square, out of breath again. "It's a good song," she says, by way of apology.

I put my arms around her. "You sounded so good," I say. "In a real band and everything."

Carter thanks Miss Rosalind Salem and then lets everyone know this will be the last tune of the night. "But there will be hats going around for donations for the protesters to pay off their fine. If any of you all should see fit to put some change or a dollar inside, it would be greatly appreciated. And either way, to all of you, we thank you for coming out and listening."

The band passes around their hats and each of the protesters has brought one too. The guitar player's green hat, Billy Deep's knit cap, which I can't believe anyone would touch, and some of the boys running things add their Red Sox hats to the mix too. The hats start going around and then, suddenly, they're multiplying. I swear there must be nothing but bare heads in Menamon tonight because everyone has taken off their hats and is filling them with nickels and with bills. I put a dollar in every hat that comes my way, and five bucks in an empty Yankees hat I swear is Leah's. I don't see her, but who else would have such a thing?

Carter hits the first chords of his last song and I know what he's playing. So does the crowd. They cheer before he even starts singing. It's "Leave Your Shoes Behind," the one about the whiskey-eyed dame, his one big hit, the one he wrung out of Marta before ditching us, the one they have all come to hear him play.

I think of Marta, and how she loved this song so much even after he was gone. How she was so proud that she wanted it in her obituary and I thought she was a fool for not seeing the truth. But when Carter moves into the chorus, you can tell this is not a musician playing his number one song for the millionth time, jaded and running through the motions. Not the way he plays it. The way he bangs out the big chords and then quietly moves into the sweeter finger picking makes my throat catch tight. Goddamn if the way he plays doesn't make you think it still means something to him. I watch him and know, just like that, that he still loves my mother.

Loving Marta Winters was never an easy thing. I can tell you, because I love that woman too. It's not something I would say out loud, but there were times when I thought about running. When she was screaming irrational things, just to test me, or making me beg and fight just so she would take her pills. When I felt like I had to be more of a grown-up than she was, and couldn't stand the way she forced me into it, again and again. I didn't run, because that's not what I do. But sometimes I wanted to, and it occurs to me now that it's possible a person could have loved her, but run anyway. That those two things might not be mutually exclusive. *Can't it be both?* Marta said.

I have an urge to visit her weeping willow down in Mystic so she'll know that I get it now. That I've followed her *please* all the way to the end. I want to climb up in that willow's branches and spend the night there, just in case she's forgotten all about us two people who love her, like the forgetful dead sometimes do.

Carter finishes the song, wishes everyone a good night, and says he hopes they get home safe. The crowd starts to get up and disperse, but I stay put. I will never stop missing my mother. And that's the way it should be. Carter maybe has been missing her awhile too. It's possible, I admit, that I was not the only one grieving when Marta Winters died. Possible I am not the only one who has been feeling random, alone, and full of holes. It's possible that in hoarding my grief, denying Carter the heartbreak that was rightfully his, I've prevented us from portioning out the load between us. And mutual heartbreak is what a family is built of, I think. People need to be all broken and busted up first in order for their parts to heal fused together.

Rosie and I help Joseph break down his barbecue. We load plates with some leftovers, supporting both sides of the paper with our hands, and the three of us head over to the gazebo, where everyone is milling about, eating food and drinking beers. Billy is sitting on an amp and messing around with Carter's guitar, no longer plugged in. Carter is sitting on the platform. His shoes are off and around his hairline he's sweaty. He is drinking an Allagash.

"Great show, boys," Joseph says. Carter turns to Rosie and me and nods.

"Hey," I say.

"Quinn," Carter says. No bullshit "Miss Winters" stuff this time. No "hey, girls." There's something about him, postshow, that is earnest and stripped of agenda.

"That last song," I say. "It was pretty good. You got that one on CD?"

The other guys crack up.

"Sure enough," Carter says. "I think we've got that one laid down somewhere."

"You never did get sick of playing that song, Carter, you bastard. I told you last time we played it I wasn't never playing it again," the mustache guy says.

"How long's it been, Carter?" the drummer asks. "Since the last barn show?"

"Fifteen years, you fool," the guitarist says.

Carter turns to me, serious, nervous. "Listen," he says, "I hope you didn't mind we worked up your tune. It's a good song. I just thought—"

"It's fine," I say. "It sounded good how you guys did it."

And then he hugs me, wrapping his arms around my head, his beer cold against the back of my neck. Before I can react I feel a second set of arms coming from behind: Rosie, not wanting to be excluded, not even for a second, hugging on to both of us. Goddammit, I think. This is it. This is it.

Squatting on the ground, Joseph Deep, ever reasonable, is counting the money from the food and the donation caps. He's got piles of bills on the grass and he whispers numbers to himself.

"What we got, Joseph?" Carter says.

Joseph Deep clears his throat. "We're more than two hundred dollars over. The food and all the fines aside, we're two hundred dollars over what we needed." He pats the stack of bills and stands up, cracking his back straight.

WE WALK HOME half dreaming. Carrying beers with us through the street because it feels like a holiday. Even the buzzing of the substation sounds like a fantastic song as we walk by, and by the time we clomp up the one thousand wooden stairs to our apartment, Rosie and I are singing about the whiskey-eyed dame.

As Rosie puts the keys in the door I run my hands up and down her sides. The key catches wrong in the door once, and twice, and she says, real low and sweet, "How am I supposed to get us inside when you're doing that?"

We get inside and I kiss Rosie in the dark. She drops her keys on the floor. They hit, heavy as a fruit, and she wraps her hands around my neck and kisses me back. We don't stop, and we're walking backward like one animal, toward the bedroom, when we realize that the phone is ringing.

I flick on the lights, too bright now. It's the house line, which no one ever calls. A faded olive-green phone with a curly cord mounted on the kitchen wall.

"That thing works?" I say.

"Not for good news," Rosie says. She goes into the kitchen and lifts it off the cradle. "Hello?" she says. Then, "Hi! How are you? What are you calling at this time for?" Next there are a lot of yeahs and um-hmms. But the way they sound starts off neutral and gets worse and worse.

From what I can piece together, a family friend has called Rosie's parents. Someone who saw her up onstage tonight. Peter McKenzie, who works for the town. Apparently he's got Rosie's parents convinced that Rosie is up to some dangerous shit and that she's hanging out with all these older men and do they really think that's appropriate?

For one batshit-crazy moment I consider getting on the phone and letting them know that's the least of their worries.

"But, Mom," Rosie says, "it's not like that. I'm just helping with singing and stuff. It's—" She gets cut off for a while. I see her shoulders slump. Finally, she says, "Have you been looking at my Polaroids? Have you seen what they've been doing to the house? Did you see the picture from last week?" And then she's crying, like I've never seen Rosie do before. Like a little girl. "Mom," she says. "Mom, I want my time capsule back. You remember my time capsule?" She's leaning against the wall, the lights on in the kitchen and black everywhere else. Black in the living room, where I'm standing. Rosie's cheek is against the wall and her hair is in her face, which is pink and wet, and she's pressing that plastic olive-colored phone harder against her face as she tells them that she's not coming to Florida.

I'm standing there uselessly. All I want is to help, but there's nothing I can do, so I go to the bedroom to give her some privacy. I lie on the bed and stare at the ceiling. She was happy just one hopeful minute ago and I can't believe her parents have spoiled it. I wonder if there's any way to rewind the evening and get us back to how we were.

It's quiet, I realize. Rosie's hung up the phone.

I sit up. She's standing there in the doorway, watching me.

"Were you having deep thoughts?" she says. "Or just hiding?" Her face is wet and her hair is falling into it, blond and too straight and parted right down the middle. Her lips are red and chapped and her eyelashes tear-separated. The way she tries to smile despite it all just about kills me.

"I'm not hiding," I say. "I was trying to think of ways to cheer you up."

She walks over and pushes me, just a little, almost like she means it. "I thought maybe you were hiding," she says. "Because you saw me crying."

"Definitely not," I say. "You can cry. You can cry every day and on your birthday too. You can cry on Presidents' Day and Arbor Day and even Christmas."

She comes over and squashes herself against me, her face on my neck. "I love you," she says, "for serious."

My limbs all feel like rubber. I take a deep quick breath and let it out real fast. I kiss her ear and talk into her hair. "I don't want you to golf," I say.

"I won't," she says, letting me get a look at her so I know she's serious. "They can't make me. I'm *nineteen,*" she says. Like this is an argument that has ever worked before. And yet she says it so fiercely I believe her. I pull her down on the bed with me, and we lie there for a long while, cupped together. She's too skinny these days and her curves are disappearing. I stroke her hair, and I can tell by the heave of her chest she'll fall asleep soon.

I list things to her as she falls asleep: "I don't want you to drink orange juice, and I don't want you to drive a fan boat, and I don't want you to swim with manatees, or eat at Waffle House, or watch NASCAR, or anything," I say. "But if you go, I'll come with you."

35

Leah

The Monday after the benefit I walk into the *Star* feeling sick to my stomach.

Charley and Quinn have rearranged the desks so they face each other, one big megadesk. They've got the files organized and laid out. A spider plant Charley's been wishing dead for months is in the middle of the desk and she is ashing into it.

It was magical seeing everyone happy and dancing at the concert. It was everything I'd dreamed up Menamon to be. But there I was, hiding out on the far corner of the green with Henry, hoping no one saw us. I tried to enjoy myself, but Henry was so tense, standing rigidly beside me, and my newspaper brain just kept turning. I kept coming up with ways I could describe the crowd and explain what this kind of show of support meant for the Dorian property. How the tide was turning, a person could feel it, watching Carter perform. Of course, I knew I would write no such story. My stomach twists.

"Morning," I say.

"So," Charley says. "You covering the townie beat today or are you going to help us out over here?"

"I can't," I say. "Stop giving me a hard time. You know I can't."

But I want to, so badly. Not working on this piece feels like sacrificing up a little piece of me and who I like to be. I know I should give that piece of me over, feed it to the thing that is Henry and me, together, to help us grow. But when I think about not putting my name on this piece, I think, How could anyone ask me to not do this thing that I want to do? I say to myself, It's not fair, and after all, this is *the news*.

"Can I think about it some more? Can you hold the piece awhile?" I say to Charley, even though the truth is I wouldn't still be standing here, lurking around their desk, if I didn't already know what I wanted to do.

"No time," Charley says. "We've got to run it by next Monday latest. If we wait any longer the house will be too far along to do anything about it, or, more likely, Carter will open his mouth and we'll be scooped by the gossip mill."

"I feel sick," I say.

Quinn holds up a trash can for me.

"You can be sick later," Charley says. "Are you gonna do this or are you gonna make Winters pull the copy out of her ass?"

"You ungrateful favor whore," Quinn says. "After I wrote you one million human-interest stories about wasp's nests and christenings?"

Charley reaches across the table and pats the tops of Quinn's hands. "You know your charms, Winters, and they are many. But let's be real."

"I'm a smoker again for the day," Quinn says. She takes Charley's cigarettes and starts packing them. "This doesn't mean I haven't quit," she says as she lights one.

It would be so easy to sit down with them. "You talk like it's so easy for you. With Henry," I say.

"It's not," Charley says. "And I love him. But he's got to know that if he's not going to do what's right, it'll all come falling down around him."

"This won't make him go back on the boat," I say. Charley shrugs and starts organizing the papers on the desk. I look at the way she's got the Dorian property files organized into stacks. "Why are they like this?" I say. "You're not actually going to lead with the loons, are you? Is that why these are in the first pile?"

"People love the loons," Quinn says.

I look to Charley for support. She shrugs again.

"You're both insane," I say. "If you want to start it off right, you have to begin with a hook. Something about how the land deal seemed shady to begin with. Or just a declaration of the facts. Something that straight out says, 'Money has changed hands illegally.' "

Quinn drags. Charley puts her arm around my shoulders. "You know, Leah, we might really botch this story if you didn't help out."

Quinn nods. "I'm a total fuckup," she says. "Who knows what I'll do."

"You just want it done right," I say to Charley. "That's the only reason you want me here."

"Eh," Charley says. "Your charms are many too, Lynch. Don't make me enumerate."

"Fine," I say. "We won't put my name on it, but I'll help." If Charley has anything to say back, I don't hear it, because I'm too busy flipping through the papers, arranging them into piles. The correct piles. I am busy putting this article in order.

36

Quinn

Leah's writing up the biggest part of the piece, the one that lays bare all the details about the money. The fiddly fucking details that I know are the most important thing, but don't have the patience to write about because it's boring, and there's no glory in it. Me, I'm writing about deer fencing, the protests, and the loons. You better believe no one has ever pleaded the case of the fucking loons like I'm going to.

It's quiet except for the mad clacking of keys and the coffeemaker *shhhing* a new pot every hour on the hour. It's raining outside but we keep the door open because all three of us are chain-smoking. Leah keeps reading things out loud, trying them out on us.

"'Ever since the construction of the Elm Park development,'" she reads, "'Menamon has experienced an unprecedented culture shift.'" Unprecedented Culture Shift. Why can't I ever come up with stuff like that?

And even Charley's writing. She's covering what she calls the Deep Background. The stuff about the original deal and what made all those Penobscot families sell in the first place. The stuff, she points out, neither of us From-Aways was around for. I loiter nearby and read over her shoulder. There's a description of the waterfront as it was when Charley was a kid that chokes me up a little.

"Holy shit, Charley, you've been holding out on us," I say. "You can *write*!"

"This place is built on my fucking bones," Charley said. "Don't talk to me about holding out."

I consider the fact that I may be the weakest link in our chain here.

We work until late. Charley heads home at ten but Leah and I keep going. I'm exhausted. I'm no marathoner.

But then I get a crazy idea. One that could make me as useful to this operation as Leah and Charley are, even if I can't write like they can.

"I keep thinking about Woodward and Bernstein," I say.

"I just assume that's your resting state," Leah says, pencil X-ing something out.

"I think we need to call the Dorians for comment," I say.

Leah puts down her pencil and rubs her eyes. "Quinn, it's eleven o'clock at night."

"It's almost midnight," I say. "They'll be asleep in New York. Their defenses will be down." I think of all the late-night calls Woodward places and how the sleepy fuckers always give away more information than they mean to.

"Okay," she says. "You're right. You call."

We move our chairs together and I flip to a new page in my notebook. Leah pulls their number from her cell phone. "Are you ready?" she says. I nod. I call.

It rings three times and I think they won't pick up. I'll be connected to their high-tech answering machine or their maid. Just when I'm brainstorming what kind of a voice mail I should leave, there's a woman's voice.

"Hello?"

"Elena Dorian?" I say. I feel like I'm playacting, but also like, This Is It, it's finally happening, the part of this job I was made for!

"Yes, who is this? Do you know what time it is?"

"I do, Mrs. Dorian, and I'm sorry. This is Quinn Winters from the *Menamon Star*."

"And?"

"I was just calling because some records have been brought to our attention that imply that you wrote several large checks to the town of Menamon to bend building code for the construction of your new house. I wondered if you had anything to say about that?"

"Good God," Elena says. I write down on my steno, *Good God!* "That's absolutely ridiculous," she says, "and I hope you'll understand why I have nothing to say to you."

"So you don't want to give any comment?" I say.

"Comment?" she says, surprised. "No, I don't want to give any comment. Your whole town has been nothing but trouble, and if I'd known what kind of lot you all were, I'd never have bought there. Good night." She hangs up.

I write down the rest of what she said. Leah looks at the pad, reads my scrawl, and grins. "She really said that?"

"I'm taking notes, aren't I?" I say. "Don't you always fucking tell me to take notes?"

Leah slaps the notebook. "We'll put it in tomorrow," she says. "Let's go to the bar."

AT THE UNCLE we sit in the back, next to the jukebox, which someone has spent ten dollars to monopolize for the night. The next twenty plays are all slotted for Patsy Cline. I look around at all the grizzled men turning their whiskey glasses over in their hands, each one equally unmoved as Patsy sings about falling to pieces.

We drink gin. "Was it like this," I say to Leah, "when you were at the *Gazette*?"

She laughs. Her hair is down and kinked where she tied it back earlier. "We didn't have to take turns with the laptops at the *Gazette,*" she says. "And I didn't get to wear boots to work." She kicks her feet out from under the table. She's got on knee-high, size-ten green rubber boots. The bottoms have a tide line of dried mud.

"No," I say. "I mean the deadlines. Worrying you won't get everything done on time and working late." Bernstein drinking one million cups of coffee waiting for an informant to crack. Woodward creeping around parking garages to meet the shadowy man in a trench coat. I was dying to have that, but now that it's here, all I feel is exhausted.

"Sure it was," Leah says. "But I was never worried about, hey, what's my local fishmonger going to think when he reads this?"

"Or your husband," I say. "How did things go over with Henry?"

Leah spins the glass between her enormous hands, some gin sloshing onto the table.

"You've got to be kidding me," I say. "You haven't told him?"

"I was thinking he wouldn't have to know," Leah says.

"You're not serious," I say. Leah takes a long drink and shrugs. "Holy shit, you're totally serious."

"I figure if I don't put my name on it, that's mostly all that matters," she says. "The byline. And he'll never have to know I've been helping with the research and writing." She looks at me, pleading. I exhale a long breath.

"Lady, I know you want me to give you a pass here, but I can't. That's a terrible plan. You've got to tell him now. If he finds out later it'll be way, way worse."

"I know," Leah says. She covers her face and mumbles into the hollow of her hands, "I know, I know, I know, I know."

"So when are you going to tell him?" I say.

"Soon," she says. "Tomorrow."

WE HAVE A couple more drinks, and then it's late. Leah pulls in her legs and clomps her boots together. "All right," she says. "I'm going back."

"You want a ride home?" I say.

She shakes her head. "Back to the office. I'm going to sleep on Charley's couch. I'll be up in a few hours anyway."

My heart sinks. This is what real journalists do. They don't go home to their girlfriends and tell them all about the top-secret articles they're writing.

"I'll come too," I say.

"Let's go, Woodward," Leah says, and throws her arm around my shoulders.

IN THE CAR, I see Leah texting.

"That Henry?" I say.

She nods, and keeps tapping. "Yeah," she says. "If anyone asks, I'm drunk and crashing at your place."

"Okay, I'll remember that in case your mom calls my mom."

"Don't give me a hard time," Leah says.

"I'm trying to help," I say, turning into the *Star* parking lot. "I'm a helpful son of a bitch, and enough of a fuckup to know one when I see one."

Leah chucks her phone back into her purse. "I know," she says, "I know, I know, I know, I know."

INSIDE THE *STAR* it's dark and we don't even bother to turn on the lights. We go to Charley's office, where the air is warm and close. Behind Charley's desk is an enormous brown plaid couch that's been around since the seventies. According to Charley, her grandfather lugged it in here and slept on it three or four nights a week back in the good old days.

I take off my jacket. Leah is bent in half, struggling to get her boots off.

"Stand up," I say. She does. I step on the toe, where her foot isn't. I reach my hand down into her boot and grab her ankle. "Now lift," I say.

Her foot slides out.

"Hey," she says. "Thanks."

I step on the second boot. Her other foot comes free, and I chuck her boots over in the corner. "You smell like wet dog," I say.

Leah yawns. "It's raining," she says. I pause to listen and realize I can hear that the rain has started up on the roof again. A tinny, drumming sound. Leah lies down on the couch, her head tucked against the arm. I take my sneakers off and slide in behind her, my feet at the back of her head. I'm asleep before I can even wonder whether Woodward and Bernstein ever fell asleep together like this—on watch, in the car, in the office—waiting for a late-night call.

THE COFFEEMAKER, CHUGGING through a new pot, wakes me around seven. Leah is towering over it in sock feet, solemnly watching coffee accumulate.

Charley's in by ten and I've managed to be sitting at my desk by then. She has a box of apple-cider doughnuts, two new tins of coffee, and a sample layout from the printers. "Look at this newsroom!" she says. I've never her seen her so happy.

The layout looks good. A five-page spread showing where the

text will go with the pictures already blocked in. Some of them are Rosie's Polaroids of the construction. We whited out her messages to her parents, all the *Love, Rosalinds*. We gave her a real photographer's credit.

By noon, Leah is electric. She circles the table with the documents on it like a shark, like she isn't looking for anything in particular. Then she snatches up a paper and takes it back to her desk. I keep reading my same sentences over and over.

By three o'clock I've got a lot of my material written, and I'm feeling good, but then I start reading over what I've written and the sentences don't make sense. I've got some basic statistics flipped and my pronouns could be referring to either the local police force or the loons.

By six o'clock I'm delirious.

"You're a champion, Winters," Charley says. "Come back tomorrow for the homestretch."

At home, I pull into the parking lot and see that the Stationhouse is shut down. The Daily Specials menu chalkboard is ten feet out in the parking lot. Over the ghost of a spinach pie special is a pink-lettered announcement: CLOSED TONIGHT FOR SPECIAL EVENT.

Sitting on the porch, with the fans spinning round, I see Rosie, Carter, Billy, Joseph, Jethro, Cliff Frame, and Sara Riley. They all look up as I walk toward them, jingling keys in my hand. They've got a pitcher of lemonade on the porch table.

"What's up, Rebel Seven," I say. They look at me like they're glad to see me, their faces respectful. Something is wrong. And then I know: Carter, Rosie, or both of them have told them about the documents. "What the fuck," I say.

"We won't tell nobody," Billy says, and he does some Honest-Injun Boy Scout crap with his heart and hands. Rosie looks delighted. She's wearing my red number nine T-shirt, and it hangs on her, because she's still getting smaller. Carter's got his hair tied back in a knot at the base of his neck, which makes his profile more hawkish than usual.

I say, "You know that if you leak this before Monday, our article won't matter at all, right? It will just be some town gossip culled and reprinted in the newspaper."

"Which is why no one's going to say anything," Carter says.

The rest of the group dutifully nod assent. Jethro looks like someone's pulling strings to make him do it, a clumsy puppet bob to his head.

"Jethro," I say, "I will kill you myself if you get drunk and start—"

"That's just hurtful," Jethro says, and drinks some lemonade.

"If you don't let us do this right, then we can't help," I say.

"That's why it's just the seven of us," Rosie says. "Or eight," she amends, pouring me a glass of lemonade and sliding it across the table.

"I don't want any damn lemonade," I say. Rosie makes a face.

Carter says, "We're planning an event to happen in tandem with the piece. We wouldn't have had time to organize if we waited for you to run it first. This way"—he taps his pencil against a few things written on his pad—"the article comes out Monday morning, and by that afternoon we're down on the green, outside town hall. So when people get mad there's a place for them to go."

"People are already mad," says Jethro. His pad's got nothing written on it. It's covered in doodles of arrows pointing in all different directions. "I keep telling you, we can do more."

"Flyers," Sara Riley says to me. "We've got to have them printed ahead of time. There won't be time on Monday."

Joseph Deep nods. "It's the best way, Quinn."

"The demonstration is going to be amazing," Rosie says.

They all go quiet. Carter puts a hand on her hand, which is

bone white, clutching the lemonade pitcher. He says, "Rosalind, you can't come."

Rosie shakes her head. "Of course I'm coming."

Billy says, "C'mon, Carter."

"I'm sorry," Carter says. "Billy, you're a minor, and after the last time I don't think it's such a great idea that you be there either. You and Rosie will be a special team. You'll hand flyers out all over town. But I want you both far away from the green."

"After everything I've done?" Rosie says. "You want me to babysit Billy? After—"

"You really think two high schoolers with flyers are going to help anything?" Jethro interrupts. He's loud but talking down at his pad. Drawing more arrows. "If you think that, you're nuts. If Joseph talks to the guys at the dock, and Billy talks to the boys—"

"I'm *nineteen*!" Rosie says.

"Jethro," Carter says. "This is the plan. You like it or you don't but this is it."

"I don't know why you think we have to do what you say, Carter," Jethro says. He smacks the table and stands up. "I'm not marching in some parade."

He heads down the stairs, heavy-footed, then hustles angrily to his truck. He has to climb into it through the passenger side because the driver's-side door won't open anymore, no matter how much he's tried to bang it out. He slams the door shut and guns the engine as he pulls out.

Joseph Deep shakes his head. "What you guys will be doing is important," he tells Billy and Rosie. "And Jethro's wrong about the green. So you guys canvass. And that will be that."

"I'll get you the flyers tomorrow morning," Sara says. "You decide what you'll do with them Monday."

"Fucking Rebel Seven," Billy says. "This is a joke."

Rosie just keeps gripping the lemonade pitcher. A wet-smelling spring breeze blows in and I smell the skunk cabbage growing by the creek down south of the tracks.

AN HOUR LATER Rosie and I are at the bar. She's complaining about not being allowed at the protest and I'm almost listening but mostly playing with her hands, stroking the backs of them and squeezing.

"They think this is just a phase. They don't even think of me like a real grown-up who's been helping them. But who do they think arranged all that stuff for the concert? Elves?"

She's too mad and distracted to care what I'm doing, so I just keep mm-hmming her. I stick my finger into the waist of her jeans and crook my finger, add an inch or two of space. I shake my head. "Let's go home, Rosie. I'll cook you something," I say.

"I'm fine," she says.

But I feel like raising my glass of gin and giving a eulogy for Rosie's hips. Another for her ass. I would speak of the splendor of her erstwhile curves, and how they will be missed. Let us all take a moment, bar patrons, to reflect and mourn.

We walk out into the parking lot weaving and bumping into each other. It's not that late. There's time for me to be functional in the morning and finish the piece, which, even as I'm talking to Rosie, is still rattling around in my head.

I hear a clang. Billy's sitting on the hood of his father's car, knees all crooked up and feet on the bumper. He's got a handful of gravel and he's throwing stones at an empty can on its side. He hits it, and the target moves. He chucks another one. It misses, pinging off a car hood.

"Hey," he says. "We got to talk." It's Rosie he wants, not me. But I answer anyway.

"Billy, go home," I say. "Go back to school."

"School's practically over," he says. "We've another month left, maybe. Rosie, listen."

Rosie stands up straight, willing herself sober.

Billy says, "I think Jethro is right."

"Billy, Jethro's a nut," I say.

Billy shakes his head. "You really think a bunch of people marching around on the green is going to do anything? It won't. We'll have the protest and you'll write a nice story about it and I'll finish school." He hops off the hood and starts pacing around. "And then, when it's time for me to take over the store, there won't be anything left. It'll be some lobster underwear tourist trap."

Rosie says, "He's right."

"Rosie, seriously?" I say. "You're not giving up on the power of song that easy, are you?"

"It's not funny, Quinn," she says. "You're doing something, okay? You don't know what it feels like, them telling us to hand out flyers like kids. They love me beaming and singing for Menamon, but when it's time to actually *do* something, they try to send me home."

"What do you want to do?" I say. "What else is there to do?"

"I don't know," Billy says. "But I bet Jethro does."

"Then you're a nut too," I say. "C'mon, Rosie."

Rosie sighs and says, "Good night, Billy. I'll see you tomorrow."

"Yeah," Billy says. "We've got a lot of flyers to pick up." He gets in his car, and when he flips on his blinker, it's flashing left. Rosie watches him pull out. To get to Billy's house you make a right.

Rosie and I, we amble home. Arms looped in the darkness.

37

Leah

Henry is working nonstop, which is the only reason he doesn't notice that I am working nonstop too. That probably I wouldn't be clocking quite so many hours if I were really covering delays in the construction of the Poverty Hollow Bridge and the senior center's Sadie Hawkins dance.

When he comes to bed at night, half the bed sags away as he falls in. He breathes a kiss near my ear before rolling over. I feel so guilty. I keep planning to tell him I have changed my mind, but then I think that maybe this is the best way: a secret compromise. We both get what we want. Henry gets to be happy, thinking I'm not involved and seeing no Leah byline on the article. And I get to be happy too, grinding out this story, feeling useful in my job and good for standing up for what I believe in . . . without him ever having to know. It's a lie. But a lie of omission! Marriages are full of these, I think. Sometimes a lie can be helpful. Sometimes a lie is best for everyone.

ON SUNDAY NIGHT, we finish. We sit on the desks in a circle and I read the whole thing out loud for the second time.

"It's good," Charley says. "Now let go and give me that." She takes the hard copy from me and she takes the little chip of file too. She's straw-haired and wearing a soft flannel shirt that no way belongs to her.

"You're sure he's still there? The printer?" Quinn says.

"I know he is," Charley says.

"How many copies?" I say.

"A thousand." Charley grins. "You feeling big-time, Lynch?"

"For certain," I say. "What size shirt does he wear? This printer you know is there?"

"What time are you coming back?" Quinn says.

Charley laughs. "I'm not coming back, Winters," she says. "We're done. Go home. Celebrate. I'll see you tomorrow morning."

IN THE CAR, we roll down the windows. I can hear water rushing through all the streams that run in the roadside ditches. The energy of the thaw is in everything.

Quinn lolls an arm out the window. "I have postpartum depression," she says.

"That's normal. When you see it in print you'll feel better."

"And then?" Quinn says.

Then. I take a long pulling curve in the car and drive into the Stationhouse parking lot. Then, I hope that Henry doesn't find out I've been contributing to the piece. Then, I resolve to never do anything like this again. If only he doesn't find out this time,

I swear, I will never do it again. I'll be just as good as he thinks I am. And maybe the Dorian job will fall through, and he'll go back to selling plants and climbing sick trees. And I will keep on at the *Star*. And we will keep living here and nothing will have to change. Menamon will be the way it is in Henry's stories. Someday we will have children, and they will ride the oldest carousel in America and swim in the Atlantic and buy lobsters from Deep's and be braver than he or I ever was and we will love them for that, our small brave children. He will never have to know the part I played in making all this possible.

"Then we write about something else," I say to Quinn. "There's always something else to write about." Quinn is staring up at her apartment above the restaurant porch, the smell of car exhaust creeping in our windows. "Are you going to go get your girl, or what?" I say.

"I am," she says. She clicks open her seat belt and jogs around the house and up the stairs. The porch is empty but the way the plastic chairs are left behind I can imagine a family getting up after a meal, full and sleepy as they lay their soft bills down for Rosie. I imagine wives saying to the men, "What a nice girl that waitress is, I hope you gave her a good tip."

Quinn is back. She slams the door after her. Does not buckle up. "She's not there," she says.

"Maybe she's at the bar already," I say.

"Maybe," Quinn says. "She might be out with Billy, picking up their flyers for tomorrow."

I can imagine Rosie and Billy on the balcony of the Stationhouse, tossing down pink leaflets. Spreading the news. Shouting from the Stationhouse porch.

"Maybe we should swing by Deep's, give her a lift," Quinn says.

"Let her do her thing," I say. "I bet she'll show up later."

THE UNCLE'S PARKING lot is full of trucks. You can hear the bar from outside. We push in the doors and the heat and the noise of the crowd is something to be waded into. Every fisherman in town is here and has a half-dozen empty glasses in front of him. The jukebox is pumped full of quarters.

We push our way to the bar and try to order but Sara Riley is nowhere to be seen.

"Can I get a whiskey?" Quinn shouts down the bar. No one answers.

A man holding a glass in each fist notices us and says, "There are women! Whose women are these? We said no wives!"

"I'm no one's wife!" Quinn shouts.

I see Joseph Deep at a corner table, smiling and nodding at some bearded man. "Joseph!" I shout.

Joseph sees us and excuses himself. The guy he was talking to lifts his glass and shouts, "To the DMR pulling their heads from their asses!"

Joseph lifts his glass in return, and comes over.

"What the hell is going on?" Quinn says.

Joseph smiles. "The Department of Marine Resources just released a study that says the lobster population is on the rise. They're lowering the minimum-size catch." I look to Quinn for translation but she is looking at me. "It's good news," Joseph says. "We're allowed to bring in more lobsters. You here to celebrate as well?"

"It's gone to press," I say. "But I wasn't really working on it. Just Charley and Quinn."

Joseph gives me a look that shows just how little he believes that, looking down his nose at me. "Really?" he says.

"Really," I say. This is when I realize I have made a terrible mistake: no matter what the byline says, no one is going to believe I kept my hands off this piece.

"Come join the party," Joseph says, and motions us over to a table.

We pull up seats. "Leah, did you—" Quinn starts to say, but is interrupted.

"Marks!" someone shouts. "Hey, Marks!" I look around for Carter but don't see him. Quinn is doing the same. Then I realize the man is pointing at Quinn.

"I think he means you," I say.

Quinn wheels around to face the guy. "Me?" she says.

"You're Marks's girl, ain't you? What number is that song of his?"

"J42," Quinn says, and she turns around. The jukebox starts singing about the whiskey-eyed dame.

A red-haired guy sits at our table. He puts down a bottle of Old Crow bourbon. "It's a good enough day, hey, Joseph?" he says.

Joseph reaches out and they clasp each other's arms. "It is," he says. "You know Quinn and Leah?"

I stare at the new man, trying to place his face. He looks familiar. He sees me looking and says, "Frank. I bought the bottle, if that's what you're thinking. Thought it would be easier than going back and forth."

"Smartest thing I've heard all night," Quinn says, and shakes his hand before filling a glass with Old Crow.

"Were you out on the water when they radioed it over?" Joseph asks Frank, his face almost splitting open in a pumpkin grin.

"I couldn't get a clear channel for ten minutes," Frank says. "Every channel I tried had someone whooping on it." He settles into the chair and kicks his legs out. A dark Celtic tattoo winds around his calf. *But give me a kiss and I might let you,* he said.

"You run the carousel," I say.

Joseph and Frank start laughing. "When I'm not on the boat,

sure I do. Joe Sanford told me to take care of the thing when he moved down to Carolina," Frank says. "And you, Mrs. Lynch, are still too tall to ride."

"Who's taking care of it now?" I say, thinking about the Dorians.

Frank looks at me sideways. "Well," he says. "If someone wanted a ride about now . . ." He pulls a ring of keys from his pocket, holds them up, and fingers a little brass one. "I suppose they'd need this."

"Can I see that?" I say.

He hands me the whole heavy snarl of keys. I examine them, and remember when Henry and I had just moved here, months ago, when I thought the carousel had the gears that kept the town running. Maybe it's the whiskey, but with Frank sitting here with the keys, the carousel still, and every able-bodied man in the bar tonight, I can't help but wonder: What is running Menamon tonight? It feels like some natural rule has been suspended. Like our parents are away or the whole night is happening off the record. The carousel is not yet gone, but it's not running either.

Quinn pours me a generous glass. "Have a drink," she says. She grabs my face and squashes my mouth into a couple of grimaces. "What's wrong? We're supposed to be celebrating."

I sit there, my face squished in her hand, and say nothing.

"You didn't tell him?" she says. "Tell me I'm wrong. Please. Tell me you told him."

"I didn't tell Henry," I say.

"Oh, lady," Quinn says, and exhales about three people's worth of air from her lungs. "You're in deep trouble."

She sits back and grabs her glass, clinking it against mine where it sits on the table. "Well, there's nothing to do about it now. You'd better make merry while you may."

How bad will it be? I'm thinking now. Will there be yelling or just quiet disappointment? Will he leave for the night? For longer? How bad was it, how bad am I, and was it worth it? That I don't know yet. Won't know till I see how everyone reacts when the article comes out. How Henry reacts.

I drink my whole glass down to the film at the bottom.

"There you go," Frank says, and fills it up again.

Sometimes I lean too heavy on the rational facts. I put too much stock in being right. And why can't it just be that if you're the one who's right, you won't need to plead your case so hard? I finish another whiskey.

I see Joseph watching me. He has been listening. I see that he understands everything.

"What do you think the over-under is on how long it will take him to forgive me?" I ask him. "A week? A month? What?"

Joseph shakes his head and leans back, away from my question. "It's hard to say, Leah, with things like this."

"Hey, buck up, Bernstein," Quinn says. She puts her glass down for a refill, too hard, and I know she's feeling the booze too. Sometimes a drink will hit a girl at just the right angle to upend her. Quinn shouts loud: "Someone put on a song that will cheer this lady up!"

An up-tempo country song starts playing on the jukebox. A couple of the guys get up and start stomping, dancing. A few men do drunken little jigs.

"Time for dancing," Joseph Deep says, and pulls me up by the hand.

Frank looks Quinn up and down. "You dance?" he asks.

"Hell yes, I dance," Quinn says. "But if you think I'm dancing with you, you're zonked."

We take to the floor and I feel light and dizzy as Joseph and I do a little country four-step turn around the dance floor. The men form small circles and move surprisingly lightly for the number of heavy boots in the room. Quinn and Frank are dancing, not together but *at* each other. Quinn might be winning. The song ends and Frank says, "Trade partners?," to Joseph, and I say, "Sure." I cut in and grab Quinn's hand.

I put a hand on Quinn's waist, which doesn't really exist. She snorts, but dutifully makes her arms into a triangle with mine. I start us off with a hop and then I'm leading us around in a waltzing gait.

Quinn cracks up. "Look at Frank's face." She laughs. Sure enough, Frank is watching us, then looking at Joseph, who extends a hand, which Frank slaps away.

Quinn and I spin around the dance floor, me drawing her under the tall bridge of my arm, her dragging me under hers. The men start whooping. We go faster, one spin feeding another. The reel moves a million beats a millisecond and the men start stepping and hopping in time to the fiddle. I let myself forget about Henry for a minute, here in the heart of the Menamon I was trying to save. We have done it! I think. This is it. Tonight in the bar is the way Menamon is supposed to be. Quinn and I have written our article and soon we will be heroes and everyone will know that we, we two From-Aways, are the ones who have set things right so this place doesn't have to change, or grow up, ever.

The song winds down and then it's gone. The men are clapping and cheering and the two of us are heaving in unison, like we're both pulling from the same reserve of air.

"I'm sweating, Bernstein. Are you sweating?" Quinn says. "Holy shit, everything's still spinning."

I say, "Thanks for the dance, Miss Winters." The whole room is tilting on its floor planks back and forth.

"That's the Old Crow, not the dancing," Frank says as he saunters over and pours us new drinks.

Joseph Deep says, "My play," and feeds the jukebox. The first chords of Joseph's song play out and someone says, "Aw, Deep, how old are you anyhow?" The men instinctively tighten their circle around the yellow burbling jukebox. A trilling drumbeat pipes through the speakers and then the floor feels like it's about to give way as every man in the bar starts stomping along. When the first keening *"Ohhh!"* sings out of the speakers, all the men join in: "Ohh!"

The singer in the jukebox starts rattling off a list of things he'd like.

> *"And a little drop of wine wouldn't do us any harm and a drop of Nelson's blood wouldn't do us any harm. And a little slug of gin wouldn't do us any harm, and a night up on the shore wouldn't do us any harm."*

And then they start singing,

> *"Roll the old chariot! Roll the old chariot!"*

Quinn and I are jumping up and down. We start singing along to the chorus as well, then suddenly the room goes dark and the singing a cappella. There's grumbling in the silence.

Frank jumps up on a wooden chair and starts improv-ing: "And a couple million bucks wouldn't do us any harm! And a week of summer weather wouldn't do us any harm! And a night without the wives wouldn't do us any harm! And a pot all full of bugs wouldn't do us any harm!"

Everything dissolves into shouting and clapping and Frank hops off the chair and into the dark.

"Power's out," Joseph says.

"Power's out!" The men cheer and clink their glasses, then sit back down and start talking like nothing's wrong.

Quinn and I are left standing there alone by the dead jukebox in the semidark.

"Seriously?" I say.

"What about the music?" Quinn says.

"Isn't there a generator?" I say.

"Let's go look," Quinn says.

We go out the back. It's dark outside. I know there are houses across the street but I don't see a single window lit up. "They lost power too," I say.

"It must be the substation," Quinn says. "It could shut everything off."

"Look up," I say. With all the other lights off, the sky is bright; there seem to be more stars than usual.

We crane our necks, lose our footing on the gravel, lean against each other for balance, like elderly people. Quinn sighs. "Yeah, there's a whole lot of flickering cosmos up there." She spins around.

I look past her. There's a low shed at the back of the lot. "Generator!" I say. I pull Quinn across the parking lot, laughing. It feels like we are up to no good, doing something important. We have to do something important because we did something important with the article and no one knows about it, so it feels like it was nothing, which is terrible. It is terrible because it leaves us wondering what's next, which is bad.

We unbolt the door. Inside, it is dark and smells like pine and diesel. I stoop, because the ceiling is low. The floor is covered with wood chips. The tank of the generator is like a sleeping animal, curled at the back.

We both stare at it.

"I know I said I wanted to turn it on but I don't know how," I say.

"I got it," Quinn says. We are whispering, though I don't know why. Quinn slinks back and starts feeling around for something that might start it.

Because Quinn can do anything. She can be a girl and sing and fix a generator and cheer me up, and fine, she's only okay at writing newspaper articles but there will be *music* again soon, because Quinn and I are always making something happen. We are a team. We are in cahoots. We are Woodward and Bernstein. I start to tell her this, but then the generator switches on and it is so loud I can't hear anything except the roaring.

38

Quinn

At the end of *All the President's Men* they never show what happens after Woodward and Bernstein get the story. They crack it, they write it, then they make you hold your breath as you wait to see if they'll be able to run it. Spoiler: They do. And then the movie's over.

Of course you know what happens because you already knew what happened when you started watching it. It's a historical fucking movie. Still, after the story is done, it feels like a copout, that spinning newspaper montage.

What happened to those men, together, after?

How do you celebrate a thing like this?

In the shed, it smells like cheap pine two-by-fours. It smells like the saw that buzzed through the pieces to cut them and make planks. It smells like the one one-hundredth of an inch of wood that you have to account for in your measurements, because it disappears when the saw runs through. That much of it, just gone. This is where we are, Leah and me, right now, in this shed. We are on that line you draw between the one part of the plank and the other, and once the saw goes through it, it will be gone. Sawdust.

I'm leaning back into the corner, over the generator, trying to figure out how to turn it on. I find the switch for the power and I flick it. The noise the generator makes is so loud it feels like someone's slammed me on the ears. The shed's board walls glow, beams filtering in all crisscrossed between the uncaulked boards. The lights are back on at the Uncle. Leah has this look on her face and she's saying something but I can't hear her, so I say, "Hold on!," and I reach down to turn the generator off again, but I'm having trouble finding it because it feels like the world's about to shake itself to pieces. And then Leah grabs me and spins me around and makes her mouth say the words big and clear so I can see them.

Sirens. Sirens, she mouths to me. And I figure this is it. They're coming to get us. The Dorians.

Leah pulls me by the hand out of the shed. My ears are ringing but I hear them. The sirens get louder as we run across the parking lot. And there they are, not police cars at all, but fire trucks, two of them, headed east. I didn't think Menamon had two fire trucks. Guys start coming out of the bar, looking around, sniffing. And then I smell it. The smoke. It doesn't smell like campfire. It's more chemical. Other men come out of the Uncle and soon we're a crowd standing in the parking lot. We all stare off toward where the fire trucks disappeared. "Look," someone says. He points off to the east. I squint hard and see something awful glowing through the trees.

39

Leah

The woods are on fire.

People push out the front door of the Uncle, and I can hear the jukebox playing from inside.

We see a man coming out of the tree line. He is carrying something.

It's Patsy Cline, I think. On the jukebox.

And it's Jethro, coming through the trees, but what is in his arms I cannot tell.

40

Quinn

I thought she would wake up," Jethro says. "But she's still sleeping." His face is covered with soot. Rosie lolls in his arms like a heap of blankets too big to carry right. She keeps sliding out of his grip. Her face is sweaty. There's blood in her hair. Why would there be blood in her hair? She looks very small and I worry about her eating again.

I say, "Jethro, get your hands off my girl."

And he says, "Quinn."

I say, "I mean it." She's drunk, Rosie, and Jethro is carrying her around like a prize. I think that she must be drunk. Too drunk.

"You have to get her to a hospital," he says, and holds his arms out like I should take her but I can't because I can't move. I just stare at his face. His eyes refuse to settle on any single person in this crowd.

Billy is standing beside Jethro, crying like a kid. Joseph comes running through everyone and he slams into Billy like a collision. And then he's squeezing him. He's squashing Billy against him, and I've never seen Joseph move that fast, or touch someone this way before.

"Are you fucking crying, Billy?" I say. I can see part of his sooty face underneath the cage of his father's arms.

"Quinn," Leah says.

"Take her," Jethro says again.

And I say, "Rosie, hey, Rosie." I want to show Jethro there's no reason for him to be touching her at all. That he should just put her down on her feet. She can hold her liquor fine.

Leah says, "Here." She is so tall, Leah. Her arms are long enough that when she extends them, open to receive, and Jethro pours Rosie into her arms, it's no problem. Rosie is so much smaller than she was before, so light now, it looks easy when Leah cradles her. She puts her face close to Rosie's hot sleeping face, her ear near Rosie's mouth. She nods.

"Joseph," Leah says. "Can you drive?"

"What's wrong with her, Jethro?" I say. I can't move. "Jethro! What the fuck did you do to her?" And Jethro looks at me, his arms still half out where he's let go of Rosie, and then he starts walking away. Away from the awful glowing, through the western bank of trees, and then he's gone.

I take two steps to follow him but Leah says, "Quinn, get in the car. Come on." It's me and Rosie and Leah in the backseat and now I'm holding Rosie, who is sleeping, who is wearing my red number nine shirt, who is bleeding on both of our shirts, who reeks of gasoline. She's breathing against my neck so slowly. Too slowly. I feel the air go in and out of her and it does not seem like enough.

"Hey, Rosie," I say. I say "Rosalind" loudly, but she doesn't wake up.

In the front seat Billy is all hunched over, just crying and crying. I think he'd crawl into the driver's seat, into Joseph's lap, if he could.

Joseph says, "Mercy General is closer but they might not have power. I think we should go to Saint John's."

41

Leah

This is the news:

Late this past Sunday evening Miss Rosalind Salem and a local boy (not named due to his status as a legal minor) assisted Mr. Jethro Newkirk in setting fire to the Dorian estate, formerly known as the properties of Penobscot Road. They used gasoline or possibly, further investigation suggests, boat diesel, to soak the perimeter and infrastructure of the house. The structure was midconstruction and largely composed of exposed timber and insulation, which burned quickly, soon spreading to the surrounding wooded area. The fire spread through the tree line to the local power substation, where a minor explosion shorted out power on the east side of town, which has remained in blackout for the past twenty-four hours. Miss Rosalind Salem of Menamon sustained fatal injuries after being struck by a piece of collapsing wreckage subsequent to the explosion at the substation. According to the male accomplice, who at this time is not being charged, Mr. Newkirk convinced the children to assist him in the arson. Their plans were related to but not sanctioned by a small group of residents intending to stage a protest of the construction of the Dorian property the next day, Mr. Carter Marks being the most vocal member of said group. The boy has stated that Marks had no knowledge of the arsonists' actions and indeed had instructed him and Miss Salem not to participate in a demonstration slated for Monday afternoon. Mr. Newkirk is awaiting trial and is expected to receive the maximum ten years for felony arson.

42

Quinn

All over town the lights are out. I wander around Carter's house, room to room, flicking the little plastic switches up and down, each one clicking uselessly in its tracks. No matter how many times I do it, nothing happens. But that can't last forever. Soon I'll flick a switch and Rosie will walk into the room, yawning. She'll give me a hard time for staying up all night, worrying about nothing.

It's four. Carter is sleeping.

I knock around in Carter's drawers and find the butts of several candles. I stick them on the kitchen table and I light them up. I'm going to wait this out. I'm not a patient person but what else can I do but sit here and wait for it to be over. I find a book on one of Carter's shelves, one with pictures in it. I put it down on the table. I flip the pages, fast fast fast.

I need a drink. I get a glass, and then I open the freezer drawer and a cool breeze puffs out at me. The ice tray is full of puddles. Right, of course: the electricity is the refrigerator too.

The unstable ones are always the ones I like, but to black out the whole town? Let me tell you, Rosie, you win. We get it. You are the bravest girl, the biggest girl. We believe you. You can play with the big kids. Just come on out now. Please.

Soon the lights will come back on.

But when we left the hospital this morning at two, they didn't say to come back. They didn't tell us about visiting hours. They just kept saying, *We're so sorry, is there family you'd like to call?*

I said, *Carter Marks,* and they said, *What's his number?*, and I said, *J42.*

I think they mean Rosie's family, Quinn, Joseph said. *Someone else will take care of that. We'll take you home.*

No, I said. I couldn't go home. I couldn't think of a single place I wanted to go. A person I could call. But then I knew. I didn't like it, but there was no one else.

Where is Carter? I said.

We'll take you over there, Leah said.

I get up, flick the lights again. Incredible, that she did this.

I shouldn't have gotten out of bed.

They dropped me off and I went inside. I sat on the sofa with a camping lantern while Carter talked to Joseph. I heard him close the door and I looked up. He was half slumped in the frame, leaning on the door like a felled tree, not quite fallen yet.

The lights are off, I said.

He didn't move.

So I got up and I went over to him, tapped him on the shoulder that was hunched up half covering his face. *Hey, Carter,* I said. *It's dark in here. You got any more candles?*

Carter unhunched himself, but his face was all wrong. It was crying, his face.

Quinn, he said, and I said, *I wish everyone would stop calling my name.* Because that's not a normal thing, you know? To call a person by their name, directly, all the time? The only person who ever does that is Rosie.

I'm very tired, I told Carter. I leaned up against him.

I have a room for you, Carter said. He stood up and started walking and I tried to do the same but there was something about that wall. The door. The idea of before that was outside it. I didn't move.

I can just sleep here, I said. *I don't want to put you out.*

Carter watched me from across the room and then he came back. *Would you stop talking that way to me?* he said. *I can't take it if you're going to keep on talking to me that way. Something terrible has happened and I'm your goddamn father and you're going to sleep in a bed and you're never putting me out. Got it?*

I shrugged, and slumped a little. I was crying then too. Because once Carter said it, I knew it was true: Something terrible had happened. Something that couldn't be fixed. I felt that too-familiar black nothingness pluming inside me. Everything seemed very far away. It was different, but it was the same, and I couldn't do it. Not again. I kept thinking, I have just crawled out of here. I have just clawed my way halfway out of this pit, you can't possibly think I can do it again. So soon.

Carter reached down then and picked me up, like I was nothing. He carried me into a little room down the hall.

There was a single bed and paintings of colors on the walls. Just shapes and colors. There were books on the shelves about all sorts of things. Georgia O'Keeffe. Amelia Earhart. A child's guide to camping and woodland survival. There was a jar of moon shells on the bookcase and a plastic horse figurine. There was a small replica ship, and what looked like a taxidermied turtle. *What the hell are you doing with a little room like this?* I said to him.

He put me down in the bed and pulled the covers over me. He got on his knees by the bed and he put his big hand on my head, pressing it gently against the pillow. *I am so sorry,* he said. *I am so goddamn sorry. If I hadn't told them to do flyers. Or if I had—*

You're so stupid, Carter, I said, and I closed my eyes, which is actually a lousy way to stop yourself from crying. *You didn't do anything. The only thing you have to be sorry for is being so stupid you think any of this is your fault.*

Because I didn't have any time to spend worrying about him. It was Jethro's fault, maybe. Or I could blame Billy for helping or Leah for not wanting to go look for Rosie, but really, when you get down to it, no one ever made Rosie Salem do a single thing she didn't want to do. I can see her pouring gasoline, that girl. I see the red plastic drum with the skuzzy spout, and I see how the drum started off too heavy for her to hold right, her pouring erratically trying to manage the weight, and then, once it got half empty, her adjusting it in her arms. I can see her moving around with it, pouring the gasoline out in circles and figure eights, tracing the fucking infinity symbol in gasoline on the floor of what should have been the Dorians' living room. I can see her doing all of this, very pleased with herself. Panting a little but humming. I can see her putting down the drum and wiping her gasoline-smelling hands off on her shirt. On my fucking T-shirt.

It would be easier if I could blame someone.

Carter shook his head and squeezed my arm. *Try to sleep,* he said, and then he left.

I thought Rosie was safe to love. She and I were going to be the cozy kind of normal family I always wanted. But now she's gone and done it. She's as bad as blood, breaking my heart like this. Bad as any Winters. Any Marks. It doesn't matter if they're blood or not—if you let a person in, make them family, they'll wind up breaking your heart one way or another. Good ways and bad ways both.

I should have stayed in the bed. But I couldn't. So here I am.

I close the book of pictures. I put my head down on the kitchen table and stare at the dark part in the middle of the candle flame. The dark part of the candle makes me see spots, so I close my eyes. I still see spots. I keep them closed.

When I wake up, the candles are hard puddles and there are still no lights on. There's blue-gray light coming in the windows and it's morning.

I can hear Carter strumming his guitar quietly in the next room. He's playing the song. The one about how I'm mighty.

43

Leah

I find Henry in his boyhood room upstairs. He is lying in bed, a T-shirt wrapped around his eyes.

"Henry?" I say.

"The moon is too bright," he says.

"The house," I say. "Did someone—"

"The soil is water repellent," Henry says. It is strange to see his mouth move while his eyes are covered by the shirt. "The fire will have made the soil water repellent. And now that everything's burned, there are no roots to hold it together, so it's unstable. It will erode. Just blow away." He lifts his hands as he says this, to show how the soil will leave. The one thing that is supposed to stay put.

"So you can't grow anything there?" I ask. I ask him this because it is easier than asking him if he knows about Rosie because of course he does not know about Rosie. If he did he would not be talking about the soil. And then I realize that maybe no one knows and so many people will have to be told. Who is going to tell all those people?

Henry sighs and takes the T-shirt from his eyes. "Nothing will be able to grow there for at least a year." His face bunches up, then releases. "Maybe longer, depending on the building materials that burned. Not that they would want to live there now anyway." He's looking at me. It's dark except for the moonlight. Henry squints. He says, "Are you dirty?"

"Henry," I say.

He says, "Do you smell like gasoline?"

I kneel on the floor next to the bed and I tell him the news.

Henry sits up. "No," he says.

"It's true," I say. I am dirty, from carrying her.

Henry shakes his head. He looks at me again. He draws his knees to his chest. He sits there like that, squeezing his own strong legs.

"I wish I didn't always hear the news from you," Henry says.

I SHOWER MYSELF scalded pink. I am congested from crying and I am breathing through my mouth. I was the one who told Quinn to let Rosie do her thing. I cannot unsay it now.

I tie my hair back tight. It is slicked against my head like a seal's. I put on a dark blue sweatshirt inside out, the fuzz showing. I don't bother to flip it around.

In the little room, Henry is still lying there on the bed, not sleeping. He is watching the mobile circle around. I lie down with him. We stay there for what feels like hours. Eventually, Henry extricates himself from our tangle. He stands up and goes to the window. I kneel on the bed so I can see what's out there too. The moon is big and the sky weird, from the smoke maybe.

"Once," Henry says, "when I was a kid, I woke up in the middle of the night and looked out there. The snow in the yard had frozen over and the way the moon was shining, it cast this long reflection across the ice, just like it does on the ocean when it comes up. And I thought it *was* the ocean. That the tide had come all the way up and that was just how it was going to be from then on. Ocean everywhere. That's how it felt most of the time anyway, with my dad."

I get up and go to him, because I think that this is the truest story Henry has ever told me. I clutch at his T-shirt and I kiss him. "I love you," I tell him. Because I do.

"Hey," Henry says. "I love you too." He squeezes me. Then he picks up all the blankets and quilts from the bed and gathers them in his arms. "Come on," he says, and I follow him out the door and down the stairs.

Henry does not stop when we get downstairs. He keeps walking till we get to the back door. And then he opens it. He does not stop when we are in the middle of our yard. I hold on to Henry's elbow and I go with him, out to the beach.

Our house dinghy is tied up to the dock, covered in a green tarp. Henry pulls it in by the rope. He flips the tarp and lays it down in the dinghy's hull. He lays one of the quilts on top. He tosses the other blankets in.

"There," he says. "Get in." I look at him, but he's waiting for me to go first, so I lower myself down into the hull. I wobble, standing for a moment before I drop down fast, crouched in the blankets.

Henry gets in next, and the whole thing rocks like it might capsize. Henry's arms go out to his sides, like he's taking off, but then he balances, and lowers himself into the hull.

He rolls a quilt up for a two-person pillow. We lie down and pull the blankets over us. I slide up next to him and put my head on his chest. The dinghy rocks back and forth. We have made it. We are safe. Above the sides of the boat we see a dark slice of trees and sky. There are still many stars, the same ones I saw earlier. I think I can smell the burning but mostly I smell the ocean. I hear the waves rolling up on shore then sinking back. We rock there and soon I fall asleep.

IN THE MORNING, when we get out of the boat, the *Menamon Star* is there on the doorstep, its plastic sleeve covered in droplets.

HENRY IS SITTING at the kitchen table, drinking coffee, his eyes wide open and staring at some kind of nothing between him and the wall. I shell the paper from its sleeve and put it down on the table. Our story is the front page. Here it is, straight off the presses, and already it's old news.

"It ran today?" Henry says.

"Yes," I say.

Henry picks up the paper, glancing at the byline with my missing name. He's on the third paragraph when he looks up at me and I know he knows.

Henry says, "I seem to remember once reading a *Gazette* article about an 'Unprecedented Culture Shift' in Bed-Stuy."

"Henry—" I say.

"Eight-foot fences, it says here," Henry says. "Interesting that they'd have known how tall the fences were gonna be."

"I was going to tell you," I say. "But then—"

"Obviously you weren't. Obviously you left your name off the byline and were hoping I was dumb enough not to recognize your copy when I read it."

"Yes," I say, because I am busted and what can I do? "Not like that, but yes."

A muscle in Henry's cheek twitches. He holds the paper out in front of him, like evidence, but does not read it. I shouldn't have done it but I just wanted to so badly. It seems so stupid now, after what's happened. Me making so much fuss over words. One article.

"I've been thinking I might go away for a while," Henry says, still looking at the paper.

"Away?" I say. I think: Don't go. It is all too terrible and you cannot leave me alone now even if I deserve it.

"Back to New York. Just for a week or two. Get my head straight."

"Because of this?" I say. "Henry, I'm sorry. I am so, so sorry." Outside, a siren whines.

"Not just this," Henry says. "You could say *this* doesn't even matter anymore, in light of everything." He flicks his wrist, cracks the paper straight.

"Would you say that?" I ask, and I hope, somehow, that this will have gotten me off the hook. Then I realize how disgustingly awful that is. I don't want to be let off the hook like that. Not by Rosie.

"I don't know," Henry says.

"Henry, don't go away. Not now," I say.

He looks up at me, lifting the newspaper. "Do you want this?" he asks. He has asked me this so many times. In New York, on sleepy mornings, he would have finished the current events and sports pages, and he would hold up the paper in this exact same way to see if I was done. Did I still need the arts? The books? The world news and politics?

"No," I say. "I've read it."

He nods and gets up. He opens the cabinets under the sink where we keep our recycling. He puts the paper on a stack of other old papers. I watch as he methodically binds the stack up with twine. Cutting it. Knotting it.

"I'm going out," he says.

"Henry—" I say.

But Henry lifts the stack by the strings and through the screen door I see him taking it out to the end of the drive where we leave our recycling.

And this will be happening all over town. Our story will be used to wrap up fishes at Deep's. It will line the floors of pets' cages. It will get crumpled into balls and used for kindling. It will blow away down the docks, the four-squared pages opening and closing like moths' wings. It does not matter so much as my newspaper brain thinks it does. It doesn't matter like humans do.

And then there is the other kind of news, the kind about Rosie. The kind that you give squatting next to your husband's bed, reeking of gasoline. This news is different from the news in the paper. It is the kind that will make its way through town whether people read the *Star* or not. People will phone people. People will see people, in the supermarket, at the gas station. Parents standing around the carousel will talk in muffled voices as their children ride around. *Have you heard?* someone will say. And someone else will say, *Heard what?* And that is when it truly is the news. When you are the one who has to instill in your voice the exact right balance of kindness and seriousness with which to tell someone something that she doesn't really want to hear.

SOME COMPANY MEN are brought up to repair the substation. People talk about what happened in quiet voices. And they do not stop talking about it.

In this town, people understand a death by drowning. It happens yearly. Men are yanked overboard by ropes tied wrong. There are undertows and riptides. Drunk children and drunker adults go swimming. There are squalls.

But there are no fires. To lose a girl this way is something this town has not practiced for. There will be no funeral because Rosie's parents will have the services in Florida. They have said they will not be returning to Menamon. It is mentioned, about town, that their faces haven't been seen around here in quite some time anyway.

And if the Salems do not come back, and if there is no funeral, perhaps it will be easier. It will be easier to think instead that Rosie has just gone down to Florida, a troublemaking kid collected at last by her parents. We imagine Rosie sulking over breakfast on her parents' patio. We imagine her refusing all the fruits, and juices. We imagine her complaining about the noisy chattering bugs in the palms, the kinds that are bigger than the ones we have here. We imagine warm air stirring wax-green Florida leaves. We see her staying pale. Wearing SPF 80 and forgetting to rub in a spot between her shoulder blades. We think of the postcards she will send us, idyllic beach scenes with notes on the back saying things like, *This is dreadful. Give my regards to the Uncle. Love, Rosalind.*

But then, we see her slowly unfurling. She starts cooking her parents Stationhouse specials for breakfast. She sits with her father on the beach. They both wear Red Sox caps, but sometimes, if the Sox aren't playing, we imagine them rooting for the Rays. We hear it when Rosie starts to sing again. Murmuring little songs as she convinces her mother to dye her graying hair blond. We watch as Rosie starts a shell collection, favoring the ugly twisted ones with secret pink insides. We see her line the shells up on the shelf in her bedroom. We notice that she has started to think of it as her bedroom. And we see how she forgets all about us here in Menamon. And we are glad it is this way. We are glad when we see Rosie in an alligator-green bathing suit and a silly sun hat of her mother's, standing knee-deep in warm Florida water. She is smiling and squinting, half blinded by the sun. She cannot see us. And we are glad.

44

Quinn

Joe Deep decides there's going to be a memorial. He runs an event listing in my goddamn paper, which is still coming out, without me. The memorial is down on the waterfront, today, at noon.

I'm not going. Like hell I'm going.

Carter says we're going. I sit on a stool at the island in his kitchen, watching him crack eggs, using his thumbs too much to do it. I shake my head. "No," I say. "I'm not going. I'm in a bad mood, Carter. My whole life is a fucking bad mood." I take a sharp breath in. I shiver.

Carter wipes egg off his hands. He leaves the room and comes back with a sweater for me. "Put that on," he says.

I pull it over my head and don't bother to pull my hair out of the neck. I let him make me food. It's been a few days, and this is what we do. I sleep. He wakes me up and says I have to eat something. I yell at him. He says, "Fine," and then starts cooking anyway. Usually I smell it and come out.

This is what Carter and I should have done when Marta died. Eaten food. Yelled at each other. Worn large sweaters as mourning garb.

This morning he's making omelets with cheese in them and spicy peppers—the way we like them. He puts a blue china plate in front of me. He gives me silverware and a cloth rag of a napkin. "Eat," he says.

I roll up the sweater sleeves and I eat. Carter watches me swallow, then forks some eggs into his own mouth. "It will be good to go," he says.

"No fucking way," I say, my mouth full of eggs.

Carter shakes his head. "No way?" he says.

I nod.

He goes to the phone. "Remember that you made me do this," he says.

When I hear the faint "*How's it going?*" on the other end of the line, I know he's bringing in the big guns.

Charley pulls up in the drive twenty minutes later. Her face is too nice.

She gives me this sad smile and says, "Get in the fucking car, Winters, or you're fired."

I sit on my stool and stare at her. "You can't be idiotic enough to think this will work," I say. "You I expected better from."

Carter excuses himself to go get ready. He leaves us alone.

Charley holds out her hand. "Please, Quinn," she says. I bite my lip. These fucking women with their fucking *pleases*.

"I don't want to," I say. "I don't think I can. Who do I owe it to, to cry in fucking public? I'll cry right here. I'll grieve just as much. Okay? I promise."

"It's not for them, you moron, it's for you," Charley says. "And for Rosie." Charley looks at the ceiling. "You know she would have loved something like this. You know she would drag you to it if she could."

"Hah!" I laugh a snotty laugh in spite of myself. It's true, this is exactly the sort of dumb thing Rosie would make me go to. Only it's her own dumb thing. Her own dumb memorial. I imagine her poking at me, pulling back the covers, handing me my clothes, saying, *We're going.*

"I'll bum you a million cigarettes, huh?" Charley says.

I scan her pockets. I see the rectangle of a pack. "I'm not changing," I say, flapping the big sleeves of Carter's sweater.

"No one gives a damn what you wear, Winters," Charley says, rubbing at her eyes. "Okay? Just come."

"Fine," I say. I hop off my stool.

Carter emerges, dressed in black. I know he's heard the whole thing. "Are we going?" he asks anyway.

We follow Charley out to the car. Carter gets in shotgun and I climb in the back. I don't put on a seat belt. Charley starts the car.

"I'd like those cigarettes now, please," I say.

Charley tosses the pack into the backseat. "Take them," she says. "I quit."

45

Leah

I have developed a fondness for the dinghy.

It used to seem like just another part of the dock, but ever since Henry and I slept in it, I've started coming down here. I scrubbed the hull out with water and bleach. The rope tying it to the dock was old, so I bought a new one. I'm getting better at climbing in. Today, I manage it without even wobbling.

I am sitting in the dinghy, in my black dress, knee length, sleeveless, my hair up in a bun, waiting for Henry to come get me so we can go to Rosie's memorial. There's something about the smell of the water that makes me feel like a real live human being. There's bigness, here by the ocean. When you look at it, how those waves come rolling in, you think, There can't really be another one coming, can there? And then there is.

"Ahoy," Henry says.

"Ahoy," I say.

He climbs into the boat. He is wearing a gray suit. He has trimmed his new beard. We sit there for a moment, rocking. I sit up taller and imagine a large oil portrait of us, the kind so big you have to step back to see it like in the galleries at MoMA. *New Yorker in Dinghy, with Husband.*

"You ready?" he says.

"I am," I say. But I am not. I keep hearing myself, that night, when Quinn suggested we look for Rosie at Billy's place. *Let her do her thing,* I said. So easy. We went to the bar instead. *Let her do her thing.*

The boat knocks against the planks. Henry pushes us off a little bit. I look down through the green water. Watch how the rope undulates in the murk.

"I'm going later this week," Henry says. "I called my old guys. They have a couple of projects they could use me on. I won't stay long. A week or two."

"You'll be working?" I say.

He nods. "It'll be good to be working. I just need a break from all this. From Menamon."

"And you'll come back?" I say.

"Of course I'll come back," Henry says, and takes my hand. He seems so tired. So joyless. It's not just me who has done this to him, but I did not help. I did not help at all.

"Wanna come?" Henry asks. "You can nose around the *Gazette* offices. We can see some friends."

"Do you want me to come?"

Henry shrugs.

New York in springtime. Trees in concrete wells will be in bloom. New Yorkers will be sneezing. Allergies, they will say, allergies. The restaurants will be unfurling blue awnings; they will be bringing out their outdoor tables. Out-of-work actors will line up for interviews to wait tables in the extra sections. They will bring their head shots to the interviews. On the subway, fair-weather fans will resume wearing their Yankees championship gear. The men who have been wearing their 1986 satin Mets jackets since 1986 will dismiss them. Both of these kinds of people will start buying the *Post* more regularly to get game updates. At the *Gazette,* they will have exactly one meeting about how they could make their sports coverage compete with the *Post*'s without the use of puns. Nothing will come of this meeting. In the parks, runners will appear. Those first few weeks there will dozens of pale chubby-legged girls, flushing red in the face, getting ready for summer. My parents will start dreaming about their summer plans. Out loud they will say, *We are thinking of going to Paris.* To themselves they will be thinking, What if we just told everyone we were going to Paris and then stayed home and did nothing? There will be ads in the classifieds for rentals in the Hamptons, Fire Island, Nantucket. This is New York in spring.

And I do not want it.

I stand up too fast in the boat. It rocks but I have my sea legs now. I do not fall. I smooth my black skirt. "Let's just go to the thing," I tell Henry. "Let's talk about this later." We climb out of the boat and onto the dock. I pick up my patent-leather heels, hop off the planks, and walk in the sand, shoes clopping together as I grip them by the straps.

I think about June. How she was so perfectly a creature of this place, born of it and lost to it, but loved. I may have gotten a late start but it is not too late for me to belong to this place, I don't think. I am not really a New Yorker in a dinghy anymore.

46

Quinn

We walk down the boardwalk to the dock. There are a lot of people there. Enough that I feel like running away immediately. I freeze but Charley grabs my wrist hard and keeps on marching me forward.

There's a wet hair-mussing breeze coming off the ocean and people take turns holding down their skirts and running hands over their heads. They're wearing nice dark clothes. Everyone in a town like this has a good mourning outfit ready and waiting to go.

Joseph stands in the center of the circle, his back to the sea, waiting. He's wearing a blue, collared shirt and jeans. Billy's not far off, wearing a collared shirt too. He looks smaller and paler than usual. He raises a hand when he sees me and holds it there. It's not quite a wave. I nod at him.

Charley drags me down to where Leah and Henry are standing. Leah makes awkward shapes with her mouth but doesn't say anything. Carter stands on my other side. Close, like he thinks I'm going to bolt.

Joseph looks at his watch, and then he clears his throat. "I want to thank all of you for coming today," he says. "Father Martineau will be leading us in a requiem mass. Father Martineau, would you begin?"

An old Canuck emerges from the circle, all in black, with a collar on. His eyes are rheumy and he has a boom box and a cup of holy water, which he sprinkles about. Holy water, I think. With a whole fucking ocean behind him.

The father crosses himself, then stoops down. The boom box starts humming some ghostly Latin something. "The 'Dies Irae,'" he says. "They are singing, 'Day of wrath! O day of mourning! See fulfilled the prophets' warning. Heaven and earth in ashes burning!'" He speaks too loud because he's old, and because he's competing with the wind. A few women make simpering noises. But what the fuck is this, anyway? Rosie hadn't been to church since she was a kid at Easter, and even then she was only in it for the chocolate eggs.

Carter has his head down, staring at the ground, and Charley's contorting her face so she doesn't cry again. They're upset, and respectful, and thinking their own thoughts.

So I just start walking.

"Quinn?" I hear Charley say. I stop at the top of the dock, on the hill, in the reeds. They're all staring at me with their mourning faces on. Even the priest. Especially Leah.

"This has nothing to do with her," I say. "If you knew the first thing about her, this isn't what you'd do at all."

I want to go back home, but if I see Rosie's unwashed dishes in the sink, or her bobby pins scattered on the counter, I won't make it another day. I start walking, and when I get to the intersection, I know where to go.

47

Leah

I don't blame Quinn for leaving. She shouldn't have to listen to this Gregorian jukebox and think about Rosie's soul.

The priest leans over laboriously and stops the cassette, then looks to Joseph. "Shall I continue?" he says.

Joseph makes a deep sighing noise. "I suppose so," he says.

"Can I say something?" Henry says. Everyone turns to face us.

Henry's forehead is creased and he is squinting, because the sun is bright, but also because he is thinking. As the faces turn to him, he musses his hair, his beard.

I think, No, whatever it is he is thinking about doing he cannot do it. It is too soon, and no one has as yet forgiven him his role in this mess. I can see it on the faces of the fishermen and fishwives, of the schoolteachers and the boys from the diner, of the Rebel Seven people miserably wringing their hands: the last thing they want to do today is listen to Henry.

"'Fiddler's Green,'" Henry says.

"Hank?" Joseph says.

Henry says again, "'Fiddler's Green.'"

Joseph's face goes soft, but the rest of the people stare desperately at the priest. They are hoping he'll start up his boom box again, shepherd them through some acceptable public grief for another thirty minutes, and then let them go home. But the old French Canadian priest seems relieved that something is happening. He is watching Henry too.

"If no one minds," Henry says. He makes a coughing noise, clearing his throat. The mourners are silent, wondering whether Henry's really going to do this. Henry doesn't notice. He starts singing.

The song he begins is sad, but with a kind of lighthearted resignation to it. Henry's voice rises and then falls dramatically; it twists itself around multiple syllables with an Irish quickness. There is a kind of maritime gallows humor in the tone he takes. He sings:

As I walked by the dockside one evening so fair
To view the salt water and take the sea air
I heard an old fisherman singing a song
Won't you take me away boys me time is not long.

Wrap me up in me oilskin and jumper
No more on the docks I'll be seen
Just tell me old shipmates, I'm taking a trip, mates
And I'll see you someday in Fiddler's Green.

Now Fiddler's Green is a place I heard tell
Where the fishermen go if they don't go to hell
Where skies are all clear and the dolphins do play
And the cold coast of Greenland is far, far away.

Wrap me up in me oilskin and jumper
No more on the docks I'll be seen
Just tell me old shipmates, I'm taking a trip, mates
And I'll see you someday in Fiddler's Green.

When you get on the docks and the long trip is through
Ther's pubs and ther's clubs and ther's lassies there too
When the girls are all pretty and the beer it is free
And ther's bottles of rum growing from every tree.

Wrap me up in me oilskin and jumper
No more on the docks I'll be seen
Just tell me old shipmates, I'm taking a trip, mates
And I'll see you someday in Fiddler's Green.

Now, I don't want a harp nor a halo, not me
Just give me a breeze and a good rolling sea
I'll play me old squeeze-box as we sail along
With the wind in the rigging to sing me a song.

Wrap me up in me oilskin and jumper
No more on the docks I'll be seen
Just tell me old shipmates, I'm taking a trip, mates
And I'll see you someday in Fiddler's Green.

A name is a funny thing. You can see people thinking a name sometimes. The way the semicircle is looking at Henry right now, I know they are not thinking, That Henry Lynch. Instead they are thinking: Hank Jr.

Joseph moves first. He goes over to Henry and gives him a good thumping hug. And then he does the same to me. And to Carter. One by one everyone lines up to do the same. With no body, and no kin, somehow Henry has ended the service gracefully and made the three of us the receiving line. Every person who showed up to that memorial gives a hug to Henry, and me, and Carter. I do not think I knew how sad I was, until each person did this. So many old-lady-perfume hugs. And cool-slippery-raincoat hugs. And warm-sweater-and-chewing-tobacco hugs. One by one they do this, and then they all file away from the docks, walking up the boardwalk and heading back home.

Charley and Carter go off to look for Quinn, which leaves just me and Henry. I put my arms around him. "Don't go," I say. "You don't need a break. Everyone loves you here. I love you. Why would you ever leave a place like this?"

"They sang that for my father," Henry says. "'Fiddler's Green.' It's for fishermen who go over." He sighs. "So do you want to come with me?" he says. "To New York? We could go to Tom's for breakfast. We could go to the park. See everyone at the bar." He strokes my hair.

I love doing all those things, but how can I leave Menamon and hide in the city while this place is busy healing? I feel like I am seeing this town for the first time now that it is burned and grieving. Menamon is not the place I thought I was moving to at all. It is not the same place it was when Henry was small, or the place from his stories, and it is most certainly not the magical New England idyll I made up for myself.

But even though it is not the town I made up in my head, the truth is that I love this place. This dump of a town. These crazy, tenacious people who are wrong and angry more often than they are right and kind.

Because here is the news: I am one of them.

And if Henry is not?

I understand there is a chance that if Henry goes to the city he will find he does not want to come back. I cannot make him promise that won't happen. Can't go with him like a chaperone to make sure he returns. He doesn't know yet, so neither do I. So I will tell him good-bye and I will kiss him and I will trust in his return. Because you cannot always know with love. If we knew how things would turn out for certain, knew a person completely, that would be far too easy.

My stomach feels heavy and my throat feels tight. I ask Henry for a ride. I ask him to drop me off at the *casa grande.*

THE BURNED HOUSE looks worse than I had imagined. Do you know what a burned house looks like? It looks like an X-ray that shows you all the places where things are broken. It looks like a black skeleton that is not strong enough to stand up. It is messy.

When you walk in a burned house, you have to look at where you are putting your feet because sometimes what looks like a floor will not hold you up. Anything can give at any time.

When you walk in a burned house, you pull your dress over your nose because it doesn't just smell like burning, it smells like insulation, and wire, and plastic. It smells like all the terrible chemicals once safely fused together to make you a house have now been rent apart.

All around the broken house you will play a game called What Did That Used to Be?

A green lump with a piece of scorched wire looped through it was a bucket.

A white plastic puddle on the ground used to be a rope.

An odd-shaped object that shines when you rub the black off it was going to be someone's very expensive bathroom fixture.

When you walk in a burned house, you should not look up. But if you do, the sky will be graphed into zones by blackened rafters and this will be the most hopeless thing you've ever seen.

Or at least you'll think so, if you don't look down again. You should not look down. But if you do, you will see a girl squatting in what was supposed to be the basement but is now just the deepest part of a burned house. The girl will have red hair tucked into a too-big green sweater, and you will see her through a large hole in the floor. You will be able to see her because the light in this house travels all the way through the roof to the basement. The girl will have black ashes all over her and her hands will be bleeding because she is pulling up pieces of concrete.

The concrete foundation of the house will have split with a fissure, and there will be a long dark crack in the floor. It is this crack that the girl will be grappling with. She will be smashing a piece of pipe into the sides of the fissure, breaking off pieces of concrete. She will be tearing them away with her hands, making the crack wider. There will be nothing hasty or emotional about the way she does this, and she will not move, even after she hears you, and turns her head to look at you. She will not care that you are there. She will go back to making the fissure wider, and wider, clawing at the foundation with her red fingers.

"WHAT ARE YOU doing?" I say.

Quinn doesn't turn or stop. My shoulders tremble watching her scrape her hands up, trying to dig her way through four solid feet of cement.

I'm standing on the foundation wall of the basement. I look for the basement stairs but they're gone. It's about eight feet down, and I don't know how Quinn thinks she's getting out of there. I take off my heels and balance them on the top of the concrete wall and leap down. I land a few feet from Quinn.

"What do you think is down there?" I say, panting a little.

Quinn still doesn't look at me, just keeps on banging, a high metal ring each time the pipe hits the concrete. Little pieces fly off in her face and she doesn't seem to care. She clears the rubble, and starts again.

"Okay. I don't need to know what you're doing," I say. "But I'm going to help you do it." There's another length of pipe and I pick it up. I look at the crevice line and then bring the pipe down hard with both hands. It bangs into the concrete and the juddering force of the blow travels through the shaking pipe, through my arms. My entire body feels it.

Quinn turns around, her lips pulled back from her mouth like she's going to snarl, or bite me, but she freezes. She looks at me. I resettle my grip on the pipe as I wait for the blow to stop traveling through my body, vibrating in my teeth.

When I feel myself again I lift up the pipe, prepared to bring it down, but before I can Quinn grabs me in a hug that is also a body lock. "Stop," she says. "I can't look at your fucking face like that."

I drop the pipe, which hits the floor with one end and then the other. An awful noise. I hug on to Quinn. "We should have gone for her," I say into Quinn's hair. "I shouldn't have said to let her be."

Quinn shakes her head. "It wouldn't have made any difference," she says, and I feel a rushing relief run through my whole body.

"What are we doing here?" I say.

"I don't know. It's probably not down there anyway." She looks at the empty crater. Chucks a little piece of concrete back into the void.

"What?"

"Rosie's time capsule," Quinn says. "A bunch of junk. Some photos and hair. A magic seashell."

"Magic?" I say.

"Yeah, probably," Quinn says. "What kind of rat bastard pours concrete over a magic seashell anyway?"

"A real rat bastard," I say, and the way Quinn's body moves up and down against me, I know she is crying. I hold on to her until she stops. I say, "Let's go to Carter's."

"As long as there's not a priest there," she says.

"No priests," I say. "Charley maybe, but no official religious personnel."

At the wall, I give her a boost up and she climbs out of the basement. I jump up and grab the top of the wall and then pull myself up and out too.

We walk all the way to Carter's. It's nice out, and it feels right to be on the road: walking on the pebbly sides, snatching at the weeds that grow there. Quinn stares at her hands like she can't believe they're hers. "We need that priest after all," she says. "Someone should sanctify this flesh. These are some holy fucking hands." She holds them up and they glow red in the sun.

Carter opens the door before we even knock. He has seen us coming down the drive. "Jesus," he says when he sees us.

He calls Charley, who is out patrolling in her car, looking for Quinn. He heats up a kettle of water and fills two basins with it. He mixes in some peroxide. He lets us sit on his couch, even though we are filthy. Quinn soaks her hands in one basin, on the side table. I have another one for my big feet, which barely fit inside. Carter sits cross-legged on the floor, watching us.

"You girls have got to start taking it a little easy," he says. "Just for a while."

Summer, Again

48

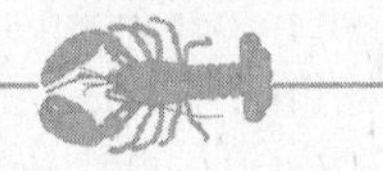

Quinn

"Hello?" I say. The kitchen is empty. So is the living room.
"Leah?" I call as I go up the stairs. "Bernstein? Where are you?"

A head appears at the top of the stairwell. Henry's. "Hi," he says.

"Hey," I say, and I climb the rest of the way up.

Henry is standing in the hallway, two huge duffel bags at his feet. He's wearing an ancient white Springsteen T-shirt with a couple of holes in it.

"Where you going?" I say.

"New York," he says.

"For how long?"

Henry looks into one of the suitcases like the answer might be there along with his jeans, some socks, a book called *A Boy's Guide to Edible Plants*. "A week maybe," he says. "Leah's down at the beach."

"Okay," I say. I start to head down the stairs, but then I say, "The Boss," and point at his shirt. "That's some good stuff."

Henry looks down at himself. "The old stuff, yeah." He hesitates a second and then says, "I'm sorry about Rosie." He braces his hands against the walls, like he's trying to push the hallway wider. "She was a cool girl. I remember when she started junior high. All the high school guys tried to ask her out and she wouldn't go with a single one."

I make a sound that is the closest thing to a laugh I've made in days. "That doesn't surprise me," I say.

"But it was the way she did it," Henry says. "She'd always tell them she would consider it. Consider dating them. And then she would send these long handwritten letters, like, in the mail, explaining all about her goals, and ideal of compatibility, and things. Telling them how sorry she was but she just didn't think it would be possible for them to take her out."

I imagine Rosie writing letters like these. I see her sitting on her bed and using a pencil and loose-leaf. I can see her signature, loopy at the bottom.

"The crazy ones are always worth it," I say.

Henry laughs. "You're probably right," he says.

"I am," I say. "I know it. I hope you know it too."

Henry stares into his suitcase. "I do," he says.

"So, you ever get a letter like that?" I say. "From Rosie? You sound like sort of an expert."

Henry laughs. "Of course I did," he says. "Two pages long." He shakes his head. "Sorry is a stupid thing to say but I am. I am sorry."

I stick out my hand and say, "Nice to know you, Henry Lynch. I hope I see you around again soon."

Henry shakes my hand, a good grip. It smarts a little. "You too," he says.

I head downstairs. "There are some beers in the fridge," he calls after me.

LEAH IS SITTING on a quilt spread in the sand. She's leaning over her knees, hugging them. Her hair is pulled back into a little broom of a ponytail. She's got an old white sweatshirt on inside out, the neckhole cut wide and showing her shoulders. She's got her jeans rolled halfway up her shins, like she's been wading. This time of year the water could freeze you blue.

"Forgot yah beeyaz?" I call, in an old-timey Mainer voice. She turns around and I lift the six-pack high.

I sit down next to her and get to work taking off my sneakers. I bury my feet in the beach.

"How are your hands?" Leah says.

I hold them out. "They're healing." Cracks and splotches of scab make them all kinds of purple and red. "I'll be able to pick up the guitar in another week."

Leah nods. "Henry's leaving," she says. She's been waiting to say this.

"He told me," I say. "Going to do some city-slicking."

"Just for a while," Leah says.

"Of course," I say. "Back in a flash. What about you? Are you going city-slicking too, you lousy flatlander?" I push on her a little, so she rocks away from me and back again. If I lose Leah I don't know what I'll do.

"No," Leah says. "I'm not. Maybe not ever again."

"That," I say, throwing my arm around her, "is fucking fantastic news."

A few yards off a sport fisherman is standing near the tide line, looking into a white plastic bucket. His pole is upright in the sand, staked. His line is cast in. It starts to jerk and he goes to the pole. He leans back and reels it in. Flapping from side to side at the end is the ugliest fucking fish I've ever seen. It's brown and mottled. There are these weblike things contracting at its sides and it has a limp spiky-looking top fin. A mouth as wide and sad as a frog's flips open and closed slimily.

The man starts cursing at the fish. He fingers the hook and works it out of its lip.

"What is that?" Leah calls out to him.

"A fucking sea robin," the man shouts back.

I whisper to Leah, "The Lesser Fucking Sea Robin is an indigenous species of the Maine coast, and is considered largely inedible by the natives."

The man flings the sea robin back, the thing flipping tail over mug until it disappears into the waves. We watch him rebait his hook and cast, the line arcing wide out over the water.

Down the way a dozen little boats are bobbing up and down in the water, each one tied up to its house's dock. One house down an old man is sitting in a beach chair. He's wearing green shorts and a denim shirt open to brown belly. He's got a three-inch-thick paperback in his hands, something black with raised gold letters. The page ends are dyed blue-green. It can't be more than seventy degrees down here, what with the wind.

"So you're coming back to work, then?" Leah says.

"Eventually," I say. "First, I'm taking a trip too."

"Don't tell me! You called your old job! You're going to do a little work for them. But you'll be back soon!" Leah flails her hands around as she says this. Then she looks at me, embarrassed over this outburst that obviously has more to do with Henry than with me.

"No," I say. "I'm going to Florida. To see Rosie's parents."

"Florida?" Leah reaches behind me to pull two beers from the pack. She opens them and hands one to me. We clink. She takes a long sip, then says, "Do they know you're coming?"

"Not really," I say. "But I think I can tell them some good things. It would have been better if I could have brought that time capsule. I thought I'd be a real hero if I could do that."

"Heroes are overrated," Leah says.

Down the way, the fisherman says, "Goddammit." He's reeled in his line once more and at the end of it is the same ugly fish all over again. Its bug eyes are embarrassed. Its fins are flapping slowly.

"It's the same damn fish!" I say. I look at Leah, whose mouth is open. Then she starts laughing, a slow build, until her eyes are squeezed shut and tears are running down her face and almost no sound is coming out. She lets herself fall onto her back, on the blanket, her laugh honking out again, hysterical. And I'm laughing too. "Of all the lousy-luck fish," I say, and we've just about got ourselves back together when the fisherman hurls the sea robin back into the ocean, a little harder than he has to, shouting, "I never want to see your sorry face again!," which sets us off all over again.

Leah pulls herself together first. "Oh," she sighs. "I'm going to miss you. Hurry back and bring me a souvenir. Some key-lime pie. A seashell."

"I will," I say. "I'll send you a postcard. And hold my job for me. I don't want to come back and find out Charley's eloped with the printer and let the paper fall to pieces."

"You got it," Leah says, staring up at the sky. "Hey, Woodward," she says. "Don't leave me alone on the beat too long, okay? There's a lot of news in this town."

"Okay," I say.

We reach our arms across and shake on it.

49

Leah

I am sitting on the front steps, picking dead leaves from the hydrangea while Henry packs up his truck. He opens all the compartments and moves around the things inside them. He's wearing a thin gray thermal with the sleeves pushed up and tan Carhartt workpants. His beard is neat and already he is a little tan. I imagine him rolling up to the city and I feel a pang. I imagine him parking his truck, taking up two parallel spots, and when he climbs out into the street, I can see him frowning at the two parking meters. I imagine a girl there, a girl like I used to be. She will be busy with her purse and her phone and her boss, but she will spot this Henry, this Hank Jr., all the same. She will stop and watch him. She will admire his easy loping stride as he walks the length of his truck and feeds quarters into both parking meters. It would start there, all over again.

Henry's got one duffel bag in the well of the passenger side.

The seat he's left empty, in case I change my mind. But I won't, because I know this is something he has to do without me. That he has to go and then come back for it to really mean something. In the bed of the truck he has a bunch of work stuff. A pair of pruning shears he's partial to. Some plans rolled up in a plastic tube. He pulls a blue tarp over everything and bungee-cords it tight.

Henry is leaving me the lobster pot to drive while he's away. This morning we brought our coffees out to the garage and he showed me the tool kit in the trunk, walked me through which tools are used to cure which rumbles, what clankings. Staring at all that stuff under the hood, I watched his hands move over the tools, pointing at the engine and explaining things like he truly believed I would be able to fix them. Everything smelled like cool morning air and coffee and motor oil. The sun was shining in the garage door but inside it was dim and I thought about trying to pull Henry down in the backseat. Having sex with him right there. But I did not. That would not have been enough to make him stay.

Henry examines two different reels of gardener's wire, trying to decide which to take and which to leave. He throws both in.

"I called my parents," I say. "They said you should come over for dinner if you want to."

"That's nice," Henry says. "I will."

"You got everything?" I say.

"Just one more bag," Henry says. He lays a hand on my shoulder as he angles past me, back into the house. He's packed just two bags, but he's bringing the good pruning shears. Henry could live for a year with nothing but snacks and those pruning shears.

I wonder if I will ever go back there, for good. I try to imagine putting on high heels and rushing to catch the express train. Watching it pull away without me because I wasn't aggressive enough on the stairs, and saying "Shit!" loud enough for everyone on the platform to hear. I try to imagine sitting at my desk at the *Gazette,* covering the low public opinion polls after the mayor institutes a new cigarette tax, and working on a retrospective comparing this year's Whitney Biennial to the past twenty. I imagine going out with the other writers after work and hashing through all the office gossip. Who didn't even get considered for the section-editor job. Whose piece got killed for suspicious reasons. And I can imagine myself doing a very good job pretending to be interested in all this, but wondering why the bar we were in didn't have a jukebox, and if it did, why I couldn't find Patsy Cline, or Carter Marks, in it. Why there wasn't a red-haired girl banging on the side of that jukebox, saying, *Hey, Leah, take a look inside this machine. Do you know this machine ate my quarter?* Just so I would give her another one. Just so she could play Guns N' Roses. Just so she could dance with her girl.

Coming up here as a newlywed, I got confused, I think. Between my husband and this town, maybe I only had enough resources to fall in love with one. To make one fall in love with me. I was so worried about Niagara Falls, but somehow it didn't occur to me to worry about the pull of an entire ocean.

It's not too late for us, I don't think. We're just good at reinventing wheels. At taking the long way. A mulligan couple. We are not good at many things, but we try to be. We are very good at continuing to try.

Henry comes outside and hefts his bag into the cab of the truck. "I'm happy to move the bags to the back," he tells me. "If you wanna ride along."

I say, "Send me a postcard. One with the Empire State Building on it."

Henry nods, rubs his beard.

"Come here," I say. I stand up on the steps and he comes.

He puts his arms around me. He kisses my face. My cheeks, my forehead, my nose.

"Bye," he says.

"Come back soon," I say. He has his hands on my shoulders, my Henry. He kisses me once more, properly. He gets into his truck. He turns the engine over and I listen to the tires breaking up the clamshells. At the end of the driveway Henry honks and waves. I wave back at him.

AROUND FIVE O'CLOCK, I am reading someone's old paperback, sunk into the couch in the living room, nursing a whiskey. I hear the front door swinging open. So soon, and already Henry has come back to me, I think.

I leap up and go to the kitchen, not running quite, but not walking either.

Charley is putting her keys down on the counter. She is carrying a six-pack. "I'm inviting myself over," she says. "Where would you like to entertain me?"

I gesture at the house. Anywhere. The whole thing.

"All right, then," Charley says. She marches into the living room and puts the beers on the coffee table.

We open the windows. There's a thrumming buzz of insects just born or waking up for the season, and the crash of the waves behind it. I sit cross-legged on the braided rug. Charley packs some new Marlboros against the flat of her palm, opens them, and peels back the foil. She opens some cupboard I've never noticed before, from which she pulls out a big turquoise ashtray shaped like a seashell. Then she sprawls, taking up the whole couch.

"I quit, really," she says as she lights one. "I'm just making an exception for tonight."

"Me too," I say as I do the same.

Charley and I drink our beers and put out stub after stub and she tells me about her romance with the printer, and I tell her about Quinn going to Florida, and we both place bets on how long it will take Henry to come back. Charley bets too high, too boldly, *two days, max,* and I know she is trying to cheer me up. Sooner or later we start to plan things for the paper, hammering out what to do this week and then the next and how it will be when Quinn gets back. What we will all do then.

When Charley heads out, around eleven, she leans heavily against the doorframe and says, "I better see you Monday at nine, Lynch. Don't think I'm going to start doing you any favors."

50

Quinn

Looking at Maine's rear end in the car mirror shouldn't make you lonesome for it. Not if your genes are wired right. But on my way out I counted doughnut shops (six), men in sleeveless shirts (three), elbows out the driver's side (a dozen), and about a million custom Red Sox license plates (BOSXFN, SOXNTN, WKDSOX), and it gave me a true pang.

I'm headed down south. My plan is to stay in Florida just long enough to piss off Rosie's ghost. Seeing her parents should be plenty, but I figure I'll do things right. Because if I hang around long enough, if I drink frozen virgin cocktails and wear long shorts to the beach, if I track down Hemingway's five-toed cats and mail Leah postcards, if I bird-watch pelicans and flirt with girls at NASCAR races, Rosie will have no choice but to start haunting me.

That's all I can hope for really. For Rosie to haunt me just a little bit. I imagine her tailing my car even now, complaining all the way. Saying, *What do you think you're doing, exactly? Do you know how interminable a drive this is? Have you even brought any provisions?*

I imagine her at every rest stop. Telling me not to buy cigarettes, please, and do I really think I'm going to be able to eat that and drive at the same time?

I'm a big fan of hauntings, as it turns out. I would take Marta's *please* to heart and let her tie her ghostly twine around Carter and me all over again, if I could.

That crafty wench. I miss her. She would have loved a Florida road trip.

My family portrait: There's me in the center, seemingly a random girl, alone in the frame. But squint. There behind me, all silvery like spider floss? Marta. Next to her is Rosie, loving how she looks all shimmery. And in the corner, just barely edging into the frame, is a guitar player's miraculously gnarled hand. Carter, sneaking his way in.

Driving down the coast like this, you see a lot of places. You look at them and you think: Maybe I could live here. Maybe I could have a pickup truck and a Rottweiler puppy, a studio apartment with a king-sized bed, a colonial home with chickens in the yard, a double-wide with satellite TV. You think maybe I could Live Right Here Forever.

I could pick any of these places if I wanted. No one's going to stop me from settling in Massachusetts, or West Virginia, or Florida, and starting all over again. But whenever I think about going someplace new, I think about Carter. I think about that little room with the lilac blanket that looked like it had been waiting for years.

I've blown out of towns enough to know what normal missing

feels like, and what it means to have a magnet strapped to your back. Waves know what that's like. To be drawn out, and to be called back home again.

I would place a bet, a big one, that Menamon, Maine, will be seeing my sorry face again.

If you hop a tall fence, electric in your mind
You'll see Saint Rosie of the high watts, Saint Rosalind.
If you find a tin box, buried, lost to time
Might be Our Lady of Penobscot's, Saint Rosalind's.

51

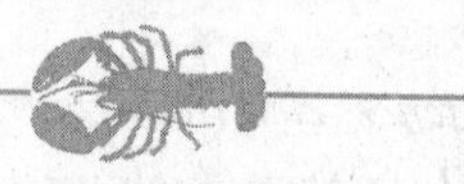

Leah

Sifting through the mail at the kitchen counter, I find a postcard mixed in with the envelopes. The picture is of a sunny little house with a dozen cats asleep on the porch. On the back, Quinn's handwriting: *Back soon. This place is a dump.*

I stick it to the fridge. The phone rings. Charley says she's coming over for dinner, and what am I planning on making?

As I leave Deep's, paper sack in my arms, I spot Carter Marks across the way, his foot up on the rail of the carousel. He is talking to Frank, who is not paying any attention to the horses careening by. Carter is holding the brass ring, twisting it in his palm so it goes all the way around and winds up at the beginning again. I start over to tell him that I heard from Quinn, but then I see it. In his back pocket. A postcard sticking out, something like a snapping alligator on it.

AT HOME, I put a pot of water on to boil and go sit on the front steps to wait.

The light gets bluer and in the dimness the clamshells in the drive glow white.

Then I hear it. Listen. The buoys, gonging in the dark.

How many times did June hear that sound while Hank was on the boat, and have to trust that he would make it home? How many times did she stand by the window, and just listen? I imagine that Henry, who is miles down the coastline, afloat in his truck, will also hear it. I know he is too close to too many rocks, but he will hear the buoys, and he will know to turn around.

Acknowledgments

I have long thought that there should be a kind of town hall message board for the universe where a person like me, who is lucky enough to have received help and kindness from an absolutely silly number of people, might post a notice of public thanks.

This is going to be a long scroll unfurling . . .

There are not enough lobsters in Maine to thank:

My editor, Kate Nintzel, for choosing *The From-Aways* not once, but twice, and for her brilliant edits, which pushed me to make this the book I hoped it would be. (Also, for pointing out that there was a totally unprecedented amount of underwear swapping in the first draft.)

My agent, Meredith Kaffel, with whom I am in cahoots. Good writers have wise voices whispering in their ears and I am forever grateful that Meredith whispers in mine. As an agent, Meredith, thank you for some Arthurian-legend-level shit. There is no one better. As a friend, I am so lucky to know a person as beautiful as you.

Margaux Weissman at William Morrow, for being the kind of lady who could hang at the Uncle anytime.

Much gratitude is owed to all the good people at DeFiore and Company and William Morrow, without whom there would be no book at all.

Cora Weissbourd, my mortal enemy at first and best of friends thereafter. You are my first and favorite reader. You knew, when I didn't, that Leah and Quinn belonged in the same book. These two women, you said, they could be friends. Thank you for dispensing this crucial wisdom, and for then taking me to the bar, and for being *you,* which is the only reason I can write about a friendship like Quinn and Leah's and know what the fuck I'm talking about.

Janice "be still my heart" Garvey, a teacher without equal and even better friend, who once struck me with an (abridged) *OED,* who first taught me Yeats, and who recited the Saint Crispin's Day speech with such glee that we all knew we were in for something special.

Jennifer Natalya Fink, the baddest-ass lady at Georgetown University. Thank you for reading all my miserable early stories compassionately, and for pointing out the path I might walk down next.

The late, great Alvaro Ribiero, S.J., whom I remember and miss every time I draw a whale around a student's run-on sentences.

Jacob Appel is owed a great debt of thanks for making sure I did not starve over the past seven years. Jacob, those samosa dinners, and words of advice, and reiterations of your totally batshit-crazy conviction that I would publish a book were just what I needed, and you knew it.

Josh Henkin of Brooklyn College once drew a diagram of

Leah and Henry's marriage on the blackboard. At the time this drove me bananas. A year later I realized Josh was right about everything. Thank you, Josh, for this, and for being the kind of teacher who truly cares about his students and sends e-mails that start: *I was thinking about your novel again the other day and . . .*

Ernesto Mestre-Reed, for sending me on a spiritual-novel-finding mission with Juan Rulfo and Somerset Maugham as guides.

The many other wonderful teachers at Brooklyn College who have helped me along the way: Michael Cunningham, Amy Hempel, Myla Goldberg, Ellen Tremper, and Jonathan Baumbach.

Other helpers, friends, and early readers who are owed a crustacean or two:

Nicole "where's my tea?" Aragi, John "djellabah dancin'" Freeman, Kelly Farber, Rachel Perry, Joe Gallagher, Tasia Hanmer, Tanwi Nandini Islam, Anna Carey, and Jake "there's nothing wrong with the present tense" Lemkowitz.

The good people of McSweeney's, but particularly Vendela Vida and Jordan Bass, for the Amanda Davis Highwire Fiction Award—the funds and emotional kick in the pants from which helped me finish this novel. Amanda's work is the very best, and I couldn't be more pleased that I've wound up being published by her same house.

The ESPY Foundation and the people of Oysterville, Washington, for setting up the most civilized writing arrangement I've ever had: stories for oysters, every Friday.

The Florida State University crew, for giving me a new writing home, and for making all the terrible jokes about Florida in this book that much more funny.

Everyone back home, I am thankful to you for teaching me

how to cut up, and how to drink whiskey. As you'll see in these pages, you all owe the town of Menamon a two-hundred-dollar fine.

My students, I love you even when you are driving me crazy and I say things to you like: "You Are All Driving Me Crazy!" Your voices and enthusiasm make reading and writing new for me every day, and I thank you for that. Particular shout-outs to my Gotham students, the Writopians, the ladies of GirlSummer, and everyone I met at CUNY.

My writing group—Ruth Curry, Snowden Wright, and Nadja Spiegelman. You came into the life of this book when it and I were at their most broken. Thank you for the love and tough love, the bourbon and cigarettes, for making me laugh and laugh and laugh. (Special thanks as well to Lindsay Nordell and Nadja Spiegelman for recording this novel's first-ever audio edition.)

The Trout Family of Writers, particularly David Greenwood, Stephen Aubrey, Erin Harte, Wythe Marschall, Chloe Plaunt, Chris Roth, Helen Rubinstein, Liz Stevens, Lauren Belski, and James Donovan: in many ways this is a book about the family a person is not born to, and so has to find along the way . . . the people in life you recognize as part of your *karass* . . . I am so lucky to have found you all.

All the Hausers in Maine and beyond, thank you for reminding me every Thanksgiving that there is a very particular tribe that I belong to.

Thank you to Goca and Tijana Igriaé, and especially Randall Joyce, who gave me my first-ever book of poems.

My grandparents Ed and Maureen Joyce. Thank you for reading me all the Oz stories, thank you for telling me long, complicated recipes over the phone, thank you for giving me my first guitar, and thank you for indulging me when I say: Can you tell me the story about X again? Again? Again?

My sister Leslie, without whom I wouldn't last a day in this world. Thank you for understanding everything, and for thinking things are funny when no one else does, and for cocking your head to the side and giving me that look that means *really?* when I need you to. I love you so much. It's SCIENCE.

My father, for teaching me the beauty of *Naturlangsamkeit,* the slowness of nature. For making me a good listener and a keen observer of the world. For telling my petulant ten-year-old self that the art of writing is *what,* Christina? The art of rewriting, Dad.

My mother, for whom an apple is always a Granny Smith green apple. For whom no moment is too small to deserve a narrative. You have always shown me how the world works through stories. You are the best storyteller I know. Thank you.

End of acknowledgments (but the thanks go on and on . . .).

CJ

Insights,
Interviews
& More . . .

About the author

2 Meet CJ Hauser

About the book

3 The Story of Lavender and Leopold

Read on

6 Down East Recipes

10 Late Night at the Uncle Jukebox with Patsy Cline

12 Quinn's Songbook

Meet CJ Hauser

CJ Hauser is from the small but lovely town of Redding, Connecticut.

Her fiction has appeared in *Tin House*, *Kenyon Review*, *TriQuarterly*, and *Esquire*, among other places. She is the 2010 recipient of McSweeney's Amanda Davis Highwire Fiction Award and the winner of Third Coast's 2012 Jaimy Gordon Prize in Fiction. A graduate of Georgetown University and Brooklyn College, she is now in hot pursuit of her Ph.D. at Florida State University.

Though ever and always a New Englander in her heart, CJ currently lives in a small white house under a very mossy oak in Tallahassee, Florida.

The Story of Lavender and Leopold

WE WERE SMALL, my sister Leslie and I. We were five and eight and on Nantucket for the summer. My family used to go there "before it was spoiled," which is what everyone calls the time that begins with the moment they themselves start spoiling a place.

But it *was* magical. Everyone wore cutoffs. No one wore shoes. The outdoor shower ran hot and we ate steamers and drank the broth from a mug, and afterward we went to the penny candy store, which smelled like Pixy Stix dust, and bought fudge and crystals of purple rock candy that we sucked on for hours even though they were jagged in our mouths. We were always sunburned at first, and after that we were naked and brown. There were small scurrying sand crabs that tickled your fingers if you stuck your hands in the sand. If you were as small as we were, you could catch just about any wave and ride it to the shore. On stormy days, when there were small craft warnings, we watched the churning sea from the window and did puzzles inside. The ocean smelled strongly of salt and dark plant matter. Everything was sticky and sandy and warped.

The writer Aleksandar Hemon once said that we make "retroactive utopias" out of places and homes we wish we could return to. Places to which we know there is no way back because they are only half real ▶

Me with Leopold, before I realized he was dinner.

The Story of Lavender and Leopold *(continued)*

anyway. I think there's something to that. How much of those summers do I really remember? How much have I imagined?

It was a less than utopian day when my parents decided that we would eat lobster for the first time. When they brought home four live creatures in a rustling sack. When they decided that it would be fine for Leslie and me to pick out which lobsters would be *ours* and play with them all afternoon in the lead-up to their becoming *our* dinner.

This is a favorite family story. It is mostly substantiated by fact. It is also the product of the four of us, my mother, father, sister and me, telling it to each other again and again. How did it happen? Was it like this? Yes, it was. Remember? Oh yes, we remember.

It was an era of purple for Leslie, so she named her lobster Lavender. I named mine Leopold. Who knows why. It sounded courtly and dignified, I think. We took the lobsters out to the lawn and watched them crawl lurchingly through the grass. We stooped close over them, encouraging them on their way. *Good job! Yes, very good!*

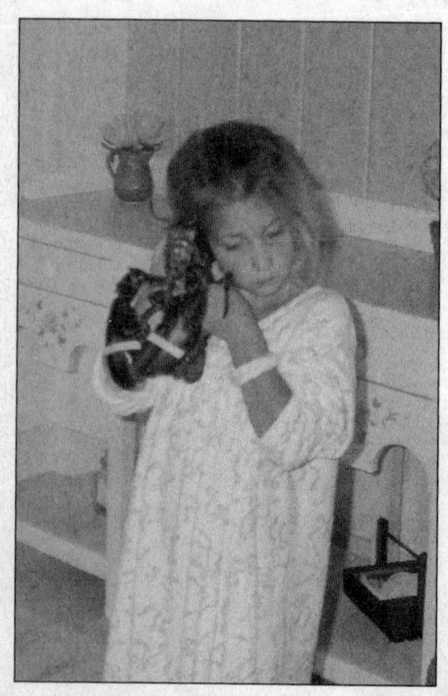

Leslie, listening to what Lavender has to say. She has just learned that we planned to eat Lavender and is very, very sad.

We brought them inside and put them on the braided living room rug. We talked to them. We discussed the details of their friendship and possible romance, but no, really, they were just friends, didn't we think?

This was certainly not humane. But neither was what happened next.

It's not that we hadn't known the lobsters were on the menu. We had heard our parents say, *We are having lobster for dinner.* And yet we had not understood that this meant killing them. That this meant the end of our play. That this was where food came from, really.

My mother had the grim job of explaining this to us. My father had the grim job of lifting the lobsters from our hands and tossing them into the pot.

We cried, of course. We sat in the

corners of the room, our hands balled, saying, *We do not want to eat them! We won't! We won't eat Lavender and Leopold!*

We were in our nightgowns by then and we pulled the fabric over our knees and tucked our heads against them and sniffled purposefully, waiting our parents out.

Our parents, however, were craftier than that. *Fine*, they said. *Then we will eat them all.*

They set the table. There was corn and butter in ramekins and elaborate metal instruments for the cracking of shells and dislodging of meat. My father brought the lobsters out on plates, placing one at each of the four places. My mother lit the candles. They sat down to table.

Are you sure? they said.

We were sure.

We looked at each other. Weren't we?

Our parents were lobster-eating pros. *Oh*, they said as they ate, *this is delicious. So good. There's nothing like it.*

My sister looked at me. Was it delicious?

She tiptoed over to the table and took her seat. She looked at my father.

He cracked a claw for her. She picked it up with her fingers and dunked it in butter and put it in her mouth.

I held out a little bit longer. I wanted the moral credit for not eating the lobster. But I wanted to eat my lobster too.

A little bit longer, but not much.

I joined them. I made a big fuss about how terrible this was and how I was only doing this because they were doing it and so forth.

Mmmmm, my parents said.

My sister poked my father. He cracked her another claw.

I dissected poor old Leopold into parts. I cried upon his shells. I ate him all.

He was delicious.

Me and Leslie, the following summer. By this point we are heartless lobster-eating pros.

Down East Recipes

Lobster Rolls

Lobster
Mayonnaise
Lemon
Celery
Celery salt
Hot dog rolls
Optional: fresh basil, paprika, roe

Boil the lobsters in a nontraumatic way (please reference "The Story of Lavender and Leopold") and, after they've sufficiently cooled, crack and remove the meat. Place the meat in a large bowl. Tear the meat into small chunks.

Adding several scant tablespoons of mayonnaise, mix the ingredients with your fingers so that the mayo lightly coats the chunks of lobster meat. If you are the sort of cook that the author's mother is, you will speak to your lobster as you do this: *That's right! There we go! That's the ticket!* This is understood to improve flavor and integration. DO NOT overdress—just enough mayo to lightly coat the lobster meat is sufficient!

Add the juice of one (or one-half) lemon depending on how much lobster you're using. Don't let any seeds sneak in.

Slice two to four ribs of celery (again, depending on how much lobster) crosswise, then halve each slice.

Add celery salt to taste.

Some people like to add a little shredded fresh basil. This is not traditional, but it can be delicious. This, of course, is up to you.

Be sure to add all components gradually and taste as you go so you don't oversalt.

Serve on toasted hot dog rolls. You may sprinkle the tops of the rolls with a bit of paprika, if that kind of thing is your kind of thing.

If you are lucky enough to get a lady lobster with red roe inside, crumble the roe over the rolls as garnish.

Yield: *Three half-pound lobsters makes about five rolls, but in my family, we like a generous roll, and have even been known to use a one-to-one lobster-to-roll ratio.*

Blueberry Slump

For the biscuits:
1⅓ cups all-purpose flour
2 tablespoons sugar
1½ teaspoons baking powder
½ teaspoon salt
½ teaspoon cinnamon
5 tablespoons cold unsalted butter
⅔ cup heavy cream
1 beaten egg for brushing the biscuits
Additional sugar for sprinkling on top of the biscuits

For the sauce:
1½ pounds blueberries
1 cup fresh orange juice
¼ cup fresh lemon juice
1 tablespoon grated lime zest
1½ cups sugar
2 tablespoons cornstarch

Yield: *Serves eight polite people or six slump lovers.*

Preheat the oven to 400° F. ▸

Down East Recipes ***(continued)***

First, make the biscuit dough:
Combine the flour, sugar, baking powder, salt, and cinnamon in a large bowl. Stir to combine evenly.

Then cut the butter into small pieces. Remember, the butter should be cold! A bit at a time, integrate the butter into the dry ingredients, using your fingers to crumble and pinch it in. Do this with all the butter so the whole mixture has the crumbly texture of bread crumbs and the butter is evenly distributed throughout.

Add the heavy cream. Mix it around with a wooden spoon just until everything comes together in a doughy way—do not overmix or your dough will get tired.

Flour your hands and knead the dough in the bowl, about seven times. Refrigerate the dough until you are ready to add it to the sauce.

Now make the sauce:
Combine the blueberries, juices, zest, and sugar in a cast-iron pot or enamelware skillet.

Bring the mixture to a low boil, stirring to dissolve the sugar. As the mixture becomes saucy, add in the cornstarch. If the mixture is not reducing or becoming thicker, you can add a little bit more cornstarch than listed here—but not too much or your slump will taste starchy, and no one likes a starchy slump. Once the mixture has thickened some, remove it from the heat.

(It is important to note that you should use the same cast-iron pot or enamelware skillet that you have cooked this mixture in for the next step. Under no circumstances should you, say, transfer this mixture into a beautiful blue glass baking dish that your grandmother gave you. If you did, the blueberry mixture would likely sizzle impressively for a moment before the dish shattered into shards, which would be both disappointing to you and alarming to any guests hoping to eat slump. Hypothetically speaking, that is.)

Now take out your dough! Using about two tablespoons of dough for each, form biscuits and plonk them onto the sauce, so they are no more than half submerged. Brush the biscuit tops with the beaten egg and sprinkle them with sugar.

Put the whole skillet or pot into the oven. Do not cover.

Bake for about twenty-five minutes, or until the biscuits are cooked through and the blueberry mixture has reduced to the consistency of a compote.

Serve with vanilla ice cream or heavy cream.

Slump time!

Late Night at the Uncle Jukebox with Patsy Cline

Selections from the Monkey's Uncle Jukebox

The Band, "Ophelia"
Neko Case, "I Wish I Was the Moon"
Guy Clark, "Dublin Blues"
Patsy Cline, "I Fall to Pieces"
Deer Tick, "Let's All Go to the Bar"
Bob Dylan, "Quinn the Eskimo"
Justin Townes Earle, "Mama's Eyes"
The Felice Brothers, "Frankie's Gun"
Fleet Foxes, "Helplessness Blues"
Guns N' Roses, "Paradise City"
Emmylou Harris, "Guitar Town"
John Hartford, "In Tall Buildings"
Hem, "Half Acre"
Jenny Lewis, "Carpetbagger"
Carter Marks, "Leave Your Shoes Behind (Whiskey-Eyed Dame)"
Tift Merritt, "Sweet Spot"
Old Crow Medicine Show, "My Good Gal"
The Pogues, "Dirty Old Town"
John Prine, "Angel from Montgomery"
Bonnie Raitt, "Bluebird"
R.E.M., "Revolution"
Shovels and Rope, "Hail, Hail"
Bruce Springsteen, "Thunder Road"
The SteelDrivers, "Where Rainbows Never Die"
Talking Heads, "Heaven"
Talking Heads, "This Must Be the Place (Naive Melody)"
Maria Taylor, "Clean Getaway"
Townes Van Zandt, "Poncho and Lefty"

Loudon Wainwright III, "Motel Blues"
Tom Waits, "Hold On"
Tom Waits, "I Don't Wanna Grow Up"
Gillian Welch, "Look at Miss Ohio"
Neil Young, "Unknown Legend"

Quinn's Songbook

"No Medicine"

Capo III

G   C   G   G   C   G
You thought I was a train, come barrelin' down the tracks

Em   G   C   D   G
I thought your heart was a white, white bird, But when it flew off it was black

G   C   G   G   C   G
You thought I was a fighter, You thought I was a saint

Em   G   C   D   G
Your face it looked like broken glass when you realized I ain't

Chorus:

G
And honey

           Em   Bm   C   G
There's nothin' to be done for that, No medicine I can give

Em   Bm   C
Can't patch up what's broke too bad, some ills you have to live with

            Cadd9   G   Cadd9
And   I've   been   living

Cadd9   G   Cadd9
I've   been   living

Cadd9   G   Cadd9
I've   been   living

F
With broken pieces

       Am
Of my own

          C   G
And no medicine at all

G   C   G   G   C   G
You thought I was a horse, come breakaway from behind

Em   G   C   D   G
I thought you'd of left this town by now, and shown how bright you shine

```
G              C      G          G    C        G
You thought I was a doctor, could fix us up with glue
   Em                      G                        C          D      G
But I wouldn't touch a single of the cracks that show what's broke in you
```

Chorus:

```
G
And honey
        Em              Bm              C              G
There's nothin' to be done for that, No medicine I can give
Em                        Bm          C
Can't patch up what's broke too bad, some ills you have to live with
          Cadd9          G          Cadd9
And        I've         been        living
Cadd9       G          Cadd9
 I've      been        living
Cadd9       G          Cadd9
 I've      been        living
F
With broken pieces
      Am
Of my own
        C           G      C        G
And no medicine, at all
G        C         G

F         Am
Be my medicine
          Cadd9         G          Cadd9
And        we          will       weather
Cadd9       G          Cadd9
 we        will       weather
Cadd9       G          Cadd9
 we        will       weather
Am    C
it    all
G          C
G          C ▸
```

Quinn's Songbook ***(continued)***

"What Bird"

Capo III

Intro:

G6 Cmaj7 G6 Cmaj7 G6 Cmaj7 Cmaj7 Cmaj7

G6 Cmaj7
What bird is at the window? A sparrow or a lark?

G6 C D G
Not an owl for sure, no. It's hours past the dark

G6 Cmaj7
What we get into last night? How'd you get here with me?

G6 C D G
We said we wouldn't do this. I made you promise me.

G

Chorus:

C D Em
But I don't care

C D Am F
'Cause I've looked everywhere for you

F C
Or someone like you

G6 Cmaj7
So I could go get coffee, While you read the news

G6 C D G
I'd come back and you'd tell me all about it, just like we used to do.

G6 Cmaj7
But what's the point in pretending it won't turn out just the same

G6 C D G
You and me drunk and screaming in the alley, me trying to forget your name

G

Chorus:

C D Em
But I don't care
C D Am F
'Cause I've looked everywhere for you
F C
Or someone like you

Bridge:

Em C G
So next time I see
Am Em
You standing cross the room there lookin' sweet
B7 Em A7 D
Maybe you won't see me, we'll be happier, we'll be free
G6 Cmaj7 G6 Cmaj7
G6 Cmaj7
What bird is at the window? A sparrow or a lark?
G6 C D G
Not an owl for sure, no. It's hours past the dark

"Saint Rosalind"

Capo V

A7sus4 G A7sus4 G
If you hop a tall fence, electric in your mind
A7sus4 G C Am
You'll see Saint Rosie of the high watts, Saint Rosalind
A7sus4 G A7sus4 G
If you find a tin box, buried, lost to time
A7sus4 G C Am
Might be Our Lady of Penobscot's, Saint Rosalind's
F
(But) I've been trying to find her ▶

Quinn's Songbook ***(continued)***

C
Jukebox songs, reminders
G
Rosie, Rosie, why'd you
A7
Have to go, and leave us here, on our own
F
'Cause this town ain't the same
C
You sent us up in flames
G A7
Oh, Rosie, Rosie, tell me you're comin' home?
C C C
'Cause if you don't
G
I don't know
G G G
(Repeat two times)